One Magic

THE BOOK OF THE CARETAKER
BOOK 2

One Magic

APRIL C. ROYER

No Agenda Publishing, LLC
P.O. Box 565, Ooltewah, TN 37363
NoAgendaPublishing.com

One Magic

The Book of the Caretaker

Book 2

No Agenda Publishing, LLC

P.O. Box 565, Ooltewah, TN 37363

NoAgendaPublishing.com

Summary: Morgan navigates the Quickening of her powerful children's magic, replacing a portal to Berios, dangerous encounters with evil men, and ancient prejudice. Along the way she forms new alliances with magical peoples and creatures, welcomes a new breed of dragon, and discovers a way to strengthen the magical connection between all of her brethren, both human and dragon.

ISBN 978-1-7320058-3-9 (Hardback Edition)

ISBN 978-1-7320058-4-6 (Paperback Edition)

ISBN 978-1-7320058-5-3 (Electronic Edition)

Library of Congress Control Number 2019947058

Cover and interior page design: MLargent Creative

Cover calligraphy constructed from an alphabet by Arthur Baker

Follow the author

AprilCRoyer.com

First Edition

10 9 8 7 6 5 4 3 2 1

FOR KATHY

Thank you for your unconditional friendship, loving encouragement,
and unyielding devotion to Caretaker Morgan's journey.
You are an amazing friend, and I love you dearly.

Acknowledgments

The Book of the Caretaker Series has been a work in progress for many years, and I am profoundly thankful to all who read, listened, critiqued, and encouraged. Since the release of *The Caretaker,* I have been blessed with meeting many new reader and author friends who have given wonderful words of encouragement that kept me going when life made that a considerable task.

Special thanks are owed to the Morgans, MoRo and MoPo, for the inspiration and encouragement to create a strong female protagonist worthy of being your friend. I am forever grateful.

Deepest gratitude goes to my wonderful editing team: Kathy Ingle, Michael Pugh, Stephanie Royer, Michael Largent, and Morgan Pope. Thank you all for the many hours of reading, editing, and discussing the story. This work is far stronger due to your skillful touch.

As always, I am thankful for my dear husband, Adam. His love and patience are much needed and much appreciated as I navigate the world of indie publishing.

To Michael Largent, for continuing to provide this series with beautiful layouts and fabulous covers. My gratitude for your skillful work is second only to that for your constant encouragement.

Pronunciation Guide

MAIN CHARACTERS

Alec	.AL·lek	Josef	.JOH·sef
Brya	.BREE·yä	Kisik	.KIS·sik
Burke	.Burk	Kyan	.KEE·yuhn
Cara	.KAIR·ä	Maric	.MAIR·rik
Christina	.Kris·TEEN·ä	Martus	.MAHR·tuhs
Daniel	.DAN·yuhl	Morgan	.MOHR·guhn
Emma	.EM·muh	Nikolas	.NIK·oh·lahs
GranMay	.gran·mey	Orin	.OR·ren
Harrick	.HAIR·rik	Qaleb	.KĀ·luhb
Hoge	.hohg	Sean	.shäwn
Irika	.EER·rik·ä	Taru	.TAH·roo
Izavela (Iz)	.Iz·ä·VEL·ä	Willow	.WIL·loh

GROUPS

Alerian	.ä·LAIR·ē·un	Nyek	.NAHY·yek
Chemerian	.KIM·air·ē·un	Perian	.PEER·ē·un
Hythien	.HĪ·thē·un	Primin	.PRIM·men

PLACES

Arshek	.ÄR·shek	Erion	.AIR·ē·on
Berios	.BER·ē·ōs	Kalias	.KĀ·lē·uhs
Chemerie	.KIM·er·ē	Veridan	.VAIR·ri·dun
Ceruk	.sur·ROOK		

DRAGONS AND NYEKS

Asira	.ä·SEAR·ä	Mythan	.MAYH·thin
Balia	.BÄL·ya	Nijel	.nah·YEL
Brit	.brit	Nulian	.NOO·lē·un
Drieden	.DRĪ·den	Palish	.PAL·ish
Elosh	.EE·lohsh	Panish	.PAN·ish
Falin	.FĀ·lin	Puria	.PYUR·ē·yä
Gerzin	.GAIRT·zen	Qin	.Kwin
Grith	.grith	Sirzi	.SIERT·zē
Helios	.HEE·lē·os	Tagien	.TĀ·jin
Hirk	.hərk	Tevish	.TEV·ish
Hytha	.HĪ·thä	Valen	.VEY·lin
Ildora	.il·DOOR·ä	Yatu	.YÄ·too
Lirpa	.LEER·pä	Zetia	.ZET·ē·ä
Manook	.mä·NUUK	Zirath	.zeer·RÔTH
Menkar	.MEN·kär	Zoli	.ZOH·lē

New Magic

"Hear me, my Daniel. Please, come to me, my mate.
Only you can save me."

"DANIEL, will you please try to stay alive long enough to meet the woman?" Morgan shouted as Alec saved him from sliding into a deep crevasse.

Her distressed brother ignored her, grabbed his torch, and took off down the dark tunnel at the same reckless pace. She and Alec caught up just as he slammed on the brakes. Daniel staggered as the woman's powerful magic and desperate plea rocked him. Morgan cringed as she felt the terror accompanying the woman's words. Daniel bolted.

"Wait!" she called as she lunged to catch him.

"She is dying! I have to save her!" he shouted as guilt and fear tore through him.

"She is not alone!" she said as she rushed forward to block his path and push calming magic with her words. "There is a huge leviathan tormenting her, and we still don't know her spirit or her intentions.

She may be your mate, or she may be waiting to kill all of us the instant we are close enough. We do this smart, or not at all!"

He was breathing very hard but nodded and fell into step behind her as they took off again. They ran hard for a few moments more, then stopped as the tunnel opened to a massive black cavern. The men held their torches up, but their light was swallowed by the darkness well before it reached the bottom or far side.

"This is not a natural structure," Morgan said as she used her enhanced sight to study the cavern. "There is a decaying spiral staircase around the edge, and the walls were shaped with tools."

"Where is she?" Daniel pleaded as he felt around the edge of the wall to find the top of the staircase.

"The bottom of the cavern is flooded with seawater, and below that is a massive portal. This must be where she arrived but — Wait!" Daniel had started down the stairs with a leap over the first broken section. "The leviathan is coming toward us."

Daniel stopped and turned back as he heard rushing water, then leapt back into the wall as the leviathan came darting out of the darkness to slam its jaw shut just a few yards below him. He scrambled a few feet back up and looked at Morgan.

"Please, tell me where she is. I believe she is my mate, and I need to save her!"

"She is in the tunnel that creature just came out of, directly across from me. You cannot rea—" She stopped trying to explain as she watched her brother and husband exchange stern nods before both rushed down the steps. Alec started shouting and waving his torch as Daniel continued to descend. "The effect of testosterone on the human mind is truly astounding!" Morgan muttered as she watched them.

The leviathan had shifted its focus to Alec for a few seconds, then lunged toward Daniel. Its jaws slammed shut right beside his body as he leapt back.

Daniel cursed and scrambled up and down the stairs while swinging his sword to slash the beast across the snout each time it struck.

"Hold!" Morgan shouted aloud and in magic. Both men went still, assuming she was talking to them, but her focus was on the enormous creature trying to eat her brother. The leviathan stopped its next lunge and hissed viciously as it turned to focus high above where Morgan stood. *"You want me. Only I will satisfy your hunger. Devour me, and you will never hunger again. Come get me!"*

The leviathan pulled itself into a tight coil then leapt with all its might. Alec moved to Morgan's side as it drew closer with each of the first three lunges. She met Daniel's eyes and nodded without lessening her magical attack on the creature's feeble mind. He took off running down the stairs, until he was above the tunnel entrance, then dropped his torch and plunged into the black water below.

He was slammed into the wall by the leviathan's thrashing tail before he could duck into the tunnel entrance. To have a sense of direction in the darkness, he rolled over to pull himself along the roof of the tunnel. His lungs burned and screamed for air before his face finally broke the surface inside a small cavern. He gasped and coughed on stale air until his head stopped spinning. There was barely enough light to make out the features of the walls, but he finally spotted a ledge a few feet above the water.

After many slips and redirects to navigate the slick stone wall, he lifted himself up onto the ledge. His insides clenched as he stared at a still form in a light-colored dress huddled in a corner.

She was silent and had no reaction to the sound of him sliding closer.

"I'm here, my Lady," he said as he reached out to lay a hand on her shoulder. "It's me, Daniel." Pain shot through his chest and slid through his veins like ice as he felt how cold and stiff her body was. "Oh, please, no." His other hand slipped in thick cold blood, and tears filled his eyes. "I'm so sorry."

"I am still with you, my Daniel. Above you. Please, come to me."

He stood too fast and cursed as his head smacked an overhanging rock before leaning out from the ledge to study the cavern above him. A small bit of light, from high in the room, reflected off the ceiling just enough to make out another ledge high above him. The wall was almost flat, and the only places to grab were horizontal fissures barely large enough for his fingers. That made his feet of little use as he pulled himself up the twenty-foot rock face.

When he finally reached the ledge, he shifted to his knees and froze as he took in the exotic form of his mate for the first time. She was the source of light in the room. Her eyes were a softly glowing amber, her skin much darker than his, and thin shimmering lines flowed along her clavicles. Her radiance grew brighter as she smiled. She bowed her head, and he felt a strong wave of gratitude wash over him.

"Thank you for coming." "Please, tell me your name."

"I am Taru, daughter of Grith."

A particularly horrible screech from the leviathan snapped him out of his trance. He moved to her side to offer a hand.

"We need to hurry. May I help you?"

She smiled and looked into his eyes as she took his hand. Their grips tightened as he eased an arm under her side. His skin warmed and tingled as he pulled her closer and lifted her to her feet. They were both lost in the sensations moving between them until he forced his eyes off of hers. As he released her, she moved to look down at the body on the ledge below.

"She was Rea, my dearest friend. She saved me."

"I need to get you free of the beast. I will return for her body later, if possible. Please, my Lady, we must go."

As she turned back to him, he noticed that she held one arm tight to her body. The ripped sleeve along it had dark stains.

"Can you climb at all?" he asked as he pointed at her injured arm.

She shook her head then glanced at the water far below. He moved to the edge and sighed.

"It is at least ten feet out and thirty down. Do you think you can run hard enough to make it, my Lady?"

She moved to stand beside him, glanced down at the water, then gave him a sly smile.

"I can make it, my Daniel."

He nodded and started to move back then gasped as she crouched and leapt. He held his breath as she flew forward, wrapped her good arm around the other, and cut smoothly through the surface.

"Well, I guess I know what those glowing lines are all about," he said with a smile as he backed up to the wall. "A little more dragon blood in the family."

He plunged into the water behind her, then wrapped an arm around her middle. They each took a deep breath, dove, and used one arm to pull as they kicked hard toward the cavern where the beast continued it efforts to reach Morgan.

As they drew closer, Taru froze, then started trying to pull Daniel back. He wrapped her tighter and shook his head as he touched her face and held her eyes. She stopped fighting him, but closed her eyes, and started to tremble. He pulled her to the staircase then carried her in his arms as he climbed.

When Alec moved to help, Daniel shook his head with a proud smile.

"I've got her."

ONCE EVERYONE WAS AWAY from the ledge, Morgan released the mind of the beast and watched it crash into the water, exhausted and confused. She turned to find Daniel's mate standing behind him, her body tense, and her head down. Daniel shifted to stand at her side and touched her back. The touch drew her closer to him but did not ease her tension.

"Taru, this is my sister, Morgan, and her husband, Alec. Her gifts of magic are how we found and saved you."

Morgan's eyes slid over Taru's beautiful form as she lowered her guard enough to feel the woman's magic. Taru flinched at the magical touch, and her heart raced as she shifted behind Daniel's shoulder.

"Taru, thus far, your magic feels pure and trustworthy. However, if you wish to be with my brother, then you must drop your guard and allow me to be certain you mean us no harm."

Taru remained still and continued to stare at the ground until Daniel took her hand and gripped it. She drew a deeper breath and looked up into his eyes.

"I trust her with my life. Please, trust me."

She gripped his hand and held his eyes as she forced a few slower breaths, then let him go, stepped forward, and bowed to Morgan.

"Thank you for allowing Daniel to save me. I owe you my life, Mistress. If allowing you to enter my mind is what my mate desires, I will not resist."

Morgan felt the storm of emotions within Taru as soon as she started dropping her guard. The woman's pain and physical weakness from blood-loss were so profound that Morgan was surprised to see her on her feet at all.

"I can help wi—"

The instant Morgan reached out for the injured arm, Taru tensed and stepped back to tuck against Daniel's chest.

"She won't hurt you, Taru. She just wants to heal your arm," Daniel said.

Taru swallowed hard, nodded, then held very still with her eyes down as Morgan stepped closer. She flinched and shivered as Morgan touched her but did not pull away.

Morgan passed healing magic to heal the fractured bone and deep gash in her arm, as well as the many cuts and scrapes over her body. She used the light touch to study her magic as her eyes moved over the glowing lines on her upper chest, then stepped back with a smile.

"I am glad to meet you, Taru. However, I prefer to get out of these tunnels before sharing more."

She let Daniel and Taru lead and stayed back a few yards with Alec.

"Is something wrong?" Alec asked as he took her hand.

"Her magic is strong and similar to mine, yet she fears me and was astonished when I healed her arm. I find that very odd. I want to get closer to Nulian so she can share in what I find through bonding."

Alec watched Daniel and Taru for a minute, then chuckled.

"In all fairness, the fear is understandable. It is rather daunting when you control a forty-foot sea serpent with only your mind, my dear." He noticed her lack of amusement and added, *"Perhaps not daunting so much as impressive, and horribly arous—"* She pushed his shoulder just in time to run him into an approaching stalactite and giggled at his muffled curse.

Sisters

TARU FROZE in her tracks as they neared the tunnel mouth. "What scares you, Taru?" Morgan asked. "I feel no danger aside from the leviathan for many miles."

Taru turned with wide eyes. Daniel wrapped his arm around her shoulders as he felt her tremble.

"There are dragons of Ceruk near. They will kill me on sight."

Morgan sent Taru calming energy as she searched around the island again.

"I do not know who Ceruk is. The dragons you feel are our brethren and are beautiful pure spirits. They will not hurt you. Let Daniel show you."

"Look within me, Taru. You will see only love and devotion between us and the dragons outside," Daniel said as he placed Taru's hand to his cheek.

Morgan noticed Taru did not delve very deep into his mind before she looked up with a small smile.

"I am amazed that a dragon of Ceruk, an Alerian dragon, could be so kind to a human. I would like to meet one of your dragon friends."

Daniel smiled and took her hand as he led her forward.

"Daniel, stop," Morgan said. He did but turned with a scowl. *"She is lying! I will not let her near them until I feel no further deceit from her. Let me do this, and do not interfere."*

He nodded and released Taru's hand as he stepped away to stand beside Alec. Morgan stepped closer to Taru and held her tearful gaze with a stern expression.

"I felt the deceit within your words and do not appreciate it in the least. You will not be welcome with us if you hold secrets from me or deceive others. Will you allow me to bond to you freely so I can see what you fear enough to lie to your mate?" Taru had dropped her eyes at first, then looked up with a dark glare, which she shifted to Daniel.

"My mate, is it your wish that I endure this punishment without resistance?"

"She is not punishing you," he said as he stepped a bit closer, matching her intensity. "She is giving you the chance to prove to us all that you are worthy of our trust. If you are who my spirit believes you are, then you will trust me when I tell you that she will not hurt you without provocation."

Taru relaxed as she held his eyes, then looked back to Morgan and nodded.

"I will not fight the bonding, Mistress. If I cannot trust my mate to protect me from pain, then I can trust no one."

"I could not agree more. I suggest you focus on that confidence as we enter bonding. It will keep you from resisting instinctively. Think of him, your trust in him, and the trust he just showed in you."

Taru blushed as she glanced at Daniel, and he smiled. When Morgan held up her hands, Taru studied the dragon markings on her palms with great interest.

"You carry the gift of the dragon?"

"That, we can discuss later. Lay your hands to mine, and I will begin. You will feel many intense sensations as I deepen the connection to reach bonding, but none of them will be painful."

Taru took one more deep breath and pressed their hands together. Morgan pushed calming emotions through the contact for a moment before deepening the connection. To limit the more intense sensations, she moved quickly into bonding. Taru gasped and braced as the feeling of weightlessness first hit her. Morgan laced their fingers and waited for Taru to get past the anticipation of pain where she could embrace the wonderful feeling that bonding is meant to be.

"I will seek your spirit, and you should seek mine."

"How?"

"Think of wanting to know the truest part of who I am. Your magic will take you there."

Morgan encountered many areas of scarring left by contact with dark magic. The darkness was familiar. It was very similar to that she had fought within the Arshek line of Erion. As she studied the woman's consciousness, she was saddened to feel such timidity and fearfulness within one who carried such strong magic.

As she questioned that, her magic located several pertinent memories. The first was of many blond-haired, green-eyed humans moving around a younger Taru on a busy street. Most ignored her. Others looked at her with disgust as they avoided getting near her. Taru had been an outcast among people that looked very much like Daniel.

The memory shifted to a new one which made her tense. Her heart ached as she viewed images of Alerian dragons attacking a village of humans and savagely killing them. She pushed those images away and was drawn to a tightly bound memory surrounded by profound love and respect. When she focused on it, she saw a huge Elder Perian dragon lying weak, wounded, and near death within a cave.

He was being caressed by a young Taru.

"You cannot die, Father. I need you. You are my only family, Grith. Please, do not go," Taru had said in dragon-tongue as tears streamed down her face. The dragon tried to croon but coughed, then spoke in a ragged whisper.

"I am going to give you a gift, my dear one, the most wonderful gift I could ever give. It will help you find your way to Erion, home of Puria's children. With the power of this gift you will not be harmed by those who serve Ceruk. They took your thoughts and attacked our brethren this day, but it will never happen again. When you are older, the gift will lead you to your magical mate and your destiny among his people on Erion. Remember all I have told you of your future, and you will do great things. I love you without limit, my dear child. Now calm your fears and trust in my love."

Morgan watched Taru lay along the dragon's foreleg as he hummed loudly. He used the sharp tip of a broken claw to trace thin cuts along her collar bones and connect them with a deeper cut high on her chest. He dropped to her middle to draw lines over her abdomen, then finished with small marks at her wrists and ankles. Taru screamed in agony until the great dragon began to drop his blood over the wounds. Each was healed within seconds, to leave behind beautiful lines of translucent scales.

With the last wound to be sealed, that upon her abdomen, his tune changed. His song grew louder and more intense as he touched his bloody snout to her belly. He focused hard for many seconds, then gave a great gasp as he lifted to look down at her once more before falling silent and still. The Elder had given not only his blood, he had given her the remainder of his life force as well.

Morgan left that painful memory and pushed deeper into the bonding to let her spirit touch Taru's without resistance. A sudden and enormous jolt of magical transfer made them both grip the other tighter. Each staggered a bit as the powerful transfer enveloped their senses. Morgan held the bonding until the transfer was complete, then let it drop with a strong push of healing to assure Taru felt no pain.

Daniel caught Taru as she pitched backward. Morgan leaned against Alec and stared at Taru.

"Nulian, did you feel that? Do we share a kindred gift?"

"Yes, my Sister. Though unlikely and unexpected, the kinship is undeniable," Nulian said.

Morgan unwrapped the top of her cloak, then knelt beside Taru to take her hand and share gentle healing energy. Taru took deeper breaths as the dizziness faded, then stared at the beautiful dragon markings on Morgan's chest. A small patch of glowing dragon scales laid between a pair of gorgeous major dragons who bowed in unison. Tears filled her eyes as she looked up to meet Morgan's gaze.

"It is an honor to welcome you into our family, my Sister," Morgan said with a smile.

"Sister?" Daniel shouted. The women laughed as Morgan helped Taru stand. "Morgan, seriously!"

Taru turned to him and laid a hand to his cheek as she shifted in close. He shivered and swallowed hard as her magic moved through him.

"The magic did not fail us, my mate. Your sister and I share dragon blood of the same ancient line. We are blood-sisters, yes, but not by human blood." Daniel's face relaxed and broke into a smile as he looked to Alec with a light laugh.

"There is way too much 'kinda related, but not really' in our family."

NULIAN, FALIN, AND LIRPA were settled on a ledge over a hundred yards away to let Taru see them without being frightened by their nearness. Taru's heart raced as she saw them, but Morgan felt only excitement, not fear.

"The Elder female you see is Nulian. She is your sister as well. It is her gift I carry. She is eager to meet you. Are you ready?"

Taru nodded. Morgan felt her honesty as well as the apprehension that rose when Nulian took flight.

Nulian landed with grace at the far end of the ledge, then bowed.

"I am honored to meet you, Lady Taru. I am amazed to find we are blood-sisters, but am most pleased with the news. Will you allow me the honor of carrying you and your mate to the castle, my Lady?"

Taru took an involuntary step back into Daniel's chest as Nulian offered a palm.

"I have never flown, my mate. I do not think I want to either," Taru said as she glanced up to where Menkar soared above them.

"I promise, it is very safe, especially aboard Nulian. She is very strict about safe transport," he said as he turned her to face him. "I would never ask you to do this if I thought you would be in any danger. Do you believe me?"

"Yes, I do believe you. However, that alone may not make my legs carry me to board the great dragon behind me."

He coaxed her into Nulian's palm by lifting her off her feet, then settled her into the saddle in front of him.

"Will it be very rough?" Taru asked as she eyed the straps he was buckling around her legs and waist.

"Not aboard Nulian. Like I said, she is all about smooth, safe transport of her human brethren," Daniel said with a chuckle.

Taru gave him a very anxious look and said, "I am quite thankful for that, my mate. Let us not tease her and make her angry while on her back, please."

"She is far wiser than her mate, I think," Nulian said to Morgan as she gave Daniel an annoyed glance.

Morgan and Alec laughed, and Taru hid her smile from Daniel. "What did she say?" Daniel asked as he glanced between Taru and Morgan.

"She feels my idea was a good one," Taru said.

Morgan raised an eyebrow at Taru's deceit, then allowed her request to connect.

"Not a lie, just a nice way to put it, perhaps?" Taru asked. Morgan nodded and moved to meet Lirpa, who was landing behind her. She stopped as Nulian crooned and nudged her gently.

"Are you troubled that I am carrying them and not you, my Sister? My thought was that she would feel safer on a larger dragon," Nulian said.

"That is fine, my dear. Just don't trade me in on a new model, just yet."

Nulian hummed to send loving devotion and thanks for her understanding.

THE INSTANT NULIAN left the ground, Taru covered her eyes with both hands and pushed back into Daniel's chest quivering.

"Lay your hand to Nulian's hide and let her help you," Morgan told her.

With one hand still covering her eyes, Taru reached down to lay her other hand against Nulian. Daniel felt her skin grow warmer under her shirt as she shivered. Nulian sang a comforting dragon song while transferring feelings of trust and safety. Taru relaxed enough to hum along and soon opened her eyes. Her eyes moved over the world around her as her fear began to turn to excitement. She pushed gratitude through the touch to Nulian, then rubbed her tingling hand before reaching for one of Daniel's.

"Oh, my Daniel. This world is beautiful. It is so healthy and new. My world, Kalias, is ancient and becoming less habitable each decade. That is why Puria left our world in search of a new home for our dragons and people long ago. She never returned to us, and chaos ensued in her absence. Without her leadership, our Alerian dragons became lax in their defenses and were soon taken by the evil magic of Ceruk. I wish I could help them, but they will not

listen when their minds are so saturated with hatred for my kind."

"Who was Puria?" Daniel asked aloud.

Nulian hummed deep in her chest at his words, and they felt the vibrations through the saddle.

"We call her The Purest and have not spoken her given name in many centuries. She is the most respected of all Chemerian dragons," Nulian said. "Her gift of blood to Lady Chemerie established the precious connection we share with our human brethren here on Erion."

Taru translated Nulian's answer for Daniel then drew quiet as she studied the beautiful young planet around her. As she shifted to ask a question, Daniel's hand brushed against a small area of velvety scales on the inside of her wrist. She shivered and pulled her arm away to cover them with her sleeve. He slid his hand over hers, uncovered them, then pushed his hand into hers as he tightened his grip around her with the other arm. His cheek brushed her ear, and she turned to let her face brush his.

"I have longed to know you for so long, Taru. I spent most nights imagining what you would look like," he said. "I never imagined a more beautiful woman, and certainly never hoped to find such lovely dragon markings." He let his thumb brush over a tiny portion of one line and smiled as she shivered and pushed back against his chest. "Never hide them from me, please."

She shifted to look into his eyes as she reached up to trace the features of his face. As her hand dropped to slide over his neck, he wrapped her in his arms.

"I have found you, just as Grith said I would. After so many years, I wondered if it was even poss—" Her words stopped when his focus shifted to her lips, and his drew closer.

He let his lips barely touch hers and paused. She lifted just enough to let their lips touch again then gasped as he deepened the kiss. He broke the kiss after only a few seconds and saw tears sliding down her face.

"Tears of joy, I hope?" She nodded and smiled as he wiped them away. The wind blew her blouse to the side, baring her shoulder and upper arm. Her instinctive move to cover herself stopped as he smiled and reached up to touch the small dragon on her shoulder. Both Taru and the dragon on her shoulder shivered at his touch.

"Oh my! I have never seen this before. Why are they glowing so brightly?" Taru asked as she studied the dragon on her other shoulder and the glowing scale regions on her chest and wrists.

"They glow for two very good reasons, actually," Morgan said to both her and Daniel. *"One, you are contacting your magical mate intimately for the first time. And two, you are near a Perian dragon. Look to your right."*

Taru turned to find Valen, a female major Perian dragon, flying close beside them. She put a trembling hand to her mouth as tears flowed down her face.

"I never dreamed I would see a Perian again. Grith was the last on Kalias. Oh, you are so very beautiful, my Lady," Taru said.

"Thank you, my new friend. I look forward to feeling our kinship," Valen said.

As they approached the city, younglings surrounded them, and Taru was mesmerized as she watched them. Morgan felt jealousy rise in Nulian at Taru's frenzied excitement over seeing Valen and the other Perians.

"Patience, my Sister. It will take her time to see the beauty in all dragons equally," Morgan said to Nulian, who nodded without comment. *"Besides, you are mine, and I do not like sharing at all."*

"Do you say that only to make me feel better, my Caretaker?"

Morgan opened herself to Nulian with no guard and said, *"You tell me."*

Nulian searched her feelings and found the fierce jealousy Morgan had felt when Taru boarded earlier. She sent deep love and friendship as she said, *"I love you too, my Sister."*

MORGAN WATCHED as Daniel held his new-found mate in his arms and enjoyed his deep happiness. She failed to raise her guard as he dropped to kiss Taru and quickly did so as she flushed.

"What did you hear that has made you so red in the face, my shy little wife?" Alec asked from aboard Falin beside her.

She shot him a sharp look, and he urged Falin away from Lirpa.

Lirpa hummed as Morgan laid her hands to her neck and both deepened their connection. Lirpa had been the first hatchling she bonded with after coming to Chemerie from Earth. They had been inseparable for many months of her first year and remained very close. Her young friend had just recently become large enough to carry her for long journeys. This was their first long flight together.

"I have news, my Queen," Lirpa said. "Hytha is two months into her first carry and grows anxious about the reaction of others. She knows that her partnership with her Perian mate was accepted, but fears her young will not be. She has been afraid to tell anyone and has not returned to Erion for many weeks. Will you go to comfort her soon, my Caretaker?"

"I will go as soon as things with Taru are settled, tomorrow, I imagine. I have been meaning to go for a visit, and that is a wonderful motivation to get there at once. I hope she sees that we are all excited to see the beautiful children which result from the crossing of Chemerian and Perian lines. I can now tell her that this is not the first time it has happened. There was definitely a crossing somewhere long ago. Otherwise, there is no way I would share the same dragon bloodline as Taru. "

Alec and Falin swooped up to them, and Alec yelled out, "Want to race, little ladies?"

Lirpa growled and put on a great burst of speed to shoot past Falin.

She then proceeded to drop behind then pass him again and again.

"You may want to stop harassing him, my dear. His feelings are sensitive of late," Morgan said.

"Perhaps it is a perfect motivation, my Sister," Lirpa said with a laugh as she nipped at his tail. He darted forward, then growled when she passed over him to shake her tail in his face.

"She is making him very angry, my dear. Why is she being so rude?" Alec said.

"You called her little, my dear. That is not a compliment for a female dragon."

"Please tell her I am deeply sorry before they do not speak again as a result of it. He is growling and about to wear himself out keeping up."

Morgan relayed the message, and Lirpa slowed down to fly beside Falin. She looked over at him and crooned as she let her wingtip clip his. He did not return the sentiment, so she snorted and moved to fly just in front of him again.

3

Destinies Merge

"WELCOME TO CHEMERIE, my Lady," Daniel whispered in Taru's ear as they crested the last mountain to look out over the rolling plains around the castle of Chemerie.

"It is so beautiful," she said. He hugged her tight as she watched all the younglings flying around them. Little Zirath came to fly very near Nulian's head and crooned to his grandmother. He caught the wind and dropped back to glide near Daniel and Taru, so Daniel reached out to touch the thin veil of his wing. Taru tensed as he did so.

"He has been my friend since he was born. I trust him with my life, and would die to protect him. Please try to let them show you their loving spirits, my dear," Daniel said. She held his gaze and nodded before reaching out to touch Zirath's wing as well.

Zirath gave a shiver and crooned before swooping off to play fight with a Perian youngling named Rogan. Daniel and Taru laughed as the two swooped and chased each other in between gentle grappling and rolling over in the air.

The party landed on the garden lawn in the middle of a huge group of dragons spread over the grounds and cliffs behind the castle. Nulian lowered Daniel and Taru to the ground in her palm. Taru scanned the dragons around her and smiled as she clung to Daniel.

"There are so many. And they act as one family. It is truly amazing."

"In Chemerie, we are all one family. You are part of our family now."

As Lirpa touched down, Morgan leapt to the ground and ran past Daniel and Taru toward the castle.

"Our children need her just now," Alec said with a relaxed smile to Taru. He gave Daniel a wink and gestured to the crowd gathered behind them. "Shall we introduce your new companion to our waiting friends?" They stepped to Nulian's head, and Alec spoke in a loud voice to the group.

"My friends, I am honored to introduce Lady Taru, magical mate to our Admiral Daniel. She has come to us from a very different place where she has received a gift similar to that bestowed upon our Queen. Please welcome her to our family everyone."

All of the dragons bowed their heads and hummed a greeting as the people bowed or curtsied and said, "Welcome to Chemerie."

Taru wobbled as the strong emotional rush from the huge number of dragons hit her. Daniel supported her. He had rather expected it given his experiences with Morgan becoming accustomed to her own magic over the past two years. He realized Taru had great magic within her but had not been around dragons since receiving her dragon blood.

Taru gathered herself, stepped a few feet in front of him, and bowed to the group of people then to the mass of dragons around them.

"I am honored to be in your presence. I have known only a few Perian dragons in my life and have not been near one for many years.

I am a bit awed by the number of beautiful spirits around me. Seeing you all together, Perian beside Alerian, as one family, is something I never imagined possible. Thank you for the welcome, pure ones," she said in dragon-tongue.

She then turned to Daniel. "May I spend a few moments with them, my mate? I very much want to touch a Perian dragon again."

"You can spend all the time you want with them, my Lady. I'll never tell you what to do."

Taru smiled then looked from Valen to a group of hatchlings and younglings.

"May I visit with them, my Lady?"

Valen looked to Nulian. Taru turned to her and blushed as she realized her mistake.

"You are welcome among us, Lady Taru. I ask that you be cautious, however. You carry a unique magic to that of Chemerie," Nulian said.

Taru nodded and approached the group, where she knelt and bowed to them.

"Hello. I am Taru. Could I please touch one of you?"

She jumped a bit and smiled when the group moved forward, hopping and jostling to get closer to her. A small Perian female hatchling jumped ahead of the group and lifted her snout to her hand. Taru gasped and flinched back as intense tingles filled her hand and made the scale areas on her wrist sting.

The hatchling moved back and crouched. Taru rubbed the scales around her wrist to relieve the sting and wiped sweat from her forehead. Once the tingling eased, she opened her arms to the hatchling.

"I am sorry if I frightened you. Please, I very much want to be your friend," she said. The hatchling moved onto her lap with a soft croon. She kept her hands on the little dragon and closed her eyes as she let the tingle spread up her arms and all through her. All of her scale regions began to glow brighter. The hatchling crooned then started to sing the Song of Connection. Taru had tears streaming down her face as all of the little ones around her joined the song.

Daniel watched her visit with a proud smile until she slumped and fell to the ground. He ran to her and flinched back when he touched her skin.

"Call Morgan," he yelled to Alec as he rubbed his stinging hands.

Alec came to him and checked Taru's heart and breathing.

"She seems to be fine. Likely overwhelmed by the magic, the same way Morgan was at first. However, Morgan never became this dangerously hot," Alec said. He closed his eyes and concentrated hard on Morgan. He connected to her with considerable effort and explained what happened.

"I will be there in a moment," Morgan said. *"Watch her closely and call if she worsens."*

MORGAN HURRIED through the castle to reach the twins as she sent them comforting reassurance. She had not been in contact with them for hours. It was the first time they had not been with either parent for so long, and the first time she had blocked them altogether.

They had bonded to one another and retreated into their own minds to control their fear. As she drew closer, they felt her and dropped their guards. She nearly tripped as their fear took her breath and sent shocks of pain all through her.

She ran into their room and rushed past GranMay, nearly giving her a stroke. GranMay had no idea what was happening since the children had blocked everyone, including their powerful great-grandmother.

The twins burst from the closet where they had been hiding and flew into her arms. She held her trembling children and passed strong comfort and love as she bonded to them. They remained in that deep bonding for many minutes as she sang a comforting tune and caressed their backs.

"I am so sorry to have frightened you, my sweet babies. It was important to protect you while interacting with someone new who has magic of her own. I should have explained it before going and I promise to never do that again without telling you."

Both children nodded and tucked their heads under her chin as they hugged her and each other. A moment later, they giggled and looked up at her with sweet smiles.

"So Uncle Daniel has his mate with him now? Is he very happy, Mother?" they asked in their normal seamless word-trading manner. Morgan smiled as she felt their joy at Daniel's happiness.

"How long have you known she was coming to us?"

"We heard her thoughts a few days ago, but were not sure if she was real," Brya said. With no pause, Kyan added, "We thought we were dreaming it because we missed Uncle Daniel and were seeking his thoughts that night."

"You were able to share his thoughts of her, without contact, and from that far away? Or was it an unintentional event?"

They both shrugged with sly smiles similar to their father's. She kissed their foreheads and held them close as her heart filled with pride, yet again. "I love you, my amazing children. Would you like to meet your Uncle Daniel's mate? I think you will find her very interesting."

They walked through the castle with each child holding one of her hands. Once down the terrace steps, they took off to leap into their father's waiting arms. Both giggled with joy as he kissed their necks and swung them in circles.

Morgan moved to Daniel and Taru where she knelt to place her hand over the point where the lines along her clavicles connected. She found a great deal of magic surging within her, overwhelming her senses. As she pulled much of it into herself, Taru woke.

"She is fine," she said to Daniel as she stood and stepped back. "However, I am concerned about the amount of magic that built within her and with how high it drove her temperature. We will need to address that soon."

Daniel helped Taru sit up and explained what had happened as Morgan joined Alec and the twins. Taru went right back to stroking the younglings around her, but did not leave herself in contact for long periods.

Daniel glanced between her and his sister's little family with a hopeful smile.

"Well, you kissed her in under an hour. I would say you are on pace to have kids within a few months for certain," Morgan chided him. She giggled out loud as she felt the embarrassment in her shy older brother, then turned to see flush cheeks highlighting a bright smile.

"You told me once of how amazing it was when you touched Alec. I think I finally understand, and completely agree. It is awesome," Daniel said. *"The magical link between us makes it feel so right and natural. I feel like I have known her my whole life."*

"I am very happy for you. And so are your niece and nephew. They're eager to meet your mate."

Daniel smiled and turned to lay a hand to Taru's shoulder.

"I would like to introduce you to Morgan's children."

Taru stood, turned, and her eyes widened as she stared at the children.

"Are they twins?"

"Yes, and special in many ways," he said with a smile as he took her hand to lead her forward. Brya and Kyan took hands and moved to stand behind Morgan, peeking out at Taru as she knelt in front of them and bowed her head.

"I am Taru, and I am honored to meet you, little ones. I am very glad to learn my mate is your uncle. My dragon father told me I would one day use my magic b—"

"Mother will not let you take Uncle Daniel away!" Kyan shouted.

Brya added, "And we will not go with you either!"

Morgan's eyes never left Taru as she calmed her children with magic and urged them to step back.

"Children, go with your father to Nulian." Alec scooped them up and headed for Nulian, who offered a palm. Morgan glared at Taru as Nulian took off, then stepped closer to her as she forced her way past her guard. Taru gasped and stood to step back against Daniel.

"It is clear that you have intentionally and effectively withheld important information from me. You will tell me the truth, freely and in full, or you will leave this country!" She shifted her gaze to Daniel, who nodded and stepped back. When she looked back at Taru, tears were streaming down the woman's face. "Drop your guard completely, offer no resistance to my search of your thoughts and feelings, and tell me what my children just felt or heard within you."

Taru dropped her guard and offered her hands. Morgan took them and gripped them hard as she deepened the connection very near bonding. Taru was breathing hard and beginning to sweat from the intensity of Morgan's search but focused on offering no resistance as she spoke.

"I am sorry I could not trust freely before. I was truly scared of your power and what you could force me to do. When you bonded to me, I concealed my dragon father's words about my destiny. I knew the Caretaker and her twin children were on Erion, but had no idea of the relationship the powerful woman entering my mind might have to them. I acted to protect them I had no idea it was you I was protecting. The children heard my thoughts of hoping you, they, and Daniel will help me free the dragons and people of Kalias. I would never force any of you to help me. It was only a hope. Please, push us into bonding, let me share the memories of Grith explaining, so you will not question my devotions again."

Morgan relaxed and let the deep connection drop as she shook her head and released Taru's hands.

"No need, my Sister. I viewed the pertinent memories as you spoke because they passed to me when we first bonded. I am grateful to know you were willing to risk yourself to protect us from possible danger. I do not understand how Grith knew of us, but I am thankful the magic has brought you to us."

The crowd around them applauded as they embraced, then even more joyfully as Daniel took Taru into his arms to lift her in a tight embrace.

Nulian had landed and the children ran to them with exuberant giggles. Morgan knelt to catch them and relaxed enough to smile as she felt their joy and heard their thoughts.

"What is so funny, munchkins?" Daniel asked and he knelt beside them.

"Aunt Taru was willing to die to protect us from Mommy, and Mommy was ready to kill her to do the same. It is ironic and funny, is it not, Uncle Daniel?"

"Absolutely hilarious," he said as he attacked them with tickles. They took off and he bolted after them. Alec moved to Morgan and kissed her forehead as he pulled her to him.

"You are still very tense. Did she not ease your worry?"

"I did not hear her thoughts, they did. That is because I was not properly connected to her as I should have been. I trusted her based on our blood-link, and that was naïve. I feel foolish and irresponsible at the moment."

Taru was watching Daniel play with the children and a group of younglings when Morgan moved to her and took her hand. She took in a quick breath but smiled as she met her eyes.

"I will earn your trust properly in time," Morgan said. *"I expected you to offer it as freely as our Chemerian brethren do, and that was wrong of me. That said, I will remain connected to you more than you may appreciate until we both feel that limitless trust. I have to protect my children. I hope you understand."*

"I do. I would do the same."

They both laughed as they watched Daniel pretend to trip and let the children and younglings crawl over him. He noticed them watching and stood to head toward them. They both gave him wicked grins, and he lifted an eyebrow.

"What is so fu—"

They laughed as Zirath, who had snuck up behind him, leapt and tackled him. Daniel grabbed him in a headlock as they twisted over one another.

"You are getting quite big, my friend. You need to consider that if you still climb on Morgan like a youngling," Daniel said as they relaxed.

Zirath froze and looked to Morgan with wide eyes.

"No, you have not hurt me. But you are growing quickly, for certain. Your mother would be proud of your girth and your coloring, as I am."

The dragon swelled with pride then started toward her with his head held high.

"Thanks for that. I've been trying to work up the nerve to tell him for days," Morgan said to Daniel. He smiled then ran to return the sneak attack on Zirath.

The two wrestled for a minute more before Daniel let out an "Ouch!" as he caught a claw in the ribs. Zirath looked mortified and touched his snout to the wound as he hummed the dragon healing song.

Morgan started toward him, then stopped as the twins hurried to his side. They stacked their hands over the wound together and hummed along with Zirath. Daniel smiled as the wound warmed and tingled under their hands. The pain left him in seconds. With only a minute of focused effort, the twins lifted their hands to reveal perfectly healed skin beneath.

"Thank you, munchkins," he said as he kissed them both and

hugged them tightly.

They kissed his cheeks then took off after the younglings, having declared themselves 'it'.

"When did they start healing anyone except you two and each other?" Daniel asked as he moved back to Morgan, Alec, and Taru.

Alec smiled at Morgan as they squeezed each other's hands. "Just now," she said.

"Really? Goodness, I feel honored."

"Don't be. They just couldn't stand to hear you whine any longer," Morgan said with a quick leap away from his reach. As he grabbed for her, he bumped Taru, and Alec grabbed her arm to steady her. Morgan went still and lifted an eyebrow when she saw her mate's palm markings glow at Taru's touch. That had only happened with her touch or that of a Perian dragon. She reasoned that Taru carried Perian blood and forced a slower, deeper breath as she looked away toward the children.

"Easy, my Queen. I am yours," Alec said as he moved to stand behind her and kiss her head. *"I have never known you to be so prone to jealousy. First of Nulian, and now of me. What is making you so edgy, my love?"*

"We will most definitely discuss it later, dear," she said to him before stepping away to focus on the others.

"Dinner is waiting. Shall we eat?" she called to Daniel and Taru while using a magical touch to summon the twins. The children soon came running past the others to reach her, where each took a hand and fell into step.

"THEY ARE BEAUTIFUL CHILDREN, and obviously have a unique bond to their mother."

"Everything about them has been unique since they were conceived. They were born in far less time than normal and continue to grow very fast."

"How fast?"

"Well, they are only eighteen months old."

"Oh! They appear to be of at least five or six years! Is the dragon's gift responsible? Were they actually born bearing markings?"

"They have only the small patch of scales you see on their chests. Morgan expects that their Crest markings will appear once they go through their Quickening, as will their Caretaker markings in their palms."

"Do you think our children could have markings also?"

Daniel's face fell as he slowed his pace to let the gap between them and the others increase.

"I doubt it, my dear. I do not have the level of magic Alec does. The men of the Caretaker line have a very small amount, which is of no actual use to us, other than our drive to protect the women of our family."

Taru felt his worry and stopped with a gentle tug to pull him back to her. She waited for him to meet her eyes, then smiled.

"I just want our children to be healthy and happy. Magic is not important."

"You are bending the truth again, my Lady," Daniel said with a skeptical look. Taru scowled as she gripped his hand tighter.

"I am not. I do not care if they carry magic, as long as they are ours and we can love them together."

"And I completely agree," he said as he pulled her closer.

He kissed her as to leave no reason to doubt his sincerity. The magic between them built very fast, which left both breathing faster and her face was flush as they eased apart.

They resumed a slow walk to give themselves time to calm before joining the family. When they neared the bottom of the steps to the terrace, Taru skipped ahead and leapt to the very top of the ten steps with ease.

"How did you do that?"

"Do what?"

"How did you leap that far? You did a similar giant leap in the cave," he said as he climbed the steps.

"It was part of my gift. I have more strength, flexibility, and endurance than most humans I have met."

"It seems I will be challenged to keep up with you, my mate," he said with a broad smile as he took her hand to lead her into the castle.

TARU NOTICED EVERYONE looking at her and stopped eating. Her cheeks flushed as she forced the large mouthful down and looked at Daniel.

"Well, if you don't eat for three days, you have a great deal to make up for," he said as he laughed. Everyone laughed along with him and resumed their meal.

"*Do your skills of endurance and strength come with a higher requirement for sustenance?*" Morgan asked Taru.

"*Yes, my Lady. I can go for long periods without eating, but I am quite hungry in general, especially if I exert myself very much. I believe my metabolism must work at a higher rate than normal.*"

"*I imagine that is the reason your body temperature climbs so rapidly when your magic surges within you. We will need to address that. Do you need to exercise more than others as well?*"

Taru paused and frowned a bit as she glanced around the table.

"*I do not know. I have never been around anyone healthy enough to exercise. Rea had painful joints, and the few others I knew as a child were far too old. I was no more active than my dragon siblings, but I suppose that is an unfair comparison,*" Taru said. Morgan laughed, and Daniel looked up at her.

"Just talking with Taru. Don't be nosy, big brother."

Brya and Kyan were giggling behind their hands to each other and shooting Daniel furtive glances.

"What are you little rascals laughing about over there?" he asked.

"We heard your response to Mother, Uncle Daniel. Sorry," Brya said.

Morgan raised an eyebrow and stared at Daniel.

"Do I need to stay more connected to you, my Brother? Are you saying rude things to me while I am so kindly guarding from hearing your thoughts?"

Daniel blushed and cleared his throat as he eyed the children. Taru laid a hand to his arm and his focus returned to her.

"We need to talk about appropriate verbalizations, my munchkins," Morgan said. "Some things you keep to yourself, as they were not intended for your ears."

"But we did not use our ears. We used our minds and that we cannot stop, Mommy. How can that be wrong?" Kyan asked.

"You may not be able to avoid hearing the private thoughts of others, but you must realize they do not always wish to be heard. It is often kinder to not let the person know you heard them, so you do not embarrass them. People think far more than they verbalize, which is a very good thing. They use manners and simple good judgment to decide what they share. Our skills are special, and you must learn to use them kindly and wisely, my dears."

Both children listened and nodded then looked at each other. They both had thoughtful expressions as they looked back to their mother.

"So, when we hear things like Daddy thinking Taru is very beautiful, that is the kind of thing we should keep to ourselves as he probably would not have said that out loud?" Brya asked.

Daniel and Alec both nearly choked during the middle of that question.

"Yes, my Daughter! That is exactly the kind of thing you should have kept to yourself!" Alec said as he scowled at Brya. She and Kyan both looked down at his harsh tone.

"I can understand your confusion, little ones," Taru said with a smile that slid into a smirk as she continued. "Even now, I am hearing things from people all around me that I know were not intended for me. I am choosing to be safe and not react at all. For instance, I just heard what your mother had to say to your father about your news and chose not to laugh out loud."

Morgan and Alec both burst out laughing along with Taru as Daniel looked very frustrated to be left out of the joke. Alec looked at him and shook his head.

"Let us just say it was very rude and included many of your favorite expletives," Alec said. Daniel laughed as Morgan blushed magnificently.

4

Changing Things

MORGAN WAS HEADED for a swim when she saw Daniel showing Taru the vaulting technique they had developed for boarding the dragons. He leapt from the dragon's front leg with his left foot then threw his right leg over the saddle as he flew up. Taru followed, but took off from the ground, without using the dragon's leg, and landed soundly in front of him.

"Nice leap, my Lady," Menkar said with a chuckle.

"Do you two want to join me for a swim?" Morgan asked them. They dropped to the ground and jogged to walk with her.

"Alec will bring the children to join us when they wake from their power nap."

"Sleep actually strengthens their magic?" Taru asked. Daniel and Morgan laughed together.

"It is just an old Earth expression. It refers to a short nap with normal rejuvenation properties," Daniel said.

"What does 'Earth' mean?"

Morgan chuckled as she patted Daniel on the shoulder.

"There is much to learn about each other, for certain."

She took off her robe and plunged into the water in a new swimming outfit she had the seamstress make. It was not the wonderful spandex of Earth but fit well. It was made of many layers of a light material that moved with her while preserving her modesty well.

Daniel started taking off his clothes, to wear only his shorts in the water, until he saw Taru's obvious discomfort.

"Would you rather we just wear all our clothes?"

"No. Do what is comfortable for you. Please, go ahead. I will be in soon."

"Please, do not do anything which makes you feel that uncomfortable, my friend," Morgan said as she stopped and turned to focus on Taru. *"How can I help you feel more at ease?"*

Taru thought, *"Be honest,"* then answered, *"I am used to swimming alone and at night. I am not accustomed to being seen by anyone when not well covered. I want to come in, but I am anxious that Daniel will not like my markings. He said he does, but he has not seen all of them. And...I have some scars. Rea said they are rather unattractive."*

"Are you wearing an undershirt and undershorts?"

"Yes, Rea brought me proper clothing before we left."

"Then wear just those and dive in. I can promise you that my brother is eager to see more of you, especially your dragon markings. He likes them far more than I care to share," Morgan said as she gave Taru a broad smile and gestured to Daniel's furtive glances at her.

Morgan could not help but glance herself as Taru removed her top shirt. As she unlaced it the neck fell off one shoulder to give a clear view of the gorgeous minor dragon shifting around anxiously. When she reached down to lift her top shirt, it lifted her undershirt to show her lower torso. Her lower back was peppered with long thin scars. However, the dragon markings on her belly were lovely. Thin flowing scale lines arced across the top of her abdomen and more were just visible above her shorts. What caught and held Morgan's gaze was a dark, yet striking, set of dragon wings that began at a small thin line of scales at her navel and stretched across her muscular abdomen.

"Oh my..."

"Turn your head, you donkey," Morgan snapped at Daniel. He flushed and turned to swim hard for the opposite bank.

Taru's face fell when she saw him swimming away.

"He is retreating because I overheard his thoughts as he saw your beautiful belly. He most definitely approves," Morgan explained. *"And for good reason. Your markings are truly beautiful, my Sister."*

Taru joined them in the water and swam with amazing agility and speed. Morgan was a rather fast swimmer but could not keep up with Taru's natural stoke.

"Is this a very deep lake? Can we dive into it safely?" Taru asked as she looked up to the high ridge far above the water.

"No, it is definitely not deep enough for that," Daniel said.

"He means he is not willing to watch you try it. However, I know something you might enjoy."

She called to Falin and Lirpa to join them.

"Are we to enjoy the activities that you love, and Nulian hates?" Daniel asked with a wide smile.

Morgan smiled as the dragons soared toward them. Lirpa dove and Morgan did the same. A moment later both burst from the water with Morgan standing atop Lirpa's back. As Lirpa swooped up into a rolling loop, Morgan let gravity pull her off and made a graceful backward dive into the water.

Next, she met Falin as he swam toward her along the surface. He put his snout up to her feet as she held her body straight and arched her back up. She was body surfing the water as he propelled her along, then both dove out of sight. They again burst from the water and she was propelled far and long across the lake.

She dove back into the water just as the children and Alec arrived.

The children cheered and begged to do it as Alec shook his head.

"The only thing that is going to be throwing you in the water is me," he said as he scooped up Kyan and marched into the water to toss him over his head.

"Me now, Daddy," Brya yelled. She was soon flying as well.

Everyone had a great time playing together and Taru astounded them all with her athletic ability.

"Like what you see, dear?" Morgan said to Alec who watched Taru with focused interest.

"She is remarkably strong and flexible, my dear. It is impressive, for certain."

"Yes, very impressive," Morgan said as she swam away.

Alec swam to catch her and turned her around to face him. *"Stop with the jealousy. I am not interested in any other. Do you truly think I would be?"*

"No, she is just really gorgeous, and her markings are fabulous. I am a bit jealous and can understand why you stare," Morgan said. Alec kissed her Crest and sent shivers all over her then smiled wickedly as he pulled her closer.

"I hope the children did not overhear that one, my dear," she said. His eyes widened as he turned to look at them. She laughed, splashed him, and swam to play with the little ones.

Zirath came to play with them and let the children hold onto his neck as he slid along the surface very fast. At one point, he carried Brya to the opposite end of the lake.

Kyan watched with worried eyes then ran full speed and dove into the water after them. He was not a strong swimmer yet, so Alec dove after him to scoop him up. Even when he came up sputtering, he fought to free himself as he stared at Brya across the lake.

"She is not going away, Kyan. She will be right back. Watch from my shoulders," Alec said. He put the boy up on his shoulders so he could see and held fast to his legs.

"She is scared, Daddy," Kyan said through his own sobs.

Morgan had already asked Zirath to come back. She had also felt Brya getting upset. Zirath swam hard then circled Alec in tight circles.

"Come along, my Prince," Zirath said. Kyan jumped from Alec's shoulders, and the three went gliding across the water together as the children giggled.

"He could have killed himself in that attempt. The instinctual pull they share is beginning to worry me, my dear," Alec said. Morgan nodded while closely monitoring her children with her magic.

As the sun began to set, Morgan and Alec coaxed the twins out of the water and carried the irritable little ones back toward the castle.

"The area is all yours, big Brother. Enjoy," Morgan said as she looked back with a wink.

Daniel smiled as he heard her. "That was nice of her," Taru said. "You heard her?"

"Yes, I do not think she realizes how much of her thoughts I can hear. I am concentrating very hard to keep my thoughts from her, but do not know if I am successful."

Taru's face reddened as she glanced toward the castle, and Daniel laughed.

"You just got corrected on that one, didn't you?" She nodded and they laughed together.

"I am going to block you both to give you privacy for a while. If you need me, just concentrate hard. I will feel it. Goodnight."

Daniel looked into Taru's eyes for a long minute then swam toward her as he said, "Privacy is appreciated."

OVER THE NEXT FEW DAYS, Daniel and Taru spent every possible moment with each other. They spent many hours filling each other in on their lives. She was amazed to learn he and Morgan had been raised on yet another planet. He was surprised to find she had little understanding of her magic and its uses.

Her physical skills continued to shock him as well. He taught her sword fighting skills, and she soon mastered the basics. Between her enhanced strength and speed, it was enough to fend off even the most skilled Knights. She loved to spend time with the dragons and was especially tickled to meet the Elder Perian males who reminded her so much of Grith.

"She seems to be settling in well," Morgan said to Daniel one afternoon as they watched Taru play with a group of younglings. "What have you noticed of her magic thus far?"

"She uses it well for communication and is enjoying the touch of the dragons' magic. I'm just worried about how affected she is when she touches them," he said as he watched her.

"She has a great deal of power but has not been taught to control it. Remember how easily I was overwhelmed when I first came to Chemerie? I was using far less than she can at the moment. I expect that, without her added strength, she would probably be passing out with any attempt at deep connection or bonding. Nulian and I plan to take her to Berios to train soon. We were just giving you two a few days together."

"I would like to c—"

"No. Sorry, but your presence would undermine the purpose of going there. We need a non-distracting environment."

Daniel sighed but nodded as he continued to watch Taru. After a moment, he shifted closer and dropped his voice.

"How long should we wait to marry? I mean, I want to be appropriate. How long is long enough, and still as soon as possible?"

"I think you marry whenever you feel you are both ready. The magic has already linked your spirits. A wedding is just our opportunity to celebrate that link with you."

"Thank you. I needed that answer, and you knew it. I love you, little sister," he said before he kissed her head and moved off toward Taru, where he stopped and bowed.

"Lady Taru, will you join me for a private dinner at dusk?" he asked in a formal tone. Taru nodded, then watched him sprint across the lawn to where Falin visited with Willow and a small group of hatchlings. As he reached them, she turned to look at Morgan and shrugged.

"You need to come meet my seamstresses. Follow me, my friend," Morgan said. Taru started to toward her but halted a few steps later and turned to glare at Daniel. Morgan felt her anger a second before intense pain buckled Willow.

"Taru, Stop!" Morgan yelled as she leapt down the steps and took off toward Willow, who was now unconscious in Daniel's arms. Taru's magical attack halted, and Willow started gasping deep breaths as she jerked awake. Morgan reached her and took the lingering pain while trying to calm her.

"What was that?" Daniel asked as he continued to support Willow's back. "What happened?"

"Your mate happened! Her jealousy and ignorance of her magic are a deadly combination." Morgan shot a glare at Taru, who was hovering a few yards behind her, then refocused on calming herself and Willow.

Daniel was looking at Willow as his neck and face flushed.

"This is not just her fault. I will explain my feelings to her as best I can. Please, be angry with me, not her."

Willow sat up and shifted her gaze between him and Taru before setting a fierce glare on Taru as she stood. She was shaking with fists clenched as she took two steps closer.

"I am blessed to have Daniel's friendship, and would never

dishonor him by seeking anything more when it is clear he feels a link to you. I care not if you trust my word, but it sickens me that you have so little trust in him! If you knew him at all, you would never question his honor!"

"Enough," Daniel said in a calm tone as he shifted between them. Willow focused on him as she stepped back. "I should have been completely honest with her sooner. It was ignorant of me not to consider her awareness of my thoughts and feelings."

"You have the right to think and feel anything you wish. It is what you choose to act on that determines your honor! Perhaps you should explain that to your mate!"

Willow spun and marched away from them. Morgan gave her brother a flat stare.

"Taru would have killed her had I not been so close. There can be no more secrets, not of feelings such as those. Share them with her, all of them, any intimate touches or moments you and Willow shared before realizing you were not linked. Do it now, Brother. Once she is calm, send her to me, and I will help her prepare for your dinner."

Daniel nodded then waited until she had caught up to Willow near the castle to turn and face Taru.

"I kissed her, once, because I did care deeply for her and was desperately seeking my mate. I do not have your magic. To detect such a link requires a touch more intimate than holding hands or embracing. I am sorry if you see it as a betrayal. But I will not apologize for caring for her, nor do I intend to stop being her friend. I love you, Taru. I will never touch another intimately now that I have found you. While I love knowing you are jealous of my affections, you must trust me enough to know I am yours and will never reach for another."

Tears were sliding down Taru's face as she lifted her head and met his eyes.

"I did not mean to hurt her. I have no idea what I did or how I did it. I was jealous, I was angry, but I would never have done that on purpose."

He stepped to her and wiped tears from her cheeks. She had shifted back against Falin, so he stepped closer.

"I know you did not mean to. So does Morgan. If she thought you hurt her dear friend on purpose, you would not be standing in Chemerie."

"She should send me away."

"Now that you know how dangerous it is, perhaps you will not argue when she insists on taking you away from the castle to teach you more control."

"No. I would leave now if she asked."

"Well, she isn't. Instead, she is asking that you go to spend time with her until I return to pick you up for dinner."

He pulled her off of Falin and kissed her cheek. She gripped his sides and held him still as she moved her lips very close to his.

"How did you kiss her?"

He did not hesitate to kiss her softly on the lips for two seconds before leaning back.

"Was there more?"

He lifted a hand to softly caress her face.

"I did this just before I kissed her. Beyond that, we only embraced as friends."

She nodded, and he started to shift back. His breath caught as she pulled him sharply back to her and kissed him deeply for a far more intense two seconds.

"I am very proud you are mine. And I will never stop being jealous of your affections."

She turned and took off for the castle, leaving him smiling like an idiot as he vaulted aboard Falin.

Morgan was waiting for Taru on the terrace and gave her a small smile as she leapt up the stairs in one effortless move.

"I do envy your agility, my friend. Once you have proper control of your magic, you will be a formidable woman for certain. Until then, I ask that you focus on not allowing your temper to rise for any reason. If it begins to, immediately focus on me and call my name repeatedly in thought. I can help calm you, even from a distance. Agreed?"

"Yes, my Queen. May I apologize to Lady Willow?"

"Not tonight. She needs to calm a bit more. I do think you should, but not when she is likely to go off like a feral animal. Her temper is not quick, but once it snaps, she is slow to calm."

"I deserve her anger. I just need her to know I had no intention of—

Morgan stopped her comment with a lifted eyebrow. She sighed and went quiet as she fell into step beside Morgan.

"I did think of wanting her away from him. Was that enough to make my magic act against her?"

"I think it far more likely to have been your desire to pummel her as you felt Daniel's emotions rise."

Taru blushed and nodded, which made Morgan laugh as they reached the seamstresses' workroom. Morgan introduced her to the wonderfully skilled ladies, then left her in their capable hands with a request to use light materials and consider showcasing her friend's lovely markings.

DANIEL SLID DOWN Falin's leg and ran into the castle to speak with the cook, then collected a few items. He then hurried to shower, change clothes, and speak with GranMay.

"How quickly can this castle pull together a wedding?" "When would you like it?" GranMay asked with a chuckle. "Tomorrow," he said with a huge smile.

"It seems both of my grandchildren believe in wasting no time when it comes to love," she said as she laughed. "Would you like a small private ceremony, or a full grand affair?" Daniel gave her a blank stare, so she patted his arm and shoved him toward the door.

"I will handle it. Off you go, to actually ask her, I imagine." Daniel kissed her cheek and turned to hurry toward the kitchens.

He packed up the picnic basket the cooks had prepared, then ran to the gardens where he acquired a few roses. He was loading all his supplies onto Falin's harness when Alec joined him.

"You have a plan then, I see. Are you sure a night alone prior to the wedding is a great one?"

"I believe you slept in my sister's bed a couple of times before you were married," Daniel said in a flat tone without turning to him.

Alec scowled until he realized Daniel was referring to the times Morgan had healed him after severe injuries. He had lain asleep from the pain and exhaustion in her bed.

"That is funny, but I would like to talk seriously a moment, my friend. I hope you will not think it too forward. I mention it out of friendship, I promise."

Daniel stopped loading and turned to face him. Alec took a few more steps to get closer as he glanced around them.

"I obviously noticed the amount of dragon scales on Taru. I wanted to make sure you were aware of their unique sensitivity," Alec said.

"Unfortunately, I have witnessed the effect when you touch Morgan's. I get it. I appreciate the concern, but I think we will be fine."

"She has no idea what to expect, Daniel. She has never been touched by anyone, much less by her mate. I am concerned she will be overwh—"

"I don't need advice on touching my mate!"

Alec nodded as he backed up and turned to leave.

"Stop. Wait," Daniel called as he rubbed his face. "I'm sorry. Look, I may joke about such things easily, but I do not talk seriously about it, ever. I appreciate the warning, and I do hear you. OK?"

Alec nodded again with a light smile but said nothing else before returning to the castle.

Daniel and Falin took the goods to prepare for the night, then flew back to the castle, where he paced the courtyard as he waited for Taru.

He froze when he saw her; she quite literally took his breath away. A beautifully cut outfit of light gray wafted in the breeze. Thin shoulder straps supported the crossed material over her torso, and a split in the front allowed her lovely belly to be seen a bit as she moved. Long fitted pants and a sheer cloak finished it off. He remained mute and transfixed as she moved toward him.

"You look amazing, my Lady. Please, join me," he said, inviting her to board Falin first.

She smiled as she stepped past him, then leapt up to the saddle. He vaulted aboard and helped her buckle into a waist strap, with care not to touch the scales on her midriff. He admired the woven straps draped over the low back of her blouse as she leaned forward to stroke Falin's neck.

As Falin took off, she shifted back to settle against his chest. He wrapped his arms around her loosely and kissed her cheek as she turned her face to his. Their connection caused them both to become warm within seconds, so he loosened his grip.

They landed beside a cabin built near a beautiful mountain stream. He dismounted then turned to catch her against him as she slid down just after him. They both shivered and smiled as he pulled his hands off her sides and took one of hers.

He led her to the back porch of the cabin, where her eyes lit up when she saw the beautiful setting he had prepared. A table covered in white linen was set with two intricately carved candles that cast a soft glow over the fine plates and silverware around them. One end of the table was filled with a spray of fragrant pink roses. Their chairs were covered with soft blankets, and a wooden settee near the table was covered with plush cushions and pillows.

"This is wonderful. Thank you for all the effort."

He kissed her hand, led her to the table then insisted she sit as he unpacked their food and served their plates. Her attention shifted between him and taking in the details of the candles, plates, and roses until he took his seat.

They ate in comfortable silence as they watched the sun set over the river.

"Would you like to take a walk, or just sit and enjoy the view?"

"How about a short walk, then sit and enjoy one another," she said.

He smiled and followed her down the stairs to the path along the river.

They walked and talked for a few minutes before Taru stopped him with a slight frown.

"Are you well? You seem anxious."

"I am more than well, Taru. I seem odd because I was thinking about how much I feel for a woman I have only known for a few days.

It seems crazy that I am standing here with zero doubt in wanting to be with you for the rest of my life." He took her hands in his. "I am so thankful that the magic has given me such a strong connection to such an incredible woman. I do not want to wait another day to start our lives as husband and wife. Will you marry me tomorrow?"

Tears slid down her face, and he felt a rush of emotions coming through their touch.

"Yes, my Daniel. Tomorrow is perfect."

He pulled her to him and slowly dropped his head to let his lips brush hers. She lifted to her toes, wrapped her arms around his neck, and kissed him with passion. When her skin grew very hot, he broke the kiss, slid a hand into hers, and urged her to resume their walk.

As they headed back to the cabin, she stumbled. When he grabbed her waist to steady her, his hand slid over the small line of scales at her navel, making them gasp and tighten their grip.

He started to pull away as he felt the intense rush of magic, but she covered his hand with hers and pressed it against her scales as she looked into his eyes. The surge of magic passing between them made their hearts race as if they were sprinting, and Daniel felt her skin temperature climb again. Her eyes glowed their brightest yet, then faded just before she collapsed in his arms.

He cursed himself as he laid her down, then concentrated on Morgan, calling her name in his thoughts again and again.

"What's wrong?"

"She held my hand to her scales too long and passed out. Her breaths are shallow and fast, her heart is racing, her skin is hot as fire, her lips are turning blue, and her face is pale."

"I'm coming! Keep your hands off of her!"

MORGAN LEAPT FROM LIRPA and hurried to kneel beside Taru. She placed one hand over her own Crest and the other to Taru's on her stomach. As she passed healing energy, she focused on dropping Taru's heart rate and allowing more efficient blood flow through her body. As her heart slowed, her breaths deepened, her lips pinked, and she woke with a jolt.

"It's all right now. Morgan helped you," Daniel said.

"What happened?" Taru asked as she sat up. "I was enjoying the sensation of your touch and... "

"You almost killed yourself, Taru. You sent your heart into a very fast and inefficient rhythm, which deprived your brain of oxygen. Had I not been near, you would have died. Sorry to be blunt, but if you two try to consummate your marriage now, you could both die from the uncontrolled transfer of energy. You must consider putting the wedding off until Nulian and I can teach you to wield your magic with enough skill to make being with your mate safe for you both."

She shifted to help Taru stand, then swatted Daniel's hands away as he reached for her. He scowled but did not reach again when Taru swayed a little before Morgan let her go.

"Tomorrow, you come with me to train. When you are ready, we will include Daniel in your training as well." She saw concern cross Daniel's face and held his gaze. "Normally, I block your personal thoughts and feelings. This time, I can't. You will have to put your modesty aside if you want to be with her safely. No limits this time, big brother." She turned and headed toward Lirpa as she said, "Only one house call a night. Keep your hands to yourself, please."

Daniel shook his head and smiled as he watched Morgan and Lirpa fly away.

"And to think, I made her blush when I caught her kissing Alec for the first time."

Taru was silent as tears slid down her face. He wiped them and lifted her chin to look into her eyes.

"We have the rest of our lives. I'm not going anywhere. I don't mind waiting if it means we can be together without worry or limitations. Do you?"

She shook her head and pulled his shirt gently to suggest a kiss. He shifted to kiss her cheek lightly before pulling away to smile at her scowl.

"Sorry, but that really scared me, and I have no desire to live through it again. Let's sit and talk. I brought a favorite dessert."

"I am still very warm. Do you mind if I go for a swim?"

"Do you mind if I don't join you? It's a bit cold for my taste."

"No, that is fine. I will not be long. I just want to cool down, so I can relax."

She walked upriver while Daniel returned to the porch. As he raised a glass of wine, he glanced toward her and froze.

He knew he should turn away, but could not help staring at the beautiful woman standing in the river. Water glistened over her dark skin, and her scales glimmered in the moonlight. His heart filled with pride as he realized that exquisite woman was to be his wife.

He watched as she started to swim upstream, pacing the current to hold her body in one spot as the water rushed past. After a moment, she swam harder to reach a small waterfall and stood beneath it. When she turned toward him, he looked away and busied himself cleaning their dinner plates and serving the dessert.

"Would you like some fruit salad?" he asked when she leapt up to the porch with grace.

"Yes, thank you." She ate the entire portion before he was halfway through his.

"I'm full. Would you like more?"

She gave him a skeptical look so he traded bowls with her and moved to sit down. When she sat down, he felt the heat still radiating off of her. He kissed her head as she laid it to his shoulder and smiled as he felt her happiness.

"I love you, Taru."

She shifted to look into his eyes and pushed a strong rush of love and devotion over him as she leaned in.

"And I love you, my Daniel."

He smiled but stopped her with a finger to her lips. "Patience, my dear. I am very shy after all."

She smiled and laid her head back down. They settled against each other but were careful to not let their skin touch as they discussed the traditions of weddings and marriage in the Chemerian culture.

"WHAT?" Morgan asked as she jerked awake. She was bombarded with answers from both Daniel and Menkar, then blocked out Daniel's frantic chatter to understand Menkar.

"Lady Taru is very hot with fever, my Caretaker. Sir Daniel cannot wake her," Menkar said. She reconnected to Daniel with a strong push of calming magic.

"Menkar is bringing you to me at my terrace. Relax. You will be here soon, and we will sort it out."

Menkar landed beside her terrace and transferred Daniel to the railing. As Alec took Taru from Daniel's arms, Morgan noticed that the glow of his palm markings was now barely visible. She quickly connected to Nulian and Valen.

"Please join me at my terrace. Quickly, please," she said to the Elder dragons as Alec laid Taru down. With their confirmation, she looked at Daniel. "I need you to go for now." He hesitated, but did not argue as Alec gripped his shoulders to urge him inside.

With them gone, Morgan knelt beside Taru and laid a hand against the scales along her stomach to study her condition.

"How is Lady Taru, my Caretaker?" Nulian asked as she hurried toward the castle.

"She is in a fever-induced coma. The question is, what caused the fever? Contact with Daniel cannot be the only issue. She has been exposed to many new things. The new planet, its people, its climate, the dragons, as well as the food and drink she has ingested. It could have something to do with her magic or simply be an allergic reaction. Or, it could be much worse."

She continued to monitor and study all she felt in Taru as Nulian landed and dropped her head over the railing.

"Join me in another search. Perhaps you can sense something I could not or did not recognize."

Nulian touched her snout to Morgan's back as she pushed to connect to Taru. They searched for the source of the fever and found nothing obvious. Both pushed the connection into bonding and still found no explanation for her condition.

She released the bonding and sat back, frustrated.

"The only thing I feel is an enormous amount of energy within her. It is as if she cannot release the energy she receives from others. I wonder if Grith did not give her too much too soon in his gift," Morgan said.

"May I help her by taking her energy into myself, my Lady?" Valen asked. "I have taken the painful energy of injury from others. However, I believe taking on this excess magical energy is perhaps the truest application of this skill of the Perian dragons."

"I do not like it, but I would never tell you no when I feel your heart aching so, my friend. Will you allow me to try a few things first?" Morgan said. Valen nodded but crooned a mournful sound.

"GranMay, I need your advice," Morgan said as she gently touched her grandmother's mind to wake her.

"How may an old woman help you, my dear?" GranMay replied. Being a Caretaker, with considerable magic and skill, she had felt the anxiety accompanying Morgan's call.

"Taru holds a great deal of magical energy trapped within her. She is in a coma. What are your thoughts on my channeling the energy within her through myself into others?"

"I see your desire to strengthen me through this. If you think my taking energy from her will help, I will obviously do it. But I do not want you choosing this route for my sake. Only do this if it is the best move for Taru." GranMay said. Morgan looked at Taru whose breathing was growing more shallow and sporadic.

"I will let Valen try her skill first, but please join me." Turning to Valen she said, "You are right, my friend. I think your unique skill may be the answer. Can I help you at all?"

"I would not feel comfortable with you involved in the bonding, my Caretaker. I have never done this with a human, and would not want to hurt you by accident. Please, move her closer to me, then step back."

Morgan pulled the lounge chair closer to Valen then sat next to Nulian's head to watch. Nulian touched her and hummed to give her comfort. Morgan deepened their connection to relax them both. GranMay came to sit beside them and took her hand.

Valen blew against Taru's torso to waft her shirt away from her belly, then gently touched her snout to the dragon wings and scales there. She shivered as she began to hum the healing song of the Perian dragons. Their version was a little different, yet of the same basic structure as that of the Chemerian dragons.

"Go slowly, my friend. Be sure only to take and not to give," Morgan said to Valen.

Valen sent light thoughts of agreement in return, but kept her focus on Taru. After a moment, her song changed and Morgan felt the energy begin to flow to her from Taru.

Seconds later, she shot to her feet and lunged at Valen with all her might. She slammed into the dragon's snout as hard as she could to break the contact to Taru, then watched as the great dragon collapsed. She hurried to leap to the railing, to Nulian's palm, and then to Valen's back. Nulian hummed the song of healing along with Lirpa and Falin who had hurried at her call.

Morgan focused on Valen's heart, which had stopped. She pushed healing as hard as she could and still Valen's heart sat dormant. After a pause to let her magic build, she pushed a burst of magic to the dragon's heart which contracted twice before falling still again.

She let her magic build again then felt it suddenly amplify as four little hands pressed against her back. As it built so high that her Crest burned, she pushed all of their energy in one powerful jolt. Relief filled them all as Valen's heart jerked and started to beat at a stable, even rate. Valen took in great unsteady breaths so Morgan pushed more healing at a fast pace until her breathing became steady as well.

With her friend stable, Morgan disconnected from the healing and turned to see the beautiful faces of her children wearing proud smiles as they moved into Nulian's palm. Once on the terrace, the twins moved to Taru and stood near her head. When they reached out, Morgan stopped them from touching her.

"She needs to use it, Mommy. We can help her. Please let us," they said together.

"I do no—"

"How must she use it, children?" GranMay asked as she laid a hand to Morgan's arm with a push of patience. Morgan responded with a stronger push of annoyance. *"Hear them out before you say no, dear."*

Morgan conceded and nodded to the twins.

"She can use it to change things and does not know how. We do, and we can help her do it," they said.

"What do you mean by 'change things'? What are you changing?" Morgan asked.

"If you have enough energy, our magic can rearrange the atoms into another shape of the same amount of matter."

Morgan sat down with a plop. *"Alec, come here, now,"* she said as she stared at their calm, rational faces.

Alec and Daniel moved to stand between GranMay and the children, looking expectant.

"Can you show us what you mean before involving Taru, please?" Morgan asked.

The twins looked at each other for a few seconds, then Brya moved to the edge of the terrace to scoop up a handful of sand. She poured half into Kyan's hand, then both closed their hands around the sand. They smiled as they closed their eyes and began to hum.

Morgan did not recognize the tune at first then heard Taru humming it within a memory she received when they first bonded. The children hummed for a minute more, then opened their eyes and hands. Each held a small glass dragon figurine in their palm.

"One Chemerian and one Perian, with amazing detail," Alec said as he knelt to study them closer.

"I wonder if I will ever get accustomed to your surprises, my children. That is a wonderful skill," Morgan said.

"You can do it too, Mommy. Why do you not?" Brya said.

Morgan raised an eyebrow and said, "I did not know I could, my dear."

"Morgan, can they help her or not?" Daniel asked.

Morgan told him and Alec what happened to Valen, and both

were scowling as they looked between the children and Taru.

"Children, we are very scared for you," Morgan said. "Valen almost died in her attempt to help Taru. What do you plan to do, exactly?"

"Only give her something to change," they said. "And sing along with her."

"You will not touch her?" Morgan asked. They shook their heads. She and Alec both let out a deep sigh of relief at not being forced to make a very difficult choice between their children's safety and Taru's life. "Alright, what do we need to do to help her?"

"May we have a large lump of coal?" they asked together. Daniel bolted from the room and returned to shove the coal into Morgan's hands before stepping back from Taru again.

She looked to her children.

"Hold it between her hands, Mommy, and sing along with us."

The twins began to sing as soon as Morgan wrapped the coal with Taru's hands. She covered Taru's hands with her own, then focused on assuring all energy flow from Taru went into the coal. When she started singing along with the children, she felt the magic flowing and focusing in a familiar, yet unique way. It reminded her of how it felt to draw, paint, or even to view fine art of others. It was the very essence of creativity.

The mass between Taru's hands got smaller and smaller as they sang. Morgan considered what she knew of coal. It was mostly carbon, in a very irregular crystal array, with a great deal of free space between the atoms. If the volume was shrinking, she figured Taru was forming it into a more regular crystal array such as graphite or even...

The children stopped humming as the energy flow stopped within Taru. Morgan released Taru's hands and let their contents fall to her belly. She smiled as she saw a small perfect diamond gleaming in the moonlight.

Taru's body temperature was near normal, and both her heart and lungs moved at a reasonable rate. Kyan and Brya bent over to kiss Taru's head then ran into their parents' room to climb up on the bed with happy giggles.

Daniel followed them and pulled both into a huge hug. He held them to him and said, "Thank you for saving her, munchkins. I am so thankful to have you with us. I love you both very much. You know that, don't you?"

"Of course we do, Uncle Daniel, we feel it every day. And we love you and Aunt Taru too," they said as they hugged him back. He beamed and kissed them both before returning to Taru and the others.

"You can touch her now. Just avoid her scales, please," Morgan said to him.

He knelt and caressed Taru's arm with just the tips of his fingers. "You did not cause this. It was her magic alone. Touch her normally.

She is ready to wake," Morgan said as she and the others went inside.

DANIEL WHISPERED in Taru's ear as he stroked her cheek with the back of his fingers.

"Wake up, my love. I am starting to think you are avoiding me."

He saw a faint smile cross her lips as she began to breathe deeply.

His eyes reddened as he fought tears.

"My heart cannot take too many more of these, my love. Please talk to me and let me know you are truly all right," he said hoarsely. She rolled her head toward him and opened her eyes with a sleepy smile.

"I had the strangest dream. I dreamt a terribly handsome man asked me to marry him, then watched as I swam in a river. He was very naughty in watching, don't you think?" Daniel blushed and kissed her cheek.

"Yes, he was indeed, and he apologizes most sincerely."

"No need. I would not have looked away, had the roles been reversed."

He caressed her cheek again as she looked into his eyes, and both fought tears.

"Do you feel all right? Are you in any pain?"

"No, I actually feel cool for the first time since coming here." Daniel held the diamond up so she could see it and she smiled.

"That was certainly a dramatic way to go about getting a diamond ring for your wedding, my dear." She smiled as her eyes closed, then drifted back to sleep.

Daniel asked Morgan to make sure she really was just sleeping before settling down on a lounge chair next to her.

ALEC HAD THE TWINS snuggled up next to him when Morgan climbed into the bed.

"Goodnight, my wonderful family," she said as she kissed all three. Brya reached up to touch her face and smiled.

"Mommy, you change things every time you heal. You fix what has been all messed up. That seems much harder than organizing silicon dioxide or carbon, don't you think?"

"What amazes me is you discussing silicon dioxide and carbon at eighteen months old. You were born with access to so much knowledge, and are growing up so fast, my little ones. Just promise me you will never get too big, or too smart, to be our little munchkins."

5

New Lessons

GRANMAY WOKE DANIEL with a soft caress of his cheek as she settled on the lounge beside him.

"Are you still intending to wed today, my boy?" she said with a smile. His initial smile fell as he looked over at Taru.

"No, Taru almost died from a few seconds of touching last night, so getting married and..." Daniel's face turned bright pink as he stopped mid-sentence.

GranMay chuckled, "That is exactly what I expected, so I did not plan anything. I knew you would both be a bit surprised at the intensity within Taru's magic. You will have your hands full, my boy. While she is away training, I would like for you to spend some time with me. I miss our time together, and I think this may be my last chance to have you to myself." Daniel heard the abnormal tone of her voice and sat up to kiss her cheek and hug her.

"You can have me to yourself anytime you want, GranMay. Just call, and I'm yours. I love you like crazy, and I'm sorry if I haven't shown it."

"No apologies," she said as she patted his cheek. "I am thrilled you have found your mate. You have much to accomplish. I would never get in the way of that."

Daniel raised an eyebrow and asked, "What is it I'm supposed to accomplish?" GranMay looked to Taru and then back to him.

"You are the mate of a woman with strong magic and a special kinship to the Perian dragons. Your role is much the same as Alec's. Your children will be very special as well. You will carry the same heavy responsibility Morgan and Alec do with the twins. You are not simply your sister's protector anymore. You and your mate have your own unique roles in the future of Chemerie."

"You clearly know far more about our future than you have let on. Does Morgan realize how much you really know, or do you hide it from her?"

GranMay blushed a little as she glanced toward Morgan's bedroom window.

"I have been able to understand a great deal more since the twins were born. I have benefited from their magic as Morgan has. But no, I have not actually discussed it with her. She has enough going on and does not need to worry about such.

"Unfortunately, she is so worried about my coming time of passing, that is all she sees when she is near me. She focuses so hard on my health that it is easier to hide my thoughts."

"But why would you hide that you have seen glimpses of the future through the children? I don't understand."

She took his hand and used her magic to speak to him privately.

"Morgan is not ready to hear what I have learned about the children's future. It is kinder not to tell her now, and I ask that you mention none of this to her," GranMay waited for a nod of agreement from him before continuing. *"Their rate of growth will not slow, and they will begin fulfilling their role within the year. Morgan and Alec will be forced to let go much sooner than any of*

us imagined, and it makes my heart ache to think of the pain it will cause them."

"Will they simply grow and become more independent, or will they leave Chemerie?"

"I cannot say, my boy. It is unclear to me. I do know there is much anguish around it for Morgan."

Daniel and GranMay both jumped when Morgan spoke from the door.

"You have hidden nothing from me, GranMay. I have felt your worry and have heard your thoughts about this for months. I said nothing because I knew you did not wish me to know. I too have glimpsed bits of their future, and have shared it with no one, not even Alec. It is too hard to think about, so I choose not to. I focus on enjoying them as much as I can while I have them." She moved to GranMay and placed her hand to her cheek. "I do worry about your health, just as you do mine. That is where I put my focus when I am near you because I love you dearly and do not want you to hurt in any way I can prevent. You are precious to me, and I intend to keep you with us for as long as my magic lets me do so."

GranMay took Morgan's hand off her cheek and held her gaze with a stern expression.

"No, my dear. I will stay for as long as my magic says I should. Then, I will let my life end naturally. It is my choice, Morgan. You must let me die my way."

Morgan's eyes filled with tears as she nodded, then left in silence. Daniel took GranMay into his arms and held her tight as tears streamed down her cheeks as well.

"I FEEL YOUR GRIEF. What has happened?" Taru said to Daniel as she woke.

"Nothing. Well, nothing yet. We were just dreading the approaching end of GranMay's life. It is hard to think about."

"Is she to die soon? Can Morgan not heal her?" Taru asked as she sat up.

"I don't know how long they mean. Morgan's ability to heal is a difficult issue. GranMay wants to die naturally when she feels it is time." "I imagine Morgan's heart is breaking a little every day. How awful for her," Taru said. "It makes the ability to heal feel less like a gift, and more like a terribly heavy burden."

MORGAN LEFT GRANMAY, walked into the bathroom, and closed the door behind her. She buried her face in a towel and cried hard for a moment before feeling Alec's approach.

She laid a hand to his cheek and shared the discussion of Gran-May's decision. He kissed her forehead and squeezed her tight to him.

"Please try to focus on the gift your magic is. Your abilities were meant to make life better but not to stop the cycle of life altogether."

Morgan nodded and laid her head against his chest.

"We will be letting our children go far too soon, my love. They will leave us to fulfill their destinies. I am not sure when, or how, but I am sure we will not have them with us for long before they are grown and ready to follow their own path."

Alec tightened his hold on her and was quiet for a moment.

"How long have you known this? Have you tried to spare me from it and faced it alone?"

"I started feeling it and seeing bits of their future a few months ago, but only felt the impending loss last week. I tried to convince myself it was loss associated with the experiences we are missing because of their brief childhood. Now, I realize it is much more than that."

"Then we must focus on cherishing them every day. We love them as much as possible and enjoy their spirits every possible second. What else is there to do?"

"You are right, of course. I just said that to GranMay and Daniel. It is just so hard to hide these feelings when I am with them. I feel like

I am lying to them by omission, and it feels awful."

Now it was Morgan who was startled to find she had been over-heard when Kyan spoke.

"Do not worry, Mommy. We will not die or leave forever. We will only start our travels," Kyan said.

"We will come home between adventures, always," Brya said. Morgan and Alec lifted them into their arms and kissed them.

"It is not nice to eavesdrop, you know. You should not have heard our conversation," Alec said. Morgan felt the irritation rise within Kyan and smiled as she kissed his nose.

"I know you cannot help hearing with your mind. This time I am glad for it. You have eased my worries, and I am grateful. However, eavesdropping is rude. You should not have been listening with your ears outside the door," she said as Kyan looked down to trace her Crest. "I was guessing about that part, but I see I am right." Kyan looked up with a wicked little smile very much like his father's, and she could not help laughing.

LIRPA HELPED DANIEL AND TARU down from Morgan's ter-race, and they walked the gardens as Daniel explained all that hap-pened the night before.

"I did not know anything about using my magic to alter things like this. How could I have done this and not known how?" she asked as she stared at the diamond in her hand.

"The twins. Their natural understanding of their magical skills is amazing. Morgan wasn't aware of this use either," Daniel said.

"It is baffling that they are so young and can do things she can-not," Taru said.

"She feels the same way," Daniel said.

They walked out of the garden and headed for the lake.

"Will you be joining me for a swim? Or would you prefer to just watch again?"

He smiled and kissed her cheek before picking her up quickly and running to the water to throw her in, fully clothed. He laughed loudly as she surfaced, then folded his arms with fake haughtiness.

"I will gladly join you as long as you respect my chivalrous nature and keep your distance. I wish to remain quite innocent until we are properly wed, my Lady."

"That will not be a problem, Admiral," she said as she turned to swim away from him.

"I was joking around, Taru. Are you actually mad at me?"

She did not turn around but smiled wickedly and slowed her pace. When he approached, she dove deep and pulled him down by his feet. She swam down below him and waited for him to surface and take a breath before pulling him back under again.

They wrestled playfully until Daniel ran short on air. When he tried to surface, she kept wrestling. He pushed her away and hurried to the surface. He broke the surface gasping for air, then turned on her with a deep scowl as she surfaced.

"Ease up! You almost drowned me!"

She was silent and flinched as his anger hit her, but he was still too rattled to calm down. He swam for the rocks by the falls and climbed up on one to rest. Taru swam after him but stayed in the water a few feet away.

"I did not mean to hurt you. I was only playing. I was not out of breath, so I did not realize you were."

"So, you can hold your breath for a long time as well?"

"I do not know if it is considered a long time. I cannot hold it as long as the dragons."

"Show me."

She took a deep breath and submerged to look up at him from under the water. He counted off the seconds for three minutes before moving to pull her up and to him.

"I'm sorry I yelled at you. Most humans can't hold their breath for more than a minute or so without passing out. I got a little scared when I felt that point approaching, and you pulled me back down again. I really am sorry."

"I learn something else by making a mistake first. I am growing tired of this method of educating myself."

They laughed together then lay on the rocks in the warm morning sun. Daniel rolled to his side and reached over to trace the gorgeous dragon wings on her torso. He could see them through the sheer material of her shirt and smiled as they shifted at his touch.

She shivered then sat up to lean in for a kiss.

"Whoa, we need none of that," Morgan said to both of them. Taru flinched, and Daniel jerked as if smacked. *"Taru, it is time for you to come with Nulian and me so we can help you control your magic. We will be gone for a few days. Say goodbye to Daniel, then join us near the gazebo, please."*

"Days? Must we be apart so long?" Taru whispered to Daniel.

"She knows the effect on you each time we touch and also knows we have difficulty being near one another without touching. The sooner you learn to control it, the sooner we can touch each other freely. I want to be able to hold your hand and kiss you without worry. Please go and put your heart into the training, my love. Then return to me so we can marry and spend every day together."

Taru smiled and stole a quick kiss before he could dodge away, then dove into the water. She was making quick work of crossing the lake when she said, *"That was wonderfully put, my dear. I will train hard and have enough control to hold you in my arms without worry very soon, I promise. Be well, my mate."*

She waved at him as she exited the water and broke into a fast run across the lawn to meet the waiting Morgan and Nulian.

"IT WAS A BIT INSENSITIVE not to let them kiss goodbye, my Sister," Nulian said as she nudged Morgan.

"We need no more excitement from her uncontrolled magic, my friend," Morgan said. She watched Taru running toward her with envy of her speed. Taru was breathing only a bit faster than normal despite the two hundred yard sprint.

"Would you like to change into something dry before we go?"

"The coolness of the wet clothes feels nice. I am fine if it does not bother you," Taru said.

"Then off we go," Morgan said as she gestured to Nulian's back.

Taru leapt to land within the saddle and moved back as Morgan took a few steps to vault up and land in front of her.

"Ready whenever you are, my Sister," Morgan said as she patted Nulian. Nulian lifted off with fluid grace as always and flew low over the waving Daniel.

"Spend some quality time with GranMay. She is weakening more each day," Morgan said.

"I will. Try not to worry and enjoy getting to know your new sister-in-magic, OK?" Morgan waved at him then laughed hard as Zirath came crashing through the falls to tackle him into the lake. She, Taru, and Nulian all laughed as they left him wrestling with the youngling.

NULIAN AND MORGAN both forgot to warn Taru about the significant drop into the main cavern of the Chamber of Elders. She shrieked and grabbed Morgan, who pushed an apology and calming energy at once. Taru's anxiety level rose very fast while they plunged into the dark cavern.

Nulian was too large to circle down. She had to let herself drop well within the cavern, then open her wings to stop just as the cavern widened near the floor. Taru did not enjoy the experience in the least and leapt to the floor the instant Nulian touched down. Morgan slid down Nulian's leg and pushed more calming energy as she apologized again.

"We can walk from here if you prefer," Morgan said. Taru nodded and glanced toward Nulian.

"You have not offended me, my Lady. I am sorry we failed to warn you of the drop," Nulian said.

Morgan and Taru led the way as they traveled through the cave system to the portal room. As they entered the darkest of the tunnels, Morgan noticed Taru did not seem bothered by the darkness.

"I see you also have enhanced vision from the dragon blood within you."

"What do you mean, my Caretaker?"

"Average humans cannot see in this darkness. The fact that you can is part of your gift."

"But, I cannot."

Morgan stopped and moved her hand in front of Taru's face. "You did not slow your step at all. I assumed you could see."

"No, I am just quite used to dark tunnels. I learned to use my hearing to keep myself in the center of them," Taru said.

They walked on and eventually entered the portal chamber. As soon as Taru's feet touched the dense liquid surface of the portal, she froze.

"Are you taking me away?" Taru asked with fear in her voice.

Morgan took her hand and deepened their connection.

"Feel the truth of my words, Taru. We are going to a different world to train, but you need not worry. It is a very safe place. It is where I take my family to protect them from harm."

Taru closed her eyes to focus on the connection to Morgan and calmed as she felt her honesty.

"What will it be like when we get there? I was not expecting to end up underwater when I traveled here and would like to be prepared this time."

"You will find yourself standing on a large ledge overlooking a deep valley. You will not be in any distress, my Lady," Nulian said.

Morgan took Taru's hand and pulled her over to the middle of the portal to stand near Nulian.

"Nulian and I will sing the song to activate the portal. I will not release your hand, but join our song when you learn the tune."

Morgan felt Taru's anxiety spike as the sensation of water climbing up their bodies started. She gripped her hand a bit tighter and smiled as she heard her ordering herself to trust in her Caretaker.

TARU SMILED as she opened her eyes and saw the gorgeous world around her.

"It is old like Kalias, yet still so healthy. It also feels familiar somehow. Is this planet near Kalias?"

Morgan, unsure, looked at Nulian and received a quizzical look.

"No idea," Morgan said.

"I will examine the stars tonight and see if they are familiar," Taru said. "Shall we begin? I would like to learn quickly and return to Daniel."

Nulian snorted and looked away. Morgan held her tongue for a bit to control her tone.

"We will not rush through this, Taru. You nearly died twice in the last days due to the unusual amount of magic within you and your inability to control its intensity. If you do not learn to control it, you will be a danger to yourself and others. I am most concerned with your effect on Daniel. I know how easily the power of bonding with your mate can become overwhelming. You could kill him if you are not in control."

"I am grateful for the training and am taking it seriously. I only wish to progress as quickly as possible, my Caretaker," Taru said.

"I understand. Climb aboard," she said.

Nulian carried them to a large lake with a magnificent waterfall crashing into it. Morgan felt Taru's desire to go swimming in the cool water but did not offer.

After both women dismounted, Nulian lay down, and Morgan sat on her foreleg. Taru remained standing, looking uncertain.

"Sit wherever you are comfortable," Nulian said. "You may sit on my leg with Morgan if you wish."

"Actually," Morgan said. "I would rather you not be in contact with Nulian, for now. Do have a seat and get comfortable though."

Taru sat quiet, waiting for further instructions.

"I want you to start the way I did. Find every dragon spirit on this planet."

Taru gave her a blank stare and glanced between her and Nulian.

"Close your eyes and use your senses to seek their spirits. Start with Nulian and move further and further away. You felt the presence of Nulian and our other friends outside the cave at the oceanside. I believe you will feel the dragons here if you try," Morgan said.

Taru closed her eyes and reached out to feel Nulian's spirit.

"You do not need to connect. Only touch them enough to sense them," Nulian said.

Taru broadened her reach. "I can feel two others nearby."

"How can she have so much power and not sense them from any distance?" Morgan asked Nulian.

"It is as though she has not Quickened and is only using her most basic skills. Perhaps we should try our method of initiating Quickening with her."

"Are you sure that is wise, given her intense magic? Will it not overwhelm her?"

"Difficult as it may be, if she has not Quickened, she will never have control."

Morgan looked to Taru again.

"Did you ever have a profound change in your ability to use the magic where it increased a great deal in intensity?"

"No, I have had most of the skills I use now since Grith gave me the gift."

"We believe that since there were no dragons near you to initiate it, you may have never gone through a Quickening. There are Elders of both breeds here on Berios who can likely initiate the change now. Given that you already carry dragon blood within you, we expect the process will be quite intense. Nevertheless, without full use of your magic, you will never be able to control it. If you wish it, I will bond with you and complete your Quickening. It is a profound level of bonding, and will likely be an intense experience for both of us. Knowing that, and the high likelihood of considerable pain at times, are you willing to let us try to help you?"

"I trust your judgment, my Caretaker. I will do what you and the Elders feel is best."

Morgan moved to sit beside her and explained the symptoms she experienced when her Quickening was initiated. She described the gradual increase in the power of the magic within her and the hot flashes and tingling that came increasingly often as the Quickening neared its end.

"My Quickening was completed by my mother and the Elder dragons of Chemerie. They passed knowledge to me through the intense bonding. You already have a great deal of knowledge within you and have had some of it available over the years. However, you may find there is much more that will become available once your magic is properly Quickened. You may also find that new skills develop. If we are successful, you will finally know the full breadth of Grith's precious gift."

A tear slid down Taru's face as she looked at Morgan's Crest. "Gaining more from his gift would be wonderful, but I will never have what you do, my Caretaker. You get to feel the profound link you share with your blood-giver every day. I would give all of my magic away if it meant touching Grith's spirit again."

6

Gift Exchange

LET US CALL OUR FRIENDS together and begin, my Sister," Morgan said to Nulian as she moved into the cold lake with Taru. They were soon surrounded by both Alerian and Perian Elders.

Nulian's twin brothers, Panish and Palish, lay to Nulian's right, and her mate, Gerzin, lay to her left. Three Elder Perians of Berios joined them to form a large half-circle around the bank of the lake. Morgan felt the heat of Taru's skin rise as the dragons drew near her and was reminded just how crucial their task was.

"Lie down in the water and trust me to support your shoulders and head," she said. Taru did as she was told, and Morgan took hold of her to push a strong rush of calming and confidence. "Open yourself to the dragons. You must let them in with no resistance of any kind. Trust in them and trust in the magic. When you are ready, relax your body, and close your eyes."

Taru let her body float free with her head resting in Morgan's arms. She focused to not tense and offer no resistance then took one more deep breath as she closed her eyes. The dragons began to sing a beautiful song together. The two breeds had slightly different versions, but the two mixed in a lovely harmony as if two parts of the same symphony.

"They will begin now, my friend; try to stay relaxed. When it is time, I will take your hands and bond with you to complete the process. No matter what it takes, I am with you, my Sister."

Taru struggled to take in her next few breaths as her temperature climbed much higher, and her entire body began to tremble.

"It really burns," Taru said as she gritted her teeth and tightened with a muffled cry of pain.

"I know it hurts, but do not block them with your mind. They are almost finished with this part. Trust in their pure spirits."

Taru forced herself to relax her muscles and opened her mind again. Tears streamed from her eyes, but she did not cry out.

The dragons stopped their song of initiation and shifted to a hum that conveyed profound trust and respect. Taru's shaking continued a few minutes more. She was incredibly hot but the cool water kept her conscious. Morgan moved her through the water to cool her more efficiently while passing healing magic to ease the lingering pain.

Once Taru's temperature was near normal, she stood on her own trembling legs. Morgan supported her as they moved toward the bank. They managed only a few feet before Taru buckled with the next round of Quickening.

Morgan pulled her back into the deeper water and continued to move her around to keep her as cool as possible. That episode lasted twice as long, and her body heat climbed even higher. She stopped for only a minute before it started all over again.

"If this worsens, she could drop into a coma again. Her temperature is far too high already. Any suggestions?" Morgan said to Nulian and the other Elders.

"Can you help her use the energy the way the children did last

night?" Nulian asked. Morgan nodded and reached to the bottom of the lake. She drew up a small bit of sand and a few stones. One stone had a vein of silver metal running through it, and Morgan had a thought.

She placed the stone between Taru's hands and held them tight with her own. As soon as Taru's shaking dropped again she spoke in a soft voice in her ear.

"Focus on the metal trapped within the stone. Make the atoms move more rapidly, so the metal becomes liquid. Then, reform the metal into a dragon amulet. Focus only on the metal and the shape you want it to be. Sing along with me as you work." She began to hum the song she learned from the children and smiled with relief as Taru began to hum along.

Morgan could feel the metal liquefy and pour from the stone onto Taru's belly. It did not run off. It slowly reformed into a circular disk with a proud dragon sitting at its center. Her temperature dropped quickly as she used the excess magic to reshape the metal.

"Very nice. Now for the details. The dragon's markings and scale features," Morgan said. Taru laid her hands down over the metal form and breathed deep as she focused. Morgan felt her temperature drop a great deal more as she worked.

A few long moments later, Taru lifted her hands and opened her eyes. She smiled at the amulet in her hand and stood carefully.

"Thank you. I was quite scared until you helped me focus and use the energy. Can we give this to Brya? I can make another for Kyan."

"That is a wonderful idea. I think you will need to make a few before we finish this task."

They both smiled and walked to the shallower water. Morgan placed the amulet on her clothes pile and walked back into the water where Taru waited.

"How long might this go on, my Caretaker? I am getting fatigued and sore."

"I do not know, but I can help with that part," Morgan said as she took her hand and passed healing energy. She was still connected when the next wave of tingling hit Taru, and had to break the connection abruptly as the sensations passed to her.

After many minutes of intense surges of magic, her temperature was dangerously high and still climbing.

"Focus on the water this time. Slow it down and organize it into perfect ice crystals all around your skin. Each water molecule surrounded by four more in a tetrahedron. Use your magical energy to form the ice and let the radiant heat of your skin melt it away. Focus now, and sing with me."

As she and Taru sang, Morgan could feel and see the layer of ice form then disappear on Taru's skin. Taru pushed her focus in a rhythm of freezing the water and allowing time for it to melt away.

Taru was able to gain control over her temperature herself using that technique. Morgan got a little frostbite from the process, but was very relieved to feel her friend calm as she gained control of the situation.

The episodes took over two hours to subside before Morgan was confident they were ready to complete the Quickening. She exited the water, dressed, and sat down to lean back against Nulian's side. She called for Taru to come sit in front of her.

"Focus and freeze all the water on your body and in your clothes so it can pull heat from your body as we proceed. Let's enter this stage with that bit of insurance," Morgan said.

Taru focused and hummed the song again. Morgan watched her clothes become brittle and glisten in the sunlight.

"Shall we begin?" Morgan asked Nulian and the other Elders.

Nulian nodded, and the other Elders gathered closer. Nulian crooned as she dropped her snout to nudge each of the women. They smiled as they stroked her and returned the rush of devotion she shared.

"You will feel a great deal of intensity," Nulian said. "The magic you each carry will move between you, and be known to both in the end. It cannot be prevented. Therefore, you must both be willing to share all you are with the other. Are you each willing to do this?"

"Are we sure we are ready, my friend? Are we to share all the knowledge you have given me?" Morgan asked Nulian.

"It is the only proper thing to do in light of her skills. To know and trust her is the best course of action, my Sister. Do you agree?" *"Yes, of course,"* Morgan said.

Taru had looked down when Nulian asked the question. She was silent, and Morgan felt her anxiety level rising.

"Do you still have things you do not wish to share?" Morgan asked. Taru looked up with tears in her eyes and struggled to gather herself as she held Morgan's gaze.

"There are things that I am ashamed of. But, I will trust you with them, my Caretaker. I ask that you not share them with anyone else. They are my burden, and I ask that you keep my secrets."

Morgan felt Taru's shame and was not sure she wanted to know whatever it was that haunted her so fiercely.

"Is this something I am going to be able to keep from Daniel? Do not put me in a situation where I need to lie to him Taru. I will not."

Tears slid down Taru's face as she held up a trembling hand to suggest sharing of the information. Morgan placed her hand to Taru's and deepened their connection to receive the haunting memories.

Her heart ached and she felt sick as she viewed a horrible memory of Taru's abuse at the hands of an evil warlord, Lord Hoge. The hateful man had used dark magic to torture her as a child.

Morgan fought to control her own emotions as she pushed the memory away. Without lessening the intensity of their connection, she took Taru by the shoulders to look her in the eyes.

"That was in no way your fault. You have no place being ashamed of it, Taru. Do not blame yourself for the hateful actions of others. Daniel would never see you as anything other than a victim in this.

He will see it for exactly what it is. Do you hear me?" When Taru averted her eyes again, she flooded her with love and compassion, while pulling her into a tight embrace. "You were a child, and he took advantage of your inability to defend yourself. I am so sorry to know you suffered such abuse. But you cannot let it hurt you a second longer."

Taru cried hard for a moment, then pulled back as she gathered herself.

"Thank you for those words, my Caretaker."

Morgan laughed and said, "Taru, please, call me Morgan." Taru smiled as she wiped her tears on her sleeve.

"Well, go douse yourself again and freeze up so we can do this thing," Morgan said.

Taru soon settled back down and focused to freeze the water on her. She opened her icicle-covered eyes and nodded. Morgan held both hands up with a smile. They joined hands and laced fingers as magic flowed fast between them.

Morgan focused their connection and entered bonding in one move. They both took a deep breath as the blissful weightlessness of bonding washed over them.

As Morgan opened to the dragons, they all began to hum to activate the transfer of magic and knowledge between the two women.

The dragons' Song of Quickening resonated within the women's heads, and the thoughts each held began to swirl through their minds in a great blur. The sharing of information was intense, and far too fast to process.

Morgan felt herself flinch involuntarily at some of the memories transferred to her. While she could not tell their content, she knew them to be of horrible events. Other memories gave her intense feelings of serenity and blissful elation. It all mingled together as her Crest burned hot on her chest.

Her entire body tingled, her muscles tightened, and her heart raced. When the dragons' song stopped, she released the bonding. As the blissful weightless feeling of bonding was broken, they dropped back into simple connection where all of the physical sensations returned in full force. Both gasped as pain rocked their bodies. Each released their grip to drop the connection and fight their own pain.

Morgan fell back against Nulian as Taru fell to her side clutching her chest and writhing in pain. Nulian and Gerzin hummed their Song of Healing and touched their snouts to the two women. All of the Elders joined the song. As their pain faded away, Morgan and Taru both sat up to offer the other a huge smile.

"I am burning up. How about a swim?" Morgan said. "Definitely!" Taru said as they both hurried toward the water.

As they dove in and began racing for the falls, Morgan was elated to find she had received a bit more than knowledge from Taru. She was keeping up with her powerful friend, stroke-for-stroke.

When they reached the base of the falls, they fought the current and climbed the boulders to let the falling water massage their shoulders and backs.

NIGHT FELL WHILE THEY RELAXED in the falls, and Morgan noticed Taru studying the horizon with a smile.

"Enjoying your night vision?"

"Yes, it is wonderful. You can also use the increased strength and stamina, I noticed."

"It is like the ability to reform matter. These were abilities that were within us all along, we simply were not aware of it," Morgan said.

"I wonder what else we are capable of and do not know it. It is amazing, is it not, my Sister?"

"We are blessed by the magic for certain. We must use it responsibly and to the betterment of our brethren," Morgan said.

"Oh my, I can see so far away. Can you see how Nulian caresses that little Perian hatchling as well?" Taru asked.

"Yes, that is a new hatchling of our friend, Asira. She is just behind you on the ridge above," Morgan said. Taru started to turn around. "Do not use your eyes. Feel her presence. Concentrate on the essence of a dragon's spirit and search with your magic."

Taru closed her eyes and smiled. "I feel her and many more nearby. They are of both breeds, but there are younglings of only Perian. I can feel them so clearly now."

"How many do you feel exactly?" Morgan asked.

Taru focused for a moment and said, "Counting Nulian, I find fifty-nine."

"That means Hytha is still here. Excuse me while I speak to her," Morgan said.

"I am delighted to hear of your news, my friend. Will you come spend some time with me?"

"With joy! I have missed you, my Queen."

"Can you bring Tagien along? I would like you both to meet someone very special," Morgan said. Hytha agreed, and Morgan soon felt them both approaching. "Follow me, Sister."

She and Taru sped across the lake to the bank where their clothes lay beside Nulian. Once dressed, she hurried to hug Hytha as soon as she landed. Both pushed to connect and then moved into bonding. Morgan felt the presence of the little ones and touched the spirit of each before letting the bonding drop.

"There are six little ones developing very well, my friends. I am so happy for you both," Morgan said to Hytha and Tagien. She reached a hand out to Tagien, and he moved to her with a deep croon.

"I want to use you to test a new magical friend. She has strong magic, and we are challenged to teach her to control it as soon as possible, so she is not overwhelmed by its strength.

"Tagien, you will find her quite interesting, because she was given her gift of dragon blood by a Perian. I call her Sister, not because she is my brother's mate, but because of the dragon blood we both carry,"

Morgan said with a smile creeping up her face. Hytha caught what she had said and arched her neck to look at her directly.

"You are saying that the line of Nulian is the same line of the Perian who bonded to your blood-sister. There was a crossing of the breeds before ours, and hatchlings survived and prospered?" Hytha said. Tagien moved to rub Hytha's neck as he heard her words.

"Yes, my friend, there was definitely a crossing before yours. So you need not worry about their health or their acceptance. We are all excited to see the beauty of your young and consider them very precious. Now, do you mind if I see if Taru can detect your young?" Tagien moved in closer and dropped his head to her.

"She will not hurt my family, will she, my Queen?" he asked in a quiet and deep voice.

She was startled by his reference to her as his Queen. The Perians of Berios had no allegiance to the country of Chemerie on Erion. He had taken her as his Queen despite never having been to Chemerie. She bowed to him to acknowledge the reference before answering his question.

"I would never let her near our dear Hytha if I thought there to be any possibility of danger, my Brother."

"Thank you, my Queen."

Morgan caressed him for a moment and shared her love and respect before she called to Taru, who approached and bowed. Morgan made polite introductions with no detail.

"I want you to connect deeply to Nulian, and then to Hytha, with touch. I will then ask a few questions about what you learned," Morgan said. Taru did as she was instructed then turned back to her. "What did you learn of their age?"

"Nulian is far older than Hytha, by many years," Taru said. "And of their lineage, are they related?" Morgan asked.

Taru thought for a moment and said, "Not as far as I could tell, my Caretaker. However, I only received a few generations from Hytha."

"And what of their mates and their offspring?"

"Hytha is mated to Tagien, and Nulian to Elder Gerzin, who lies beside her. Nulian has had many clutches and has sadly lost many young to battle over the years. Hytha has not had any clutches hatch as yet, my Sister," Taru said. She had glanced at Hytha as she finished her summation. Morgan said nothing but raised an eyebrow to Taru. Taru looked from her to Nulian and Hytha.

"My Sister, is it my place to speak of a clutch currently held within a dragon?"

Morgan smiled and asked out loud, "What of clutches not yet laid, my Sister?"

"They both hold an unborn clutch, my Caretaker."

Morgan turned to stare at Nulian for many seconds before moving to lay a hand to her cheek. She felt the little ones at once.

"When did you conceive them? I have not felt them until now."

"Earlier this week, my Sister. I only felt them about an hour ago,"

Nulian said. "You were quite busy, and I felt it pertinent to protect them from the Quickening ceremony. I would have shared it with you when we had a moment alone, my Caretaker."

"I know. Forgive my childish jealousy. I am very proud for you, my dear," Morgan said as she pushed them into bonding. Gerzin joined them, and all shared their joy as they touched the spirits of the little ones. Taru caressed Hytha until Morgan dropped the bonding.

"I am sorry, but I did not know what else to do. I knew you had not felt them yet, but I could not lie to you."

"It is all right," Morgan said as she continued to caress Nulian. "I am too happy with the news to let my disappointment in the way I found out bother me. I was afraid my dear Sister would not conceive again after an awful wound to her abdomen last year. I am too happy for this gift to worry about much of anything." Gerzin crooned and nudged her against his side with a bump against Nulian's snout. Nulian moved to touch her at the same time as the dragons reinitiated bonding to her.

Taru walked to Tagien and bowed. "I am Taru of Kalias, my Perian Brother. May I have the honor of touching your beautiful hide?"

Tagien bowed in return.

"A child of Kalias and a friend of my Queen may certainly touch me, my Lady."

"How do you know of Kalias, my friend?" Taru asked as she moved to touch him. The instant she touched his hide, she had her answer. She connected and then bonded with his permission. Tears filled her eyes as she leaned her head against his neck. After a moment, she pulled back from the bonding and smiled at Morgan, who now stood beside her.

"Tagien is of Grith's line, distant, but the same line. The Perian dragons here are from Kalias," Taru said.

Morgan laid a hand to Tagien and sought his heritage. Once she knew what to seek, she also felt the connection. It was fainter for her, of course, but she felt it.

"We are all brethren in spirit and by blood, my friend," Morgan said to Tagien with a smile. He crooned and nudged both her and Taru against him.

"Asira, will you tell me the legend of how your line came to this planet? I would like to understand the connection to Kalias and Erion," Morgan said to the Elder Perian female standing beside Nulian.

"Our ancestors came here from Kalias many generations before Puria went to Erion. They chose to stay here because they foresaw the fall of the dragons on Kalias and sought to save our breed by living away from the evil of that world. It was said that the evil would weaken, and a pure child of Kalias would come to us. The strength of the dragon-child would allow us to be triumphant where we alone could not," Asira said as she looked to Taru. "I believe I have just met the child the legend speaks of." Taru blushed as Asira bowed to her.

"Are you saying there is a portal from here to Kalias that you can access yourself, my Lady?" Taru asked.

"Indeed. It is within that mountain," Asira said.

"May I see it?" Taru asked as she looked at the mountain.

Morgan felt Taru's desire to return and free her people rising within her.

"I do not think that is a good idea, Taru. You are not ready to go back and free your brethren yet. You have much to learn, and you need to explain your plans to Daniel. You owe him that."

"I would never leave him. I will never return if he does not accompany me. I need him, and I want him with me, always. Even now, I ache to have his spirit near me. I am here without him only because you tell me it is necessary."

Morgan smiled as she felt Taru's sincerity.

"My heart is comforted by your love and devotion to my brother. I did not mean to offend you so, my Sister. I apologize." Taru nodded as her cheeks flushed again.

"I would be glad to take you to the portal chamber, my Lady. Would you like to go now?" Asira asked. Taru glanced at Morgan then looked back to Asira.

"No, my Lady. I will stay and train with my Caretaker. Thank you for the offer. I do hope to see it before leaving this lovely world," Taru said.

"You may as well go now. We will train no more tonight."

Taru gave Asira a wide smile

"Please, come aboard," Asira said as she proffered her foreleg in the manner Morgan had developed with the Chemerian dragons.

Morgan turned to find Nulian rubbing snouts with Gerzin. She seemed far more interested in him than in the trip to see the portal chamber.

"Hytha, will you carry me, my friend?"

"Of course, my Qu—" Hytha began.

Morgan had taken only one step toward her before she heard Nulian growl low in her throat. Anger and disappointment had flashed within her powerful sister, so she redirected her steps to her at once.

"I only intended to give you time with Gerzin, my dear. I thought a celebration was warranted after your news today. I asked Hytha, not the other way around. Be nice," Morgan said. Nulian shifted to nudge her against her side as she gave Hytha an ugly glare. *"That is just plain rude, Nulian. She was helping me at my request."*

"She knows I am your first and should have been more hesitant to accept the role in my place," Nulian said as she continued to glare at Hytha, who had dropped her head with respect.

"My first!" Morgan said with a smile. *"I have felt that way for some time, but I did not realize you felt that way, as well."*

"I do not wish to have you fly with another if I am available. I love your mother and grandmother, but it does not compare to the way I have come to love you, my Sister," Nulian said as she rubbed her snout to Morgan.

"I love all my dragon and human brethren. But I am yours first, for certain," Morgan said. Nulian nudged her into her palm then moved her to the saddle as she crooned.

"Firsts forever, my Sister," Nulian said.

Morgan stroked her and told Asira they were ready to go. As they lifted off, Morgan thanked Hytha for her willingness to help and promised to spend more time with her before they returned to Erion.

THE GROUP FLEW to the end of the mountain range behind the lake and dropped into a massive cavern. They flew through a long wide tunnel leading back toward the lake for about two hundred yards before the tunnel dropped down a few hundred feet. Morgan could hear water rushing overhead when they landed in a vast main chamber that held the portal.

"We are under and behind the falls?" Morgan asked.

"Yes, my Sister, and it is quite cool because of it. I suppose Taru is quite comfortable, but I find it chilly," Nulian said as she shivered a bit. Morgan giggled as the dragon's shaking made her slip sideways.

Morgan and Taru dismounted and walked forward to inspect the large purple pool. Taru knelt and touched her hand to the surface. She rose with an odd look on her face and stepped back from the pool.

"I think this portal may have been used recently, my Lady. Do you feel it too?" Taru asked. Morgan knelt and touched the surface.

"I do feel magic unique to that of the portal itself. I am not sure if it is from use, or from a source on the other side. We do not know where it is located on Kalias. It could be near a strong source of magic," Morgan said. Taru took three more steps back, stopping only when she bumped into Asira's leg.

"I recognize it now. It is the magic of the dragons that serve Lord Hoge! This portal must lie within or very near the Castle of Ceruk. Why have they never used it?" Taru asked as she scowled at the portal.

"Portals are a gift of the magic. It requires strong magic and a pure spirit to access it. One must also speak the language in which it was first created, most commonly dragon-tongue, as well as the song which activates it," Nulian said.

Morgan's stomach flipped as she pictured Brya and Kyan leaving her via a portal. Nulian heard her thoughts and hummed to push calming as she touched her side.

Taru had left the cavern and was trembling by the time Morgan caught up to her.

"I am too scared to go back. I know I need to return and save those with pure spirits, but I am too weak of spirit myself. I could never do it."

"You are among the strongest I have met, Taru. You will save your people one day, but you should not feel like you need to do it now. You have a great deal to learn, and you deserve to live a happy life for a while. Do not feel weak because you have the good sense to be afraid of the evil they represent. Weakness is an unwillingness to fight when the time comes. I am certain you will fight with all that you are when facing a dark enemy."

"Thank you for your confidence, Morgan. It means so much to know you think well of me and are beginning to trust me."

"I just bonded to you deeper than any human other than my mate or my children. I trust you with my life because I felt the nature of your spirit and know it very well, as you now know mine. You are my blood-sister, and I am your friend in every way," Morgan said. She then pulled Taru along as she said, "I am starving. We may be able to wait for days, but I do not like the feeling of hunger if I can avoid it."

They soon flew out of the chamber tunnels into the clear sky above. Nulian and Asira took them to the gazebo, and the women ate their fill of sandwiches and vegetable pieces.

As Taru was changing for bed, Morgan glanced her way and smiled.

"It seems that completing your Quickening has allowed Grith's gift to mature even more, my Sister. That is absolutely magnificent. Daniel may pass out when he sees it."

Taru was confused until Morgan's eyes dropped to her middle. She looked down to see the great elder Perian dragon now standing proud on her abdomen. Her eyes filled with tears as she touched the dragon. It shifted and opened its wings with a flourish that made her shiver and laugh.

"His coloring is like fire dancing on your beautiful skin. Please, warn me before you let Daniel see that. I prefer not to hear those thoughts."

They both laughed as they settled into bed and soon fell fast asleep.

MORGAN BOLTED straight up in bed as she felt panic and fear in the early hours of the morning. A tremendous crashing sound from far in the distance filled the night. Taru was awake a second behind Morgan, and they both sprang from the bed. When their feet hit the floor of the gazebo, they realized the whole structure was vibrating and moved out onto the ledge.

Nulian roared as she approached at a fierce speed.

"Taru, get ready to mount the second she lands. Something is very wrong," Morgan said as she moved back to give Nulian the full platform. Nulian made an abrupt landing, and both women vaulted aboard and held on tightly.

Nulian launched at once and flew hard for the other end of the valley as her heart raced. She was picking up speed so fast that Morgan and Taru had to lie flat to her back to remain stable in the saddle.

"I feel too much fear from too many to focus on the pain," Morgan said. *"Who is hurt?"*

"My dear brothers. They were guarding the portal to Erion. They do not answer me."

Nulian cleared the last ridge separating them from the portal valley and roared.

"Is this not the location we arrived on this planet? Where is the portal?" Taru asked as they studied the mountainsides. Despite their enhanced vision, neither could make out the portal ridge. Morgan struggled to reply as the horror of the situation hit her.

"The quake has broken the entire side of the ridge away," Morgan said. "The portal to Erion is gone."

7

Fracture

NULIAN DROPPED INTO A STEEP DIVE toward the rubble pile in the deep valley below. She circled as she scanned for her brothers. Morgan used sight and magic to search for them as well.

"Over there!" Morgan said. *"To the left, under the rubble against the base of the mountain. It is Panish. He is still alive."* Nulian landed, and Morgan vaulted off her shoulder onto the rubble pile. She found Panish and crawled under and between massive boulders to reach him.

"He is broken many times over and bleeding inside and out," Morgan said. "Taru, come, I need your skill." Taru leapt with acrobatic grace over the boulders and landed beside her.

"Place your hands to my shoulders, and let the magic build within you. I will need to draw from your excess magic to save him. You must not let me pull too much, too fast. Give me what you can safely."

Taru nodded as she placed both hands to Morgan's shoulders.

Morgan focused to heal the internal injuries first to stop the bleeding, and let his heart rate increase a bit. Then, she addressed the many deep gashes and major broken bones.

"Nulian, I need you to move the debris off of him. You must free his leg and wing before I can work with them."

Nulian came from the opposite side of Panish and stepped very carefully. She gave a mournful croon when she saw his broken form but went to work, carefully lifting the large rocks with her claws and teeth. When Panish was uncovered, she pulled his leg free and cringed at the sound of the broken bone scraping on itself.

"Hold it in the approximate position it would naturally fall and let it relax a bit," Morgan said. She crawled up and laid her hands to each side of the break, focusing her healing energy on that area. Though the splintering of each side mended well, she grew weak before the reconnection of them was complete. Her hands had started to tremble until Taru gripped her shoulders again to offer a large bolster of magic.

Once his leg was finished, Morgan climbed over his chest to the opposite wing. Her heart sank when she saw part of it was completely severed. She was studying it when Nulian crooned again.

"Please try, my Caretaker," Nulian said.

"You know I will. Lift his wing and hold it steady." Morgan crouched under the connection point. "Taru, I need you to hold each bone in place while I bind them."

"Just do your best, my Sister," Nulian said as she shifted around the broken wing. "If he cannot fly, I will carry him." Before she could act, Gerzin landed and moved to them. She crooned sadly and let him lift the mangled wing to hold it in place.

Nulian turned to look around her and jumped to the side. Morgan's breath caught, and pain shot through her chest as she shared the intense loss that filled her dragon-sister when she found Palish's body directly beneath them. Nulian let out mournful croons as she began to shift rocks to reach him.

"*Does she realize* —" Taru asked.

"*She knows,*" Morgan said as she focused on blocking Nulian's grief.

Morgan directed Gerzin and Taru to hold Panish's wing in just the right position as she moved along, mending the delicate flesh and bone. When she finished, she was relieved to see blood flowing back into the tips of his wing. He began to wake in pain, so she moved back to his head and sent him healing energy to heal the remaining cuts and deep bruises before he fully woke.

As she finished, he opened his eyes and held her gaze while fighting to remember the last few seconds before he had lost consciousness. She experienced the tremendous loss he felt when he could not locate Palish's spirit. Though she sent love and support, she knew it was but a fraction of what he needed to deal with this loss.

"I am so sorry, Panish. He was gone before we arrived."

He slowly rose and moved to where Nulian and Gerzin lay beside Palish's broken body. The others moved aside as he covered his brother's body with his own and roared in grief.

Morgan held her guard high to block enough of Panish's grief to manage walking. She sat beside Nulian and joined the Elder dragons as they sang the Song of Connection to say goodbye to Palish.

GERZIN AND NULIAN carried Palish to a high mountain crest and covered his body with kindling. Morgan used her supplies to start the fire and flew with Nulian during the burning to honor him properly.

Taru stayed at the gazebo and watched with Asira, who explained the meaning of the ceremony and Song of Connection. When the burning was complete, Nulian took Morgan back to the gazebo.

Nulian turned to search the valley.

"He has gone. He flew west as the burning neared its end and would not answer me. Give him time to mourn, my dear. His heart aches more than we can know," Morgan said.

Nulian dropped her head and lay down. Gerzin lay next to her and crooned as he rubbed her neck with his snout. Morgan tried to soothe her for a moment, then left them alone. She returned to the gazebo, lay down on the bed, and cringed.

"You are hurt, my Sister. Can you not heal your own wounds?" Taru asked.

"Hush! Say no more aloud about it right now. I am fine and do not want to worry Nulian. I will heal fine," Morgan said. Taru looked up, and Morgan sighed as she felt Nulian right behind her.

"Let me see it, please," Nulian said. Morgan rolled off the bed and took off her shirt. Taru gasped at the sight of her back. Morgan realized she was not reacting to the cuts along her ribs, but to the horrible scar in the middle of her back.

"A story for another time. For now, lay your hands to each side of my wound while our friends sing their healing song. Focus your mind on mending the skin, and feel the magic work. It may help you learn to do basic healing on your own," Morgan said as she lay back down.

Taru scowled as she looked between Nulian and Morgan. Morgan raised an eyebrow with a strong push of annoyance, and Taru stepped forward. She turned her head away and gritted her teeth as Taru laid her hands against her side.

Nulian and Gerzin began to hum their healing song, and Taru flinched at the sensation of the powerful magic flowing through her. She focused on Morgan's flesh and felt the flow of energy begin. Morgan flinched when she tried to push more energy at a faster rate, so she lifted her hands away. Nulian nudged her.

"Continue, please. Just go more slowly, my friend," Nulian said. Taru placed her hands back to Morgan and focused on the skin again. She saw the cuts knit together, and the bruising fade away.

"What is left? I feel something is not finished, but I do not know what it is," Taru asked Nulian.

"Search her body through bonding and find the problem," Nulian said. Taru focused but only managed connection.

"My Caretaker, will you lower your guard and allow me to bond to you, please?" Taru asked. Morgan allowed it. Taru soon found the broken rib, then told Nulian of the problem.

The dragons resumed her healing song, then stopped before the bone was healed. Taru stopped to look at Nulian.

"Finish it yourself. You have the skill. Focus on the need and send your magic there to accomplish the reordering. It is just like the ice in the lake, my Lady. Order the pieces their natural way," Nulian said. "Focus your magic on the task, and do not allow it to warm your skin. Morgan is being kind in not telling you that your hands are very hot."

"Sorry, my Sister; I will try to do better," Taru said as she moved to the water fountains and wet her hands to cool them. She formed ice on them a few times and moved back to Morgan.

Morgan sighed and relaxed her muscles when she laid her cool hands against her again. Taru tried to bond but was blocked again.

"Please —"

"Sorry," Morgan said as she dropped her guard and formed the bond herself.

Taru focused and found the unhealed bone. She visualized the fully healed bone in her mind as she pushed magic to the area. The bone gradually began to heal. It took many minutes, but Taru finished the healing on her own. When she finished, she flopped down on the bed exhausted, and Morgan laughed.

"It is wickedly satisfying to see someone else struggle with it just as I did at first. You did very well. Thank you," Morgan said.

"Thank you for not telling me just how badly I actually did in giving you more pain than necessary. You are brave and kind, my Caretaker."

"It could not be too bad if I am healed. You successfully healed the first time you tried. That is rather amazing, don't you think?"

"The dragons healed. I watched and donated magic to the effort," Taru said. Morgan smiled and shook her head.

"They only helped for the first minute. After that, they did not push magic at all. It was all your doing, my Sister. Sorry to trick you," Morgan said. Taru smiled and her face reddened as she realized what she had accomplished.

"Thank you so much for everything you have given me today. I owe you so much already," Taru said. "I hope that I can soon be of use to you in serving the dragons properly."

Morgan's weak smile faded as reality crashed back in. She looked to Nulian as her heart ached, then lay back and closed her eyes.

"We will get home somehow, my Sister. You will be with your family again," Nulian said. Morgan rolled to her stomach and buried her face in a pillow as grief and exhaustion took her.

HER WAY HOME to Alec and the children was gone. Morgan woke to that reality and the possibility that she may never see them again. The only possible way home she could see was via Kalias, a world with a history of darkness so fierce that the dragons chose to seek others to call home. Her mind raced around those thoughts until she made a decision and climbed out of bed to get dressed.

"Taru, is the portal you traveled through from Kalias to Erion serviceable to the dragons?"

Taru woke confused by the question, then sobered as she understood Morgan's reasoning. She swallowed hard and considered it.

"The portal itself is plenty large enough for any dragon, but the tunnel is very narrow in two spots after many quakes over the years. The smaller dragons such as Hytha may make it, but the largest could not without finding or making another entry point to the chamber. I am sorry," Taru said as she glanced toward Nulian. Morgan dropped her head as tears filled her burning eyes, then stood and walked from the gazebo.

Nulian followed her to the far end of the ledge. As she touched her back, Morgan turned and laid against her snout.

"How can I leave you, my Sister? How can I when I know I may never see you again? My heart is ripping at the thought of it," Morgan said through sobs. Nulian had tears streaming down her cheeks as she lay on the ground to curl around her. Morgan sat on her foreleg and leaned against her neck as they shared a deep connection in silence for half an hour.

"You must go to the children and to Alec," Nulian said. "I love you and will miss you very much, but you must return to Chemerie. We will see each other again. I am sure of it."

Morgan felt no true confidence in those words within her dragon Sister, but understood her need to feel confident in them.

"I will never stop trying to reach you again, my dear. I love you too much to settle for goodbye. Never say it to me, my Sister. Not ever." She walked a few feet away, then turned to look into Nulian's eyes. "I will find you a way home. I am not about to accept my children growing up without their GranNulian."

Nulian hummed to pass love and respect as she chuckled along with Gerzin. Morgan returned to the gazebo to pack a large bag. Taru had already packed all she could carry in food and water. She told Morgan to pack the warmest clothes she had brought as the weather on Kalias was mid-winter. Morgan had brought nothing warm, so she carried a blanket on her pack.

They boarded Nulian and Gerzin, then Morgan spoke to Hytha during the flight.

"As you know, our portal to Erion has been destroyed. I know you have your mate here, and could live here happily forever, but I need you, my friend. You are the only Chemerian dragon here small enough to reach the portal to Erion on Kalias. Any Perian

dragon will be killed on sight on Kalias. Will you accompany me, my friend?"

Hytha did not answer at first. Morgan felt her fear and dread for her young if trapped upon Kalias.

"Never mind, my friend. I have no guarantee you would be able to escape to Erion, and I would never want your precious young to fall into the hands of the wicked men on Kalias. I should never have asked. Please do not think of it another moment."

Nulian moved into the portal chamber to find Panish waiting.

"You are too big to reach the portal to Erion, my Brother. I am sorry," Nulian said as she touched her snout to his.

He barely touched her, then pulled back as he spoke in a harsh tone, completely devoid of his natural humor.

"I am going to help our Queen reach the portal to Erion. I will find my way back here or die there. I am going, Nulian. Do not speak of it again." He turned, walked onto the portal pool, and sat to wait for Morgan and Taru.

Nulian walked to him and rubbed his snout until he nuzzled her in return. She then dropped her head to hold her snout against Morgan.

"Until our spirits touch again, my Caretaker. May the magic keep you," Nulian said. Morgan hugged her tight then moved to Panish's side. Taru said her farewells, then joined Morgan and Panish.

Morgan turned in circles to read the writing on the walls until she memorized it. Taru did the same then joined Morgan and Panish as they started to sing the unique song to activate this portal. The portal fluid began to climb their legs, and faint light emanated from the pool below their feet.

Morgan held Nulian's gaze as she said, *"I will have you with me again, my dear Sister. I love you."* Though she disconnected and focused on the song, her eyes held Nulian's until she was eclipsed by the portal's activation light.

Kalias

MORGAN AND TARU both flinched at the roaring of dragons the instant they appeared on Kalias. Both women pushed against Panish's side as they used their magic to take in their surroundings.

"Well, it could not have been too much worse than this. We are trapped with a large angry group of dragons who will likely wish to kill us on sight. Lovely," Morgan said as they all moved off the portal.

They now stood in a pitch-black cavern in the bowels of the Ceruk castle dragon hold. Even with their dragon-sight, the cavern had barely enough light to see each other.

"We must hide our dragon markings. To get out, we must wait until the dragons are needed for battle," Taru said.

"You two can surely get out through the bars of a gate, my Queen," Panish said.

"No, we will not leave you here," Morgan said.

"You will save yourself, my Queen!" Panish said as he gave

her a sharp glare. "You must return to Chemerie to care for our brethren. I am of no consequence in that matter."

Morgan nodded as she felt his anger, conviction, and the grief driving both. She pushed love and devotion as he moved to the opening of the cavern to peer down the tunnel in both directions.

"I feel over a dozen dragons nearby. Can you tell the number within the hold, my Queen?"

"Oh yes, I feel them alright. I have found thirty-one dragons filled with hate for humans of all kinds. We will need patience and a great deal of luck to reach the gates." She looked over the great Elder dragon and patted his shoulder. *"Can you hide us under your wings?"*

Panish raised his wings a bit to let them climb up and lie along the main bone of his wing. He looked odd with the extra bulk, but given his size, it was not too noticeable.

He moved at a slow pace through the tunnels as Morgan guided him to miss the other dragons for as long as possible. When they could avoid them no longer, Panish tucked his wings a bit tighter and took a deep breath. He growled low in his chest as he approached a small group of females.

The female dragons moved to the side and crouched lower to the ground as they watched him. He growled constantly to let them know he was in no mood to be tested as he moved past.

His successful intimidation ended as he rounded a corner to face a massive battle-scarred male near his own size. Panish side-stepped to flank the Elder male and dropped his head to show submissiveness in hopes of moving by unchallenged.

The Elder ignored him until he side-stepped into another male who emerged from a small tunnel. The smaller male growled and reared to strike. Panish made a quick shift back to protect the women under his wings. That move encouraged the Elder male to advance on him.

"Fight, Panish! We will hold on," Morgan said.

Panish reared and struck the attacking Elder with a great roar and pushed him hard with his chest. He knocked the male over and stepped on his neck while growling. The Elder went still as he felt Panish's teeth against the tender underside of his neck.

Morgan's heart ached as she felt fear and pain from the trapped dragon. That compassion turned to fear as his roar brought more males into the cavern to surround them.

"When I engage them, run, my Queen," Panish said as he held off their attackers.

"Wait!" Morgan said. *"If you try to fight, they discover us while enraged, and we are all dead."*

"That feels inevitable at the moment," Taru said as growls rattled their bones.

Morgan blocked Panish and slid to the edge of his wing with a hard look at Taru.

"Hold, but be ready to bolt, my Sister."

Morgan dodged Taru's attempt to grab her and dropped to the cavern floor. There were many hisses as the crowd spotted her.

Panish crouched low next to her. She focused her gaze on the injured Elder snarling at her.

"I want only to heal your wounds. I will not hurt you, I pr—"

The dragon lurched to bite her, but went limp as Panish struck to end him. Morgan backed up to Panish and climbed to his back. Taru followed, and another round of hisses broke out. Panish turned as he swung his tail and snarled with bared teeth.

"Bold attempt, but hardly helpful, my Queen," Panish said.

"Agreed!" Taru said.

"Either of you have a better idea?" Morgan snapped.

"Daniel spoke of you using suggestion to control the minds of others. Can you do that to dragons?" Taru asked.

"Doubt it. They are far too intelligent. But I'll try," Morgan

said as she connected to the minds of all the dragons around them. *"Rest, you are very tired. Lie down and rest."*

The cavern went silent, but the dragons around them did not lie down. They looked at each other, and her, with obvious shock.

"I am a friend," she said aloud in dragon-tongue. "We are not the cruel people of Ceruk. We do not wish to hurt you. My friend only killed to protect me. He loves me, as I do him."

"Hold your lies, Human! We will hear none of it. The lies of humans have led us to evil deeds too many times," the largest male present said.

"Have you ever known a human you could trust?" Morgan asked. "No, not one! They use us for our ability to fight and control us with their power of mind. They feel nothing for us. We are only animals to them."

"Then I feel very sorry for you," Panish said. "You have known only the lowest form of human possible. I have been blessed to live among kind and loving humans who mean as much to me as my dragon brethren. I will die for this woman because I love her, not because she controls me. She would never ask me to do anything that I did not wish to. You may choose not to believe me, but you can let her show you and judge for yourself. Or, are you so afraid of the magic that you would not allow it?"

Many growled at his accusation of fear and advanced toward him. A second later, they all quieted and moved back. A great Elder female moved into the chamber and to the body of the slain male dragon. All of the males moved further back and bowed their heads to their Eldest Female.

The enraged female raised her head slowly and moved toward Panish with her body low in an attack position as she growled and snarled.

"I do not know you, dragon. You are not of this family. You have slain my brother. I will now take your life in return. If you wish your humans to have any chance of survival, I suggest you put them aside," the Eldest Female said as she circled Panish, and he moved to keep his head between her and Morgan.

"My Elder, he only killed to protect me," Morgan said. "Please, consider his reasoning. Your brother was injured. I wanted to heal his wounds, but he chose to strike at me before hearing my words." After many seconds of being ignored, she took a bolder tone. "I would expect the Eldest Female to have more self-control and use her intellect before her brawn."

The Eldest Female stopped and glared at her before raising her head and sitting down.

"You ask for thoughtful consideration and trust when you have drawn first blood. Why would we trust the word of an outsider who has just slain our kin?" the Eldest Female asked as she turned her glare on Panish. "You say you love this human, and claim she loves you. I have heard of this only in ancient fables of the old world. I do not believe it possible given what I have seen. But, I admit that I hear sincerity in your words."

The Eldest Female stared at Panish for a long moment in silence, then looked to Morgan again.

"Show me what you will, Human. However, do not touch me!" Morgan focused on the Eldest Female's spirit to connect to her.

"If I push through your defenses by force, I will cause you pain. You must allow me to connect with you by choice, or I cannot share with you. Will you drop your defenses, please?" Morgan said. The dragon hesitated then gave a small nod.

Morgan focused again and found she had dropped them half-way. It was enough for her to share information, but nothing more.

First, she sent all she felt for Panish as she worked to save his life, then shared his loving response. She sent her love for Nulian, the last words they shared, and the intense rush of love she received from her just before falling through the portal. When she opened her eyes, she saw a look of complete bewilderment on the Eldest Female's face.

"You traveled to our world from another through the great portal below? From where did you come?"

"An ancient home of the dragon. We are trying to get to a second portal on this world, so we may go to our homeworld."

"What is the name of your homeworld?"

"I do not think you should be honest, my Queen," Taru said only to Morgan. *"These dragons are not to be trusted."*

Morgan shifted to look at Taru and shook her head as she spoke aloud.

"We must think of the future, not the past. If they are to be our friends in the end, we cannot start with lies," she said as she gripped Taru's hand to push reassurance. She turned back to the Eldest Female, who was studying Taru.

"My blood-sister does not wish for me to tell you the truth because she grew up here, on Kalias, fearing you. She has great love for dragons, but also has profound memories of the carnage your breed has done to humans here. I wish to look to the future, and the hope that we can become friends. Feel the truth in my words through our connection as I say that we are from Erion, home of the children of Puria."

The room filled with growls. The Eldest Female quieted them with an angry roar, then stepped closer to Panish. He turned to protect Morgan from a quick lunge. The Eldest Female gave him another harsh look, then addressed Morgan again.

"I have heard that name in old fables, but know very little of its significance. How can we possibly believe you human? What proof do you have of this great love for the dragon? How do we know you are not controlling your mount as the Ceruk control us when they wish us to kill for them?"

"Do you believe a dragon can be forced to share magic with a human?" Morgan asked.

"Never!" the Eldest Female said among many hisses and growls from those around them. "Forceful sharing would never be possible! No dragon would give magic to a human. No human is worthy of that trust or power."

"What would it mean to you if a dragon did share magic with a human?"

The Eldest Female did not answer at first. She looked to many of the Elder males and females in the crowd as she conferred with them in thought.

"It would mean there are pure-spirited humans, and we have never met one. We are not likely to believe that. Humans have never proven themselves worthy of trust so deep, nor love so profound."

"I have shown you the love I have for this dragon and for his sister. In fact, his sister is my dearest friend. It was she who gave me her blood and her Heraldic Crest," Morgan said as she untied her wrap and allowed it to fall open to reveal the scales and markings on her chest.

The entire chamber went silent. The Eldest Female shimmied forward to see it, but Panish stopped her with a low growl. Morgan placed her hand to Panish, which made her Crest glow brightly.

The Eldest Female stepped back and arched her neck at the sight of the glowing Crest while many around her dropped low to the ground.

"I have never seen such a marking. I believe I have just met a race of humans unlike any on this planet," the Eldest Female said in a respectful tone.

"No, you have not!" Taru shouted as her entire body trembled. "There are many humans of pure spirit on this planet. They are my people, and we are also capable of profound love for a dragon." She was sweating, and her entire body was very hot as her magic surged. Despite her fury, she thought to freeze the water on her skin, cooling herself as she continued. "I was raised among dragons here. They were my family, and I loved them dearly. I too was given the gift of blood by my dragon father before he died." She opened her cloak and let them see the scale lines along her clavicle and sternum. She was fighting tears as she spoke but held herself together.

"Your Dragon Markings do not glow as does the other. Why is that?"

Taru tensed and stayed silent for a moment. Morgan was proud she chose to give an honest answer despite the possible response.

"I received blood from a Perian dragon, not an Alerian."

The cave filled with growls again. The Eldest Female did not hush them as her face darkened.

"I should kill you where you sit! Perians have taken the lives of too many of our kind to forgive. If you carry their blood, then you carry that burden," the Eldest Female said as she took an aggressive stance.

"You will have to kill me first," Panish said as he matched her fighting posture. "I will die for her because I have felt her spirit and know it to be pure and beautiful. I do not care what the dragons have done to each other on this world. I know all dragons are pure of spirit, and I know that both of the women on my back have love for all dragons of all breeds." He growled and moved sideways away from the female as she stepped forward. "You will be surprised to know that the woman you just threatened to kill has intentions of saving your brethren from the Ceruk, for no reason beyond her faith in the purity of your spirits." The female growled in return and swung her head in frustration.

"This talk of love for humans makes me think you are indeed controlled by them. Clearly, their control is great if they forced an Elder to give them the gift of blo——"

Panish cut her off as he rose up to his full height and roared with rage before speaking in a booming voice that rattled Morgan and Taru to the bone.

"You should be ashamed for being so narrow-minded and ignorant of your heritage! Have you no ancient knowledge that shows you the true nature of the bond between humans and dragons? Do you know nothing of the day of Puria, when all humans wore the Heraldic Crest of their dragon family?"

The Elder Female dropped her head and backed up a few paces as her anger faded.

"Most of our knowledge has been lost through many decades of magical torture and control. Our knowledge of the old days and the old ways is limited, existing only as untrustworthy fables," she said. Panish calmed and softened his tone as he stepped closer to her.

"My Queen can share much with you, if only you will let her. What is there to lose in the gain of knowledge?"

"Do you know of our ancestors here on Kalias? Do you actually know of our lineage?" the female asked Morgan.

"I have a great deal of knowledge of your lineage because your line is the same as the blood within us," Morgan said as she caressed Panish's neck. "Puria was of Kalias. She traveled to Erion with a few others. Their blood is within both an Alerian and a Perian line on Erion. I will gladly share the details I carry. Perhaps that information will convince you that we are worthy of your trust. However, you will have to show some trust in order to receive the information. I will need to touch you to bond deep enough for such a transfer."

The Elder Female nodded as she settled to the floor. Morgan started to dismount, but stopped halfway and remounted.

"I feel the distrust within you, and a bit of deceit as well," Morgan said. "You intend to take me away from Panish to question me in private. That is not acceptable."

Looks of shock were exchanged between the dragons around them.

"I had no idea you could hear my thoughts. It is true, I do not feel trust for you as yet, and your mount makes me uncomfortable," the Eldest Female said as she shot Panish another sharp glance.

"She makes me anxious as well. She is quite large, my Queen," Panish said only to Morgan. She lifted an eyebrow and fought to not smirk as she felt Panish's profound attraction for the fierce female.

"YOU WILL HAVE TO TRUST to receive the information, my Elder," Morgan said as she dismounted to stand against Panish. "I will not leave my friend's side. You must trust us to approach close enough for me to touch you while in his protective reach. If you strike at me, he will kill you. Trust, or not, it is your choice." She held out her open palms and showed the Elder female the dragons upon them. "I am a Caretaker of dragons. I would never hurt a dragon of any kind unless it was trying to kill me or my brethren with malice in its heart. Will you trust, my Elder?"

The huge female dropped back to the ground and inched forward as she shot furtive glances at Panish. She laid her neck on the ground before them as she held her body tense and ready to jump back. Panish moved to keep his head beside Morgan to stop any quick move toward her.

Morgan waited a few seconds then reached out to lay a hand to the neck of the great female dragon. The dragon sprang back and shivered. She eyed them as Panish chuckled low in his throat.

"That is the magic of the Caretaker, and the magic of the dragon blood within her, that you feel. It is not painful, only a very intense sensation. True?" Panish said in a low gentle voice.

The Elder female nodded and inched forward. Morgan knelt and placed both hands to her again, being careful not to allow much transfer as she connected for a moment.

"Hello, Qin, I am Morgan. I am going to slowly increase the depth of our connection in order to reach full bonding. You will feel a great deal of sensation. I am currently holding most of it back. Are you ready?"

"Yes, I can handle it, Human."

"Her name is Caretaker Morgan, my Lady," Panish said with a slight growl to his voice.

Qin gave him a sharp look then corrected herself to say, "I am ready, Lady Morgan."

Morgan was careful as she increased the connection toward bonding. Qin's hide shivered beneath her hands as she felt intense waves of both fear and amazement from the anxious Elder. She passed calming confidence as she continued and felt Qin relax a little.

"I will now initiate full bonding. It is a very different sensation, unique to what you have felt with another dragon. Ready?"
"Yes."

Morgan initiated the bonding and sent Qin her knowledge of the dragons which came from Kalias to Erion long ago. She shared her limited understanding of their life on Kalias prior to crossing over. Next, she shared some of the knowledge she gained from Taru during her Quickening. It was information concerning the early days on Kalias when Alerian and Perian were loving brethren.

More of her ancient knowledge rushed forward as she focused on the need. It confirmed that the darkness of Ceruk had affected the Alerian dragons more than the Perians, causing them to separate on Kalias and flee to other planets to preserve their races. Other memories explained that the Caretaker line carried the magic of Puria's mother, Alerie, due to the bonding of Puria and Lady Chemerie long ago. Before breaking the bonding, she sent a strong sample of her love of Nulian and her desire to bring her home.

She was careful to give Qin as little discomfort as possible while dropping out of bonding by pushing her healing magic at the same instant. As she finished, she moved back against Panish's side. Qin lay silent and trembling from the effects Morgan could not prevent.

Panish hummed the dragon healing song and touched his snout to hers. The Elder Female flinched, then allowed his touch a few seconds before backing away. Morgan stepped away from Panish in order to vault up, but was blocked as Panish offered his palm.

"What was that for? What has you worried?" Morgan asked as she knelt in the middle of his palm to let him lift her to his shoulders.

"It is more formal, my Caretaker. I wish to make a good impression." Morgan smiled as she wrapped her blanket around her as a cloak.

"What could be funny at a time like this?" Taru asked.

"The magic is forever entertaining, if only you keep an open mind to see it. Think of all the things that happened to put us here with Panish today. Now I see it was orchestrated by the magic."

"I do not understand, my Caretaker."

"Panish has just found the mate he has searched for his entire life," Morgan said as she gestured to the Eldest Female.

"Surely, you are joking!" Taru blurted aloud as she looked over at Qin in disbelief. Morgan laughed as the tension of the last hour began to lessen, and the wonder of the magic filled her.

Qin looked to the Elders surrounding her, then turned back to Morgan and Taru.

"We will not harm you, my new friends. You are all welcome here. Please, follow me, Elder Panish."

9

Pure Forgiveness

QIN LED THEM DOWN A LONG TUNNEL and into a great room full of hot springs. The chill in the air made the hot spring pools look very inviting to Morgan, but she was not that relaxed just yet.

Qin lay down and dropped her tail into one of the pools. She gestured to Panish to lie across from her. He did so only after insisting all the other dragons clear the chamber, so none were near enough to hurt Morgan or Taru. He lay down, and the women dropped to the ground to stand beside him.

"I enjoyed touching your spirit, Lady Qin," Morgan said. "You have a great deal of scarring from years of contact with the darkness, but your spirit is still a pure one capable of much love. That is excellent news to me. I was worried about the effect of so many generations in close contact with strong dark magic. I have seen, from the memories within Taru, just how dark the Ceruk magic is."

Qin looked at Taru, then dropped her head to stare at the water.

Taru said nothing as she also stared blankly into the pools.

"Forgive them, Taru. Openly, right now. You must make the first step of forgiveness," Morgan said.

Taru looked at her and trembled with anger as she said, *"I am not ready. I remember too clearly the day they killed my entire village."* Morgan held back her response as Qin raised her head and turned to Taru.

"I can never ask you to forgive the acts committed by my breed against your people, my Perian friend. I can only tell you that we are acting at the hand of another every time we are allowed out of this hold. I cannot explain it. I can only say I am ashamed of the things we have done. You must believe me when I say that we have had no ability to fight their control for many generations. We can keep our thoughts from them, but cannot fight their magical commands," Qin said.

Taru did not meet her eyes.

"You need to speak openly, my friends. You are both hiding recognition of the other, but I feel it all the same," Morgan said to Taru and Qin. "Tell me, my Sister. All of it, please."

Taru looked at Qin with fury in her eyes and held the Elder's eyes with her body primed to fight. "This dragon killed my human father and sister. I have no doubt it was her, my Caretaker. I am sorry, but I am not ready to forgive that!"

"Do you remember her as well?" Morgan asked as Qin released Taru's glare and looked back into the pools.

"No. However, I do remember making a choice because of her. I chose not to kill a great Elder Perian because he begged that he see his human child again. I could not believe his words to be true, that he could love any human. Nevertheless, I could not kill him when I felt his anguish. It is the only time I have ever been successful in not following my orders in full. I was the last in the cave, so I left him alive."

She turned to Taru as she said, "I later learned that a female child with magic of her own had been held within the castle for many days.

I have wondered many times over the years if the Perian had been truthful." She watched Taru a few seconds. "I am right, am I not? It was the Elder named Grith who gave you that gift?"

"Yes, it was!" Taru yelled as she stood. "Am I to now forgive you for killing my human family because you spared my dragon father? Do you expect me to thank you because you left him alone to suffer?"

Qin growled and said, "I expect nothing from any human, much less understanding and forgiveness."

Silence fell as the two angry females stared at one another.

"My Sister, look past your anger and say what you truly mean," Morgan said. Taru dropped her head and cried silently as everyone else kept quiet.

"Thank you," Taru said at last. "Thank you for showing mercy to let Grith live. Had you not, I would not have been able to say goodbye. His gift was wonderful, but saying goodbye meant everything to me. Thank you, Lady Qin."

Qin was dumbstruck and had no reply.

"Try 'you are welcome'. It seems appropriate," Panish whispered. Qin gave him a sharp look and he chuckled. Morgan smiled and fought to stifle her own laughter as Panish's amusement cut through the tension in the room.

PANISH WATCHED QIN'S every move. His intense emotions and surging magic were making Morgan grow warm sitting against him.

"Now that you have found her, will you speak to her directly about your link?" Morgan asked him.

"Please do not meddle, my Caretaker. This is both private and delicate."

She scowled and kept her head down while sliding to the edge of a pool, where she took her shoes off to dip her feet into the hot water. It was wonderful.

"Are you not hot just from the steam? I am burning up in here,"

Taru said. Morgan touched her skin and shook her head.

"You cannot let your temperature climb this high. Use the magic at once. Freeze the water around you for a bit."

"I was very upset. Also, our large friend is putting off some very strong energy," Taru said as she sat down. She closed her eyes and commenced to freeze the water on her and let it melt away. She did this for about five minutes and finally cooled down to a safe level.

"Sleep far from the pools and do not snuggle up to Panish," Morgan said. Taru nodded and moved to the wall to open her blanket. As she settled on the hard ground without pause, Morgan moved to lay down beside her.

"I will not be offended if you sleep near Panish rather than by me. He seems uneasy with your move away from him," Taru said.

"He is fine. He has other matters to attend to and has asked me not to meddle."

"He actually said you were meddling? How rude!"

Morgan chuckled as she snuggled in a bit.

"He is an old dragon and has finally found his mate. He does not want anything to mess it up," Morgan said.

An hour later, Morgan sprang to her feet as a loud roar rumbled through her body. Qin was atop Panish's neck with teeth bared, and both were growling. Taru started to get up, but Morgan grabbed her as she felt the emotion between the two dragons. She sat down, moved back under the covers, and urged the trembling Taru to lay back down.

"They are just testing one another. It is a normal first step of courting among adult dragons. Leave them be unless one hurts the other badly," Morgan said.

"Badly? Do you mean that hurting their mate to some degree is acceptable?"

"Yes, they will nip or claw, and sometimes draw blood, but it is not a worry, my friend. I believe you and Daniel have had a

few wrestling matches in the lake already, have you not? If you did not understand human customs, that could look violent and not playful. Just roll back over and stop staring, please."

Qin continued to growl low in her throat as she moved her snout across Panish's chest and up his neck. He growled as well but made no move to fight her off of him. When she reached his snout, he nipped at her. She nipped harder, biting his lip. He flinched and growled loudly with the pain of it. Qin rubbed it with her snout to soothe the pain and crooned low in her throat.

Morgan smiled at the mingling of the growl and the croon. She felt the love growing between them, and her heart ached.

"Alec, Brya, Kyan, Daniel, GranMay everyone. Will I ever see them again?" she thought as she drifted toward sleep. *"Have they missed me yet? No, I have only been away for two days. They have no idea how our future is threatened. I am thankful for that at least."*

TARU LAY AWAKE FOR HOURS listening and watching the dragons' courting. She had never seen such interactions and could not help but watch. They were rough, yet gentle as they wrestled with each other. They would take breaks where they lay far apart and sleep. Then one would start aggravating the other with nips and pokes.

Finally, Qin laid her neck against his and crooned low in her throat. Panish wrapped his neck around hers and crooned in return. They slowly brought their cheeks together and hummed a deep reverberating tone.

"Their first bonding, how wonderful," she thought. She watched and listened for a moment more before she realized she was in trouble. *"Hot too hot must focus!"*

Morgan woke with a jerk as Taru's fear shocked her. She found her friend red and sweating at the same instant she felt the magic emanating from the dragons.

"Panish, please stop! You are affecting Taru badly," Morgan called. Panish released the bonding, and Qin responded with a deep growl. He moved between her and Morgan as he nipped his mate in warning.

"Lady Taru has not yet learned to control her magic. We were risking her life by producing so much magical energy, my mate," Panish said. Qin looked to Taru and nodded as she saw her condition.

Morgan helped Taru focus the magic on the water in the air around them. They froze the water, and tiny crystals fell to the ground in a symphony of tinkling sounds. Taru cooled after a long effort then fell fast asleep.

Morgan moved to the dragons and stood beside Panish's neck as she bowed to Qin.

"I am very sorry to have interrupted such a special time. I would not have done so had it been any less critical. Please understand, my Lady."

"Is she sincerely worried about my feelings?" Qin asked Panish.

"Yes, I am. I felt the love between you two, and have shared in the bonding of dragon mates before. I know it to be both powerful and precious. I am truly sorry to have stopped your first."

Qin looked at Morgan with an expression of awe. She crooned, touched her snout to her hand, then left with her guard held high.

"Did I offend her? I felt a jumble of emotions just then," Morgan asked Panish.

"She is trying to deal with her world turning upside down, my Caretaker. She is happy for it but remains conflicted. Despite Lady Taru's understanding and forgiveness, she struggles to forgive herself, and doubts her worthiness for such forgiveness."

Ceruk Castle

WHISPERING THOUGHTS woke Morgan the next morning. There were many dragons in the small caverns around them, and all were talking about her, Taru, and Panish. She woke Taru with a gentle touch of love and friendship. Taru rolled over with a sweet smile on her sleepy face.

Morgan moved to get them a bite to eat from their pack. She split a sandwich between herself and Taru and sat by the hot water pools to warm up.

"My Caretaker, you and Lady Taru can make your escape easily through the main gate given your skill of controlling the weak-minded," Panish said.

"I am not leaving you, Panish. We must figure a way to get you out with us," she said.

"I do not wish to leave without Qin. We should find a way to free them all from the darkness. Can you do it, my Queen?" Panish asked as he nudged Qin, who lay beside him once again.

Morgan swallowed hard as the weight of that request hit her. She looked between Panish, Qin and, Taru. She knew the only correct answer was to try.

"Panish, you know my responsibilities to our Chemerian brethren, and those to my own children. Nevertheless, I cannot leave them if they truly desire to be free of the dark magic. Of course, we will try."

She handed her food to Taru and looked to Qin.

"Have you truly decided to trust me, Qin? Can I walk freely around your brethren without fear of death?"

"I have instructed that no one harm any of you. My brethren will do as I ask, my Lady. I will accompany you if you wish it," Qin said.

"No, thank you. I would like to study the magic around this place more closely. I ask only to be left alone, my Lady. Taru, you need to practice holding your guard against force. Panish will surely help you while I am gone, if you ask him. I seem to remember he enjoyed his involvement in my training." She smiled at Panish only to feel guilty as his thoughts went to Palish and the way they teased Nulian.

She walked to the tunnels which lay the highest and farthest away from where the humans entered the hold. Dropping her guard in small increments, she opened herself to the hold and beyond.

The many dragon spirits in the hold were filled with curiosity about the newcomers, rather than hate as before. She found a large number of eggs and hatchlings in a smaller hold. As she pushed further, she found many non-magical human spirits in the city around the castle and more within it as well.

A few women within the castle had a small bit of magic. None near the level she had after Quickening; their power was barely more than Alec's.

She searched further into the castle and tensed as she felt a darkness she knew far too well.

"Harrick!"

The dark spirit of Alec's blood-father was within a large suite on the third floor of the castle. He was weak, but it was without question the same evil man she had fought the year before.

"Now I know why I could never find you on Erion. But how?"

She felt another spirit approaching him, one which carried the dark magic of his line. Careful not to be detected, she listened to their words.

"How are you, Grandfather? Can I have anything brought to you?" the teenage boy said.

"Do not treat me like an invalid, Martus. Even weakened, I still have greater magic than you, boy. Leave me be. Go practice your control over the beast."

"Yes, Grandfather," Martus said as he bowed to Harrick.

Morgan felt the resentment within the young man as he left the room. She followed his progress as he headed down a long hallway toward the far end of the castle, and searched the rooms ahead of him as he continued. Her breath caught, and her chest ached as she recognized a spirit she had touched before.

It was a Perian youngling of Valen's, the only one she was unable to free from Harrick. They had assumed him dead because she had been unable to locate his spirit on Erion. He now lay motionless on the floor with large metal bands around his wings and jaw.

Angry tears rolled down her face as she put all the pieces together. Harrick's black spirit could never have activated the portal. He had used the pure-spirited dragon as a key by forcing him to sing the activation song. Her heart raced as she realized they could also get to Berios if they learned of the portal in the dragon hold.

Her fury spiked as Martus entered the youngling's room, walked straight to the dragon, and kicked him hard in the side. It was all she could do to stay undetected as she watched the boy drop to his knees and grab the youngling's head.

"You are mine! You will serve me all of your days. Serve me, and you will be given all you can eat and the mate of your choice. Deny me, and you will live as my slave. Make your choice, Nijel!"

Martus used his magic to push into the mind of the youngling. Morgan felt Nijel's pain as he was flooded with darkness and raised her guard to protect herself.

"No!" she screamed as anger seared through her. Taru and Panish both heard her and felt her rage.

"What pains you, my Queen? What did you find in your search?" Panish asked.

"I will explain in a few minutes."

She took some time to consider the new circumstances before returning to them and leaning into Panish's neck. He and Qin crooned, and Taru moved to sit next to her.

"I failed a youngling and he has suffered unimaginable pain as a result."

She shared what she had seen and heard with them all. Taru and Qin did not appreciate the pain this meant for Morgan, but Panish did. He pushed strong waves of loving support and devotion before explaining more to the others.

"Harrick is a Son of Arshek, a family line of dark magic which has tormented many countries on Erion for centuries. Our young Queen defeated Harrick last year."

"It seems I did not." Morgan stood and began to pace around the pools. "My inability to locate them has haunted me. I search almost every day. Now it makes perfect sense...I was so blind!"

"My Queen, you broke him. The evil of Arshek is no longer a threat to our family," Panish said.

"Wrong. His family's wicked magic grows strong again in his grandson, Martus. The boy's pleasure in hurting and controlling Nijel was as dark as anything I have ever felt within Harrick. I failed because I hesitated the first chance I had to kill Harrick. I chose mercy where it was not deserved. I failed Nijel that day, and I have failed him every day since!"

Taru started to follow as she left the chamber, but Panish stopped her.

"Give her time to herself, my Lady. She must deal with this in her own heart first."

"It makes no sense for her to blame herself for the youngling's suffering. She had no way of knowing about the portal," Taru said.

"Her heart is devoted to the dragon and her role as Caretaker in ways you do not yet understand. She takes the suffering of any in her care as her own failure. Even if she is not directly responsible, she feels she should have done more to prevent it. I agree that she is in no way responsible, but as I said, she must deal with this in her own heart," Panish said. Taru nodded then picked up where Morgan left off in pacing around the pools.

WHEN MORGAN RETURNED her face was set and her plan in place. "We must move quickly to free the dragons here, including Nijel. I cannot speak with Nijel. We know all too well he cannot prevent Harrick or Martus from taking his thoughts. It is wise to assume Hoge has the skills to affect a Perian as he has the Alerian line," Morgan said.

She turned to Qin as she felt her anger rise at the knowledge that the youngling was a Perian.

"If you are to be part of our great family, you will release your prejudice toward the Perian breed. They are as pure of spirit as the Alerian breed, and we love all equally. If you cannot see past your hatred and help him, tell me now. I will not free your brethren if they will harm him or any of my Perian brethren."

Qin considered her for a long minute showing no expression then bowed her head to her.

"Since meeting you yesterday, I have learned much. I have felt the love you have for the dragon and cannot help but believe in you. I choose to put my trust in you, Caretaker Morgan. I believe your spirit to be honest and true. I will make sure all my brethren know not to harm the Perian youngling, nor fight any others we meet. Any who refuse my order will be left behind when the time to leave comes," Qin said.

Morgan felt the sincerity in her voice and moved to stroke her. "Thank you very much, my friend. I am honored by your words and your trust." She continued to caress Qin as she faced Panish and Taru.

"Here is my basic idea, you need to help me fill in the gaps. Taru and I will use our skill of reforming matter to remove the obstacle of the metal gates on this and the hatchling hold. I will use the power of suggestion to control the guards, perhaps put them to sleep. Taru and I will use our strength and flexibility to scale the outside of the castle to reach the youngling and free him. There I need help from you, Panish. Nijel has never flown and may not be able to at all. I need you to carry him to safety. Once he " She froze as she searched the hold.

"Guards are searching the hold for any other injured dragons. They seek the reason for the death of Qin's brother. Panish, hide us under your wings again, please!" Panish quickly shifted to hide them and lay against the back wall in the shadows.

When the guards entered, they moved around Qin and toward Panish. He growled low as they neared him and received a sharp jab in a hip with a spear. He growled in anger and started to shift around to face them, but Qin distracted the men with deep growls behind them. Morgan felt the pain within Qin as the guards jabbed at her to make their escape from the angry Elder dragons.

As soon as the guards were away, Morgan and Taru hurried to heal the dragons' wounds. Qin passed worry to Morgan as she laid her hands to her.

"The guards will inform Hoge, and he will come to punish

you for acting against them. I will not let him, my dear," Morgan said as she healed her.

"I worry for you, my Lady. Surely he will feel your magic if he gets this near," Qin said.

"We must move. Hoge will come now. Panish, I need you t—" She squinted as she raised her guard much higher. "He will be here any minute now, he knows of Qin's fight, and is not pleased. Let us go to the portal room," she said as she took off running. She and Taru mounted Panish on the run, and he moved quickly through the tunnels behind Qin.

Morgan and Taru both doubled over and groaned as they were hit by the force of Hoge's dark assault on the dragons when he entered the hold. Qin buckled, and Panish moved on past her. Morgan focused on blocking Hoge and helped Taru, who was pale and almost unconscious.

"Fight it! Hold your guard high and tight, Taru. Use Panish's magic to boost your own."

She could feel both Hoge and Harrick approaching them through the hold tunnels. She considered the danger in her options.

"My friend, I do not want them to find the portal. I am going to lead them another way. Take Taru back at once. She has no chance against them. I can at least defend myself. Go now, please," Morgan said.

She jumped and rolled away from him then started running fast up a side tunnel as Panish continued on as she had asked.

As she doubled back for the front gate, she allowed Hoge and Harrick to feel her magic pushing back against theirs. Both redirected to follow her path. She intended to intersect with the men near the gate.

Her path shifted, and her pace doubled as she felt Qin rushing to reach the men before her.

"No, Qin, do not fight for me. I intend to let them take me to the castle. There I will be in a better position to help Nijel. Do

not let them know you care for me, my friend. I will need you later tonight."

She ran into the chamber just as Harrick and Hoge entered from the other side. Qin had respected her request and stood against the side wall watching in silence.

Morgan glanced at the gate, then back to the men trying to pass her guard with their dark magic. She was able to block them from her mind, but the intensity of their dark attack had her shivering.

Harrick hobbled forward and raised his hand with the intention of entering her mind through touch. She countered his movements to stay away from him, and he grew weak from the chase. She kept herself aware of all around her and felt the guards closing in on them.

"Are you going to let him torture or kill me before we even get to meet properly? Am I not more interesting to you alive and intact, than broken, Lord Hoge? I dare say you would find my skills of interest in many ways," she said. Hoge's face split into a wicked smile as he glanced over her body.

"I dare say I would indeed, my Lady," Hoge said.

"Not a chance, but keep thinking so, you idiot," she thought, allowing only Qin to hear her. The dragon hid a snort of amusement with a low growl as she eyed the guards near her. *"And now to impress the power-hungry heathen."*

When Harrick stopped his chase, she stood tall with her defensive guard high. She placed her hands over her Crest and let the magic build within her until her slight tremble ended and she felt strong again. As it rose enough for her Crest to glow brightly in the dark cavern, she offered Hoge a wicked smirk. He matched her expression as he glanced at his guards.

"Take her."

"I think not," she said with a bored tone as she connected to each guard and used suggestion to hold them in place. They struggled but could not move their feet. She had not broken her eye contact with

Hoge, nor let her smirk slip from her face. She could feel Harrick's extreme weakness and Hoge's fatigue in fighting against her.

"I can do this all night, gentlemen. Can you? I have no hope of escape and am smart enough to see that. What do you suggest, Lord Hoge? Shall we fight to the death here in this filthy cave? Or would you like me to accompany you, as your guest?"

Hoge gave a deep chuckle as Harrick gave him a covert look of disgust. Hoge dropped his attack and held himself tall as he continued to hold her gaze.

"I like the second option, my Lady. Will you consent to join us as our 'guest' for dinner then?"

"Only if I have your word that you will not allow this foul man to touch me. I do not wish his wretched hands on me. He carries the mark of our last encounter and apparently holds a grudge," Morgan said with a haughty air. Hoge laughed again and moved toward her.

"He does, indeed. I believe he wishes to see you suffer for your actions, my Lady. I will prevent that for a time, I assure you. You are far too interesting to let him have you just yet. Please, come and let me make you feel welcome," Hoge said.

Morgan side-stepped Harrick and moved toward Hoge and the gate. She knew she could defeat either of these evil men alone. However, if one made skin contact and the other assisted in the attack, she was doomed.

"I expect manners, Lord Hoge. You will keep your hands to yourself, yes?"

Hoge nodded and moved ahead of her. She stayed to the side and waited for Harrick to move ahead of her as well. He did not move until Hoge turned to look at him and used magic to order him to move.

Harrick reached her position and lunged for her. She struck him hard in the chest and knocked him back a few feet to land on his buttocks. Hoge came back with a sauntering gait and laughed as he looked down at Harrick.

"You picked the wrong woman to offend, Cousin. Now, do get your sad self up and move along. Dinner awaits, and I am famished after such a rousing activity."

MORGAN FOLLOWED HOGE into the castle of Ceruk. She felt the presence of a few women with meager amounts of magic and Martus. While the women did not concern her, the darkness and hatred within Martus certainly did. She gave him a haughty smile when he stepped into their path in the main hall.

He moved to his grandfather only to be pushed away as Harrick hobbled out of the room. She understood Harrick's shame but had no sympathy for the evil man.

Martus glared at her as he moved closer.

"We meet again, Caretaker. I will have to do better this time around," Martus said.

"Planning another cowardly stab in the back, little boy?" she said with a challenging glance.

"No!" Hoge barked as he shifted to block the young man's lunge toward her. "She is my guest for dinner, and you will not interfere. Your skills are nearly strong enough to defeat your grandfather, but you are still well away from matching me. I suggest you remember your place." Martus gave the large man a respectful nod, then backed away.

"When you have finished with your guest, I request a moment of her time, my Lord," Martus said.

"Gallantly put, Martus," Hoge said with a chuckle as he directed Morgan into a dining hall. "Now, leave us."

Morgan watched as three women of various ages entered the room and seated themselves at the table.

"Leave us, Ladies. I have private business to discuss with my guest," Hoge said to them. Morgan heard the thoughts of all three as they reacted to his order. The eldest was angry and jealous, the middle-aged one was mildly insulted, but the reaction of the youngest was far more interesting.

"Gladly!" the young woman said to herself. *"Any time away from you is a blessing. I hope she can defend herself from your evil magic."*

"I intend to, my Lady. He will not touch me without a great deal of help. Are you his daughter?" Morgan asked.

The young woman glanced at her and said, *"Thank the magic, no! I am unfortunate enough to be the third wife of the great beast. If the chance ever came to be away from here, and free of him, I would take it without pause, my Lady. Good luck to you."* She gave Morgan a small smile as she rose and turned to leave the room.

Hoge caught Morgan glancing at his young wife. "Do you approve of my wives, my Lady?"

"They are lovely. However, I see no need for three if one is doing her job properly." Hoge's loud barking laugh filled the room as he moved to pull out a chair for her.

"I completely agree. Please sit, my lovely Lady, and eat a good meal. You look starved," Hoge said as his eyes slid over her form yet again.

She focused to keep her face placid and her tone light as she flirted with the nasty man. His protection from Harrick and Martus would be useful, as long as she could avoid his advances.

As she sat at the far end of the table from Hoge's normal seat, he moved to sit next to her. She sat on the very edge of the chair, ready to make a quick move away if needed.

Servants moved into the room and served their meal. Morgan connected to a young woman who had served her plate and asked, *"Should I eat this?"*

"Yes, but do not drink the wine, my Lady. The young master tainted it," the woman said. Morgan kept her eyes on her plate and Hoge as she thanked the young girl. When Hoge lifted his glass of wine, she raised a hand to halt him.

"Do you trust Harrick and Martus so much that you would drink wine which was opened out of your sight?"

"Are you telling me something, my Lady? Have you just saved me a terrible illness or even death?"

"Perhaps, my Lord, perhaps," she said with a smile.

She picked up her fork and began to eat. Hoge called for fresh wine glasses and a new, unopened bottle. He stood to open the wine himself. He leaned far closer than was necessary as he poured hers. She leaned away from him and gave a shy smile.

"I am sure I smell of dragons. I do apologize if it is offensive to you."

"I find nothing about you offensive, my Lady. However, I will see you have the opportunity to freshen up after dinner," Hoge said as he reseated himself. "May I ask you a personal question, Lady Morgan?"

"You may ask. Answering is my choice, of course."

"Are you actually married to the son of Harrick? A son of the dark magic?"

"Indeed, I am not prejudiced as to the nature of magic. I am simply attracted to the power of it. I find the combination of a strong magic with mine to be greatly satisfying. That being said, you should know my husband is not the angry beast his father is. My hatred for Harrick is as much for his horrible manner, as it is for his misuse of power." She concentrated to guard her deceit, knowing he was seeking it. A purposeful push of confidence and honesty with her words seemed to satisfy him.

He studied her a minute, then leaned toward her and spoke in a deep tone.

"So why is a married woman wandering around on a distant planet all alone?"

She put her fork down and looked him in the eyes as she took a drink of wine.

"Two reasons really. The first is that I have unfinished business with Harrick and Martus. I cannot very well let the young man who tried to kill me run around free, now can I? The second reason is profound curiosity about the source of the powerful magic I felt as soon as I crossed over to this world. I believe that source is mostly within you, but there seems to be more. Do you have family with similar magic here?"

"Yes, my wives all have magic, and our children will as well."

"Will?" she said with a raised an eyebrow. "You do not have children as yet?"

"No, not yet. However, one is on the way as we speak. My youngest wife carries my child. She is three months along." Morgan had seen the flash of annoyance cross his face at her question and felt wicked satisfaction.

"Congratulations! An heir is a wonderful thing, indeed. Especially when young Martus thinks he is in line to take your throne at this point," Morgan said as she raised her glass to him.

Hoge met her glass with a dark look in his eyes. He moved his hand to purposely make their fingers touch. She shivered at the sensation of his magic, and he took a deep breath as he felt hers.

"Ahh, yes the combination of strong magic is indeed an exquisite sensation, my Lady. I have never met a woman with magic so near mine before. I am quite glad you came to hunt my cousin," he said in a low smooth voice. She nodded, then continued to eat.

"This meal is delicious. I thank you for your hospitality. I am glad to see you are a very different man than your cousin."

"Yes, very different, indeed. I assure you. Would you like to have a bath and fresh clothing before we visit a bit more?" She stood as he did, but did not take the hand he offered.

"That would be lovely. I am feeling quite dirty from visiting the dragon hold."

HOGE LED HER to a small suite and entered with her.

"I will have a maid bring you fresh clothes. I will also assure you are not disturbed for an hour."

"And you will be watching my every move with your magic, I am certain. So you would suggest that I not try to escape," Morgan said with a wink. He smiled wickedly as he stepped closer to her.

"You are both powerful and wise, a treat indeed." "You have no idea, Lord Hoge."

His smile changed to a look of frustration, and he moved toward her, reaching for her middle. She stepped back and raised a hand of warning.

"Patience, Lord Hoge," she said with a calm expression. "Allow me to freshen up. Perhaps then, you will honor me with a dance?" He glanced at her glowing Crest and the dragons on her hands as he stepped back and bowed. "It will be my pleasure, my Lady." He left the room and stationed three guards outside the door.

She moved into the bathroom and faked the movements of a woman undressing and readying herself for a bath as she opened to find Nijel.

He was in the company of both Harrick and Martus, being treated horribly. She swallowed her anger, then found the young wife of Hoge sitting alone in a suite nearby.

"Did you mean it when you said you would take an opportunity to escape Hoge?"

"Yes, but go quickly! He is coming!" the young woman said.

Morgan backed away enough to hear and see but not be detected.

She watched Hoge enter the room and move to his young bride. "How is my child this day? Have you eaten properly and rested?"

"Yes, my child is fine, my Lord," the woman answered matching his cold tone. Hoge raised his arm to slap her but stopped short.

"Be thankful you carry my seed. Your tongue will earn you much pain after he is born. It would serve you well to earn my forgiveness before that time. You will accept that I am your husband and serve me, or you will live a wretched life in solitude. It is your choice, Cara!" He turned for the door, then stopped to look back at her with a haughty smile.

"You should know that I will spend the evening with a beautiful woman with powerful magic. If her magic is as great as I believe, I will no longer need you."

"Show jealousy," Morgan suggested to Cara.

"I expect you to return to my bed this night. My disappointment may cause our child to fall ill. Do not hurt me so when our child is still fragile," Cara said as she moved closer to him with tears welling in her eyes. He moved back to her and kissed her.

Morgan felt the woman's revulsion as she let him have the simple kiss without flinching.

"It is very pleasing to feel such jealousy for my attention, my Cara. Lady Morgan has great power that I can use. But I care for you, Cara. You will wake with me by your side," he said before kissing her again. She smiled and rubbed her swollen belly as he left.

"That was very smart, my friend. And thank you for assuring me a safer night. Now I have to ask how far you are willing to go to escape," Morgan said.

"I would rather die than hand my child over to him. If there is any chance my child will be born with a pure spirit, I want them to grow up free of the dark magic of Ceruk. What would you have me do, my Lady?"

"Is the young man, Martus, at all interested in you? Could you lure him away from the youngling dragon and Harrick?"

Cara gave a loud laugh.

"I could distract him quite easily. He has watched my every move since coming here last year. He even tried to talk to me once and was pummeled by Hoge. But what do you expect me to do with him?"

"Nothing at all. Just make him think he has a chance at some-thing with you, so he will leave the dragon. When you get him away, I will move to free the youngling. I can deal with Harrick without making a scene. Could you find a way to detain him?"

"I will go for the direct approach. I will knock him out then shove him in a closet."

"Sounds like a good straightforward plan. I will contact the dragons and get back to you on the timing. Thank you, Cara."

"HOW ARE YOU, MY FRIEND?" Morgan said to Qin.

"I am worried about you, my Lady. I want to help you but have no way to get to you."

"Did Panish get Taru away safely?" *"Yes. He has not returned."*

"I am sure he is talking with Nulian, considering options. Please, do not worry. You will be with him again, Qin. He loves you already and will not accept being without you. He is simply trying to be of the most help just now."

"I understand he has responsibilities, my Lady. Tell me how I can help you."

Morgan smiled as she felt Qin's pride in her link to Panish, as well as her annoyance in discussing it.

"I am going to use suggestion to have the guards at your gates open them. You must subdue them then move your brethren out and away. I will have the guards at the youngling gate open it just after yours so you can get them to safety as well. Send your brethren to the cave system Taru described, and have them begin searching for access to the portal room. My hope is that they can find a way by clearing debris, or perhaps another tunnel system will reach it. Ask them to spread out and search quickly.

"Your task in this is rescuing me and Nijel. He is a bit large now, but very weak from being bound all the time. My intent is

to time it such that I reach his room, unbind him, and open the window just as you are approaching. Are you ready for this, my friend?"

"Yes, my Lady. However, you have forgotten the control Hoge has over us. If he finds out we are escaping, he will attack our minds again. We may not be able to prevent hurting you. That I do not want to contemplate," Qin said.

"I assure you, I have not forgotten. I will have him occupied while you are escaping, my dear. Once all but you are away, I will free myself from his company and go straight to the youngling. Trust that I will give your brethren the opportunity to get away. And as for you, I will be there to help you fight him. Do you trust me enough to do this, Qin?"

"Yes, my Lady, I truly do."

She spoke back and forth with Qin and Cara to get the plan fully in place, then readied herself to face Hoge. She would need a great deal of magic to block him while communicating with Qin, Cara, and Nijel.

Once again, she placed her hands over her Crest and focused to let magic build within her. When her skin grew warm and tingled like mad, she was ready.

When she felt Hoge approach her door, she focused on the guards at the gates of the dragon holds. She found four at each and took their minds with ease.

"Unlock the gates quietly," she suggested until they had finished the task.

She met Hoge at the door with a smile and pushed her magic onto him to block his reception. She used suggestion to keep his focus on her as she took his hand with her gloved hand. As they walked down the hall together, she smiled at him and connected to Qin.

"Are you free?"

"Yes. My brethren are taking the younglings and eggs now. I

will hide and await your call. Be careful, please."

Hoge led her into a small hall which was occupied by a small orchestra. The musicians began to play the instant they entered, and Hoge swept her into a waltz. She could feel his dark magic through the gloves and her dress where his hand rested on her waist. It took a bit of focus to suppress its effects and regain control.

"Go get Martus and take him back to your room. I will alert Hoge to his treachery when you are ready," she said to Cara. She had to take a few deep breaths to maintain her focus as she managed this magical multitasking.

"You are quiet, my Lady. May I ask your thoughts?"

"I would embarrass myself were I to discuss all my thoughts, Lord Hoge. But I will say that you are a gallant dancer and I find this quite pleasant. A surprise, I admit. I expected to find a harsh ogre when I came here. Instead, I find a handsome man with wonderful manners. A delightful surprise, indeed."

Hoge pulled her closer to him as they continued to dance. She held his gaze as she tracked Cara's movements.

Cara walked down the hall and cracked opened the door to Martus' room. She smiled at him and gestured he come to her. He moved without hesitation.

MORGAN DID ONE FINAL SEARCH of the castle to assure all was in place. Martus was in Cara's room, and Harrick was pacing the room below, leaving Nijel unguarded. It was time to act.

She stopped dancing and looked into Hoge's eyes with alarm.

"Do you feel fear? It is a young woman your youngest wife she is very afraid," Morgan said as she dropped her block of Hoge's magic to allow him to open to locate Cara. "Is she friendly with Martus? He is with her."

Hoge moved quickly to the door and stormed down the hallway.

"Start the yelling and fighting, my friend," she said to Cara

while hurrying to free Nijel.

She heard the ruckus of Martus getting pummeled by Hoge as she climbed the steps and laughed aloud.

"Qin, I am nearly there. Take flight above the castle, please," she said. *"Cara, run to me as soon as you can get free! Go while he is distracted with beating Martus."*

She reached the youngling's room to find it secured with two locks. With a hand laid over each, she focused on the metal to melt the key portions. Morgan slammed a shoulder into the door of Nijel's room just as Cara came running up the stairs. They shot into the room, closed the door behind them, and moved toward Nijel. He was very agitated. Morgan felt his warning just in time to duck a hatchet aimed at her head.

Hoge's eldest wife had been hiding in the shadows behind the door and shrieked as she attacked. Morgan blocked the second strike and took the woman to the ground. Cara slammed a fist into the old woman's face to knock her out as Morgan hurried to free Nijel.

She located the three evil men as she worked. Martus was being dragged off by guards, Hoge was searching the small hall where he had left her, but Harrick was only a few yards from her.

"Cara, help Nijel to the window while I open it. Hurry, we are about to have company," she said as she moved to the window. *"Qin, drop to us."*

She broke the handle off, melted it, and started to reform it as she moved to help with Nijel.

"Alright, lift him to the window with me," she said to Cara. Her new strength made the task possible, but still very difficult. She lifted the large youngling to the window ledge and passed trust and confidence as Qin approached.

"Nijel, you must jump and trust her to catch you. Quickly, go!" He hesitated, so she nodded to Cara and they both shoved him hard.

"Catch him, my dear. Carefully, please," she called to Qin.

Qin caught the youngling just as the door behind Morgan flew open. Morgan stepped back into Harrick and pushed Cara to the window.

"Jump, my Lady," Qin called as she circled back around.

Morgan was wrapped around the neck by Harrick, who was using every ounce of his remaining magic and strength to hold her physically.

"Go, Cara, jump now," Morgan said. Cara did not hesitate and landed safely on Qin's back as she swooped below the window.

With them safe, Morgan grabbed Harrick's arm and attacked as she lowered her guard. He roared with pain as she shredded through his feeble guard to flood him with pure magic. As he wilted to the floor, she knelt to grip his throat. She looked into his eyes as she pushed him to the brink of death, then stopped.

"Remember this mercy, Harrick! It will never be offered again!"

Hoge entered the room with a snarling curse just as she reinforced her guard and leapt toward the window. He caught her and dragged her back into the room.

"I think not!" he said as he slammed her against a wall and spun her to face him. He used his considerable weight to pin her, gripping her hair with one hand and her neck with the other. "We are far from finished! You owe me a warm bed and an heir!" He tightened his grip and attacked her guard with dark magic. "I will enjoy breaking you, Woman. You will submit, or you will die at my hand you bi—"

Morgan's Crest burst into light the second she unleashed a fierce magical attack on the arrogant man. His arms weakened, allowing her to slip free. She gripped the dagger she had formed from the window latch, buried it in his side, and punctuated each word with a piercing strike of magic as she said, "Submission Is Not In My Nature!"

"CATCH ME, MY FRIEND," Morgan called, falling fast toward the rocky ground below.

Qin dropped into a steep dive and swept under her just in time. She landed hard and cursed as one leg buckled beneath her.

"Are you injured, my Lady? Shall I land?" Qin asked.

"Please, get us to the portal as fast as possible! I will address the injury when we are safe on Erion."

They flew on for a few minutes, then Qin made a horrible sound and lurched as she threw her head. Morgan quickly blocked Hoge to protect Qin's mind.

"Hoge's attack is stronger than usual," Qin said.

"He is using the magic of Martus to strengthen his own."

Qin jerked as they heard a great roaring from the cave system ahead and felt the rage growing within many of the dragons ahead of them.

"Some are not able to fight him and have attacked the others. My brethren are killing one another, my Lady," Qin said.

"Turn back to the castle and let me fight Hoge to give them more time."

"I cannot do that. You are injured, and it is too dangerous," Qin said.

"We are not likely to make it to the portal with your brethren enraged. Turn back, please!"

Her plea was unnecessary as Qin saw a large group of her brethren dragons headed for them on an attack mission. She turned back toward the castle with a dramatic roll and flew hard.

"Perhaps we can make it to the other portal before they catch us, then you can go to Berios," Qin said as she headed that way.

"I can stop him and give them time if you can just keep them off of us for a bit."

She glanced back and saw the group had gained on them and were very near now. Qin was carrying a great deal of weight and growing tired. Morgan saw the very dire situation and saw but one way to handle it.

"You will have to drop weight, fly over..." Morgan started to say. She went quiet as she felt the presence of dragons approaching them from the castle.

Qin jerked to the right just as six huge dragons, three Alerian and three Perian, rushed past her. Morgan's heart leapt as she felt the presence of Nulian, Panish, Gerzin, Asira, Tagien, and Tagien's mother, Tevish. She also felt Taru clinging to the harness on Nulian, and her anxiety climbed. Nulian and the others were swarming the attacking dragons and Taru was right in the middle of it.

"Lady Taru is fine. I am keeping her away from them. Defeat the dark ones, my Queen. We will give you time," Nulian said.

Morgan focused on the castle and on Hoge. She closed her eyes, placed her hands over her Crest, and used the sum of her abilities to push against him. Even from her distance, she felt his pain as her magic hit him. She held nothing back. She pushed her magic against theirs with more force than she had ever used before.

As Hoge weakened, she attacked the mind of Martus and forced him to withdraw. Both men dropped to their knees, shaking and roaring in pain. Her pure magic was shredding through their guards and destroying the dark magic within them. At last, she felt all the dragons calm and stop fighting.

"Direct the effort to find a way to the portal, my friends. I will stay here until it is time to fly there and go home. Have them search all tunnel pathways. Find a way home for all of us," Morgan said to Nulian and Taru.

"We will indeed, my noble Queen," Nulian said. Morgan smiled as her friend's love filled her.

"How are you smiling when you are sweating from the pain of a broken leg and fighting two evil men with your mind?" Cara asked as she tightened her grip to hold her steady.

"Love and friendship. It cures most anything."

She maintained her focus on the men and kept them subdued and unable to fight back. Asira and Panish approached, and Morgan felt Qin lift and fly with much more ease as Asira took Nijel from her. As Asira swooped away, Qin lifted again and stopped her wing beats. Panish had moved under her to carry her along a bit and let her rest. Morgan felt the love between them as they crooned to one another.

They soared in wide circles around the castle while the dragons searched for a way home, and she kept the evil men at bay.

"We have cleared a path, my Queen. It is time to go home," Nulian called. Morgan felt the desire to return to Berios from those who lived there.

"I thank you for your help, my friends. We will see you again soon. This world will be a bridge to reach you when necessary. Please, be vigilant in guarding the portal at all times now that these evil men know of its existence. Give my love to everyone on Berios. May the magic keep you all." She waved to Asira, Tagien, and Tevish as they flew back toward the lair and the portal to Berios.

Qin landed near the mouth of a large tunnel entrance. The dragons had dropped large boulders on the side of the mountain to gain access to the largest tunnel system leading to the portal chamber. They cleared the debris away, so even the largest could reach the portal.

Panish and Gerzin went through first to deal with the sea serpent, and find the path it used to reach the open sea. That would be the way for the dragons to exit the portal chamber. They returned as she and Qin arrived. Morgan felt Panish's injury at once.

When she started to move from Qin, Cara grabbed her.

"Have you forgotten you have a broken leg?" Cara yelled. Morgan squinted as the woman said that out loud. She had been blocking her pain from the Elder dragons and Taru so they would not worry and stop their efforts to get home. As she expected, the Elders and Taru came to her and made a fuss.

"My friends, my magic allows me to fight the pain very effectively. Let us worry over it after we are home, please. I am fine."

Nulian moved to her and held out her palm with a stern expression. Qin had dropped her body and head as Nulian approached.

"Qin, this is Nulian, sister of your mate and my dearest friend. I shared my love for her with you. Please do not take offense. I want and need her touch just now. Thank you for protecting me. I am grateful for your friendship."

Qin turned to nod to them both.

"It was my honor to help you, Caretaker Morgan. I remember the sensation you shared of your love for Lady Nulian and would never stand in the way of such a friendship. I am in no way offended."

Morgan moved into Nulian's palm and then onto her back with care. "Taru, will you please free the youngling from his bindings and control his pain?"

"It is already taken care of, my Caretaker. Nijel is settled with Elder Gerzin for his trip home," Taru said as she moved over to Qin's back to ride with Cara. Morgan smiled and nodded as she laid forward to rest against Nulian.

"Oh, my Sister, I am so thankful to have you with me again," Morgan said as her throat tightened and her eyes burned.

"I am very glad to feel your spirit as well, my dear one. I was tortured by the thought of never feeling this again," Nulian said as she moved into the tunnel behind Panish.

"Move up beside him and lift his tail to me so I can help him. He is hurting more than I can accept, my dear," Morgan said to Nulian.

Nulian did as Morgan asked so she could heal the great gash along his hind leg. As she finished, he crooned in thanks and quickened his pace. They reached the portal chamber, and she insisted she and Nulian be the last to go through.

"I will not leave another behind, my dear," she said when Nulian grumbled.

They arrived back on Erion to the sound of many dragons roaring with happiness. Morgan saw that Taru and Cara had dismounted Qin to climb the ancient staircase that circled the chamber.

"She cannot hold her breath as we can and may not make it through the underwater tunnel. I will escort her up on foot and meet you there, my Queen," Taru said.

Morgan nodded and smiled to her as Nulian turned for the tunnel entrance.

"Take a deep breath, my Queen, and hold on tight," Nulian said.

Morgan was taken on a fast and twisting ride through water-filled tunnels before they broke free of the rock and shot up out of the sea.

"Now that was a great ride! We should do that more often," Morgan said.

"Perhaps I will give Menkar a race one day and show him how it is properly done, my friend." They both laughed as Nulian glided around the island containing the portal.

Morgan focused on Chemerie and connected to Alec, Brya, Kyan, GranMay, and Daniel

"I am home, my family. I will be with you soon." All of them hit her with a barrage of questions. She laughed at the rush of worry and love from them. *"It is a long story. I promise to give it justice when we are together. I love you, and am very glad to feel your spirits. Let our country know that I have a few new friends with me. Meet us in the garden in about an hour."*

"Why the long delay, my dear? Where are you?" Alec asked.

"At the beach."

Family Gathering

"I AM GRATEFUL that my children are so proficient at healing already," Morgan said to Nulian. *"This will be more than Taru is ready for. I still find it profoundly annoying that I can heal almost any wound in others, but not my own."*

"I agree. Perhaps it is something you can work toward. You will certainly have ample opportunity for practice given your tendency to put yourself squarely in the middle of whatever could maim you."

Morgan patted her hard and laughed, then grimaced. Nulian hummed her healing song again. *"Thank you, my dear. It has been a very trying couple of days."* She laid back and began to relax at last. Her eyes grew heavy, and she drifted in and out of sleep.

Feelings of great fear jolted her awake. The dragons from Kalias were turning back at the sight of the Perian dragons approaching from the castle.

"In Chemerie, we are all family, and all are of pure spirit," Morgan said to all the dragons from Kalias as she pushed friend-

ship and devotion. *"You are all welcome to be part of our family. Trust in me, my new friends, and allow these wonderful spirits to prove their kindness. Do not mark them an enemy based only on their appearance. Release the hatred instilled by the evil of Ceruk. Make your own decisions, and your own choices."*

Qin moved ahead of the group and flew toward the Perians without a sign of worry. She was greeted with croons and deep hums of welcome, which she answered with notes of respect and gratitude. Her brethren followed their Eldest Female's lead and the two groups soon mixed to form one massive fleet heading back toward Chemerie.

"Look, my Sister, now you cannot tell who originated from which world. We are one family sharing one magic, just as in the days of Puria," Morgan said as she watched some Chemerian younglings begin to play with those from Erion.

"You have accomplished so much, my Queen. You have surpassed even my predictions of your greatness."

"It is the magic which does great things. I am just its tool for the day. Our next task is to build a new portal. We must reach our family on Berios. I believe I am beginning to better understand the type of tasks my children are meant to help me accomplish."

Moments later, the large group of dragons landed and overfilled the castle lawn. Many landed on the surrounding cliffs and in the lake area. Nulian set down with her usual grace in the center of the group, and they cleared a path for her to reach the gazebo where Alec and the children waited for Morgan.

"Come to me, little ones. I need your help," Morgan said.

The twins ran forward to meet Nulian, who lay down and put a leg out for them to climb up. They hurried to kneel beside her injured leg. Alec was right behind them and frowned when he saw the leg lying in such an odd position.

"That looks like a thorough break, my dear," Alec asked. She nodded and looked to the children as he took her hand.

"Your father will pull the bones into alignment, and you need to mend it there. This is a much larger task than you have done before, so take your time and learn as you go." They both nodded and placed their hands to her leg very lightly. As her pain dropped away, she smiled and took a deep relaxing breath.

She nodded, and Alec pulled her ankle hard to set the bone sections in a straight line. She gritted her teeth and dug her fingers in between Nulian's scales as her pain shot beyond the twins' block. The children began to sing the healing song of the dragons as they worked. Her pain faded, and the bones were healed in less than a minute. They continued to heal the torn tissue a few minutes more until she felt no noticeable discomfort at all.

"I am very lucky to have you two around. As Nulian says, I seem to place myself in the middle of trouble quite often." They both gave her serious nods of agreement then burst out laughing as she grabbed them and tickled them fiercely. Alec helped her slide to the ground, then took her into his arms.

"I feel your fatigue, my love. What have you been up to?"

"Taking the long way home." She kissed him passionately and deepened their connection. He held her tight and matched her intensity for many seconds before easing her back to breathe heavily against her lips.

"While I am deeply grateful for a kiss like that on any occasion, I expect an explanation for such desperate feelings later, my mate."

MORGAN GATHERED HER FAMILY around Nijel, where she knelt to caress him and survey his injuries. She looked from him to his mother, Valen, who was curled around him and many of his siblings.

"He has a great deal of damage from his mistreatment at the hand of Harrick and Martus. His leg has healed in a very poor position, as have the main bones of his wings." She then looked into Nijel's eyes as she passed her most sincere love and friendship. "I very much want to free you from your pain and give you as much mobility as possible. I can repair much of the damage, but I will have to break the bones to reset them. I may not be able to block all of the pain as I do such intricate work. Do you wish me to do this, Nijel?" The youngling looked up to his mother.

"You will not fly if you do not let her try, my Son. I have given my allegiance to this woman, as my Queen and Caretaker, because I trust her with my life. I ask that you trust in me," Valen said. Nijel looked to Morgan and nodded.

"Alec, Daniel, I will need both of you, please," she said as she stroked Nijel. When the men settled beside her, she looked to the twins. They had settled beside Nijel's shoulders and waited with focused expressions. "To help our new friend, I need your help to control his pain. I will focus my efforts to reset the bones. You will focus only on his pain and send him constant healing energy to keep him as comfortable as possible. Try not to push so hard as to run short of energy before I can finish. That may still happen because this will take me many minutes. I will monitor his pain and shift some of my magic to that effort if needed. Do your best and learn as much as you can." They nodded and placed their hands on Nijel's neck. She felt Taru's eagerness and nodded for her to move closer. "Lay a hand to me, and simply feel how I direct the magic with focus on each task. Give nothing unless I ask." With a nod from each in the group, she looked to Nijel and pushed a strong wave of devotion.

"Here we go," she said as she nodded for the children to begin easing his pain. To the men, she said, "Put gentle pressure on his leg until you feel me break the bone. Then use greater force to pull the bone back into place." The men nodded, and she focused on the ill-fused area of the thick bone of his thigh.

They all worked together as she focused to repair the bone and what she could of the damaged muscle tissue around it. It was not perfect, as the damage was severe, but it would now bear far more weight.

Shifting focus to his wings, she moved from bone to bone, breaking and resetting them to maximize his wingspan and strength. They were still going to be small for his body. She hoped they would bear his weight.

Nijel never flinched through it all, and Morgan never detected pain from him. Brya and Kyan had their eyes closed, and their Crests glowed brightly in the morning sun as they maintained a strong connection with the young dragon.

"I am done, little ones," she said. They looked up with broad smiles. "You have every right to be proud. That was wonderful, my dears."

They beamed as Nijel crooned to pass his appreciation, then wrapped their arms around his neck.

"Welcome home, Nijel," they said together. They started finishing each others' sentences as they introduced themselves and told him how much they loved his mother and his siblings. Nijel stood to try out his new leg and wing. Many around them roared in celebration as he gave his wings a strong beat to lift himself off the ground and land without pain.

The youngling was in high spirits, which made Morgan very happy. Her guilt for his suffering lessened as she watched him crooning to his mother and his siblings while the children crawled over all of them. A gentle touch of magic made her turn and meet Taru's eyes as she stepped closer.

"I understand why you sent me back, but it was very hard to take, my Queen. I apologize if you heard my angry thoughts," Taru said. She then shot a sharp scowl at Nulian as she added, "I very much wanted to return and help you. Unfortunately, Lady Nulian would not allow it until she was ready to take me herself."

"She is fiercely and persistently protective, for certain," Morgan said as she patted Nulian, who had just dropped her head down to touch her back. "While I know quite well how frustrating it is to be held back when you want to fight, I am proud she did not let your fear and anger guide you.

"Keep in mind that my dear Nulian has had plenty of practice in managing me. You did not stand a chance of getting past her protective nature. Do not be upset with her. She does it because she loves you as much as I do." Taru lifted an eyebrow, then looked away. "Yes, Taru, I do love you very much." She pulled her into a hug, then laughed and held her at arm's length to meet her eyes. "But you are still not ready to marry my brother."

Daniel groaned a bit louder than he intended and everyone laughed. Taru sobered as she saw Willow change directions to avoid their path.

"I will see you all in a bit," Taru said as she kissed Daniel's cheek. He gave her a small smile and nodded before she hurried to catch up to Willow. Morgan gave Daniel a smile and pushed confidence as he watched his mate and best friend begin talking.

"So when do we hear about your adventure?" Alec asked. "After we eat!"

"*Which should be after a proper bath, my Queen,*" GranMay added from behind her. She laughed at Morgan's blushing and took her arm to walk to the castle with her. They walked at a slower pace to let the others stroll ahead of them.

"Valen's youngling returned, many new dragon brethren among us, yet you are filled with loss," GranMay said. Morgan stopped and looked into GranMay's eyes as she shared the loss of Palish. She knew the twin dragons had been precious to her during her term as Caretaker, and passed all the supportive magic she could with her words.

"Thank you for sharing that with me, my girl. I would like to go speak with Panish. Go clean up. I will see you in a bit."

DANIEL AND TARU showed Cara to a guest room and then continued on to Taru's room. Daniel closed the door and held her tight for a moment before releasing her.

"I missed you very much. Are you alright? Were you injured in this adventure?"

"I am perfect now that I am with you again. We will marry soon. Morgan completed my Quickening so I will have much greater control now. I still have much to learn, but it will not be very long, my love."

Daniel kissed her cheek and said, "That is excellent news." When he turned to leave, she pulled him back to her with insistence.

"I have enough control already to not accept only that before you go, my mate," Taru said as she kissed him deeply.

Daniel did not fight her in the least. She remembered Morgan's warning about hurting him and stopped their contact the instant she felt her control waver.

Daniel was a little flush as he stared into her eyes.

"I long for the day when we can continue that kind of kiss without fear," he said. He kissed her hand, bowed, then backed up while holding her eyes until he reached the door.

DANIEL, ALEC, AND THE REST of their closest family gathered in the dining hall as Morgan and the others freshened up. Daniel and Alec were both solemn as they looked out the window at all the new dragons.

"Somehow they went from Berios to Kalias. Another portal, I suppose. To have freed the dragons from Ceruk, I assume they had an encounter with the evil Lord Hoge that Taru spoke of," Daniel said.

"Yes, I believe they had a difficult time of it. Something is haunting Morgan. We both know there had to be a profound catalyst to drive her to Kalias so soon. There is something significant we do not yet know," Alec said as he stared out the window with thoughtful, worried eyes.

"Very perceptive, my husband," Morgan said as she neared the dining room with the children on her heels.

Alec smiled as he turned just before she entered the room. *"Why thank you, my wife."*

"Have I mentioned I missed you fiercely, my ridiculously handsome husband?"

"No, and my heart is heavy from the lack of attention."

She smiled at his flirtatious tone and lifted to her toes to kiss him gently, before moving to meet GranMay at the door with a hug.

"I trust you met Qin," Morgan said as she escorted GranMay to the table and eased her into a seat. It took all of her self-control not to pass healing as she felt her pain and fatigue.

"Yes, she is a strong spirit and seems quite devoted to Panish already. She was jealous of my touching him. That worried me until I realized they had not yet taken their first flight."

They laughed lightly together as she offered Cara a smile and directed her to take a seat.

"Everyone, our lovely new friend is Cara. She comes to us from Kalias. She helped us escape, and I returned the favor by welcoming her to live with us. The rest of the details will be shared after we eat. Please, introduce yourselves while I stuff my body with food."

She dug into the wonderful meal. Alec watched with amused interest as she finished a second plate of food.

"Is there something new I should know, my bride?" Alec asked. She stopped chewing and gave him a blank stare. Taru giggled as she gestured to the empty plate. Morgan swallowed the large amount of food in her mouth and smiled.

"The dragons and I helped Taru through her Quickening. I gained some new magical attributes in the process, as did she. I seem to have gained a bit more strength, agility, and stamina as well as the accompanying appetite. In my defense, we have barely eaten for two days, my dear."

"I cannot wait to help you investigate the extent of your new skills, my dear," Alec said with a wink. Daniel rolled his eyes.

"They came in handy yesterday, for certain," Morgan said as she ignored her brother and started to eat again.

Everyone who had not been involved was staring at her with interest.

"My Sister, you start the tale while I finish my little dinner," Morgan said to Taru.

Taru explained about the efforts to complete her Quickening, and the skills they both noticed were transferred. As she neared the destruction of the portal, she stopped and looked back to her. Morgan nodded and washed the last of her food down with a glass of wine before scanning the anxious faces around her.

"I have very bad news, my family," Morgan said. "Our friends and the sanctuary of Berios are not very accessible any longer. The portal on Berios was destroyed in a quake."

She stopped to take another drink and put her emotions in check.

"We also lost one of our Elder dragons. Palish, twin brother of Panish, was killed in the quake." The room was silent as the loss moved through everyone. Most present knew and loved him, as she had. GranMay's pain was profound. Her bond with the twins was among the strongest she had ever formed.

She proceeded with the story of their traveling to Kalias in the hope of getting home. "When I opened to search the planet, I found two people I have been seeking since we freed the Perian dragons enslaved by Arshek."

"Harrick and Irika's son," Alec said with a heavy sigh.

"Yes, they used the injured youngling I failed to save to activate the portal. He has been their prisoner all this time and has suffered constant " she stopped as her voice cracked.

"Do not blame yourself. You did all you possibly could. Let go of that silly notion," GranMay said.

Morgan nodded to her and gave a weak smile before continuing. As she told the tale, she had to be careful not to react to the many thoughts she overheard from Alec and Daniel. However, there came a point where she paused.

"I had no intention of letting the man touch me, my dear. I simply used his weakness against him." Alec nodded, but she felt his jealously and protectiveness boiling still. She continued the story without interruption until she reached the explanation of Cara's involvement.

"You carry the child of Hoge?" Taru asked with a look of disgust.

Cara's face reddened as she stared at her plate.

"Do not make her feel guilty. Apologize right now!"

"I am sorry. I did not mean to sound judgmental. It is just that...I...have a past with him and felt sorry for you having to know him that well. Sorry for my tone, my Lady."

"What kind of past do you mean, Lady Taru?" Cara asked.

"Careful with your words, my Sister," Morgan said as she glanced at the children.

"I was once an unwilling guest at his castle. We can compare war stories another time," Taru said. Cara nodded, but still looked sad as she rubbed her swollen belly.

"You are worried the child will have a dark spirit like the father," Alec said. Cara looked surprised that he understood and nodded. "Well, I can tell you, from experience, that blood does not determine the spirit of the child. I struggled with the identity of my own father and was shown that the true nature of a person is determined by the life they lead and not by their blood parents. Since you have had the misfortune to spend time with him, it might surprise you to know that I am the blood son of Harrick." Cara's face showed the shock he expected as she looked to Morgan for confirmation. "I was raised among those of pure spirits, and bare absolutely no connection to the darkness. When I learned about my blood lineage, I feared just what you do now. My dear mate, her family, and the love of my Chemerian brethren helped me see the truth. You will be able to explain the truth to your child from the beginning."

Cara stared in disbelief, then her eyes filled with tears as she trembled.

"I hear the logic in your words, King Alec, and I thank you for them. But...my heart is still terrified that the evil of that man will be within my child."

Morgan moved to kneel beside her and placed a hand to her swollen belly. She bonded to Cara and then sought the spirit of the little one. Once she found it, she directed Cara's focus to let her feel the spirit of her child.

"Your child has a beautiful spirit, just like her mother," she said as she let the bonding drop away. Cara burst into tears, so she held her until she could calm down.

"Thank you so much for letting me come here with you. I have had dreams of having a family around me ever since I lost mine," Cara said.

"How did you lose them?" Taru asked.

"My parents were killed when I was an infant, and my aunt when I was two. Then I lost my uncle and cousins in a great dragon raid on my village. I was very little, yet I remember their love," Cara said. She looked to Taru with a longing expression on her face. "You remind of my Aunt Halei. Your magic reminds me of her touch so much."

"W...what was your uncle's name?" Taru asked with wide eyes. "Rone. Did you know them?"

"What an amazing coincidence, Mommy," Brya said as she and

Kyan smiled and bounced in their seats.

"What coincidence, little one?" Cara asked Brya.

Morgan gave Brya a stern look, making her clam up and blush. She and Kyan covered each other's mouths and sat back, still beaming. Cara looked to Taru, who was still staring at her with wide eyes.

"Please, Lady Taru, if you know something about my family, I want to know. Good or bad, I just want to know."

"I did know Rone and Halei of Dobitch village. They were... my parents."

"What? But, I never —"

"Mother lied when she told everyone she had lost her last baby. She took me to live with dragon friends in the mountains."

"Well, no wonder your magic feels so comforting. Nice to meet you, Cousin!" The two smiled brightly and flew into each others' arms. Brya and Kyan bounced in their chairs again as they clapped, and everyone joined them with happy laughter.

"Alright, children, time for you two to head to bed," Morgan said as she returned to her seat.

"We need to know what happened, Mommy. Please, let us hear it with our ears," Kyan said. Alec snorted as he was taking a drink. Morgan gave him a questioning and annoyed look.

"At least they are honest. We know their tendency to hear everything eventually through thought. You may as well let them hear it first hand, my dear."

She conceded and continued the story. She told them of the battle with Harrick and Hoge and of her merciful refusal to take their lives.

"Is it wrong to kill someone who would kill you?" Kyan asked.

"No, not if your life is in danger at the time," Daniel answered. "If you seek them out to kill them, it is wrong indeed."

"Mommy, your life was in danger. Why did you not take his, and stop his evil from harming others?" Kyan asked.

Morgan looked at his innocent face without answering him. Alec grasped her hand as he felt her heartache.

"Son, you are blessed with the power to save lives," Alec said. "After you have fought to bring life back to someone near death, you will understand why your mother would find it hard to take a life when given a choice."

Kyan and Brya looked at each other as they discussed it in silence then both nodded.

"We did not mean to hurt you by asking, Mommy. We just want to understand why killing is sometimes acceptable and other times considered wrong," Brya said.

"I do not mind the questions, love. But sometimes you are going to find that adults still ask the very same questions and have no perfect answer," she said as she forced a calming breath. "I was not able to open myself enough to search the entire planet, but, to our knowledge, there are no dragons left on Kalias. That should mean that those three evil men are trapped there. The bad news is there are still pure-spirited people there who will need help getting out from under the cruel hands of these men. We will have to go through Kalias to reach Berios unless we learn to construct a new portal," she said with a huge yawn. Everyone took that as a sign to head to bed and started to shuffle out.

"Can we learn to build a new portal, Mommy?" Brya asked.

"I consider it my job to find out, my sweet girl. We will all work on it together. Now, off to bed. I will be up in a moment," Morgan said as she rustled the twins' hair.

She smiled as they ran ahead of her. They raced along, darting between everyone while laughing as usual.

"I think they grew another inch while I was gone."

"They barely ate or slept. But yes, they did grow a bit," Alec said. "They do not like separation from one another at all. But I did not expect it to be as bad with my absence as that," Morgan said.

"I did. They are quite attached to you, my love. Did you not realize they get nervous when you visit the ancestral lair or go riding with Nulian for many hours?"

"Yes. I have felt their concern and was aware they used their magic to follow my movements. I just did not realize my absence would upset them so much," Morgan said. "I dare not think how they would have reacted if I were unable to make it back."

Alec took her hand to connect to her as they walked, and she deepened the connection.

"I would have taken care of them, of course," Alec said. "But our hearts would never have been whole again. I am glad we did not know how close we came to losing you. My heart aches at the mere thought."

They tucked the children in and sang them to sleep. Morgan was still solemn as they entered their chambers. Alec pulled her into his arms and caressed her face as he studied her eyes.

"You have suffered the possibility of never seeing us again for days. Your heart has been breaking a bit more each minute. Let yourself cry, my dear. Relax now. You are home. I am sorry for your pain and so very grateful for your magic, which brought you home."

Morgan let the tears come and tucked deeper into his arms. He held her tight as they entered bonding. After only a moment, he lifted her in his arms and carried her to the bed where she fell fast asleep.

DANIEL WALKED ALONG the hall with Taru with a smile on his face. "What are you thinking?"

"Can you not hear all my thoughts like Morgan?"

"Like Morgan, I am being courteous, and not listening. Would you be alright with my staying connected to you so I can hear all your thoughts?"

"That is not a good idea, my Lady. I would be uncomfortable with you hearing my thoughts as they come to me."

"I think it would be wonderful and allow us to get closer."

"Yes, well Listen, I know you are very tired, so I will go. Get a good night's sleep. If you need me for anything just call. Goodnight, my dear," he said as he kissed her cheek and turned to leave.

"I do not understand why you need to hide your thoughts from me, my mate. I will respect your wishes, but am hurt by the lack of trust," Taru said in an angry tone. Daniel stopped and spun around to face her.

"Taru, I was simply sparing us both the embarrassment of my very personal thoughts about you. It was not a question of trusting you. I hope you can understand that because that is all I care to explain." He turned and moved down the hall as his face reddened.

"Mercy, you are shy. Aren't you?"

He kept walking but smiled as he said, "In some ways, yes. But not altogether, my dear. Once we are married, there will be no holding back of anything, I assure you."

"Good, because I am eager to know all of you, my mate," Taru said. Daniel smiled and hoped she did not hear all the thoughts that came to him as a response.

Painful Past

DANIEL WAS TOO AMPED to sleep, so he jogged to the lake and plunged into the cool water. He swam a few quick laps, then set a lazy pace toward the falls. He dove to swim under the churning water and was startled by a hand grabbing his ankle. He looked down to find Taru floating up to him as their link burned within him.

"I can use the water to control my body temperature, my dear. Hold me, please," Taru said as they surfaced.

"Are you sure? I do not want you fainting again."

"I am sure."

She moved into his arms and connected as she kept her guard high.

When her body grew warmer, Daniel started to push her back. "Wait," she said with a smile as she held him close. "Whoa! What was that?" Daniel asked with a shiver.

"I am using the excess magic to freeze the water near my body. Heat pulled from my skin is used to melt it away."

"That is pretty ingenious."

"Your sister is rather brilliant, my mate."

"And I am very grateful for that. I am holding my fiancé without worry. I am very grateful, indeed," Daniel said. He held her close for a long moment then whispered, "Can you handle a bit more, my dear?" "Yes."

He kissed her as they floated in ice crystals and held each other tight for many minutes.

"It is getting late. We should go back," Daniel said as he pulled back from her.

"I have perfect control. I am not overwhelmed at all."

"It is not your level of control I question at the moment. Come, let's get some sleep," he said while swimming away.

She caught up and dunked him before darting past. He grabbed her and dunked her in return. They had reached the shallows where they stood looking at each other with a hint of mischief in their eyes.

"I challenge you to dunk me again, my mate," Taru said.

"I would not want to hurt you, my dear."

"I dare say, you cannot."

Daniel laughed and started to circle her as he said, "I have seen your impressive physical skill. But, do you actually think I would fail in a real attempt?"

"I do. If you are bold enough to try, I will enjoy the match. However, I doubt your willingness to push yourself to your fullest against me. Nothing less will gain you victory. I will not hold back to let you win." She turned to keep him in front of her and side-stepped as well.

"Do you promise not to be mad if I hurt you or win?"

"I will hold no grudge. But you will not win!"

Daniel's mischievous grin shifted to a focused scowl.

"Are there any rules to this match I should know about?"

"None. Our goal is simply to dunk the face of the other by whatever means necessary. Are you game?"

"Absolutely."

They maneuvered around each other for a few seconds before Taru made a quick leap at him. She slammed into his chest with her palms. He stumbled back without going under, then quickly grabbed her wrist. After sweeping one of her legs to throw her off balance, he twisted her arm behind her back, then wrapped his around her chest to bend her back and make her unstable on her feet.

"Are you still so confident, my love?" he asked as he kissed her ear.

She slammed her head into his forehead, then used his second of shock to break away and move to the side.

"I certainly am," she said with a laugh.

"So we fight at that level, do we?" Daniel asked as he rubbed his head. "Alright then, your rules."

This time he took a defensive approach to the game and waited for her move toward him. She continually moved to the side, trying to grab him from behind. He countered her moves with ease and smiled at her annoyance.

She made a quick move to grab his knee, pull it to her, and lift. His other leg moved from under him, but he gripped her neck and shoulder. He then slid to her back and locked his legs around her middle. She was now supporting his weight. Her annoyance climbed as she tried and failed to throw him several times.

"It is a draw if we enter the water together, yes?" he asked.

"Not if you go in first," Taru growled as she leaned over and placed him near the surface of the water. Her flexibility and strength to hold his weight in this position was incredible. He could not help but admire it. He was not ready to lose, however, so he jerked his leg free and pushed her away hard.

They were both a bit winded from that exchange and smiled at each other with eager intensity. They clashed and struggled to pull or push the other over a few more times. The match ended when Taru made a quick and acrobatic flip over his head. She landed behind him and grabbed him from behind to pin his arms at his sides.

"Deep breath, my love," she said as she picked him up, spun, and slammed him in the water just before her.

They surfaced with Taru giggling. Daniel had a very intense look on his face.

"You do not have to be physically dominant to own my heart, Daniel. Do not be mad," she said as she moved closer to him.

He grabbed her, pulled her to him, and kissed her.

"Best two out of three, my dear. Go!" He pushed her back and set his feet. Taru stood docile.

"You do not like to lose. Do you, my mate?"

"Are you not willing to beat me again? I can handle it. Let's play."

"Only if we move from the water and make this a proper wrestling match. I used to wrestle the dragons and am rather good. Want to give it a try?"

"I have done a bit of wrestling as well," he said as they moved onto the lawn. "Our rules were to pin the shoulders of the other for three seconds. What are yours?"

"Make the other give up or fall unconscious. But your rules will do."

"No, yours are better," he said with a wink.

"Are you sure? A loss of that kind will be hard to swallow for a prideful male."

"And for a boastful female, my dear."

Taru gave him a mischievous smile, and they began.

They grappled and twisted over one another, trying to get the other into a compromising position. Their efforts lasted for several minutes with many intense situations. At one point, Daniel had Taru pinned. He put torque on her arm, and she grunted. He released her and she moved away with a giggle.

"That was easy. You will have to be willing to cause me pain to get me to concede, my love," she said through a wide grin. Daniel stood and stared at her, breathing hard.

"I can't hurt you on purpose."

"Then you will lose," she said as she attacked. She hit him hard and slammed him to the ground. He lifted his hips and used her momentum to flip her over his head and onto her back. He pinned her with a familiar wrestling move from his high school days on Earth.

She struggled against him for a few seconds, but could not break free. When she snarled, he chuckled.

"When was the last time you found yourself the loser in a physical challenge, anyway?" he asked as he used most of his strength to keep her pinned.

She went very still, clenched, roared with rage, and sent a white-hot flash of magic through them both.

"Aahhh!" Daniel yelled as he released her and jerked away. She rolled and scooted away from him, panting fast, her eyes and crest brightly aglow.

He hurried to drop his scalded hands in the lake water as she bolted.

"Taru, wait!" He gave up calling after two more tries, then focused on Morgan as he studied the blistering skin on his hands.

"Meet me on the terrace," Morgan said.

"I need to find Taru. She ran off."

"After I heal your hands. Meet me!"

A moment later, Morgan took his hands in hers to heal the deep burns with a frown as he looked out over the garden.

"Will you explain this, please? I was blocking you to give you privacy, so I have no idea what happened."

He explained as she finished, then pulled away and turned.

"I'm going to find her," he said as he moved toward the steps.

"Daniel, wait," she said as she stepped forward to touch his arm and pass concern. "There is an explanation for her overreaction to being held down, and to your question."

"Like what? What are you talking about?" She gestured for him to wait and connected to Taru.

"Do you want me to explain, or do you want to? You must trust him to understand, my Sister."

"No! Please, Morgan, do not tell him. Ask him to come to me in the rear of the garden. Thank you for healing the wounds I inflicted, my Queen. I am so sorry."

Morgan told Daniel to join Taru, then spoke to her again as he hurried to her.

"Do not feel bad. You will learn to control such reactions. For now, just trust him. He will not blame you for your reaction once he understands."

DANIEL SAT ON THE BENCH beside Taru and took her hand, gripping it tighter when she tried to pull away. He kissed her hand until she relaxed, then traced the dragon on her wrist. She rubbed his palms lovingly and kissed each as fresh tears ran down her face.

"You asked a question, and the answer made me remember a very painful event. As I thought of it, my anger flared, and I lost control of the magic. I am so sorry. I never meant to hurt you. This is exactly what Morgan was afraid of. We should stay apart until I am competent enough to be safe," Taru said. She stood and started to walk away.

"So, rather than trust me to understand, you are going to shun me? Do you think me too shallow to understand, or simply too ignorant?"

Taru did not turn to look at him, but stopped and dropped her head. He moved to gently turn her and took her into his arms.

"Morgan says there is something I need to understand that will explain your reaction. You do not have to explain if you are not ready. But do not think I do not want to understand, or that I'm not capable of handling whatever you tell me. Give me more credit than that, Taru."

"You do not want this information. It is very...unpleasant."

He eased her back and lifted her chin so she would look at him. "I want to know everything about you so I can be the best husband possible. Share with me and help me do that."

"I will show you, but I cannot speak of it," she said. He nodded and lifted her hand to his chest.

"I do not want to hurt you again. Morgan must be involved," she said as she pulled her hand away. He hesitated for only a second, then nodded.

"My Queen, will you mediate a bonding between Daniel and me? I am going to share with him but do not want to hurt him. You know the intensity of the event and the likelihood of my losing control."

"I would be glad to. I am sure Daniel will find it uncomfortable, but you are being very responsible by asking me. I will meet you back on the terrace," Morgan said.

They joined her moments later. This time Alec was with her. He rubbed his eyes as he yawned, but sat down near them without complaint. Morgan gestured for them to sit on the lounge chair next to her.

"Are you sure about this, Daniel? This is an extremely personal and intense memory that you will be experiencing just as she did. You could just have the basics in words. It would be much easier to take."

"Show me the truth and let me deal with it. I love her and want to know her completely."

She smiled and nodded as she held her hands out to them. As each took a hand, she connected to them and passed calming feelings.

"Are you ready, Taru?" "No, but I must do this."

"I am simply mediating the energy flow. You are in control of the process. I will initiate bonding, but you will choose what is shared."

Taru nodded, so she deepened the connection to bonding. Daniel took a deep breath as the sensations hit him. Morgan eased the flow to him for a bit to let him adjust, then deepened it further to allow easy sharing of information.

Taru and Daniel held each other's eyes as they felt the powerful sensations. They each sought the other's spirit and spent a minute enjoying it before continuing. Taru forced a deep breath as she directed him to her memory of the horrible days being tortured by Hoge as a child. She nodded, then closed her eyes as she gave him full access to all she had experienced.

Daniel's anger and pain both climbed as he watched the abuse. His body trembled with rage, and he became queasy as he experienced how Hoge tortured her in so many physical and magical ways for many days.

Hoge had tried to break her spirit, to make her use her magic for him willingly. Despite his considerable efforts, he did not succeed on his own. He used other magical people to help him force his way into her mind and take her memories. The evil man had laughed in her face as he told her he was going to have her dragon family killed and thanked her for her help.

Taru had grabbed Hoge's throat as she roared with rage. Hoge's retaliation was both physical and magical. It was pain greater than any Daniel had ever imagined. Hoge had held her down, laughed in her face as he attacked her mind with magic, and struck her again and again.

Daniel lurched and pulled his hand free of Morgan's.

The bonding was broken at once, causing him horrible pain. He lay on the terrace floor, shaking and groaning as he cried silent tears. Morgan helped Taru with the pain of the sudden drop and passed calming before letting her go to Daniel.

Taru knelt beside him and placed her hand to his shoulder. She passed healing energy, and he soon relaxed his muscles. He was still panting and trembling as he sat up to take her into his arms. He held her and cried with her.

Morgan moved to sit beside Alec while wiping her eyes.

"I am not asking for details, but I felt the emotions you experienced. Am I right in assuming Hoge did a great deal of damage when she was with him?" Alec asked.

"Yes, the worst kind imaginable, my love. Daniel just experienced it through her eyes."

"Good gracious," Alec said as he pulled her to lean back against him. They were silent as they watched Daniel and Taru connect to deal with the reality of her abuse.

"Thank you for trusting me with this," Daniel said to Taru. *"I am so sorry you had to endure such a thing. I am disgusted that I touched you in a way that made you think of it. I will never hold you forcibly again, not even in play. I will never hurt you. Tell me you know that. Please, tell me you know I meant no such thing."*

"I know your spirit, and I know you would never hurt me. It was just a reaction to your question. I love you, and do not question your love for me."

Daniel kissed her and held her tight to him. He then pushed her away so he could look at her again with fierce intensity.

"Morgan showed him mercy, but if I ever meet him, I will not! I never want you near him again. If you must go back to Kalias, I will be with you. He will never hurt you again, Taru. I will die before I let that happen!"

13

New Pathways

TARU SPENT SEVERAL HOURS each day over the next few weeks training with Morgan. She loved her new control and attacked each task with enthusiasm. Using the excess magic that built within her required conscious effort, but she enjoyed finding new ways to do so. A favorite for both her and Morgan was to form jewelry out of various metals and crystalline gems. While diamonds were their favorite, they discovered many more as they experimented.

At breakfast one morning, Morgan was chatting with GranMay about what she had learned of the metal the Knights' swords were made of.

"It takes a great deal of magic to reform it. I consulted the Book of the Caretaker and learned that Lady Chemerie herself formed the swords when the evil of Arshek came to be a problem. That means they have held their edge for hundreds of years without tarnishing or weakening at all."

"Yes, I know. I had the same curiosity years ago. Does your

curiosity have something to do with the portal boundary rings?" GranMay said with a knowing smile.

"Yes. I believe we can learn to form one ourselves. All that is left is to understand the purple liquid and how it works."

"Is that all?" GranMay asked as she chuckled. "It all sounds like a great task, but I will help you with it as much as I can." Morgan felt her change her wording but did not react. GranMay had first meant to say, '...as long as I can,' but changed it to not upset her. Even her grandmother did not understand her skills.

As they left the dining room, she reached for GranMay's hand and noticed her avoid the skin contact by taking her arm instead.

"I will not heal you unless you ask. Please do not avoid touching me, or connecting to me. Trust me not to heal you against your wishes. I want to be as close as possible while I have you," Morgan said as they strolled the garden.

"Thank you for respecting my wishes, my dear. I will trust you. For now, no healing, but please do touch spirits with me, my dear girl," GranMay said as she held up her hands.

Morgan touched her hands and tensed as the profound difference in her grandmother struck her. GranMay pushed confidence and encouragement as she laced their fingers and pushed them into a deep connection.

"I love you, and I love our family here. But I know it is nearly my time and I long to be with my husband and your parents again. I hope to help you reach Berios and rebuild the portal. When we do, it is there I will stay. You will return here and let me go, my dear. Do not pity me. I am ready for the next part of my spirit's journey."

"I am trying to understand. Handling Father's sudden death was awful, but this is much harder. I will do my best to focus on enjoying your spirit, and not on the day I will lose it," Morgan said as tears filled her eyes. They hugged and held each other for a long

time as she cried. It tore her heart to not pass healing energy to her tired and pained grandmother, but she did not.

Frustration mingled with sadness as she thought of her children leaving her as well. GranMay took her arm to resume their walk.

"You have a right to be angry, my dear. You will experience the loss of me and the children within the year. But remember, the twins will return to you. You will have many years with them, and their own children, I imagine," GranMay said. "Besides, you will have other things occupying your mind, my dear."

"Yes, the portal rebuild is a difficult ta—"

"Oh, my dear, you have been so focused on others lately, you have not taken time for yourself to meditate. Please do so right now," Gran-May insisted.

"That sounds ominous. Am I ill?" Morgan asked as she sat down on a bench. GranMay maintained the same stern expression as she sat down. Morgan had to focus more than usual to release her connections to those around her, and focus on her own spirit.

Tears slid down her face as she found what GranMay was referring to. GranMay placed a hand to her shoulder and joined her in the bonding.

"I believe this new child will keep you busy, indeed. Your next year will have a great mix of love, life, and loss. You need to enjoy the ride, my dear. Am I right that you carry a little boy and are nearly a month in?"

"Yes, and his spirit is beautiful and strong. He already has strong magic within him, much like the twins carried at this age." They held each other as they touched the spirit of the unborn child.

MORGAN PLANNED TO surprise Alec with dinner at the river cabin and share the news of their new child in private. As she sat to work with Taru that afternoon, her thoughts lingered on the child and the arrangements.

"Congratulations, my Sister! When did you learn of it?" Taru asked. Morgan looked a bit annoyed, and Taru looked down.

"You did nothing wrong. I only learned this morning when GranMay told me to meditate. I will tell Alec tonight, so please keep my secret till tomorrow," Morgan said. She raised an eyebrow as Taru looked down again.

"What is it, Taru?"

"He may already know. The children told me last week. They asked to let you feel him for the first time yourself."

"What? They told you before me?" she barked.

"Please, do not be angry with them. They only figured it out when they were experiencing the spirit of Cara's child and realized they had felt that sensation before within you. They did not intend for me to overhear their excited discussion of it, but it was too late. We did not mean to anger you, my Sister. It was an honest discovery on both our parts."

Morgan looked away and focused to calm herself.

"Come to me, right now," she said to her children. To Taru she said, "I am not mad with you, but I need to talk to my children. Please, go and enjoy a day off with Daniel."

Taru saw the children running toward her as she left, but did not dare tell them what awaited them.

As the twins neared the gazebo, they slowed their pace and joined hands. They crept up the stairs to stand behind where she now sat with her legs crossed.

"Sit down in front of me, please," Morgan said. They sat and scooted against one another as they met her eyes. "I am very hurt that you did not come to me the instant you realized I carried a new child. I just found out that you knew through Taru. I ask that you never hide anything from me again. Promise me, right now," Morgan said.

The twins looked at each other and back to her in silence.

"What else are you hiding that has tied your tongues? Tell me voluntarily, before I seek it myself. No secrets."

Their anxiety was climbing, but she let them feel her anger for a bit longer before she calmed herself.

"Mother, we only wanted you to feel his spirit for yourself and share it with Father yourself. We knew that was a special experience and did not want to spoil it for you," Kyan said.

"Do not evade my question. Tell me all you hide. Now." Kyan dropped his head and Brya gripped him tighter.

"There are many things we have not shared, Mother," they said together.

"Then begin."

"We know that Zirath will find his magical mate among the dragons from Kalias, and that GranNulian carries four healthy eggs, and that one of them will not survive to hatch."

"Why would you not have shared each of these things with me instantly? Why would you keep anything from me?"

"You are so busy, and so worried, for so many. We did not feel we should worry you since these things are not critical. We feel your worry for the loss of GranMay, and of our departure, and do not want to add to it. We did not mean to hurt you, Mother," Brya said as her eyes filled with tears. Kyan put his arm around her and hugged her tight to him.

Morgan opened her arms, and they moved into her lap, careful not to put pressure on her belly.

"I must know that you will share everything with me, rather than try to protect me. Our magic is strong and our responsibilities to our brethren are great. That makes our connection to one another very important. Can you now promise me that you will hide nothing from me again?" They looked at each other and paused for a few seconds before both nodded.

"What did you need to consider before answering?"

"We had to agree to share even those things which will hurt you.

It was not an easy promise to make, Mother. We do not want to cause you pain, but we will keep our promise," Kyan said as he traced the dragons on her chest.

"Should we now share what we have learned about our tasks?" Brya asked.

"Yes, absolutely. If there are things you know that I may not, you should share it. I will do the same as you grow and it is appropriate. Do you have things to share with me now?"

"Yes, we searched our knowledge while you were gone to Berios and Kalias. But you will not like it, Mother," Kyan said.

"That is not the point, my love. I must know as much as possible to serve you and all my brethren properly. Now, let us bond and have you open to me completely to share all you know. We will do this every day from now on and will all be open and honest in all things," Morgan said.

They all bonded and the children passed more information to her than she expected.

"Well, there was good and bad news there. I do not like it all. But I cannot change it either. Better to know and be prepared, my dears. Thank you," Morgan said as she kissed their foreheads.

She hugged them tight, then tickled and bit at their neck and shoulders until they were almost out of breath. They were all lying on the gazebo floor laughing when she felt Alec's approach.

"How about you two go share the sensation of your little brother with your father. I want to watch and feel his reaction from here."

The children jumped up and ran full speed to him. They both leapt into his arms and knocked him back a step. They had grown a great deal and were the size of average six-year-olds now.

Each placed a hand to their own Crest and one to his cheeks. He looked up at Morgan as a huge smile filled his face.

"That is fantastic news and a wonderful way to tell me, my bride."

He kissed the children all over as he swung them in circles. When he put them down they ran behind him as he sprinted to the gazebo. He scooped her into his arms and spun her around as he kissed her.

"Congratulations, my love. I am so very proud," he said as he lowered her to the ground with care. He touched his hand to her belly as he gazed into her eyes. "Let me feel his spirit as you did the twins."

"Later, my dear, when we are a bit more alone," Morgan said as she blushed under his intense gaze. Alec started to argue but stopped as he heard Daniel and Taru approaching.

Daniel looked at Alec's hand on her belly then at her.

"Are you?"

"Yes, I am carrying a new nephew for you."

"Congratulations, I am very happy for you both," Daniel said as he kissed her cheek and patted Alec on the shoulder.

"I apologize for my anger earlier," Morgan said to Taru as she gripped her hand.

"I understand, my friend," Taru said. Morgan nodded, then her face dropped a bit.

"Everyone needs to take a seat as I share something the children have told me that concerns us all," Morgan said.

"KYAN AND BRYA tell me that we must return to Berios in order to form the replacement portal. That may seem obvious, but I had hoped to be able to manage it from this end. The issue is, while the metal ore needed is on Erion and Berios, the material we need to form the portal fluid is only on Berios. Given its size, all of our family's magic will be needed to have any chance of accomplishing the build. The dragons will add their magic to ours, but it will take a great deal of strength to make it large enough to allow the passage of the Elder dragons."

Both Daniel and Alec had tensed at this news.

"We must all travel via Kalias to reach Berios," Daniel said with a heavy sigh. "I do not like it, but I see the necessity. May I suggest a force of Knights go through first to clear the way for you, Taru, and the children?" He clenched his fists, and she heard his thoughts.

"While Harrick, Martus and Hoge are not our primary concern, they will be an issue. I prefer to not engage them, to pass through undetected." Daniel looked at her with relief and gave a slight smile. "However, we will not go until Taru is ready to fight. There is a good chance we will not be able to avoid detection altogether."

"I would like the opportunity to address my people if possible," Taru said. "I believe there are more that are like-minded to Cara and are ready to fight if they see hope ahead of them. We can offer them that hope."

"If a safe opportunity presents itself, I will support your efforts to help them. However, I do not think this first trip through is the appropriate time to expect it, my Sister."

Alec took her hand by habit as he considered the danger in this venture.

"I feel your concern for the child within me, but please remember I can shield him completely. I will not take undue risk, however. I, GranMay, and our dragon brethren will prepare Taru well, and she will be able to defend herself and perhaps defeat him."

Taru's eyes widened.

"That is wonderful news. Does that mean she is ready to marry me, as well?" Everyone laughed at Daniel's enthusiastic outburst. He did not join them.

"We will begin testing her soon. I will tell you then," Morgan said. Daniel nodded and turned to Taru.

"Perhaps you should not add to the stress by giving me that look, my mate," Taru said to him. He smiled and blushed as he looked away.

Morgan could not help but giggle. She then took a deep breath as a warm rush of loving sensation poured over her. She looked down to see Brya rubbing her belly and humming. Kyan lay against Alec's chest and hummed along. The children were singing the Song of Connection to their unborn brother.

"Do you two think we will meet your little brother as fast as we met you?"

They smiled and shrugged their shoulders. She felt the truth in their simple answer of uncertainty.

"I think he is quite fortunate to have a big brother and big sister like you two," Alec said. "You already show him love, and that is very special."

"I hope I can be as good a big brother as Uncle Daniel," Kyan said.

"Then you must prepare to love him deeply and protect him fiercely," Morgan said as she shared a smile with Daniel.

"You will be a wonderful big brother, and Brya will be a wonderful big sister," Daniel said. "That is a very lucky munchkin in there, for certain. He is getting one amazing family."

"Well, we should head in and inform the rest of the family of the good news and the bad," Morgan said. "Daniel, will you and Taru take the children in and arrange for the family to gather for dinner in about an hour? I would like a moment with my King."

Brya and Kyan squealed as Taru and Daniel attacked them with tickles. The four ran across the lawn and were soon out of sight. Alec pulled Morgan to him.

"Now, my love, please bond to me and let me touch our new son's spirit," he said in his low melodic voice. She had already deepened their connection and pushed them into bonding as she rested her cheek to his. They stayed in that wonderful place of limitless sharing with their new son for many minutes before she let the bonding drop.

"You know I will protect our child, my dear. But, I must assure our passage to Berios," she said as she shifted back to look at him.

"What of your confidence in Taru?"

"She is strong. But I cannot, in good conscience, send her against the three of them alone, especially not given her history with Hoge. She has no experience battling with the magic, and it is a very different use. I will assure her a fair fight with Hoge, and be there to back her up if it proves too much for her. She deserves to be the one who finishes his dark reign."

"And Daniel and I will be there to back you both up."

"We will both be there to protect our children. We have much to think about to make this happen safely."

"Let me and Daniel worry about most of it. Put your focus on the portal and our children. We will consider the situation and bring the best options to you soon."

She tucked into his arms and closed her eyes. "I love you, my husband. I am very lucky to have you."

Alec kissed her head and said, "And I, you, my bride."

MORGAN AND ALEC entered the main dining room an hour later and addressed their extended family to announce the new pregnancy. Everyone clapped and moved to congratulate and hug the couple.

The family ate a wonderful meal of roasted chicken and many vegetables as the room buzzed with happy conversation. The servants offered Morgan juices and teas rather than the customary wine. She thanked them for their thoughtfulness.

As everyone finished eating, she explained the need to repair the portal on Berios and the necessity to travel there via Kalias. Many were worried and much discussion of the options ensued.

"We will consider all the options, of course. However, the fact remains that it must and will be done. I trust everyone here will support whatever plan is agreed upon by me, Alec and the Admiralty." She stood with Alec and everyone raised a glass to toast their new child before they separated for the evening.

She and Alec tucked the children in and went to bed themselves.

They were talking when she felt the children approaching their door. *"Come in."* They entered holding hands and looking anxious.

"Could we touch our brother's spirit as Daddy did?" Brya asked. Morgan held the covers up and they climbed in. Kyan climbed over to sit on Alec's stomach and Brya settled to Morgan's other side. Each placed their hands to her belly and smiled.

She put her hands over theirs and bonded to both with ease. They both shivered when they touched their brother's spirit. Morgan withdrew and allowed them to stay bonded with their brother alone. She opened her eyes and smiled at Alec, who was beaming.

The children grew tired as they held the strong bonding, so she touched both to suggest releasing it. "He is beautiful," Brya said as she and Kyan laid down between their parents. Kyan yawned and added, "And very powerful." They were both asleep in seconds.

"I will take them to their beds in a bit," Alec said as he kissed and stroked their faces.

"They can stay for the night. They feel wonderful and we should be grateful for times like this." Her eyes filled with tears and Alec kissed her head as he snuggled up to the three of them.

As she lay cuddled with her family, she decided she could not wait to tell GranMay another bit of information the children had shared with her.

"GranMay, are you awake?"

"Yes, I am catching up with Kisik. What is wrong?"

"Nothing is wrong. I just think you should get plenty of rest to prepare for your upcoming quest. You really should get to bed."

"What are you on about?"

"The children tell me it is you who will accompany them on their travels. You may want to reconsider your desire for healing." GranMay was silent. *"Are you alright?"* She understood feeling her confusion but did not expect her disappointment.

"How can that be when I have been overcome with the feeling

that it is time to move on?" GranMay said.

"Perhaps the move you have been anticipating is this journey and not your time of passing. I certainly hope so. I just needed to tell you that. Sorry to interrupt your time with Uncle Kisik."

"Goodnight, my sweet girl."

Siblings

MORGAN TOOK SOME TIME to meditate the next morning. She spent time touching her new son's spirit, then focused on the ancient knowledge deep within her.

"I need to understand how I am to regenerate the magic within Chemerie. How am I to reinforce the magical bond between our people and our dragons? Is this to be done in my lifetime, or is it a matter of the work my children will do? How was the bond made so strong long ago?"

She soon saw an image of Lady Chemerie laying her hands to the pregnant belly of a young woman. She was singing an alternate version of the Song of Quickening to the infant, and her Crest glowed brightly as did her palm markings.

The image soon changed to the infant's birth. Lady Chemerie held the infant to her Crest and sang the Song of Connection as she bonded to the child. Moments later, she released the bonding and laid the child in the arms of its mother saying, *"Our magic is now awake within her. She will have a strong bond to the dragons."*

Morgan fetched the Book of the Caretaker from her bedside table. She wanted to search for more on this method from the knowledge of her foremothers.

She smiled as her magic touched the magic of the Book. The study allowed her to gather many more details of the method Lady Chemerie used to initiate the growth of the magic within a child. She went over the process many times to make sure she understood it.

As she replaced the Book, she searched all of the women of Chemerie and was pleasantly surprised to find twelve pregnant women. The one who interested her the most was her dear friend and distant cousin, Emma. She was the daughter of Kisik, Alec's adoptive father, and therefore had been raised as Alec's sister.

"Good morning, Cousin. How are you feeling today?" she asked Emma.

"I am sick to my stomach again and have no idea why. I was hoping to see you about this annoyance today. Will you have time?"

Morgan smiled as she realized Emma had no idea she was pregnant, and was careful to keep her emotions to herself.

"I would be glad to see you now for breakfast, if you like."

"How about after you eat breakfast. I am in no mood to be near food at the moment," Emma said.

"Sure. How about a visit with Alec and the children as well? May we come to see you at your place?" "

Wonderful. See you soon."

Morgan gathered the children and Alec and they all ate a quick breakfast before heading into the township toward the home of Emma and her new husband, Paul. Emma and Paul had been childhood rivals and had kept their distance as adults until they ran into each other by chance at a Spring festival.

They had literally run into each other as Emma chased the twins and Paul ran after his own nephew in the children's area. He had grabbed her arm to keep her from falling, and their contact revealed their magical link. Both were thrown by the news, given their bickering as children and teens. After a few days, each felt the magic urging them to find the other.

Theirs was an interesting relationship. It was a constant source of amusement for the entire family. Emma was prone to say whatever was on her mind, which was the exact opposite of the formal, reserved nature of Paul. Morgan thoroughly enjoyed spending time with them, as it was always an entertaining encounter, given her ability to hear both of their thoughts.

THEY ARRIVED to find a subdued Emma being supported by Paul. She was still sick to her stomach but put on a happy smile as the twins ran to hug her.

"Do not say a word to her about her pregnancy. I want to let her figure it out by feeling her child's spirit," Morgan warned them. They did very well to not look at her as she spoke and followed her request as they gave Emma and Paul a normal greeting.

Alec hugged Emma, as she hugged Paul. *"I will help her. Do not worry, my friend,"* she said as she passed calming feelings to ease his worry.

"Thank you, my Queen," Paul said with a bow of his head. She did not even bother asking that he call her Morgan yet again. She had accepted it was just not in his nature.

She moved to Emma as Alec released her and passed healing energy to relieve her nausea. Emma took a deep breath as the awful sensation left her and wore a more relaxed smile.

"Thank you, Cousin, that feels much better. I am so happy to hear of your new pregnancy. I regret not joining the dinner, but I could not face food at the time. Could I trouble you to search for what is making me feel so nasty all the time?"

"I certainly will. I would prefer doing so through a deep bonding. Is that alright with you?"

"I have never felt that sensation with someone so magical. Does it hurt?"

"Yes! It is excruciating," Alec answered. Emma gave him a sassy look and pushed him hard in the chest.

"You go play with my husband and leave us be, little brother. Morgan is mine for a bit," Emma said. Alec stole a kiss from both of them then moved to join Paul and the children in a game of kickball in the backyard.

The two women sat on a love seat and turned to one another.

"Take my hands and just relax. I will not hurt you." She moved into the connection with care to let Emma get comfortable with the level of sensation.

"My goodness, Cousin. This is a wonderful feeling. Thank you for the experience," Emma said as she trembled.

"This is only a strong connection. I will now move to bonding. The discomfort you feel right now will disappear. Ready?" She felt Emma's agreement and initiated bonding.

Emma gasped as the weightless sensation took her. She hummed as the feelings of love and friendship Morgan passed washed over her.

"Seek my spirit, as I seek yours," Morgan said.

Morgan was not surprised at the vivacious and bright spirit within her cousin. She took a moment to let Emma experience that sensation.

"Now seek the spirit of my child within me," Morgan said. Emma had not been expecting this so she hesitated. *"Just think of him and let your spirit reach out."*

"This is amazing. I can feel him as a separate little energy from your own. He feels beautiful, just like you. Thank you for something so precious."

"Now focus within yourself, my Cousin."

The instant Emma felt the child, Morgan was taken off guard by the massive rush of emotion. She had not been surprised like this in some time, but was glad of it. The love and joy she was sharing with Emma was wonderful.

She backed away a bit to let Emma enjoy the experience of touching her child's spirit. When Emma grew weak, Morgan eased out of bonding and passed healing to keep Emma from getting nauseous. Emma opened her teary eyes and raised her head with a look of awe.

"That was the most wonderful gift I could ever imagine getting. Thank you so much, my Caretaker," Emma said. She wrapped her in a loving hug and cried hard. Paul came into the room and dropped to kneel beside her.

"What did she find? Emma, whatever it is, we will handle it together, my dear. Please, tell me what is wrong?"

"Nothing is wrong, these are tears of joy. My dear cousin has just given me a most precious gift and allowed me to discover a wonderful truth for myself," Emma said. She moved to take his hands to feel their connection as she continued. "We are to have a child, my husband. That is why I have been so ill. It is simply the hormone changes of pregnancy."

Paul blanched. Alec caught him as he swayed, then pushed him back toward Emma. He sprang up, grabbing Emma as he rose, and lifted her into his arms.

"Oh Emma! I am so relieved you are well, and so happy for our fortune. I love you, my dear one!"

"Wow! I did not see that one coming," Morgan said to Alec.

"I am not surprised. He had just told me that he thought her to be very ill. He had tears in his eyes before coming to her."

They both flinched in reaction to Emma yelling.

"Put me down, you silly man! You really need to control those crazy emotional outbursts of yours before you harm our child!"

Paul froze and put her feet back to the floor before he realized she was joking. He smiled and kissed her with enthusiasm; he had clearly forgotten they were not alone until their kiss was interrupted.

"Uncle Paul, I thought you were shy?" Brya said with a giggle. Paul jerked from the kiss and blushed as he smiled at Brya.

"I usually am, Princess Brya. However, I am far too happy and relieved to worry about such just now," Paul said as he gazed at Emma. To the amazement of everyone, even Emma, given her emotional response, Paul kissed her again with meaning.

"My children need no more lessons today, Sir Paul. You can hold that until we have left you," Alec said as he gripped Paul's shoulder with a small laugh.

Kyan started to say something, but was hushed by a quick mental touch from Morgan.

"I realize you are aware of much more than the average child your age, but it is still inappropriate for us to allow you to see the personal interaction of others. Do not argue, my boy."

WHILE STILL VISITING with Emma and Paul, Morgan noticed Kyan was very interested in something outside. When she focused on his feelings, her insides clenched, and she shifted to connect to Alec.

"You need to field this one. Your son is quite focused on a young lady outside. I am definitely not ready, my dear." She moved to the kitchen to help Emma prepare snacks for everyone.

Alec watched Kyan and saw he had singled out a particular girl in the bunch playing in the street. He moved to squat behind his boy and asked, "Who is she?"

"She is my mate. Her name is Iz, short for Izavela."

Alec was held mute a few seconds and gave Morgan an 'Oh Mercy!' glance.

"She is a bit more mature than you as yet. I suggest you not plan to confront her for quite a while."

"I will wait until my Quickening. I should be fully grown and appear older than her by that time. She will understand, I think.

I believe she may also know of our link, but that is only a guess."

At that instant, Iz noticed her King and Prince were watching her. She bowed to them, and they returned the gesture. Iz held Alec's eyes rather than Kyan's before turning back to her game.

"Perhaps, but remember that most do not feel the link until they are older than she. When did you first feel it?" Alec asked.

This time Kyan blushed and looked to his feet. He mumbled something Alec did not understand as Brya appeared at Alec's other side with a scowl.

"He felt her last month and searched all day until he found her. He has been annoyingly aware of her ever since," Brya said before marching away. Kyan caught up to wrap his arms around her.

"My mate will never replace you. Nothing ever could. I love you, Brya. You share my spirit like no other ever will." He held his sister tight until she hugged him in return. They took hands and went back to the yard to play alone.

Morgan had been connected to Alec through all of that conversation. She was standing in the kitchen, taking deep breaths to stay calm. Alec moved to her and held her tight.

"Mercy, that boy is moving quickly, my love. Just like his mother," Alec said teasingly. Morgan tried to smile but failed. "At least he is being open, as you asked. Now you can keep track of this young lady to make sure she is aware of his special gifts and prepared for them in some way."

"And what of Brya? Did you feel her pain as she watched him staring at the girl?" Morgan said with a harsh glance at the window.

"I felt great annoyance for certain, but Kyan comforted her. And the girl's name is Iz, my dear."

"I fell madly in love with a boy when I was five, and he would not give me the time of day. Therefore, I decided I did not love him, that I actually hated him. I declared war and gave him all sorts of diffi-culty all my years...until I married him," Emma said. The tension in the room broke, and everyone laughed together.

"Are you serious? You actually remember having a crush on Paul as a little girl?" Morgan asked. Emma nodded and looked to Paul, who also nodded with a shy grin.

"I had no interest in girls yet and only saw her as a terrible ball player. Therefore, I had no idea why I would want to be hanging around with her. She did not like that at all. I paid dearly for years," Paul said. They all laughed, took the treats to the back yard, and ate with the children.

Once the snacks were all eaten, and the children settled down for a nap, Morgan turned to Emma and Paul with a serious expression.

"I would like to talk to you about a precious gift I can offer your child." Alec looked at her curiously, and she smiled. "I have not even shared it with Alec or the children yet. I contacted you as soon as I felt your child."

Emma and Paul both had serious and slightly worried expressions. "One of the tasks put before me is to bring strength of magic back to all the people of our country. I have studied memories of Lady Chemerie,and now know how to do this. I use my skills to pass magic to an unborn child, then further activate it at the time of their birth. They will have far stronger magic within them than what our brethren currently feel. That means they will have a special bond to our dragon brethren and each other. They will go through a mild form of Quickening when they come of age, and share an even stronger connection from then forward."

Everyone looked at her, stunned and speechless.

"You are offering that Emma's child be the first to be given magic in this way since those blessed by Lady Chemerie herself?" Alec asked. Morgan nodded as she looked into Emma's eyes.

"The child would have employable magic like those of the Caretaker line?" Paul asked.

"The strength of their magic will be far less than that of a Caretaker, yet, considerably more than our people carry now. The skills they develop to employ it will be unique to the individual."

"You have never done this before, nor have any of the Queens for over a hundred years?" Paul asked.

"No, Paul. I have not done this myself, as yet," Morgan said as she pushed calming to Alec, who was glaring at Paul. "However, I am confident in the skill, having spent many hours sharing in the experiences of my foremothers as they did so." Emma looked at Paul, and he looked to the floor. "I ask that you not answer now. Consider it together, and let me know when you are ready. For now, just enjoy the knowledge of your healthy child growing well."

She and Alec rose and went to pick up the sleeping children. Alec lifted both with practiced skill before she could reach them.

"Protecting your little wife? Have you forgotten my new physical skills?"

"Absolutely not," he said as he gave her his most wicked smile and kissed her cheek. She smiled at his next few thoughts and moved to let him by.

Alec said goodbye to Emma and Paul but did not stop to kiss Emma.

Morgan felt her disappointment.

"He is upset, but he will be fine. Do what your heart says is right, and let no one else tell you what that should be. Not even your little brother," Morgan said as she hugged Emma tight with a kiss to her cheek.

"IT IS TIME you come to see me, my dear," GranMay said to Morgan as she approached the castle with Alec and the children.

Morgan was surprised to locate her in the hot spring pool room of the dragon chamber. She kissed Alec, started jogging toward the castle, and opened herself to feel GranMay's condition. The brave woman was in considerable pain. Morgan felt it quite clearly, despite GranMay's attempts to guard it.

When she reached the pool room, she took off her dress and entered the hot water pool with GranMay.

"Please say you are ready to accept healing," Morgan said.

"Yes, I am indeed. I spent a great deal of time meditating today and found you were right. The journey I have felt coming is indeed the one with the children, so I must be well enough to undertake that expedition," GranMay said. She raised a hand, and Morgan gripped it tight.

Morgan healed all she could find within her dear grandmother, finishing with an extra dose of loving support. Her strong grandmother had embraced her time of dying, yet accepted her destiny is to live on. All of those conflicting emotions were moving through GranMay as her pain faded.

GranMay hummed as she moved her arms and legs with fluid, pain- free motion.

"You are so efficient at healing now. That would have taken me a far longer time. Of course, I am a bit of a useless lump compared to you, the twins, and Taru," GranMay said. Morgan felt the strong feelings of worthlessness from GranMay like a stab in her heart. She immediately sent back feelings of respect and gratitude as she turned GranMay's face to hers.

"GranMay, I will not act as if our power is not stronger than yours. But if you think I consider you useless, then I have failed you greatly. I am sorry for ever allowing you to think —" GranMay stopped her with a gentle finger to her lips.

"No, I am sorry for saying that. You have not led me to feel that way. It is the jealousy of an old woman, and I let it drag me down. It is difficult not to become envious of all the skills you have developed. And now, we have Taru with similar skills. In comparison, I find myself lacking. However, you should feel no responsibility for it. You are a wonderful granddaughter, and I would have no other."

Morgan smiled and let the calming emotion GranMay was passing add to her own effort.

"You will not be going on your quest for some time, and we have much to do before then. I will need you, GranMay. I am happy to know you will be with me through this," she said. GranMay dropped her eyes and shook her head a bit.

"Honestly, Morgan, how could you need me? What do I offer that you do not have many times over?"

"Wisdom. That is far more valuable than power alone."

"Good answer, my sweet girl. Very good answer, indeed," GranMay said with a soft chuckle.

MORGAN ASKED TARU, Alec, Daniel, and the children to join her and Nulian on the garden lawn for some training and testing.

"Alright, Taru, it is time to see how well you can control your magic under stress. We will try a few types of stress to find where we need to focus. First, try to use suggestion on Alec. Make him sit down," Morgan said.

"Fight with all you have. Raise your guard and do not give in by choice. Make her push against you," she told Alec. He nodded and focused on his bit of magic. She had been working with him to use it to its fullest capability. He raised his guard and looked Taru hard in the eyes. Taru was not committing to the task.

"He will hold no grudge if you hurt him in the effort. I will make sure it is not too much. Now focus and make him sit down. You must ignore all distraction and fulfill that task."

Taru pushed against his guard and felt him wince as he fought her. She backed off and looked to Morgan for assurance that she should push harder. Morgan nodded, so she resumed her efforts.

Morgan began adding stress at once. She started trying to push into her mind by force. Taru squinted from the sharp pain of it but raised her guard to block the force as she focused on finishing her task.

Morgan was not pushing at full strength and began to increase the intensity in small steps. Taru recognized the threat and stopped hesitating to use her own force on Alec.

"Sit down, my King," she suggested as she pushed hard against him. Alec was fighting hard enough to be trembling but was unable to resist the command and sank to the ground.

Taru released his mind and turned to face Morgan as she focused to hold her guard in place. Morgan used her magic to communicate but included everyone present so they would understand her method and actions.

"This is about half-strength. You will have to fight me to keep me out. Give me your best."

She increased her force at a faster rate. Taru knelt and closed her eyes. Daniel moved forward, but Morgan raised a hand to him as she stepped a little closer to Taru.

"This is nowhere near the power of Hoge. Defend yourself!" She felt the anger she had anticipated burst within her strong sister.

Taru reached deep within and found that level of power she had not yet used. She pushed hard against Morgan and made headway.

"Now, we are near seventy percent of my power. I will push no harder for the moment. I want you to overcome my guard at this level and hear my thoughts. You will have to focus hard and deal with all other interruptions, simultaneously, to win," Morgan said then raised her guard to Taru.

Taru did not hesitate in applying force, but Morgan held her guard with ease.

"Daniel, apply distraction. Move around her while touching her scale areas."

He moved in and touched the scales of Taru's arm. She shivered, and Morgan made an offensive strike. She almost surpassed her guard due to her distraction. Taru felt the near invasion and refocused, holding her at bay while Daniel continued his assault on her senses.

"Defense is not enough. Move against me."

She was getting annoyed at feeling no increase in effort from Taru until she was hit with a huge burst of force, which almost made it through. After countering with a matching force, she pulled back the assault. Taru sat down, breathing hard.

"Sorry to harass you, my dear," Daniel said as he sat beside her. "I forgive you," Taru said with a smile.

"You did well, Taru. You used your ability to store magic to your advantage for the first time and with a very good result. Keep up this pace, and you may be able to break my guard one day," Morgan said. Morgan felt the irritation and a bit of boastful pride from Taru and smiled. "Do you think you can already?"

"Perhaps, if there are no surprise distractions," Taru said. Morgan smiled and bowed to her.

"Then be my guest. Now is good for me. Whenever you are ready, my Sister."

"Uh Oh," Brya and Kyan said as they moved back from their mother and Taru. They sat beside Alec and watched the two women begin to circle one another.

"I agree with your irritation, my Sister," Morgan said to Nulian. *"I think a bit of humble pie is a good idea at this point, don't you?"* Nulian chuckled, and Morgan smiled as she stared into Taru's intense eyes.

Taru's pride had pushed her into this and she was not about to back down now. She let her magic build as she circled and held her guard with all her might.

"No hard feelings either way, my Caretaker?" Taru asked.

"I hope not. But that will be up to you," Morgan said with a small smile.

"Yes, my Queen," Taru said as she attacked with all she had. She was astonished by the strength of the guard Morgan now held. It was far stronger than any she had felt before. Her attack was like water thrown against a stone wall.

Morgan chuckled at Taru's reaction.

"No, Taru. You are not ready to match me just yet. I have had far more time to build my defenses."

She watched as Taru began to quiver from the effort of pushing with all her strength. She felt her force weaken and thought her done until she felt a surge of power within her. Taru was once again using her ability to store magic and thrust it at her in bursts.

She had to reinforce her guard a bit as she used that skill. She refused to let her win as it would do her no favor. Taru needed to understand what to expect from Hoge and Martus if she faced them again. Their guards were weaker than what she was facing now, but Morgan was not going to tell Taru that.

After another long moment of failed attempts, Taru withdrew and bowed in respectful acceptance of her defeat. Morgan wrapped her in a tight hug and passed pride and reassurance.

"Give yourself time, my Sister. You will be very powerful in many ways in time. For now, would you like to see if you are ready to get married?"

Daniel jumped up and answered. "Yes, yes she would." Taru smiled as he kissed her cheek.

MORGAN ASKED TARU and Daniel to sit crossed-legged in front of one another. She then sat to one side, as Nulian laid her head down on their other. Both Daniel and Taru stroked Nulian's snout.

"This is a treat. I hardly get to touch you. Morgan is quite jealous of your attention," Taru said.

"As I am of hers, my Lady," Nulian said with a deep chuckle.

"You are to enter into deep connection and then attempt bonding," Morgan said. "I realize it is intense and personal. We will experience none of it, and you will have your privacy. We are asking you to enter bonding for the first time in our presence. It is the only real test of your preparedness for extensive contact. If you can handle this, you are ready."

Daniel seemed happy with the idea, but Taru forced a deep breath and closed her eyes.

"What is wrong?" Morgan asked her.

"He is going to be profoundly disappointed if I fail. I need to relax before touching him," Taru said. A few seconds later, she looked up at Daniel and offered her palms.

"No, use the strongest possible method, please. Place each of his palms to an area of dragon scales," Morgan said.

Taru was smart about placing his hands. She started with a hand to the smaller scale area on her wrist.

Daniel hummed as the sensation washed over him, but stopped and blushed as Morgan smirked and raised an eyebrow. Taru deepened the connection with just that hand in place and allowed herself plenty of time to get control of it. She then placed Daniel's other hand to the spot high on her chest, where the two long lines along her shoulders intersected. She started with only his fingertips, then gasped when she laid his palm flat against her scales.

A fine sheen of perspiration appeared, and she began to freeze and refreeze. She and Daniel shivered as the sensations intensified, and Daniel began to tense.

"Too much, focus on his pain. Give him only what he tolerates with ease. Wait until in full bonding to release the more intense emotional energy," Morgan warned Taru.

Taru pulled back the emotions she had been pushing and deepened the connection. She reached the limit of connection and was ready for bonding.

"I will not join you within this bonding, but will monitor your energy level and the physical effect of it on you both. Taru, go slowly and be sure to monitor both of your responses. And most importantly, enjoy it!"

Morgan watched as the dragons on Taru's body began to shift and shimmy around as she initiated bonding. Daniel took in a great breath as the sensation of bonding took him.

"Good gracious," he muttered aloud.

Alec had to quiet the children's snickers. Kyan and Brya had been watching all the activity of the training session with the utmost interest as they discussed everything in silence. They were about to burst with questions, but knew that they must wait.

Morgan and Nulian monitored the couple's physical reaction to the bonding and their level of magical energy. Thus far, Taru had been proficient at regulating her body temperature and the flow of energy.

Suddenly, her temperature began to rise sharply, and her magical flow to Daniel increased many times over. Morgan and Nulian both started to reach out and stop the bonding but held back at the last second as Taru shook her head and smiled.

"I have control. I am only taking him to his limit, my Sister. He has a great appetite for this activity," Taru said.

Morgan smiled and blushed at the tone of Taru's voice while glancing at Alec who had heard and was also smiling. Nulian hummed a deep rumble at the feel of their intense bonding.

"I am jealous, I think. My thoughts go to Gerzin as I feel their energy mixing," Nulian said to Morgan.

"I understand completely. I am feeling the energy from them and from Alec as he stares at me," Morgan said. Nulian glanced at Alec and chuckled a bit.

Brya and Kyan rose and walked away.

"What is wrong, little ones?" Morgan asked them.

"We cannot help hearing their thoughts and know we should not. We will block for a bit, Mommy," Kyan answered.

"That is very mature and responsible of you. I will force against your guard if I need you." She gestured toward them and Alec followed.

After many moments of allowing the couple uninterrupted bonding Morgan laid a hand to Taru to request she back out. Taru passed healing energy to Daniel as she broke the bonding to drop back to connection. The physical responses of shivering and tingling returned to both and they flinched in discomfort. Morgan and Nulian shared their healing energy to take the effect away at once.

Daniel and Taru looked at each other as they both breathed hard with matching smiles.

"Did she pass the test?" Daniel asked without breaking eye contact with his mate.

"Indeed, she did. You are ready to marry, but must still be careful. You cannot let yourselves get too carried away. I purposefully avoided laying your hand to the most sensitive area of scales on her abdomen. That one, you two must navigate carefully, alone," Morgan said. Morgan felt anxious concern flash through Daniel.

"It will not limit your choices of activity. Just go slowly," Morgan said to him alone.

"How is tomorrow for you, my dear?" Daniel said to Taru as he smiled.

"Too soon, I would like to wait a bit longer. I am not feeling ready just yet," Taru said.

Morgan felt the deception in her words but did not react. She let her friend harass her big brother with pleasure.

The poor man looked baffled but reacted well. "Alright, just let me know when you are ready."

"We will see you two at dinner," Morgan said as she rose and fell into step with Alec.

Taru and Daniel walked hand-in-hand through the garden in silence for a minute.

"Daniel," Taru said as she stopped and tugged on his hand to turn him to her, "I think I am ready now." He gave a cheer and picked her up to swing her around.

Morgan and Alec both laughed as she blocked the all-too-private thoughts of her brother and his fiancé. They reached the lake and watched the children swim with Zirath, Falin, and Lirpa.

"That was quite intense. I could feel the intensity and passion of their connection through you," Alec said as he wrapped his arms around her from behind and kissed her neck.

"Really? I didn't notice."

He dropped his mouth close to her ear and whispered, "Liar." "I admit to nothing," she said with a smile.

DANIEL AND TARU opted for a small family wedding in the garden. All their family and dragon friends were there and excited. GranMay cried, and Morgan almost did as she and Alec performed the ceremony.

Daniel had designed and asked Morgan to make a spectacular setting for Taru's first diamond as her wedding ring. Taru had made him a detailed dragon ring bearing many small diamonds as the dragons' eyes. It was a bit large, but looked handsome on his hand.

The couple flew off on Falin and headed to the mountain cabin for their week-long honeymoon. Morgan and GranMay both cried as he kissed them goodbye. He was leaving for only a week, but it was the reality of his heart now being devoted to another that made it so profound. Morgan felt a sensation of loss but put it away instantly. She was proud to know that Daniel was loved so fiercely.

Morgan and Alec spent two hours at the reception, visiting with all their family. Emma had been subdued in the corner of the garden until the party ended and most had gone.

"Emma is coming over. Be nice," Morgan said to Alec.

"You look like you are feeling much better," he said to Emma. His tone was as cold as his expression.

"Yes, I am fine. I have not been sick since you all visited," Emma said as she shifted on her feet. "Look, we all know I reacted badly to your offer, and I am so sorry. I was just a bit overwhelmed, and it does sound a bit scary. Paul is still not convinced because he is so afrai—"

"Convinced?" Alec barked. "Emma, do you think for a second that your Queen and Caretaker would do anything to endanger your child? She would never have suggested it had she thought any harm were possible. You have been offered an honor most would die for, and you have the nerve to question its validity. She would never say it hurt her, but I will. I am ashamed of you Emma. Truly, I am."

He took Morgan's arm and half carried her to the castle. She let him, so he did not look foolish, but took her arm away as soon as they were out of sight of the guests.

"Do you feel better? That was wonderful, Alec! You just embarrassed the mess out of her. She is crying her way home right now."

"Good!" he yelled. "She should be embarrassed for her actions. Morgan, you should not forgive so easily in this. She questions your heart and your ability. It is nearly unforgivable!"

"You are overreacting, my dear."

He turned on her with a scowl and stared at her rational look with annoyance.

"How can you not be hurt by this? She is your friend and my sister. You offered her the most amazing gift, and she has questioned your competence with the magic."

"I won't act like it is not very disappointing, but I understand her fear for her child's safety. She has wanted a child for many years while she searched for her mate. This is her first and she is protective."

"You are making excuses for her. If she had proper trust in her Queen, she would never have questioned the beautiful gift you offered. It rips at my heart that my own sister has done this to you." He took her into his arms as he tried to calm his fury. She helped by passing calming feelings, but it still took a long time to abate.

"I can forgive because I feel the reason for her fear. She is terrified of the magic itself. She has been for many years. I felt her fear when

I bonded with her yesterday. The fact that she entered the bonding with me at all tells me she trusts me. I believe it has everything to do with how Cora died at the hand of Harrick.

"You need to go to her now and talk this out. Whether she wants the magic for her baby or not, she loves you, and her heart is breaking. Please, go to her. This should be a happy time, and I do not want this choice ruining it for her."

Alec dropped his head to rest on hers as she helped take all his rage away.

"I will go. Will you join me?"

"No. She needs you right now, not me."

"You have an amazing heart, Woman," he said as he kissed her forehead.

Nyeks and Iz

ALEC ARRIVED at Emma's house, and Paul answered the door with a stiff bow.

"Good evening, my King. May I help you?" Paul said.

"You know I need to speak with Emma. Please, let me in so I can apologize," Alec said. Paul stepped back to allow Alec in and led him to the sitting room.

"I will see if she wishes to see you. If she does not, I hope you will be a gentleman and leave without another outburst," Paul said. Alec nodded and swallowed the words on his tongue. He understood Paul was angry that his wife had come home crying.

Five long minutes later, Emma entered the sitting room. She did not come to him or even sit down.

"What is it, my King?"

Alec's heart ached at her tone and formal address as he rose and moved to her.

"I apologize for losing my temper. I never should have raised my voice to you, my Sister. I am very sorry for hurting you like that."

"Your apology is accepted. Goodnight," Emma said. She turned to leave and he stepped in front of her, taking her into his arms.

"I had no idea you feared the magic itself. I thought you questioned Morgan. Why have you never told me, Emma? All these years of sharing so much, and you never told me." Emma broke and cried into his shoulder. It was a hard, breathy cry which shook her whole body.

"I saw Mother's body when they brought her back for her burning ceremony. She was bleeding from her eyes and ears and had the most pained expression. I was young, but I remember it even now. The sheer power of the magic has terrified me ever since.

"I trust Morgan, I do. I have never balked at her touch. But the intensity required to transfer magic to my baby scares me so much. If the child has magic, their life will be so much more dangerous, just as yours is now. I worry for you and your family every day, Brother. The magic within you makes you a target for the dark ones."

Alec rubbed her back as he considered her words and gave her time to calm a bit more.

"The magic is strong. The evil ones do seek to destroy the pure magic. I cannot argue those points. But I can say the wonder of feeling the magic and the connections it provides makes you want to protect it with all you are.

"The magic allows a bond deeper than you can imagine with my mate. It also allows me to sense the emotions of, and speak to, my dragon brethren. It is wonderful and amazing and a precious gift. The risks are not really risks because in receiving the gift you understand its precious nature and devote your life to protecting it. As Chemerians, we all understand its value to the dragons, but we have lost the value to us.

"Morgan is to renew that level of connection between all of us. She offers for your child to be among the first of her generation to have the ability to connect with her brethren on a profound level. While the Caretaker will always have a greater power, in time, all Chemerians will carry magic and will feel it within everything they do.

"Emma, please release your fear. Let your child have this amazing gift. Put your trust in Morgan and in me. We would never hurt you or your precious child."

Emma raised her head with a devilish smile.

"I had already decided to ask Morgan to give the gift to my child, but that was a wonderful speech, little brother."

He laughed a little but held her face with serious eyes.

"I am so happy for you. You are going to be a magnificent mother. Congratulations, my dear Sister." He lifted her in his arms to hold her tight.

FALIN FLEW in large circles around the mountain where Lirpa rested atop the highest cliff. He growled low in his throat and shook with rage as he watched a dark red male major dragon from Kalias swoop over her again and again then land beside her. The male circled her as he snorted and nipped. Lirpa nipped at him each time he lunged for her then stood. The male charged her and knocked her to her side, then straddled her with one leg as he growled and drew his snout up her neck.

Falin roared as he dove for them and rammed his chest against the massive male when he landed.

"What has you so upset, youngling?" the major dragon asked. "Do you sincerely believe you have a claim to this beautiful dragon?"

"I do," Falin said as he stepped closer and dropped into a fighting stance. "Back away, Helios."

"You are not dragon enough for such a vivacious female, or you would have acted. Go hide in your chambers, youngling. Leave the mating to the adults."

Falin roared as he attacked. He slashed with his front claws into

Helios's shoulder and pushed him back. His second charge was blocked by Lirpa, who crashed into his side.

"Enough!" she said.

Falin shifted to move around her, so she lashed across his snout with her tail. He backed away as she moved to Helios and sang her healing song to stop his bleeding.

"As you just felt, we share no link, my friend. Know that I am flattered by your willingness to fight for me," Lirpa said to Helios. "Go to the Caretaker. She will take your pain and ease your anger."

Helios stood and moved around her to face Falin.

"This is not over, youngling. We will finish it when Lady Lirpa is not present to protect you."

"I will fight you anytime you wish," Falin said. He growled until Helios took flight, and Lirpa turned back to him.

"I have been of age for months, yet you have not come to me seeking a link. I assumed I was not desirable to you," she said as she circled him.

"You are the most desirable female I have ever seen, Lirpa," he said as he studied her form. "Any male would agree."

"Yet, you make no move. I had thought you my intended but perhaps I mistook our friendship for more than it was."

She turned to walk away, and Falin pounced. He knocked her to her side and moved to hold her down. Both growled as he dropped his snout to her neck. She nipped at his snout, and he bit her in return.

"You were not mistaken. I fully believe you to be my mate."

He growled and dropped the guard he had held around her for over a year. She roared with excitement as his magic and emotions hit her.

He crooned as he stroked her neck with his snout and she returned the gesture.

"I know your reason for waiting, but I do not share it. I care not how large you are Falin. You are very handsome to me and are stronger of spirit than any I have met. I love you and am deeply proud to be yours."

"And I love you, my mate."

He initiated bonding as he laid his head alongside hers, and both dragons trembled with the intense sensation. They hummed together and deepened the level of bonding as he lay down against her. Their magical link ignited within them, and both shuddered as their hearts raced. Tears of joy slid down their cheeks as they let the power of their link fill them.

They lay panting from the long bonding for only a moment before Falin stood and nudged her hard.

"Fly with me, my mate," he said as he opened his wings with a flourish and launched into the air. She needed no more convincing and shot from the ground right behind him. They soared in circles around each other, letting their excitement build, before shooting straight up to fly as high as they could together. When at their highest, they collided and wrapped each other tight.

They held each other in that intimate embrace as they dropped in a free-fall back toward the ground below. The feeling was intoxicating. Falin bit Lirpa to make her release him, just before they slammed into the ground.

"Have mercy, you two! How about being a little more careful in the future and saving me a heart attack!" Morgan said.

They soared over to her and roared their greeting as she and Alec waved. She pointed at the lawn, and they turned to see Nulian and Gerzin accompanied by Sirzi, Menkar, and Helios. Helios bowed to them and joined the others in a roar of congratulations.

"He needed a nudge, my friend. I thought Helios the appropriate catalyst," Nulian said to Lirpa.

"Thank you, my Elder. Your wisdom is most appreciated," Lirpa said as she dropped her head to stroke Falin, who soared below her.

"TIME TO SHARE, MOMMY," Brya said early one morning as the children came bouncing into Morgan and Alec's room to sit on their bed with serious faces.

"Yes, indeed it is," Morgan said as she pulled both of them close and kissed them. She and the children all bonded and shared their new information.

She told them about the initiation of a child's magic, and they told her of what they believe to be their first task. They had shared many dreams of a beautiful, magical species called a Nyek.

"We are to seek them and bring them to live here in safety," Brya said as the bonding broke away. Kyan added, "They are almost extinct, and we must help them become many again. But that is all we know." Both children were staring at her with hopeful faces, so she closed her eyes to seek any information she carried about these creatures.

"Most of what I found was verbal. The images were blurry, but the creatures appear to be small and cat-like with beautiful fur. Was that your impression from your dreams?"

Both children looked confused, as did Alec.

"What is a cat, my dear?" Alec asked. She laughed at herself.

"Sorry. It is a common pet of Earth. Let me show you," she said as she pushed memories to them all. "Of course, a common cat has no magic. Earth has many different types of cats in many sizes, from a few pounds to well over my size. As the images I found of the Nyek were from the dragons' perspective, it is hard to say how large the Nyek are. My guess is around that of a hatchling dragon."

"Did you learn anything more?" Kyan asked.

"Yes," she said with a smile at her children's impatience. "The information was from both our Chemerian dragons and from Grith's memories of Kalias I gained through Taru. The creatures inhabited both worlds at one time. It will be hard for us to tell how many are still alive because they have the power to remain virtually undetectable, much like the Elder dragons can."

"If they carry so much magic, what killed them off?"

"Humans, of course! They were hunted for their beautiful coats by people ignorant of the fact they were destroying a profound source of magic on their world. The drop in Nyek numbers has contributed to the gradual decrease in magical content of all people and dragons on Erion over the last many centuries. This is because they act as a sort of magical battery. They store great amounts of magic within them and can allow it to be used by those of magical skill."

"I cannot wait to see one, Mommy. Can you study the Book of the Caretaker and see if there are any better images of what they look like?" Brya said as Kyan nodded and bounced.

"I have not seen you two this excited since you discovered chocolate," Alec said as he grabbed both and kissed their necks to make them giggle. They were polite in letting him play but sat up with serious expressions as they glanced between her and her side table.

"Would you like to get it for me?" she asked. They flew off the bed then hesitated before opening the drawer.

Kyan took a step back. Brya stared at him hard and shook her head as she stepped back and took his hand.

"Together in this and all things, my Brother," Brya said.

"What was that about?" Alec asked Morgan.

"He just suggested she had more right to touch the Book of the Caretaker than he did because she was the female child and next Caretaker. She did not approve of that assessment."

"I understand his concern. We should talk about this with them soon, my dear." Now it was Morgan who gave him a harsh glare. *"This country has been ruled by a female Caretaker for hundreds of years. There may be controversy over the suggestion of a male standing in that position. I am not saying I agree with it, but we should discuss it as a possible issue,"* Alec said.

"It is nothing more than a matter of trust. If they trust his

spirit to wield the magic with honor, then his gender should not matter. It is a discussion for a later time."

"And one we should have before we include them, I see." He took her hand to soothe her annoyance, and she smiled as they both looked back to the children.

"It is heavier than it looks. Lift it together," she said.

They stepped forward and reached for the drawer. Both stopped with their hands an inch away and stared as the cover began to shimmer with the silvery designs their magic activated. They were mesmerized for a few seconds before touching the cover. Both shivered and giggled at the sensation of the Book's magic touching theirs. Their Crests were glowing brightly as they carried the powerful Book up onto the bed and laid it on Morgan's lap.

"As this is your quest, I think you should join me in this search," she said. They beamed as they scooted close and awaited instruction. "Just bond to me, and I will guide you. Once we are bound to the Book, ask your questions. The answers will come as voices, sounds, sights, or feelings. If it is too intense, raise your guard, and I will drop the bonding."

When her hands touched the Book, its delicate scrolling markings glowed brightly, as did her Crest and palms. The children copied her and shivered again. She initiated the bonding and waited for them to ask the question of the Nyek. They first received a number of images of the beautiful creatures sitting around small children.

The wonderful creatures reminded Morgan of a very small Lynx of Earth. They had a stocky build and tufts of hair on their ears like a Lynx, but also had a very long tail and silky fur which seemed to vary in color. Their coats also varied in pattern. Some were striped like tigers, some were spotted like a leopard, and others were rich solid colors with no pattern.

The Nyeks accompanied members of the Caretaker line as well as many other Chemerians. The magic they carried allowed them to communicate with humans and dragons, but their language was their own. Their unique capacity for storing large amounts of magic allowed them to transfer it to a Caretaker as needed.

She reviewed the images and found that many were of the same Nyek with a different coat color. As she concentrated on this trait, her ancient knowledge provided further understanding.

While Nyeks are born in various colors, they can also change color and pattern at will. It is a skill of enjoyment as well as defensive camouflage. Their most effective defense is the sudden and massive release of their stored magic. They release it in the form of white light, which blinds their attackers, or as high-frequency sound, which deafens them. The effect is temporary, allowing them ample time for escape.

The children then sought the feeling associated with the presence of a Nyek. Morgan shivered at the sensation but felt no reaction from the children. They raised their guards, so she released the bonding.

"Why did you shiver, Mommy? We felt nothing."

"I felt their presence as a chilly tickle when the dragons of my markings began to wiggle. You will feel it after your Quickening," Morgan said as she placed the book back in the side table.

The twins looked at each other and began to move off the bed. "Wait. Come back here." They moved back up and looked up with gloomy faces.

"Please do not be in such a hurry. You are growing so fast and will Quicken far sooner than any before you. After your Quickening, you will have no choice but to accept the responsibility that accompanies that gift. You need to enjoy being children while you can. Now, speaking of acting like children, why don't you go play for a bit? Zirath is waiting for you below my terrace."

They smiled and kissed her and Alec before running to the terrace and jumping to Zirath's back. He knew not to fly with them but took off running. They bounced and giggled all the way.

MORGAN WATCHED THE CHILDREN PLAY as Alec came to stand behind her. He wrapped his arms around her and looked for the children.

"I cannot see them. Are they near the lake?"

"Yes, they are swimming with younglings. Nulian watches from the ridge above. While they are distracted, I need to talk to you about their Quickening," she said as she turned to face him. "I am worried about the intensity it will have. Taru's was very painful because she already bore the Crest and dragon blood. I also viewed the Quickening of Caretakers who bore the Crest, and their pain was extreme as the waves intensified toward the end.

"Taru and I will help with their pain, and I am sure they will help each other as well. I do not expect we will be able to prevent it all. I just want you to be prepared for it."

"Will you show me what you saw? I would like to understand."

She took his hands to bond and let him view the painful experience of the magic's intense multiplication within those who already bore the Crest of the Caretaker line.

"Mercy! Was Taru's that bad as well?"

"No. I have not told her, but I believe it is because the natural level of magic within her was not as strong as those of the Caretaker line. It was her Crest, and the dragon blood it represents, that intensified her experience. Our children will have both to contend with." Alec hugged her tighter as they shared their worry.

"I am certain that you will help them find a way to limit their pain. You are strong and ingenious when a need arises, my dear. Though we wish them no pain, feeling some could serve to make them aware of the great responsibility they will then hold."

Morgan tensed and turned to focus on something out at the lake. "What is it?"

"Iz has come to speak to Kyan. Brya is jealous and very angry. We should hurry."

AS THE CHILDREN RODE across the lake with Zirath, Kyan jumped and swam for the northern bank. Nulian hit the water within seconds and lifted him above the surface.

"GranNulian, I am a very good swimmer now! Stop treating me like a baby!" He jumped from her palm and swam hard for the bank.

Nulian picked him up again.

"Do not raise your voice to me, young one. You will show respect to the Elder dragons, no matter your station among the humans," Nulian said. Kyan's face fell as he felt her disappointment in him.

"I am very sorry, GranNulian. Please, forgive my anger. I was embarrassed to be treated as a child in front of my mate," Kyan said as he glanced toward the shore where Iz stood.

Nulian was a bit taken aback as she had not realized he knew of his mate's identity. Morgan had not told her yet. She looked toward the teenager standing near the bank and bowed her head. The young woman returned the bow.

"She is very attractive and seems to know of your link, given her focus on you. Did you tell her?"

"No, but she saw me watching her last week, and may have realized why," Kyan said.

"Do not assume she knows. She may be here to ask why you watched her. Be careful of your words, my Prince," Nulian said.

"Yes, GranNulian. And thank you for protecting me from myself," he said as he held his arms up to her. She crooned as she dropped her snout to let him hug her, then set him down near the young woman before backing away.

NULIAN TOLD MORGAN and Alec of Kyan's embarrassment as they reached the lake. They walked along the opposite side of the lake to where Brya now sat, fuming. She vented her anger by making the water around her freeze and then boil, over and over.

"You are going to kill the fish within the lake if you continue.

Calm yourself," Morgan said.

Brya bolted and ran hard along the bank away from them, so they took off after her. Morgan pulled ahead of Alec and scooped her up with one arm. When Alec caught up he started to scold Brya for running away but was stopped by the pain he felt from her.

"She hurts very badly. She cannot understand his desire to be near any other than her," Morgan told him as she held the struggling child. Alec took Brya and held her to face him. Brya continued to glare at Kyan and Iz.

"Brya, does Mommy love Daniel?"

"Very much."

"Does her love for me in any way lessen her love for Daniel?"

Brya looked between him and Kyan and was silent for many seconds before answering.

"No, it does not. I see that those are two very different loves. But this is not the same, Father. Kyan and I share more than parents. We share spirits. I do not understand why he wants to allow someone to interfere with our tasks and responsibilities. It will ruin everything if our bond is not focused," Brya said. Her jealous anger still boiled within her, but she managed to keep it out of her voice.

Alec was shocked by the maturity and logic in her words and looked to Morgan for ideas.

"She may be right. They do have much to accomplish together, and it is important they be focused," Morgan said as she also looked over at Kyan and Iz.

"You are letting your own protectiveness blind you, and are not being fair to him. He cannot ignore the pull of his magical link any more than we could. Help Brya understand he has a responsibility to Iz, as well," Alec said. Morgan took a deep breath as she accepted the truth in his words.

"Brya," Morgan said as she took her from Alec. "I do understand. I am sure you noticed that I feel similar annoyance. But we are both wrong and act selfishly. Just as it would not be appropriate for me to keep Daniel from Taru, it is wrong for you to keep Kyan from knowing Iz. Trust him to always be devoted to you as his sister, as I do Daniel.

"Just yesterday, I had to watch my brother fly off with his heart devoted to another. It did make me feel as though I had lost him a little. But you know as well as I do that I really gained a new sister and did not lose a brother at all. Perhaps you should be interested in knowing the person the magic has picked to be your new sister."

"I am not interested in knowing her yet. I only want her to leave my brother alone until he is of age. I will not get in the way then. Please, keep her away until then, Mommy," Brya said as she wiggled to be let down. She moved to the water's edge and stared at Kyan with her arms crossed and her guard high.

Morgan looked at Alec, a bit unsure as to what to say. He nodded and moved to kneel in front of Brya.

"No, Brya. We will not prevent him from knowing his mate." Brya's eyes poured tears down her cheeks as her face fell with disappointment. "You will have to come to terms with this and not make your brother feel bad that he has found her early and wants to know her. I would be ashamed of you if you were not focused on his happiness in this," Alec said. He rose and walked away as he spoke to Morgan. *"That was very hard, but I think it th right answer, my dear. She must not be selfish in this."*

"I agree and am proud that you had the strength to say it where I did not. You are a strong father, my mate."

"Brya, if you love him, you will want what is best for him, no matter the difficulty, my dear. Now, let us go meet her together," she said as she took her daughter's hand to pull her along.

KYAN SLID OUT of Nulian's hand then bowed to Iz.

"Good day, Ms. Izavela."

"My Prince, please call me Iz. Only my mother still calls me Izavela, and only when I am in trouble," she said with a smile. He smiled in return and shifted a bit.

"How may I help you today?"

Iz looked across the lake at her Queen, King, and Princess and tensed as she saw them watching.

"Have you come with a question or a request for my parents, perhaps?" Kyan asked as he felt her anxiety.

"A question, I suppose. I noticed you and King Alec watching me from Lady Emma's home last week. I was wondering if I had done something wrong, or if there was perhaps another reason for your interest in me," Iz said as she watched his eyes. Kyan had opened to Alec as she asked the question so he could hear her words.

"Do I tell the truth, Father? I do not want to lie, but she may not understand since I am still so young," Kyan asked while holding his face placid.

"Look to me as if I hold the answer, and let me handle it," Alec said.

Alec smiled at Iz as he approached at a jog, then stopped and bowed as she curtsied.

"Good morning, my King."

"Good morning, young Lady. To what do we owe the honor of a visit this morning?"

"I was inquiring as to your interest in me when you visited Lady Emma. Did I do something to attract it, or was there another reason?"

Kyan felt her attempt to hide her own idea of the meaning.

"I believe she felt something too, Father," Kyan said. Alec smiled at her and then at Kyan.

"I would rather not discuss the reason just now, my dear. I am sorry, but you are welcome to join the children in a swim with Zirath if you would like."

Iz looked at Kyan, paused for a few seconds, then said, "No, thank you. I think I should go. Good day, my Prince."

"Good day, Ms. Iz," Kyan said as he bowed.

Iz turned and Kyan looked at Alec. Alec connected to Morgan and caught her up as she approached.

"I will speak with her. You play with the children and try to lighten the mood for a bit," Morgan said. She released Brya, and the angry girl shot for the water without looking at Kyan. Alec followed both into the water and caught his daughter.

"PLEASE WAIT, I would like to speak with you, Iz."

The girl stopped and turned to curtsy. She was very uncomfortable but held Morgan's eyes. Morgan caught up, then offered a smile and a slight bow in return.

"Please, do not be nervous. I would like to talk to you about what you felt from Kyan."

Iz diverted her eyes. "I was not sure if I did feel something, but have not been able to stop thinking of it. I am sorry if I offended you by not being straight forward with him."

"No, I can understand your curiosity, and your reluctance to speak with Kyan about it, just yet. Do you understand what you felt, Iz?" Iz blushed as she looked beyond her at the lake where Kyan played.

"Is he to be my mate, my Queen? Is his growth rate actually going to catch him up to my size and maturity one day?"

"Well, I am glad I do not have to explain all that," Morgan said with a laugh. "Yes. You are correct, my dear. He is your mate, and he will catch up with you within a couple of years or less. He is quite curious to know you but does not want to upset you. Are you interested in knowing him now, or would you rather keep your distance until he appears more your age?"

"If the last few nights are any indication, I do not think I could sleep if I tried to stay away altogether, my Queen. Do you mind if I spend time with him? I think it would be very interesting to watch him grow so quickly. I would know him much better and perhaps understand his special skills as well."

"The magic is an understanding force for certain. I could not have asked for an easier time of this conversation. I would be very glad for you to know him, so you are prepared for his special role. However, there is something we need to discuss. His sister —"

"— objects to my presence entirely," Iz said with a quick glance at Brya. "I need no magic to read the expression on her face, my Queen."

"Yes. I will not make it sound better than it is. She is having a very hard time with him giving attention to another. She says it is because she does not want his attention drawn from their special tasks. But I realize it is a matter of the very intense magical bond between them and the understandable feeling of possessiveness that carries with it. I cannot promise she will let go of that easily but would ask that you respect her despite her anger. She will understand eventually. I just cannot say when that might be."

"Does Kyan know how she feels? Is he willing to upset her in order to know me?" Iz said with a furrowing brow.

"Well, honestly, I am not sure. I feel his frustration. He wants to make both of you happy and is unsure how to do that," Morgan said. Iz wandered a few steps away to watch the children playing for a moment. "Will you tell him I prefer to wait, to meet him and get to know him as an adult? That way, he will feel no guilt, and Princess Brya will not be distressed. I would appreciate being able to talk with you and keep track of his life, if possible."

"That is very kind of you, Iz. I appreciate your willingness to accept hardship to give them an easier life for a bit. However, I do not think that will be a favor to either of them. Brya needs to learn to accept you, and I would never ask you nor Kyan to fight the magical link that draws you together. Come, join me and let me introduce you to your mate and his sister."

She took Iz by the shoulder and led her back to the lake. Iz shivered at the sensation of her magic but did not pull away.

"Come join me on the bank, my family. I would like us to speak with Iz together."

"No, thank you. I would rather ride Zirath some more," Brya said.

"I am not asking, young lady. You will join us, and you will be civil."

Morgan felt her anger, but was proud that her daughter held her words to herself. She of course heard them anyway, but could not hold them against her as she did not offer them.

Morgan and Iz stood at the bank as the others exited the water and toweled off.

"Kyan, come here, please," Morgan said. He blushed a bit as he walked forward, then held himself as bold as he could muster while smiling at Iz. Morgan marveled at how big he was as he gazed at her.

"As you have felt, Iz is indeed your magical mate and she has also felt the pull of the link you share. She would like to get to know you as you continue to grow."

"I am glad to know you are understanding of my growth rate and are not upset that I am so much younger than you. I will catch up very quickly, I assure you."

"I am glad to meet you, my Prince. And I am excited to get to know you better."

Kyan then blushed again as he thought, "I want to touch her hand and feel our link." Morgan heard him of course and chuckled as she thought, *"Patience, my boy."* Kyan looked at his feet as he blushed even more.

Iz stepped forward to curtsy to Brya.

"Good afternoon, my Princess, I am very glad to meet you," Iz said. Brya nodded, but said nothing. "Could I join you for a swim sometime? I have never had the opportunity to swim with a dragon and it looked quite fun." Brya did not answer until Morgan gave her a stern nudge with the magic.

"If my parents allow it, and your mate wants it, I cannot stop you," Brya said before running into the water. Iz looked disappointed, but not surprised. Kyan moved to the edge of the water as he watched Brya swimming hard away from them.

"She is tiring, Mommy," he said aloud. Zirath had been swimming under her and now came up to pick her up on his back. Kyan turned back to Iz and bowed.

"I am sorry Ms. Iz, but I need to spend time with my sister, just now. May I spend time with you later today? We could go for a flight, if Mother will allow it."

"Just call on me when you have time, Prince Kyan. I would be very happy to spend time with you," Iz said with a kind smile. Kyan smiled and held her eyes as he bowed. He then dove into the water to join Brya.

Iz watched them for a moment then turned to Morgan and Alec.

"I am blessed by the magic to be linked to your very special son. I am a little thrown to be honest. It is hard to think that cute little boy is to be my husband. I think I will just get to know him as a friend and let the magic lead me," she said.

"Very wise, young Lady," Alec said. "I am thankful for such understanding of our children's special circumstances. It is wonderful to meet my future daughter-in-magic." He offered a hand and bowed to kiss hers as she took it. Iz blushed and turned back to watch the children playing.

"Very gallant show-off," Morgan said.

Alec chuckled as he put an arm around his wife and kissed her cheek.

"Iz, would you like to join us for lunch and take a flight as Kyan suggested?" Morgan asked.

"I would love to, my Queen. Thank you for the invitation," Iz said.

"Shall I be at the main entrance to the castle a bit before noon then?"

"No, meet us at the garden gazebo. I will ask your parents if they could join us for dinner at six as well."

Iz curtsied and moved off with a happy bounce in her step. Morgan felt her happiness and was smiling as well.

"Now, we need to deal with Brya before she attacks Iz when nobody is looking," Alec said. "Agreed," Morgan said as she laughed.

MORGAN AND ALEC entered the lake and swam to join the children and Zirath. Morgan called to Lirpa and Falin and asked if they wanted to play.

"Lirpa is restin—" Falin said.

"I would love to join you, my Lady," Lirpa said. *"We will be with you soon."*

When the dragon couple arrived later, there was a tension within both of them. The twins swam to them to crawl onto their snouts. Both turned to Morgan with bright smiles. She nodded, giving them permission to speak of what they just felt.

"Congratulations to you both!" they cheered together.

Lirpa and Falin glanced around at the others for an explanation, but none was offered.

"What are you referring to, young ones?"

"You are carrying your first clutch, Lady Lirpa," they said together again.

The two dragons sat stunned for a second then crooned as they touched snouts and nudged the children.

"We hope to be going through our Quickening soon. Would you allow us to help Mother Quicken your children? It would be very special to us if we could."

"Of course, little ones. We would be honored for you to touch our children's spirits," the dragons said. They hummed very deep and loud to vibrate their snouts and tickle the children.

"Will you lift us up high so we can jump?" Kyan asked. "My Queen?" Lirpa asked.

"Just not too high, please," Morgan said. She watched and told Lirpa when to stop. The children soon leapt back into the lake with huge splashes. Everyone swam and played for an hour or so then settled down on the bank to rest before getting dressed again.

Kyan moved to sit facing Brya with a serious expression.

"Brya, I will not spend time with Iz without your support. I cannot stand your disappointment or anger any longer, it hurts too much. Please, tell me you will not make me stay away from her altogether when we know it will hurt her. She has done nothing to deserve it," Kyan said as his eyes filled with tears. As always, Brya shared the anguish within him. She also began to cry.

"I love you, Kyan. I am sorry for being selfish. I am just so scared to lose you. I cannot lose you, not ever," Brya said. Kyan took her hands in his to deepen their connection.

"I am never going to leave you, Brya. We will both have families of our own, and all will be very close. Do you truly believe I would ever leave you for any reason?"

"No, I know you would not," Brya said as she wrapped her arms around his neck and buried her face in them. "I am sorry for hurting you." They held each other and cried together as their parents struggled not to cry with them.

"You two ready to get cleaned up for lunch?" Alec asked.

Brya jumped up then pushed Kyan back as he rose to his feet. "You should bathe if you are to spend time with Iz. If she smells you right now, she may never marry you," she said with a giggle.

Kyan smiled and tried to grab her as she bolted away. They both took off running full speed for the castle.

MORGAN AND HER FAMILY were awaiting Iz at the gazebo when Alec groaned and muttered a curse. She turned to see a large

Knight with a furrowed face accompanying Iz.

"Good day, Sir Truin. How are you this fine day?" Morgan asked.

The Knight bowed with respect, but the scowl remained.

When Morgan connected to him and his wife earlier to invite them to dinner, she had opted not to tell them of their children's link that way. She planned to explain it in person over dinner.

She saw now that they had questioned Iz and found out already. Her father was upset at the news, but that did not explain Alec's reaction.

"Care to explain your annoyance?" she asked Alec.

"We have never cared for the company of each other, my dear. This is unfortunate, indeed."

"Iz, will you join the children and help them load the picnic supplies on the dragon harnesses, please," Morgan said. *"I will speak with your father. Just go relax, my dear."* Iz bowed, then moved off, causing Sir Truin to grumble. He dared not argue with his Queen, but his anger spoke his mind.

"The magic has indeed linked our children, and we have no place questioning it for any reason," Morgan said. "I will not hear any such comments. However, if you would like to better understand the situation, I would love to talk with you about it, Sir Truin."

Sir Truin was red in the face by the time she finished that statement, frustration boiling within him. Alec saw the man's stern expression and stepped forward with one of equal intensity.

The senior Knight nodded and took a small step back when he met Alec's eyes.

"A better understanding may make it less difficult to handle, my Queen. Presently it makes little sense to me, and I question the validity of the link. I ask if you have confirmed the link yourself, my Queen," Sir Truin asked in his loud resounding voice.

"No, I have not bonded to them and sought the link myself. I trust the magic within my son, as well as his recognition of the link. I feel no need to check it. Iz herself felt the link just being near him."

"My wife and I respectfully request that you confirm it, my Queen. We would not want to see our daughter invest her heart in this idea and have it injured in turn," Sir Truin said. He had given Alec a harsh glance as he finished that statement.

Alec was breathing a bit fast as his annoyance climbed. She took his hand and sent calming energy to hold his temper in check.

"Do you understand what that level of bonding is like, Sir Truin? It is very intense and very personal between any; it is far more intense between mates with profound magic between them. I am sorry, but I will not do that. It is inappropriate at this time. You will simply have to take the word of your Queen and King that this is a rightful magical pairing until the time they are both of an appropriate age for such bonding to one another."

"You should know that I courted his youngest sister. He did not approve of that, either. He has held a grudge since the day I told her that I could no longer see her in a personal way. I believe that situation fuels his anger."

"Sir Truin, fully explain your reasoning for questioning their pairing, please," Morgan said.

"Prince Kyan is but a child, my Queen. Iz is nearing her time of marriage. How can that be an appropriate match?" Morgan focused on his words and felt only a hint of deception.

"There is more, is there not, Sir Truin?"

Truin glanced at Alec then looked toward Iz and the children.

"Was my husband in any way unkind to your sister when he was seeing her? Do you have reason not to want your family to join with ours?"

Sir Truin looked uncomfortable and embarrassed as her words struck him.

"No, my Queen. King Alec acted honorably by my sister, and I would be honored to have our families joined. I am simply worried for my daughter, my Lady." Morgan stepped to him and placed a hand to his arm to pass friendship and understanding.

"This all came as a bit of a shock to me as well, Sir Truin. I understand your protective response, as I had the same one. I also considered keeping them apart for a while. After all, it is my little boy who announced he knew who his mate was to be," she said as she turned to watch the children and Iz working together. "But we have no place questioning the magic, my friend. It has allowed them to feel the link early for a reason. I believe it is so Iz will see him grow and better understand his magic and his role in our world. She recognizes that and welcomes the opportunity. We must let the magic guide us and trust in its wisdom."

Sir Truin shook his head in awe as he watched the children together.

"He looks seven or eight already, yet he is only a year and ten months. He could be marrying my daughter when he is only three or four years old. It is just too abnormal and seems unreal, my Lady. However, I will trust in the magic, as you say. I was wrong to question it. Also, you are right. I did have ill feelings toward King Alec that were wrongfully fueling my anger. I apologize."

"I am sorry if I hurt your sister in any way. I realized she was not my mate and did not want either of us to get any more attached. Please understand that I was following the magic as well, my friend," Alec said as he stepped forward and offered a handshake. Sir Truin took it with a small smile. "No more hard feelings then?"

Sir Truin nodded and looked back to the children. He smiled and said, "Iz tells me Princess Brya seems to feel a bit of animosity toward her attachment to your son. Is that to be a problem?"

"At this time, it seems to be taken care of, but I make no promises it will not be a problem from time to time," Morgan said. "The bond between the twins is very strong, and Brya has seen Iz as a threat to it. We and Kyan have discussed it with her. For now, she seems happy to get to know Iz and support Kyan's wish to know her."

"Sir Truin, would you care to join our lunch picnic?" Alec asked. "We would welcome the opportunity to get to know you better and discuss this new situation."

"I appreciate the invitation, but I must say no. I should get back to my wife and eldest daughter, Kay. She is due to have my first grandchild this month and was not feeling very well this morning." Morgan had a broad smile and Truin noticed. "What makes you smile so, my Queen?"

"I intend to pay your daughter a visit this week to offer her a very special gift. I will leave it to her to explain if she wishes," she said. She bowed her head, then moved off to join the children.

"What is she talking about, my King? What sort of gift would the Queen offer my daughter?"

Alec clapped a hand to his back and laughed lightly as he smiled.

"A uniquely wonderful gift. Our families are to be quite involved now, my friend. We will see you for dinner. Perhaps bring Kay and her husband if they are interested. See you then."

THE PICNIC PARTY traveled to a distant mountain river and cool water pool for their lunch and an afternoon of relaxation. Zirath joined them and played in the river with the children with enthusiasm.

Iz was comfortable with the children within an hour and played with no hesitation. Soon after they entered the water to swim, she and Kyan took hands as she helped him climb onto a large boulder. They both froze and stared at their clasped hands. Morgan felt the surge of magic from many feet away and started toward them.

"Are you two going to jump in or not?" Brya chided.

Kyan jumped up and ran to leap off the rock with Brya. Iz slowly sat down on the rock, where she stared at her hand and rubbed her palm.

"A unique sensation, yes?" Morgan asked as she sat beside her.

"Definitely. It was wonderful, and unlike anything I have experienced before. I felt the magic from you this morning when you laid a hand to my shoulder, but this it is definitely different, my Lady,"Iz said in a quiet, distracted voice. She stared at her hands in silence a moment before continuing. "I think I have just accepted the reality of my future. I am quite overwhelmed, my Queen. How is a simple girl like me to properly serve such a powerfully magical man as Kyan will be?"

"You are far from simple, Iz. The magic would never have chosen you were you not suited to be a wonderful wife to him. You have a special heart. That is clear in your ability to understand and welcome the complexity of this situation," Morgan said. Iz looked out at Kyan as her eyes welled with tears.

"Will his rate of maturing slow once he reaches adulthood, my Queen? Or...or will I lose him within years of our marriage?"

"I am not sure, my dear. We will have to wait and find out together," Morgan said as she passed calming energy to the trembling young woman.

"I am very glad to have your friendship in this, my Queen. I had feared you would resent me for bringing the pairing to light while he was still so young."

"You were right to worry. I was shaken when I saw him watching you, and was still considering keeping you apart even this morning. It was my dear husband who reminded me that I had no right to do that. This situation is awkward for us all, but King Alec and I are blessed by your maturity and understanding."

Iz smiled as she watched the twins playing and giggled. "Watch him, it is so cute. He will be playing, see me watching, and change his manner to seem more mature to impress me. I hope he grows comfortable enough to just be himself soon."

"He will. Just be yourself, and he will too. Go play now and treat him as you would any other friend."

Iz laughed as she got up and thought, "Or, as any other little kid anyway."

"Do not let him hear that, my dear," Morgan said.

Iz froze and looked horrified. *"Oh! I forgot about that. How do I keep him from hearing my thoughts?"*

"You cannot prevent it, I am afraid. He did not hear what you just said because I was blocking our conversation from him and Brya both. But you need to be prepared for them to hear your thoughts at all times. It will take some getting used to, and there will be times when a natural reflexive thought will embarrass you. Sorry to be blunt, but that is the truth."

"This is going to be an interesting year, my Queen," Iz said as she took two fast steps to leap into the water in spectacular splashing fashion.

Morgan smiled at the twins' approval and laughter as she moved closer to them. She waited till they had their backs turned, then leapt high above them. She splashed all three, and Iz looked amazed that her Queen was playing in the river.

"I'm it. Ready, set, go!" Morgan yelled.

All three dashed away and she swam hard for the nearest. She chased and dashed for them, giving them just enough time to escape so the game would last longer. "You're it," she said as she tagged Kyan and leapt out of reach. Kyan dashed straight for Brya though Iz was closer.

"Are you afraid you cannot catch me, Prince Kyan? Do you think me too cunning and quick?" Iz asked. He dashed at her and she swam hard then climbed up a rock to get free of him. He climbed after her and followed her as she leapt back into the water. He landed almost on top of her and tagged her as he dunked her.

Iz surfaced and darted toward Brya. She halted as she was met by a sad stare from the young girl.

"Do you wish to play any longer, Princess Brya?"

"No, thank you, Ms. Iz. I will spend time with my mother for a bit. You may have time with Kyan," Brya said. She turned and swam to wrap her arms around Morgan's neck and tuck her head in.

"Why have I not felt my mate as well? What does that mean?"

Morgan rubbed her back and soothed her through their magical bond.

"You have not felt him yet, but that does not mean you will not in the future. Perhaps your mate is not from Chemerie, or even Erion, for that matter. Think of Uncle Daniel and Taru. You must try to be patient, my dear. Besides, you have enough to worry about this year, don't you think?"

Brya smiled as she carried her from the water to join Alec. Alec had heard their conversation through Morgan and was smiling. He took his daughter into his arms greedily and kissed her head as he tucked her in tight.

"Brya, I am not ready for you to find your mate. Please, do not go any faster, or your mother will be healing me daily from a nervous disorder." They all laughed as Brya kissed him to soothe his worry.

16

Transfer of Magic

MORGAN, ALEC, AND NULIAN were returning from a long flight when Morgan felt profound worry from Sir Truin, who was seeking her at the castle. *"What troubles you, my friend?"*

"My daughter, Kay, is not well. She has a fever, and we worry for her and the child, my Queen. Could I bring her to see you?"

"I will go to her now. Meet me at your home."

The Knight took off at a sprint for his home, and Nulian flew hard to meet him. Morgan and Alec hurried to a smaller home nearby, where Kay lived with her husband, Geno. They met Sir Truin in the foyer, and all headed up to Kay's bedroom.

Alec stayed near the door as Morgan moved to the bed and laid a hand to the young woman.

"Your problem is the injury to your foot, my dear," she told Kay. "You allowed the cut to become infected." She passed healing energy to heal the cut and reduce her body temperature to normal. When she finished, she sat beside Kay and smiled.

"Thank you so much, my Queen. I never expected to have you come for something so trivial," Kay said. "I feel quite silly."

"It is no problem at all. If, in the future, you have a wound of any kind, come to me at once. Please, do not let yourself suffer." The young woman blushed and nodded. The twins and Iz arrived and were relieved to see Kay relaxed and smiling.

"May I check your child while I am here?" Morgan asked.

"Yes. Thank you, my Lady. Our child has grown a great deal since you last checked its health."

Morgan placed both hands to her swollen belly and connected to both mother and child.

"When I checked your pregnancy last, I did not offer to tell you the child's gender because I felt your apprehension. Am I correct that you would both like to know now?" Kay and Geno looked at each other then both nodded with broad smiles.

"Yes, my Queen. We would very much like to know," Geno said. "You carry a very healthy son, my dear," Morgan said to Kay. Geno beamed as he hugged Kay tight. Morgan rose to leave, but anxious curiosity from Kay made her turn back. Sir Truin stepped forward and took his daughter's hand as he looked to Morgan.

"What was the gift you spoke of last week, my Lady? I mentioned it to Kay, and she has been bursting to ask you."

"I understand if you give the gift to Kay now instead of waiting to let Emma be the first. She will understand as well," Alec said when Morgan looked at him. She smiled as she looked between Kay and Geno. "I offer your child the gift of magic, my friends. I would like to transfer magic to your child, so he will have a greater bond to his brethren, both man and dragon. Is this something you would want for your child?"

Geno almost fell over before Sir Truin directed him to sit on the bed beside Kay. The couple both stared at her, speechless, as their gratitude washed over her in a strong wave. She smiled and laughed.

"Though your mouths are not speaking, I can feel your interest. Before you agree, I want to be upfront and tell you I have studied the process thoroughly, but this will be the first time I have performed the transfer myself. I understand if you—"

"We trust you without limit, my Caretaker," Kay said. "Please, we would be honored to have our child be the first to receive this gift from you. When would you do this? Do I need to come to you at the castle after he is born?"

Brya and Kyan laughed quietly behind Morgan as they felt the excitement from Kay.

"Move back to your father, please," she said to them. They moved but put on impressive pouts as they did so. "Be patient. You will be doing these yourselves before too much longer, I imagine."

"My Caretaker, do you mean to do it now? Here?" Geno asked.

"If that is alright with you, yes. Your boy will come in a few weeks, and this part must be done prior to birth. I will also come at the birth to complete the initiation of his magic," she said as she sat down. "Kay, you will feel a great deal of sensation, but no pain. Your child will do some stretching and kicking as he feels the same tingling sensations. You need only to relax and lie back. Geno, if you hold her hand, you will feel some of the sensations as well, I believe."

Geno snuggled in beside Kay and took both hands as they glanced between each other and her. Morgan held her hands out to them with a smile.

"May I calm you first?" she said. They took her hands, and she sent calming emotion. Each took slow, deep breaths, then smiled as she slid Kay's shirt up over her belly.

She placed her hands over her Crest to focus her mind and her magic. Once focused, she laid her hands to Kay's belly with one hand on each side of the baby, just as she did with a dragon hatchling still within its egg. She closed her eyes and began to sing the unique and beautiful version of the Song of Quickening.

Everyone in the room was mesmerized by the song and the way her Crest and hands glowed brightly. The dragons of her markings also began to move about. Kay gave a little gasp of amazement as she watched them.

Morgan focused within herself to build her magic, then bonded to the child to seek his spirit. Once she had a very strong hold on his beautiful spirit, she changed the song and pushed the magic to him.

The child began to move around as the tingle intensified between her hands. She felt the essence of the magic binding to his spirit. It was a wonderful new experience. She reached a threshold where he could take in no more and took a moment to touch spirits with the child before letting the bonding break away.

MORGAN LET the very deep bonding to the infant drop to find Alec kneeling in front of her with worried eyes.

"The twins passed out, but they are waking now."

She moved to her children where they lay on the floor with their Crests and hands ablaze. They were moaning and writhing in pain. Fear filled her the instant she touched them. Their temperatures were high, and the magic was changing within them.

"I think I have initiated their Quickening. Let's get them home!" She and Alec each scooped up a child and said fast farewells to the others as they moved to Nulian.

"Am I right, my Sister? Have I brought their Quickening on early?"

"Indeed, but they were very near it already. Let us make it as painless as possible, my Caretaker," Nulian said as she began humming.

Morgan pushed healing energy to both children as they flew quickly for the castle.

"THE TWINS HAVE ENTERED their Quickening and they are suffering badly. I need your help, Ladies," Morgan said to Taru and GranMay.

She glanced at Menkar and he was away to get Taru from the river cabin at once. She and Nulian called to the Elder dragons as they flew for the castle lawn. The Elders started filling the lawn, and Nulian landed in the middle of them.

"We will sing the Song of Quickening and make sure all is initiated properly. Then we will assist you and Queen May in controlling their pain as much as we can, my Queen," Nulian said.

Morgan nodded but did not break her concentration on the pain control for her children as she and Alec moved them to the ground. She was able to control most of it and keep herself stable. Kyan and Brya held each other's hands and tried to look brave for the other.

Alec lay down to put his head near theirs and stroked their hair.

"Can I do anything to help?" he asked Morgan.

"Offer support your way, my love."

He kissed them both and talked to them in his deep soothing voice. They closed their eyes and rested their heads to his as he comforted them.

Nulian and the other Elder dragons began to sing their version of the Song of Quickening. Morgan cringed as she heard the obvious similarity to the song she had sung earlier.

"I am so stupid! Why did I not discuss my intentions with you? I have done this to my children out of idiotic naivety!"

"Do not blame yourself. I would not have known to warn you, my Sister. I have never heard of a Caretaker's child being Quickened by any other than the Elder dragons," Nulian said.

Morgan felt no less guilty. She looked into her children's pain filled eyes as hers filled with tears.

"I am so sorry, my loves. I will do my best to control your pain."

"It started when we sang along with you, Mommy. It was not your doing, but ours," Brya said. Kyan added, *"We welcome the change, Mother. It hurts now, but will be worth the result."*

The dragons' song shifted, becoming more complex, which made the children curl up in increasing pain. Alec began to sing a favorite song of theirs, and they put their heads against his again. Morgan pushed healing energy as fast as she could. She began to tremble as her magic level dropped.

"Do not go so far you have to stop and leave them unassisted, my Sister," Nulian said.

Morgan reduced the rate of transfer and focused to let her magic regenerate while still sending steady healing to them.

GranMay arrived and offered her assistance as well. Morgan felt the added energy and smiled at her Elder Caretaker with thanks.

"I figured this would be a major event, but did not expect it this soon," GranMay said.

"It is my fault they suffer early. I was transferring magic to an unborn child, and they began to sing along with me. It initiated their Quickening immediately."

"You were doing what?" GranMay said as her head shot up. Morgan explained in thought, and GranMay shook her head with a small chuckle. "It is clear that I cannot die anytime soon. I have to stay around to see all that you three accomplish. I would not be surprised if you all learned to fly next."

Morgan noticed that as GranMay talked, she never wavered in supplying a fast flow of magic to the children. Her grandmother's magic may not have the same breadth as her own, but she had great depth in the skills she had developed.

She felt the twin's temperatures rising far too high and backed off on the transfer of healing energy.

"You must use the extra magic which builds within you. Use your reforming skills, my dears," Morgan said.

Kyan reached for Alec's dagger. He held it in his hand and closed his eyes. The knife softened, and he pinched the blade in two pieces, giving half to Brya.

They both trembled and had trouble focusing but managed to reform the metal a few different ways to use the magic within them. Morgan felt their temperatures dropping as they worked.

"Will the intensity of the episodes worsen, Mother?" Brya asked.

"I am afraid so. Let us move to the lake so you can use the water to control your temperature."

The twins stood on shaky legs and took each other's hands. They did not make it to the lake before they buckled with the next wave of Quickening. They reached for each other, embraced, and put a hand to the other's Crest. They put their foreheads together as they bonded and sang the dragon song of healing together.

"You are so smart with your magic, my children," Morgan said as she knelt beside them and laid a hand to each. The twins knew the state of bonding allowed for the release of most of the physical pain. It took enough from them that she could control almost all of the rest for now.

Unfortunately, they could not hold the bonding on their own long enough to make it through all of the Quickening they would face. Morgan hoped she and Taru could supply enough energy to help them hold it through the worst episodes at least.

As that episode came to an end, the twins' temperature was very high. They rose and stumbled toward the water.

"Just us for now, Mother. We have an idea and need to do it through our link. If it does not work, we will call," they said together. Morgan stopped and let them go out into the water alone.

"Should we stop them? They are already too weak to swim," Alec asked.

"They are not going to swim. They are going to use the water in a more complex way than making small crystals. They feel the magic growing and know they have to do something with it through this next episode." They held each other as they watched their children move into the deeper water. "Have you noticed they are growing rapidly during this process? They already look a year older than an hour ago."

"No wonder they hurt so much. Add the pain of such rapid growth to the pain you saw within the others with a Crest "

They gripped each other a bit tighter as they shared the worry consuming them both.

"The next wave is starting," she said as she felt the surge of magic within her children.

The pain hit, making both Kyan and Brya stumble. He dropped under the water, but she lifted him.

"Focus, use the magic. Bond again and use it, my loves." The twins turned to place a hand to the other's Crest and touch foreheads.

"Watch closely, my dear. They are going to let their imagination run the show."

EVERYONE WATCHED IN AMAZEMENT as the children started to rise up from the water. They had frozen the water below their feet in a six-foot circle and now rose with the ice. The water around them started to freeze to form a railing around the edge of the circle.

Next, more water near freezing began to rise as a sheet from all around them and encase them in a massive transparent dome. The entire thing looked like a snow globe as it actually started to snow inside the bubble.

They held the structure for a few more minutes, then released it as the worst part of the episode passed. The sheet of water fell away, and the ice platform began to melt.

"That was amazing!" Iz said from just behind Morgan. Her face was white, and she was trembling.

"Do not worry," Morgan said. "They have found a brilliant way to deal with the magic as it surges through them. I should have known they would not need me."

"They do now!" Alec shouted as he bolted forward to dive into the water.

The twins had passed out and dropped below the surface.

Morgan passed Alec as she used all her new strength to reach them. She dove to reach Kyan.

"Brya, where are you?" she said as she searched with magic. She found her ten feet deeper. Kyan was not breathing and needed to rise. Just as the painful choice demanded action, Nulian rose from beneath and lifted them all out of the water.

Nulian laid Brya on her palm next to Morgan and Kyan as she hummed the dragon healing song. Alec climbed up and moved to Brya as Morgan worked on Kyan. Taru and Daniel had just arrived, and Taru dove into the water from Menkar as he dropped over the lake.

The twins were not breathing. Morgan passed healing magic fast and hard to Kyan while Taru climbed up and started to work on Brya. Kyan soon coughed, and Morgan rolled him to Alec as she moved to work with Taru.

Her sweet daughter was white as a ghost and her lips were blue. She checked her fear and focused to push healing magic as fast as she could. She felt nothing from Brya in response.

"Taru, bond to me and give me all you can," she said. She let Taru's magic flow through her and directed it as pure healing energy. After only a moment, she had to cut off the bonding to Taru, who had fallen to the side, unconscious but stable. GranMay had been brought to Nulian by Gerzin and laid her hands to Brya to help. Together they pushed an enormous amount of healing. Another minute passed, and still, Brya was unresponsive.

Morgan was trembling and growing cold, yet she pushed as hard as she could. She became dizzy, so she laid one hand to Nulian to pull magic from her.

"Brya!" Kyan yelled as he bolted awake. He laid a trembling hand to his sister's Crest and spoke into her ear as he cried. "You cannot leave me. I cannot live without you. Fight for me, please!

Take my strength, Brya."

Kyan closed his eyes and his Crest glowed brightly, as did Morgan's. They both pushed with all they had and were nearly unconscious when Alec started pulling them back.

"No!" Kyan screamed as he fought Alec off. He broke free of Alec's grasp, then moved above Brya to stack both hands over her Crest as he screamed her name and pushed all he had left as one jolt.

He fell back against Alec just as Brya's Crest burst into light under his hands. She gave a great gasp and coughed. Morgan scooped her into her arms as Alec did Kyan, then all shared one great transfer of love and relief.

Brya took Kyan's face in her hands and kissed his cheek as she passed magic to strengthen him. "Thank you, my Brother. But do not ever do that again. You will not die in an effort to save me! Promise me, right now!" She was crying hard as she yelled at him. He said nothing as he wrapped her in his arms and held her tight.

The family cried together as Nulian hummed to wake Taru and moved them to the shallow water. They reached the sandy bank just as the next wave hit the twins.

"Not the water again, please. How about the sand this time? You do wonderful things with sand," Alec said as he lifted them and pushed them away from the water.

The children sat in the middle of the large sandy bank, bonded, then built an intricate glass castle all around them.

"I have never been so scared in my life, my Queen. Are they going to suffer like this very long?" Iz asked as she joined Morgan in pacing along the edge of the glass castle. Morgan took one of the girl's shaking hands to pass calming energy.

"I do not know how long it will take, my dear," Morgan said. She accidentally squeezed enough to make her flinch. With a quick push of apology and healing, she let her go.

"May I stay and help in any way possible?" Iz asked. Morgan

nodded and moved closer to the children as the intensity started to fade again. She watched them fall to the ground and breathe hard in exhaustion.

"This is a lovely castle, but you forgot the door, my dears." Everyone laughed as she vaulted over the castle wall to reach them. Taru followed, and both passed healing energy to rejuvenate the children.

"We sure could use a Nyek right now, Brother."

"Mother has it handled, Sister. But a Nyek would make it easier on her for sure."

"What is a Nyek?" Taru asked.

"Our first task, Aunt Taru," Brya said. Morgan was explaining it to Taru when Brya looked at her palms and gasped.

"Look! Mother, my markings are appearing," she said. Morgan saw the beautiful dragons appearing on her hands and around her Crest. Alec heard and clambered over the wall to see.

"They are gorgeous, and unlike any dragon I have ever seen. Very unique indeed, my dear," Alec said. He kissed her forehead and hugged her tight.

Morgan felt great disappointment in Kyan as he stared at his own hands and saw nothing.

"No male has ever had them, Kyan. They may still show up, but try not to be upset if they do not. You have an enormous amount of magic. That is the real gift after all."

Brya moved to sit closer to him and put her hands down. Kyan picked up her hands to tease the dragons and make them wiggle.

"Never hide them again. Not for me or anyone else. I am very proud for you," Kyan said.

"Well said, Son," Alec said as he patted his shoulder.

Everyone stood and moved toward the wall to exit. Alec was knocked forward as Kyan fell against him when he was hit with intense pain again. Morgan started to pass healing, but he pushed her hands back.

"No, Mother. I am fine," he said. He then failed to stand as his knees buckled, making him fall hard to the ground. It was not happening to Brya this time. Brya tried to pass healing, but he shook his head. "No, please, let it happen. I feel it should be natural this time."

He rolled on the ground and moaned as he tried to hide his agony. Morgan was near moving to him when she heard his thoughts summoning Iz. Iz came flipping over the wall and moved to him. She was crying as she took his hand without a word.

She started trembling and sweat poured from her within a few seconds of touching him.

"He is blocking Iz from the pain and sharing only the sensations of the magic itself. He is comforted by her touch. However, he is holding a great deal of magic and his temperature is rising quickly," Morgan explained to those around her.

Kyan sat up and held up his other hand to Iz, who took it while staring hard into his eyes. He dropped his head and gritted his teeth through another wave of pain and then looked up again.

"My Prince, please let me take some of the pain. I want to help you." Kyan shook his head, fought through another intense round of pain, then looked back into her eyes.

"Please allow me to bond to you, Iz. Just for a moment," Kyan said. "What?" Alec asked as he started to stand. Morgan took his arm to hold him back as she passed calming magic.

"His being male is making this very different. Perhaps that is why the magic gave him his mate early. Trust him, my dear."

Iz nodded, and Kyan smiled before grimacing again. He moved her hands to his Crest and bonded in one quick move. Iz gasped and Morgan felt Sir Truin's fear behind them.

"He will die before hurting Iz, my friend. Trust him," Morgan said to him.

She connected to Kyan and found they were in a deep bonding already. Her breath caught in her throat as Kyan started humming the Song of Transfer. She felt the magical transfer from him to Iz begin and started to rise. This time it was Brya that stopped her.

"I understand now, Mother. He is giving her a gift, as you did the child earlier," Brya said with a smile.

"To an adult? How can " Morgan said as the understanding came to her. "Ah yes you are clever, my boy."

Alec squeezed her hand for more information.

"The link between magical mates is strong enough to support the transfer if the power of the giver is great enough. His power is at its highest now because he allows it to build and willingly endures great pain."

She watched as Kyan and Iz released the bonding and fell to the side exhausted. She and Alec found they were fine and laughing as they looked at each other. Brya walked over and placed her hands to her hips.

"Well, you must have had that idea for quite some time, Brother. Brave and noble, yes, but sneaky too."

"What better way to use our magic than to share it, my Sister?" They all laughed as they helped Kyan and Iz to their feet.

"We still need a door," Morgan said as she touched a wall of the castle. She focused and reordered the glass to shape a drawbridge.

"Very nice, Mother," Brya said as she bounded through. She tripped, then laughed at herself as she said, "I am not used to this height just yet. The ground is a bit further away."

GranMay grabbed her and hugged her tight. "I do hope you slow down, my dear. You are almost taller than me already. My ego may not tolerate looking up to you before you are at least two years old."

Kyan moved from the castle with Iz and stood up straight to meet the harsh gaze of Sir Truin. He released Iz's hand but did not break eye contact with her stern father.

"I understand you just gave my daughter a gift through a highly personal bonding without my permission, young man."

Alec moved toward them. *"He is just playing with him,"* Morgan said. He stopped and hid his smile.

"Yes, Sir, I gave her a bit of magic while I had the opportunity. I felt it a proper gift for my mate, Sir Truin," Kyan said, holding his stare until Truin's face broke into a smile.

"I think it a wonderful gift as well, Prince Kyan, and I sincerely thank you," Sir Truin said. Kyan let out a breath of relief as Sir Truin shook his hand hard.

"Kyan! Look at your Crest," Iz said. He looked down to find his dragon markings showing themselves at last.

"I had accepted I would have none," he said as his voice cracked. Iz traced those now appearing on his hands, and they moved under her finger. Kyan shivered and said, "That is a lovely sensation."

Alec chuckled and pulled Kyan away from Iz as he said, "I think it is time we all went in for some supper."

"Hey, munchkins!" Daniel called in a harsh voice as he stepped in front of them. "You two owe me for interrupting my honeymoon." The twins' faces fell a bit before he laughed and hugged both. "No worries, I was growing bored, anyway." He was shoved hard in the back by his new wife.

"Well, I will just go back by myself, then," Taru said as she turned and took off for Menkar.

"Oh mercy," Daniel said as he took off after her. Everyone laughed as Taru asked Menkar to lift off just as Daniel reached for the harness, which sent him sprawling into the grass. Menkar chuckled and that drew even more laughs from the crowd.

The rest of the group headed inside for a fine dinner to celebrate. Morgan was solemn despite the happiness of the others, so Alec directed her away from them.

"Talk to me."

"It is not over. That was just initiation. I have to complete

their Quickening. Now that I have seen their level of power, I wonder if I can handle it properly. It has been a while since I doubted my skill like this. Not since losing Balia."

"You will do all you can do, and no other could do more. It is that simple, my dear," Alec said. She tried to smile, but he did not. *"What is it that really troubles you? You are not connected to me as usual to hide your pain. Stop it, and tell me the truth."* She closed her eyes and dropped her head to his chest as she let tears fall.

"Kyan saved her, not me. She would have died. I could not save her."

She let herself release the tension that had built through the evening. Alec held her tight while she cried, knowing that was what she needed most.

UNLIKE MORGAN'S QUICKENING, THE TWINS' painful episodes of fast magical growth had calmed in a few days, yet their rate of physical growth was still advancing rapidly. With most of the pain at bay, they spent much of the next few weeks working with Morgan, Taru, and GranMay to study the materials and methods needed to rebuild the portal to Berios. Morgan studied all of her memories and all of the information she could gain from the Book of the Caretaker.

While she felt confident with finding and gathering enough ore for the circlet, filling it with the purple liquid was still a mystery to solve. She knew it was found on Berios, but could learn nothing of its handling.

"Alright then. We are going to make a man-size portal ring with this bit of ore. You have all studied the design of the portal to Earth, yes?" Morgan said. Everyone nodded. "Our biggest challenge is to work together such that our efforts are effective. Let's first try picturing the design as we touch our hands to the ore. Place one hand to the person beside you and the other to the ore. Bond together as one and focus on the metal."

All in the magical group did as she suggested: Brya touched Kyan, who touched Morgan on one side, and GranMay touched Taru, who touched her on the other side. She had both hands to the ore in front of her. As they focused, the metal softened and began to form five individual rings rather than one large ring.

"Stop, everyone. This is not working."

"I am sorry to say so, but I did not expect it would, my dear. It is like having many people painting the same portrait. You must focus the energy through one person, I believe," GranMay said.

"That is a lot of magic flowing through one person. It is bound to be difficult, but you are right. Let's try it," Morgan said. Everyone gathered around and laid a hand to her.

They all bonded again and she laid a hand to the metal. It worked. The metal softened and began to form into one large circle. Though she made good progress, she had to break the bonding well before the ring was complete. She slumped forward, breathing hard and sweating.

"What is the effect on you?" GranMay asked as she passed healing energy to cool her.

"The magic gets caught within me rather than passing through, it is hard not to store it naturally. If I allow even the slightest bit to move within me rather than flow through, it raises my temperature and makes me lose focus," Morgan said.

"It appears that we need a focuser who cannot store the magic as readily, thereby, allowing most to flow through. Perhaps I am a useful old bird after all," GranMay said with a wink.

"GranMay, are you sure you want to try this?"

"I am the only one who will not have to worry with the storage problem. Let me try, my dear. If it is overwhelming, I will release the bonding." Morgan raised an eyebrow, so she added, "I promise."

Morgan stood, took a small step back, and received similar

feelings of worry from the other three of the group.

"I am the Elder here, am I not?" GranMay snapped as she eyed the group. "Now, bond to me and focus!"

Nobody argued. Each placed a hand to her at once. GranMay shivered with the sudden rush of magic, but placed her hands to the ore and focused it.

She was wonderful. She allowed the magic to flow and sculpted the complete circle in perfect detail. When she finished, she stood to admire the work with a satisfied smile.

"That is pretty good for a first attempt at reordering matter, wouldn't you say, my dear?" GranMay asked.

"You have not practiced with smaller amounts as we did?" Morgan said. GranMay patted her hand as she chuckled.

"I do not have that kind of power within me, my dear. But, if I did, I now know I could wield it well," GranMay said.

Morgan kissed her cheek and said, "Of that, I have no doubt, GranMay."

"WE NEED TO GO TO KAY. It is time," Morgan said. They explained their departure as they moved away from the group. Morgan connected to Geno and told him he needed to head home to welcome his son.

Morgan and GranMay arrived at Kay's house just as Geno came running from the Knights' training grounds. He slid to a stop and stumbled as he attempted to bow.

"Let's go, Geno. Formality can wait," GranMay said. They all moved up the stairs and down the hall. Geno knocked and peeked in.

"Your Queens are here, my dear. May we join you?" Geno asked. Kay was very happy to see them all and even happier when her Queens lessened her pain.

Morgan sat beside her and held her hand to keep her pain at

bay while GranMay moved to help Kay's mother, Daris, get ready to receive the baby.

"Mother, we feel the magical child coming. We very much want to join you. Will you ask Lady Kay and Sir Geno if we may?" Kyan asked.

"It is Sir Geno who will have an objection to your being present Kyan. You are more a man than boy now, and this is very private," Morgan said.

"Please explain our need to share in this, Mother. I think it important we learn by feeling what you do," he said.

"My friends, do you understand the special magic of my children?" Morgan asked the nervous parents. With their nods, she added, "They ask to be present and witness this transfer." She looked to Geno. "Kyan is the first male to carry the Caretaker magic for many decades. That makes this request more of an issue, I realize. May he join us?"

Geno was conflicted, but Kay squeezed his hand with a nod.

"If they are to give this gift to others as you do, there is no place for modesty. They must learn, and we are happy to allow them to benefit from this wonderful occasion," Kay said.

Daris hung a curtain that blocked view of Kay from the waist down. "No need for the boy to get too much of an education today, however," she said with a smile.

"I completely agree," Morgan said as everyone laughed.

"It is time to start pushing, my girl. When you feel the next contraction, push with it," Daris said. Kay sat up and Geno sat behind her to support her back. Since Morgan and GranMay were keeping the pain away, Kay felt for the muscle contractions to know when to push.

Brya and Kyan entered the room and sat away from the bed. They both kept their eyes away from Kay, feeling awkward.

"Come closer and learn from your mother. We welcome your involvement," Kay said to them with a smile. They rose and moved to stand near the head of the bed. Kyan was discreet and polite.

"You will listen and feel the transfer, but do not attempt to join it. Only observe for now. After your Quickening is complete, you will begin to participate," Morgan said. They both nodded and stood in anxious silence, awaiting the time to bond to her and feel the new magical process.

Kay's contractions became intense. After only a few minutes, Daris leaned around the curtain with a wide smile.

"Alright, my girl. Your little one is almost ready to join us," Daris said. "Sit up, and push hard with the next few rounds of contractions."

"I will keep her pain at bay. Do your work, my dear," GranMay said with a wink to Morgan.

The instant the baby boy was born, Daris handed him to Morgan. She cuddled the wailing child to her chest, assuring his skin was touching her Crest scales. He quieted as her magic washed over him at a profound level. The twins laid a hand to her and bonded with her as she focused on the infant. Tears slid down her cheeks as she bonded to the baby boy and felt the considerable amount of magic within him.

As she started singing the unique Song of Quickening, magic began to flow to him once more. She held the bonding as she sang, focusing to not stop when the twins left the bonding and took their hands off of her. When she finished transferring as much magic as the little one could accept, she opened her eyes to find the twins offering healing energy to the now very pale and unconscious Kay.

Morgan handed the infant to Daris, then moved to the bed.

GranMay stopped her as she reached for Kay.

"She fainted soon after the child was born, and the twins moved to her at once," GranMay said. "They identified the problem just as I did. I focused on pain control as they focused on the wound. They are healing her with great care to assure she will have no difficulty carrying another child. I am so proud to see their focus and strength in a time of stress. They have become very mature in their magic." Morgan smiled and nodded in agreement as she gripped GranMay's hand.

Daris moved to hand the infant boy to his father, but he shook his head without taking his eyes from Kay.

"His mother will hold him first," he said in a gruff voice. He caressed Kay's face until she woke then lifted her up to lean back against him again. Kay was shaking a bit as she reached out, so he supported her arms and the child as Daris handed him over. The new parents took in the face of their new son with tears rolling down their cheeks.

"Children, do you feel the magic within him?"

"Yes, Mother, you did an amazing job," Brya said as she kissed her cheek.

"Thank you all for this gift, and for helping me today. There is really no way we could thank you enough," Kay said.

"I consider it an honor to share the magic," Morgan said. "I hope that we will be able to share it with all of the children born from now on. It will reestablish the wonderful connection between Chemerians that existed in the days of Lady Chemerie."

They visited with the new parents for a while, then headed back to the castle.

"Are you going to give the gift to Aunt Emma's child, Mother?" Brya asked.

"Yes, of course. I made the offer and told her to come to me when she is ready. I expect to see her soon," Morgan said.

"Especially now that you have transferred the magic to one child successfully already," Brya said.

"I still find it very insulting that she did not have enough trust in Mother to accept the gift with a grateful heart at once," Kyan said.

"Kyan, she did not hesitate out of lack of trust in Morgan, but from fear of the magic," GranMay said. "You should not judge so quickly." Kyan nodded as he thought more about it.

"I am sorry. I forget she does not feel the magic as we do. Therefore, she does not know that it is only dangerous in the hands of a dark-spirited person."

GranMay put an arm around him and said, "Very wise, young man."

Qaleb of Veridan

MORGAN JOINED THE ADMIRALTY of the Guard in the planning room to discuss the logistics of traveling through Kalias to Berios. The Admiralty's current plan was to take many Knights and dragons to see them safely across Kalias to the portal to Berios. They hoped to travel undetected at night, using the enhanced vision of Morgan, Taru and the dragons to their advantage.

"Actually," Morgan said, "I think it wiser that Taru and I be the first to go throu—"

"That's a great idea," Daniel snapped. "If we are not to worry about your safety at all!" He received a sharp look from both Morgan and Alec, but held her eyes with an intense stare. "We should send ample forces in case the dark ones are lying in wait."

Morgan glared at him as she stood and used her magic to calm her own temper. *"I share your feelings about Hoge, but I am not going to be yelled at in front of the Admiralty, nor do I appreciate the assumption you just made! Excuse yourself until you can pull your crap together and speak to me with some measure of respect!"*

He glanced at Alec, then left the room.

Alec watched Daniel leave as if he wanted to call him back or follow him.

"What would you say to him?" Morgan asked Alec as she shifted her glare to him.

"That he is right. He may say it rudely, but he is not wrong in being cautious. We remember your last visit to Kalias and how you returned to us. We have certainly not forgotten the experiences Taru had at Hoge's hand. Neither of us is willing to let you, Taru, and our children go there without heavy protection, my dear. With or without your permission, a battalion of Knights will accompany you." His anger grew as Daniel's had and his face was red despite having only communicated in thought.

"Do you actually think I would take my children to that planet unprotected, or even weakly protected? Do you honestly see me as some naive irresponsible fool, Alec?" Her face was flush as they stood toe-to-toe, staring hard at each other.

Sir Burke, Alec's brother, and a senior Knight, cleared his throat and asked, "Do you two wish to continue our discussion later?"

"No! We will discuss this until a plan is in place. Make yourselves comfortable, everyone," Morgan barked. She sat and did not look back at Alec as he took his seat.

"If you are ready to discuss the plan in a calm, respectful manner, please return so we can begin," she said to Daniel.

She leaned back in her chair, clasped her hands below her chin, and stared at the table in front of her until he was seated. As she leaned forward a hush fell over the group.

"As the question seems to have been raised, let me make something clear. I have no intention of letting my children on that planet until it is safe!" She paused and tried to calm herself, but failed. "Taru and I can prevent Hoge, Harrick, and Martus from detecting the presence of our troops. Without us blocking them, our troops' presence will be known within seconds. Our forces will be met by the Ceruk militia then have to endure a bloody battle to reach the portal. I am not willing to risk the lives of a hundred brethren to preserve my own, and I will not be told to do so when I have the skill to prevent it!

"I will be among the first to go through to Kalias so I can do my job. My job, Admirals!" she shouted, rising to her feet. "It is my duty to protect my family and my brethren as best my abilities allow. I do not care about the rest of your planning, but proceed knowing I will make absolutely sure those men and their dark magic come nowhere near my children!"

The room was silent as she calmed herself by force, sat back down, and shifted to lean on one elbow.

"Let's hear the options for the forces to be taken, the timing, and any other details necessary," she said as she scanned the shocked faces of the Knights around the table. She raised an eyebrow to Maric, who started offering methods of organizing the infiltration.

She refused to look at Alec or Daniel throughout the entire three- hour meeting. As the meeting adjourned, she rose and left without a word to either, while blocking their thoughts altogether. Alec followed her to the door but did not give chase as she bounded up the steps.

"Sorry, my friend," Daniel said to Alec once they were alone in the hallway. "I should not have spoken to her that way. She is right to be mad. Should I go apologize first, or are you headed that way?"

Alec rubbed his face with both hands and sighed as he watched Morgan return from their chambers and jog across Kindred Hall without glancing his way. "We wounded her with our quick assumption. Suggesting that she would not be fully cautious with the children is not an offense that a simple apology will fix."

"So what do we do? I can't just walk away knowing I hurt her."

"We apologize by showing her that we believe in her judgment. We must never make this mistake again. A sincere apology is warranted, of course. But we will have to wait for a while. She has no intention of being spoken to right now. She is blocking us completely," Alec said as he watched her disappear out the castle's main doors.

The two men turned to walk down the hall and heard a light laugh behind them. They turned to see Maric smiling.

"Our misfortune amuses you, Uncle?" Daniel asked. Maric clapped a hand to each of their shoulders and laughed louder.

"I have not seen her that mad in quite a while. The words did not have to be audible to know their content. You both have a great deal of groveling to do. Flowers are a good idea, my King." He walked on, still chuckling and smiling.

MORGAN EXITED THE CASTLE with her guard up to keep from venting her anger on anyone else. She had changed into running clothes and was set to take off when she heard the thoughts of a young boy.

"I bet Queen Morgan would make him stop if I told her. But, if he found out, he would hurt me even worse. She is so strong and smart. Maybe she could make him not want to hurt me anymore," the boy thought.

Morgan felt the profound sadness and fear within the boy. Her anger quickly found a new target. She moved through the streets seeking the boy and turned a corner just as his fear spiked.

Slap!

She could not believe her eyes. A huge man was raising his hand to slap the boy a second time.

"Hold!" She used her magic to stop him and hold him still as she approached.

She did not yell or even speak as she opened a hand to the boy, who dashed to her side and buried his teary face in her shirt.

It was all she could do not to act as she looked into the hateful eyes of the man before her.

"Maric, please send a few Knights to arrest a man in front of the butcher's. I will see to him until they arrive."

"You are safe now. Please wait for me on the walk for a moment. I will be right back," she said to the boy as she passed calming, loving feelings to him. He moved to the walk and huddled by the wall as he glanced between her and his enraged father.

She turned and walked toward the belligerent man at a slow gait.

"I will release your arm. Then, you will be taken to the holding cell of the castle until I consider your crime fully. If I find what I expect to when I search the boy's memory, you will leave this country."

The man was straining hard against her hold, and his thoughts were as hateful as his expression.

"I feel your desire to strike me," she said as she released him and smirked. *"Take your best shot, you great coward."* He clenched his fists and shook with rage as his eyes left her and went to the boy. *"Oh, I see. It is only children you dare to strike."*

The man lunged at her with a howl of rage. She dodged, then tripped him to let him fall hard to the stone street. Many others who had heard the boy's wails moved in to help. She raised a hand to stop them while using her magic to restrain the man.

"Wait quietly until your escort arrives," she said as she forced him to kneel and cross his wrists and ankles behind him. The hateful man growled at being controlled. He fought and strained against her hold but could not move his legs or hands from their position. She ignored his hateful cursing as she moved to pick up the crying little boy.

He tucked his head into her shoulder, gasping and sputtering as he tried to talk. She passed calming energy to soothe him again.

"He is awful, but he is my father, my Queen. Can you make him better, so he will not be so mean anymore?"

"Better from what, Liam?"

"He likes wine and ale too much. It makes him mean. If he has none for a while, he is nice, like he was before Mother died. Please, can you make him better, Queen Morgan?"

Morgan's anger calmed a bit as she felt the love the boy had for the man. She searched the man and indeed found a heavy haze of inebriation over his senses.

"Liam, I will not allow him to hurt you again. He will not be with you for a while. Once he is sober, we will see if he has the strength and will to change his ways. For now, we will make a safe home for you in the castle, alright?"

Liam tried to smile but jumped as his father shouted.

"He is mine! You have no right telling me how to raise him. He is a brat and..."

Morgan stopped his hateful words by holding his jaw still and shut while walking away. The Knights arrived, so she released her hold and asked them to lock the man away in the dungeon with no alcohol of any kind until further notice.

She carried Liam to the castle and walked straight to Cara's room. Cara opened the door and took Liam without a word of question.

"He needs love and kindness, my friend," Morgan said.

"Well, what is your name, you handsome little fellow?" Cara asked with a subtle nod to Morgan as Liam answered. "I am Cara, and I am very glad to meet you, Liam. Would you like to play in a big warm bubbly bath?" Liam smiled and she moved toward the bathroom.

Morgan turned to find Alec staring at her with soft eyes.

"She is kind to care for him without question like that. We are fortunate to have such a friend," he said.

"Yes, we are. That is what I expect of all our brethren. The boy's father will change, or leave," Morgan said as she walked past him with her guard still blocking him. "Leave me be," she said as she felt him start to follow her.

ONCE OUTSIDE THE CASTLE, she broke into a slow run. As her muscles warmed she turned up the speed. She was now able to run at a fast pace for a long distance, and it was wonderful. It allowed her time away from everyone to think, and she relished the escape. With her child growing fast within her, she would soon have to stop running so hard. At the moment it was safe, so she pushed her body. As she reviewed Alec's presumptive comments she ran even faster.

She was about an hour into her run when she felt Nulian approaching. Her heart lifted as she felt the joy within her friend.

"I will lay my clutch this night. I will then be ready to travel to Kalias with you tomorrow," Nulian said.

"That is wonderful news. I am very happy for you and Gerzin. But no, I do not want you to leave them so soon. We will wait a bit longer," Morgan said.

"Will you sit with me, as you did with Balia?"

"Thank you, my Sister. You know how much I want to be with you for that time. Just call when you are ready and I will be with you in moments," Morgan said as she slowed her pace. *"I am ready for a rest. Which of the rivers near here is the best for a relaxing dip?"*

"There is a wonderful spot just to the south."

Morgan topped the hill and found Alec waiting for her by the small river.

"Hear him out, my Sister. He aches of guilt, and it pains me. Do it for me so I will not worry so on this special day," Nulian said.

"Nulian, please! You are far too fierce to play the fragile female, and not at all convincing!"

She stood on the ridge, looking down at the lone man sitting by the river. Though she was too far away for him to hear her, he turned around as he felt her presence.

He did not try to sway her with a large smile but held up a single white rose.

"Please forgive me, my love. I am very sorry for hurting you wi—"

"I often hold my tongue when you fail to give me due credit for my knowledge or my skill of magic because I recognize that only I truly appreciate either. But today you questioned my sense of responsibility to protect my children. That is not easily forgotten. The rose is lovely, and I appreciate the gesture. But I am not ready to fall back into your arms. Give me some space and time."

She turned to leave, then hesitated and turned back to him.

"Ask yourself why you would have even considered what you accused me of today. I would like to know where I failed to make you think, even for a second, that I would allow them to face such danger without the highest protection. To think that possible, you must think very little of me."

She was off in a flash, running again at full speed. Alec tried to call her but she blocked him.

"Please take him back, and leave me be for a while," she said to Nulian who still circled high above.

"Very well," Nulian said.

MORGAN RAN for many more miles before she stopped to rest near a cliff overlooking a beautiful valley to the south of the castle. She sat in peaceful silence and let her mind open to all the living things around her.

As she concentrated to find all of the spirits nearby, she felt a faint magic. There was a young teenage boy with his own magic hiding within the wooded valley below. He was moving to the west of her. She approached his spirit and found severe heartache, great anger, and considerable fear.

She moved down the mountain to get closer, then halted as she saw heavy bruising and deep cuts on his face and arms as well as blood soaking the back of his shirt. He limped through the rough terrain with great effort to be quiet, pausing often to see if he was being followed.

She had felt his type of magic on Erion before of course. It was the magic held within the people of a small country just west of the Chemerian border called Veridan. She was aware the country was fraught with civil unrest but knew little else.

"Hello, young man. I see you are injured, and I feel your fear. I am Queen Morgan of Chemerie. I offer you help and safe refuge."

At the sound of her words in his head, he dropped to the ground, looked all around, then took off at a sprint. She followed but kept her distance.

"Menkar, I know you wish to watch over me, but stay out of sight until I can calm this young man, please," she said.

"A search party comes this way from the west, my Queen. I sugges you move away from here at once," Menkar said.

"I am aware of the group, but I am not going to leave this boy to be injured again until I understand the circumstances. He has been tortured, my friend. I doubt that search party means him any good."

"I will await your call unless I feel the danger is too great to you, my Queen."

"Thank you. If I gain his trust we will need a ride home," Morgan said. She monitored the progress of the search party and confirmed the group to be around a dozen, few enough for her to handle if need be.

"Please, let me take you to safety. The large search party approaches and you have no hope of outrunning them on those injured legs. Feel the truth in my words, I mean you no harm and offer honest help and safety."

"Am I to believe you do not know who I am? Surely they have

offered you control of my country if you help to capture me and kill the rest of my family," the boy said.

Morgan had pushed trust and friendship to him, but he had a considerable guard in place and felt none of it. She felt the search party advancing and moved to catch the boy.

He was stunned by her speed as she approached. Aware that he could not escape, he turned and took a defensive fighting posture. He crouched and held his hands up as he stepped sideways away from her.

"You have a choice, young man. Go with the group approaching us, or come with me. I offer kindness, which is a bit more promising than what they offer. Please, trust me."

She offered a hand to him and waited for him to decide. He started to relax, then jumped at the sound of baying dogs within the search party.

"Menkar, come near enough to spook their dogs. That will stop their progress for a bit."

The boy started to back away, preparing to run.

"My friend will buy you time to escape by distracting the dogs with his presence. You need to move now if you have any hope of escape on foot. Go to the north and reach the river. Use it to travel faster away from them. There is a small village about seven miles downriver. The people there are of pure spirit."

The boy ran away for many steps, then stopped and looked back. "Thank you for your help. I am sorry I cannot trust further, but trust has led to my father and mother being murdered. I am not ready to trust again."

He turned and ran at full speed to the north as she had suggested. She followed just out of sight, intending to watch his interaction with the party and learn more of his situation.

"This is a well-armed party, my Queen. Shall I disperse them for you, or would you like to deal with them as a tight group?"

Menkar asked. She smiled at his amusement in the game of herding the group of men around.

"Just back away and let them come straight at him as a group."

She moved to the side and out of sight of the boy's path while tracking him and the party chasing him. The boy tripped and slowed many times, which allowed the party to catch up. She settled above him on a rocky cliff as the party moved in to surround him.

He did not cower or beg for mercy as the group of men moved closer.

"Cowards! Killing my parents as they slept was not enough for you? What more do you want, Cregan?"

A tall, lanky man stepped from the group carrying a look of menace and conceit.

"I want to be assured of my crown, little cousin. And you and your magic offer a risk I will not accept. You will die at my hand, and I will take your power as you take your last breath," Cregan said as he stepped forward drawing his sword.

Morgan dropped down to land between him and the boy.

"I think not. You have crossed into Chemerie, gentlemen. I will not allow you to harm this boy. Leave him be, and I will not harm you."

Cregan and his men looked at each other and at her. They started to laugh as they surveyed this unarmed woman wearing sweaty clothes. Cregan stepped forward and raised his sword to her chest.

"I fear no one! Especially not a feeble fema—" Cregan started to say.

"Female? Yes," she said as she stopped his tongue. "Feeble? Hardly!" She made him kneel before her and offer his sword. She also stopped the men of his group by holding them still. The dogs followed her request as well and lay down.

"It is time you all leave Chemerie. You are not welcome here," she said as she moved forward to take the sword from Cregan's hand. She made him stand and walk backward for many paces before releasing her hold on him.

He stared in disbelief as she smiled and gave a little bow. When he charged, she stopped his feet, making him land hard in the dirt at her feet. She held him still as she knelt to look him in the eye.

"You cannot beat me, and the amount of humiliation you receive in front of your men is up to you. Now, leave this country or insult will turn to injury." She stepped away and allowed him to stand on his own.

"You will pay for this, Woman. You have defied the new King of Veridan. You will pay," Cregan snarled. He backed away and ordered his men to do the same. They filed out of the area and turned to leave as they questioned their leader in angry voices.

"Do you now trust that I mean you no harm? Will you accompany me back to the castle, so I may help you?" she asked the boy. She felt his answer and said, "Jump up to ride on my back so we can get clear of them. They are attempting to surround us again."

"My Lady, I am much too heavy for you to carry. I am fine and can carry myself."

Morgan shook her head as she picked him up, slung him over her shoulder, and took off. She headed toward a clearing nearby as she called to Menkar. He landed the second they cleared the wood line. The boy panicked and struggled to get clear of her grip. He yelled and writhed as they approached the dragon.

"Tell him to hold his tongue, my Queen. His noise is attracting the angry crowd."

"I doubt telling him will help!" She struggled to hold the strong young man until he looked at Menkar and froze.

"Did that beast just speak to you?"

"Yes, he did. He wishes for you to be quiet, and I agree!" She leapt to climb up Menkar's leg but was thrown sideways as the boy gave a kick off of Menkar in panic. They both landed hard on the ground, and Menkar growled as he moved to put his snout between them.

"Are you alright, my Queen?" Menkar asked. Morgan rubbed her back and belly but found all to be well with her and the child within her. She turned and glared at the boy.

"What is your problem, boy? I try to help you, and you fight me! Do you want to be killed by your crazy cousin?"

The boy was pale and trembling as he stared at Menkar, who had his snout against his abdomen, pinning him to the ground.

"Please, do not let it kill me. I will join you. I swear it. I will be no further trouble, my Lady." Morgan patted Menkar until he lifted his snout off of the boy.

"This dragon is my friend and will not hurt you unless you try to hurt me. If you come with me, it is by choice and not out of fear of either of us. Now choose! The men approach again." She turned and leapt up to the saddle.

"What a choice, a murderous cousin or a vicious dragon. May the magic keep me," he thought as he stood. He glanced between Menkar and the woods behind him then bowed to her.

"My heart says to trust you. May I come aboard, my Lady?"

"Yes. Step into Menkar's palm. He will lift you."

Menkar offered a palm, and the boy swallowed hard at the sight of the long talons curling around it. He glanced at her then checked his fear to climb up and kneel in the middle of the great talons.

He soon settled behind her, and they were off. He did not wrap his arms around her, choosing instead to grip the saddle's rear bolster and clench his legs.

"May I have your hand so I can relieve your pain?"

"I have heard of the healing power of the Chemerians, but my real pain cannot be healed. I have to find my older brother and warn him of the treachery at home. He is returning within the week and will surely be killed if they find him first."

"If you will share his essence with me, I can locate and warn him for you. You will have to bond to me to do so. It is an intense feeling. Are you willing to try?"

"If you can save my brother, I will endure any pain necessary. What must I do?"

"Only take my hand," she said as she turned to smile at him. She held up a hand, and he stared at the dragon in her palm for a second before taking hold. He took a sharp breath and shivered at her touch.

"You carry considerable magic, but do not use it. Why is that?"

"It is forbidden to use the magic before your age of Lordship. I am not yet old enough to train, my Lady." She lifted an eyebrow but held her rebuttal for later.

"Once I deepen the connection to bonding you need to think of your brother and his spirit."

He nodded and closed his eyes. She went as gently as she could and focused on his thoughts of his brother.

She then reached far into the bonding to examine the spirit of the boy before allowing him entry into her country. She found his spirit to be kind and noble. There were many scars left from torture with dark magic, but he carried none. His magic was pure and unique to any she had ever felt.

When she broke the bonding and dropped to connection. He cringed as his pain returned. Her push of healing energy made him gasp, so she eased the rate of transfer to heal the worst of his wounds before breaking the connection.

"Thank you for the healing. It felt wonderful, my Lady. Can you now find my brother?"

"I will try, Qaleb."

He raised an eyebrow at her knowing his name. She smiled as she turned back to face the direction they were flying and opened herself to feel magic further away.

"In what direction shall I start searching, Qaleb?"

"The southwest, near the oceanside, he was taking a vacation after his seventeenth birthday and Quickening ceremony."

She searched the area and found a group of three young men and approached each. The youngest of the three was Qaleb's brother.

"I believe I have found him. I can connect to him and let you talk through me if you wish." She offered a hand to him with a smile. He took it without pause this time, then shivered a bit as she connected to him.

"When I squeeze your hand, speak to him naturally. He will hear you."

She connected to the young man far away and gave Qaleb a squeeze.

"Sean, it is Qaleb. Can you understand me?"

Morgan felt shock from Sean, then adjusted her guard as she felt profound anger welling within him. She was careful to allow nothing beyond basic communication.

"I am speaking through a new magical friend from Chemerie. Sean, you must be careful, and you cannot return to the castle. Cregan has murdered Mother and Father and has assumed the throne for himself. He would have killed me as well if this new friend had not shown up. Sean, he will kill you on sight. Meet me somewhere, please."

Morgan was troubled by the lack of surprise she felt from Sean and was then sickened by his response.

"Qaleb, you fool! Of course, they are dead! After everything your dear father did to us, do you expect I would allow him to rule another day once I had full use of my power? Cregan, my blood-cousin, acts on my order. I am the one who had them killed!

"Our only bond died with our useless mother. I bear no loyalty to you. Either return to Veridan and kneel to me as your King, or never let me see your face again."

Morgan broke the connection and Qaleb let go of her hand. He turned around in his seat and cried in complete silence. She tried to ease his anger and heartbreak by passing gentle feelings of support and friendship as they flew on.

As they approached the castle, she connected to Alec to inform him of everything that had happened and he agreed they should help the boy and offer him a home.

"What of the darkness within him? Will you need to assess i—"

"Shockingly, I actually did think to check! It was scarring only. His spirit is pure and he poses no threat to our brethren!" She took a long moment to calm herself before continuing. *"I will speak with him more before introducing him to anyone else. If you would like to join us, we will be at the lake in about ten minutes."*

"I will be there, my Queen," Alec said. His annoyance with her temper and sarcasm came across quite clearly through their link.

18

A Taking of Eggs

WELCOME TO CHEMERIE, Qaleb. As I told you earlier, I am Morgan, the current Queen. You will meet my husband, King Alec, when we land," Morgan said as they approached the castle.

"Thank you for the kindness. I will be no trouble to you or your King before I leave, my Lady."

"Qaleb, please accept my offer of safe refuge until you are healed and rested, at least."

"That is very kind of you. I am a bit lost in this. I will never serve Sean. I cannot return to Veridan until my magic quickens." He rubbed his face hard and mumbled a curse. "I truly am a fool. I thought he cared for me and our mother. I once thought I felt the darkness within him, but my father said I was wrong and punished me for the accusation."

"We are about to land. Please turn back around and hold on a bit more securely. Menkar is quite gentle, but I prefer to be safe," Morgan said. When Qaleb turned, Morgan felt his awe as he first saw the castle and city of Chemerie.

They landed near the lake where Alec awaited them. Morgan helped Qaleb dismount and the boy moved to the water. He knelt and filled his hands to drink.

"Do not drink that, Qaleb. I will have a proper meal for you soon. Please, come and meet my husband."

He glanced toward Alec, hurried to wash his hands, then dried them on his pants. It proved pointless since his entire body was filthy, but the attempt at manners was noted all the same. He moved to stand before Alec where he dropped to one knee and bowed his head.

"I am prin— Qaleb, of Veridan. I am thankful for your Queen's kindness. I ask that you not punish her for the decision to bring me here, your Highness. I will be no trouble and will leave your land at once if you wish."

"Young man, you have a very wrong impression of our relationship. My Queen does not answer to me. You are welcomed by her, and therefore welcomed by us all."

Qaleb looked between the couple as he stood and took a step back. "Do you mean to say she is the dominant mate, that it is she who rules this country, and not you, Sir?" Qaleb asked. Alec nodded with a smile.

"That is right. I am King only because I was fortunate enough to be the magical mate to the Caretaker and Queen. She is the leader of our people, and I humbly serve her in that station. We discuss most things together, of course. However, she is the leader of Chemerie."

"OK, now you are forgiven, my mate," Morgan said as pride filled her heart. He took her hand with a warm smile.

Qaleb backed up as he stared at Morgan with a deep frown. "What about that makes you so fearful and angry?" she asked.

"I must take my leave now. Thank you for your hospitality," Qaleb said. He turned to bolt but found the cliffs around the lake were far too high to scale. The only opening out of the small cavern was blocked by the stretched out Menkar.

"You can go if you wish, but please tell me why you are suddenly afraid of me?"

"No woman could rule a country when a man stands by her side. I do not know why you lie, but I am safer alone than among those who would deceive me."

Morgan felt the truth in his belief that they were deceiving him. "Qaleb, it is clear we are accustomed to very different views of relationships and the role of women in society. Neither my mate nor I have lied to you. Use your magic, my friend. Do you feel deception from me as I tell you this?"

"I cannot use it yet. It is forbidden and...I am unable."

"There is no reason why you should not use the gift of magic if you carry it. I am sorry to know you have been kept from this gift for so long. Please, allow us to show you that we do not lie. What proof do you need?"

"If a man will follow your order over your King's, then I will believe you. Neither can use magic to coerce the man's actions."

"I have a problem with that request. I do not give orders, except in times of battle, and rarely even then. I am sorry, but that is not the way we live. We are not Lords who force our will on our people. We serve our brethren, and they choose to serve us in return. They put their trust in me to wield the magic in the best interest of our country."

At that point, a housemaid arrived with a tray of food. "Thank you, Alaina," she said.

Alaina set the tray beside her with a curtsy then withdrew. Qaleb held his stern facade despite the hunger that gnawed at him as he glanced at the food.

"The plate is for you. Please enjoy it while we talk privately," she said as she took Alec's arm and directed him away along the bank. Only after they were many feet away did the starving boy move to the tray and begin to eat.

"I understand he has had a difficult time, but to refuse the kindness you offer, and to be so disrespectful, is ridiculous," Alec said.

"You may see it as disrespectful, but Qaleb is accustomed to a woman being in the background, barely seen and never heard. It reminds me of a few cultures on Earth. Equality is an ideal their country has no concept of. It seems impossible to him that the position of power within our society has always been held by a woman."

Alec wore a frown of annoyance as he watched Qaleb.

"Give him a chance to adjust before you judge him as disrespectful. And by the way, I see us as equals, my love. I do not see you as a humble servant."

He smiled and kissed her cheek. *"I know. I was merely laying out the structure and not our personal view of it."*

They walked back to Qaleb, and he resumed his stiff, formal stance.

"Thank you for the food, Sir," he said to Alec.

"Thank us by letting my Queen prove her honesty through touch."

"Yes, Sir," Qaleb said as he held out a hand as if waiting for it to get slapped. Morgan stepped forward and brought her palm up to his to pass feelings of friendship and trust.

"I am sorry for your loss, Qaleb, and I want to help you. Feel the truth in my words as I tell you that we are not deceiving you in any way, and both welcome you into our home."

Qaleb did not pull away. He stared at her as the frown left his face.

"You felt the truth in my words, I see. Your magic recognized mine."

"I do feel it, my Lady. I feel that you speak the truth. I apologize for not trusting your word. And thank you for allowing me safe refuge in your home."

He had pulled his hand away with a glance at Alec and took

another step back as he rubbed it to relieve the tingle her touch left behind.

Morgan took Alec's arm and the three walked toward the castle.

"Do you have children, your Highnesses?"

"We have twins, a son and a daughter. You will meet them soon," Morgan said.

Qaleb's face showed the profound grief inside him as they walked on.

"Will you be offering that he live here for as long as he likes?" Alec asked.

"I will later, of course. He has had enough for today."

"Are you still hungry, Qaleb?" Alec asked. "We are about to have dinner ourselves and ask you to join us. You can meet our family."

Qaleb looked at his clothing and blushed a bit.

"I would never sit at a table like this, Sir. May I impose further to clean up before joining you?"

Alec laughed and said, "It is no imposition. I would have insisted, had you not asked."

"I am afraid I will not be joining you at dinner just yet. I will be with Nulian as she lays her clutch, my dear," Morgan said. She kissed Alec's cheek and nodded to Qaleb before taking off at a run toward the lower entrance to the dragon chamber.

"She is very swift, your Highness," Qaleb said as he watched her speed across the lawn.

"Yes, she is, indeed," Alec said with a smirk as he saw the obvious attraction the young man had for his wife.

Once they reached the castle, Alec asked a page to arrange for Qaleb to have a bath and a change of clothes. He then sought his children.

ALEC FOUND the twins playing a board game with Iz in the main sitting room and joined the fun. He teamed with Iz against the twins and made them promise not to cheat with the magic.

"You cannot turn off a river, Father," Brya said.

"Do you mean to say you could not block one another as your mother does, even now after your Quickening has begun?"

Brya and Kyan looked at each other and smiled. "We have never tried," they answered together.

"Really?" Iz said in a skeptical tone. "You mean to say that you share all your thoughts, even now, as you are maturing so fast?"

"We have no secrets," Brya said as she glared at Iz.

Iz felt the chill in that answer and glanced at Alec before looking back to the game board. Brya turned to Kyan, who was scowling at her. She looked away with a shrug, and he dropped his game pieces on the table with a clang as he stood up.

"Father, will you permit me to take Iz for a flight with Menkar? He is napping on the lawn, but offered to take us earlier."

"Certainly, but make it a short one. We will have dinner in an hour."

Kyan offered a hand to Iz as she rose and held it as they walked out together. He was near her height now but still appeared at least two years younger. Alec smiled as he noticed the hand holding.

He turned back to see the very red face of Brya, who was staring after them with her eyes brightly aglow.

"Say it. Tell me how mad you are that he is now blocking you out of anger at the way you spoke to Iz."

Brya shot to her feet and started for the door.

"Hold! Come back and sit down." She moved to sit beside him and plopped down with a huff. "Calm yourself, please."

She closed her eyes and forced herself to calm, then turned to him with less of a scowl.

"You deserve to be blocked. That was very rude." She dropped her eyes but still scowled. "I expect he asked that you apologize, and you refused. Am I correct?"

She nodded as she fidgeted with the game pieces. He moved to pull her into his side and gave her a few seconds to calm some more.

"What made you say that so hatefully? Think about it a moment before you answer."

"She assumed that Kyan would block me to keep thoughts of her away from me. He keeps nothing from me, and I do not want him to. Not even things about her."

"You cannot mean that, my dear. He will have a very intimate relationship with Iz when they marry. Surely you do not want to have that type of information shared all the time."

"Why not? It is perfectly natural to want to touch your mate. I am not embarrassed by his desires for Iz. I understand he wants to grow so she will see him as an attractive man, not as a little boy. He wants her to want to touch him. That is natural. I do not understand why she would expect him to block me from it."

Alec was about to call Morgan in for a rescue when Brya sat straight up to stare at the door. She sprang to her feet and bolted from the room. Alec followed and saw Kyan dash through a side door to Kindred Hall with Iz right behind.

"What is it?" Alec asked as he felt fear in them both.

"GranNulian is afraid, very afraid."

The twins ran hard across the length of Kindred Hall, then slowed just before reaching the door to the dragon chambers. They stopped, both fighting tears as Kyan took Brya into his arms.

"Father, Mother would like for you to join her. Take your sword with you," Kyan said. Alec moved without question.

"What is wrong, my friends?" Iz asked as she moved closer to them.

"GranNulian is having great difficulty with a laying," Brya answered through sobs.

"I will go and give you privacy," Iz said as she turned away.

"No, please stay with us, Iz. You are a great comfort...to both of us," Brya said. Iz looked surprised but hugged them both tight against her.

MORGAN HAD ARRIVED to find Nulian in the largest room of the dragon chambers. She was lying under the heated waterfall Morgan had installed to comfort the largest brooding females who could not fit within the smaller pool room.

Nulian was in considerable pain and was trembling. Morgan soothed the pain and Nulian breathed deeper as she relaxed.

"You should have called me sooner," Morgan said as she moved toward her belly without taking her hand off her body.

"Pain is normal, but this is not, my Caretaker."

Morgan laid her hands to Nulian's lower abdomen over a battle scar to check the eggs' progress. She found the reason for Nulian's severe pain and her heart ached.

"What have you seen?"

Morgan moved back to her head and stroked her.

"When I healed the awful wound to your abdomen last year, I had to remove some tissue that was too damaged. It mended in such a way that the passage is too small for your large eggs. That section of the birth canal cannot accommodate them, my dear."

Nulian crooned a sad sound as she curled to touch her snout to her belly where her eggs lay. She was quiet for a few seconds then touched her snout to Morgan.

"You must take them, my Caretaker. Please, I do not want to lose them."

Morgan caressed her dearest friend as she accepted what she must do.

"Do you want to have the children or Taru help control the pain while I work? I will not be efficient at both, my dear."

"No. Gerzin will offer his healing song, and I would like King Alec to join and offer help to you. I do not want the children here for this, my Sister. They have many years to learn of such difficulties. They do not need their first laying to be this memory."

Morgan felt the children approaching and stopped them as she explained the situation. Nulian had summoned Gerzin, and they heard his talons clicking on the stone floor of the entry hall already. He must have been waiting just outside the chamber entrance. He was humming as he entered and moved to wrap his neck around Nulian's and support her weight as she leaned into him. She gave a sweet croon, and they hummed together for a moment as they connected.

Alec entered soon after Gerzin and moved to Morgan's side.

"My heart does not want to know why you need my sword, does it, my dear?"

"No. When I healed her wound last year, I could not mend it properly. She will now suffer because of it. I will wield the sword, so no one else has to fe—" Alec held the hilt of the sword firm as she reached for it and met her eyes with a stern expression as he took her hand in his.

"You hurt for her, of course. But I will not have you blaming yourself for the damage done to her. You saved her life and pre-served her ability to carry another clutch. Today, you serve her further by saving her hatchlings. There is no reason for you to do so alone, however. Show me where to cut, and let me do it for you, please. You can then focus on the eggs and heal her as quickly as possible." He squeezed her hand as he looked into her eyes. She nod-ded and turned to Nulian and Gerzin.

"I will move to be safe and efficient, my Sister. Ready yourself. Gerzin, you will need to move so you can hold her still while the inci-sion is made and I remove the eggs. Give her all your healing strength. I will join you when I have removed the eggs. My Sister, are you sure you do not want Taru to help with this? Your pain would be far less."

"I need only you, my Caretaker," Nulian said as she rolled to her side to expose her belly fully to Morgan. Gerzin shifted to use his bodyweight to keep her still. She grunted, he lifted a bit, then she made him lie back down.

"I am ready, my Sister," Nulian said. She looked away and Gerzin's healing song resounded in the chamber as he laid his snout to her chest.

Morgan placed the point of the sword at the top end of the incision and traced the line for Alec.

"Only a few inches in. Quick, but careful, my dear."

Alec set his jaw as he nodded. He held the sword with one hand on the hilt and the other half-way down the blade for precise control of the path and depth of the cut.

Morgan kept a hand to Nulian so she could flood her with healing energy blocking her pain as long as she could. She nodded for Alec to begin and pushed a bolster of reassurance. He had to force the blade through the tough hide of her underbelly. It took great force to cut the thick layer in a controlled manner. He moved as fast as he could while maintaining control of the blade. She moved in behind him with her small knife to cut through the finer layers to reach the eggs.

The instant she took her hand from Nulian's body to reach for the first egg, the dragon gave a great roar of pain and lurched, slamming her body against theirs. Alec lost his footing against her thigh, and the blade plunged in too deep. His face blanched, and he was near vomiting as he felt the blade scrape against shell.

Morgan kept moving her blade along to reach and remove the eggs through a clean slit in the birth canal. She removed the egg Alec had pierced and laid it to the side of the others without comment. Once all the eggs were removed, she placed a hand to each side of the great wound and focused to seal it.

Alec had fallen to his knees, shaking as he stared at the damaged egg. She felt his anguish, but could not help him while focusing to split her efforts between lessening Nulian's pain and closing the wound as cleanly as possible.

Soon, the inner layers of the wound were knitted and the bleeding stopped. Nulian's muscles relaxed and her breathing calmed with her heart rate. Morgan continued to pass healing energy until the wound was sealed and she felt no discomfort from Nulian. Once her friend was at ease, she moved to Alec and knelt beside him.

"The twins told us that one of the eggs would not survive. We had no idea this was how it would occur, so I did not think to warn you. We thought it would simply never hatch. I am sorry for the pain it causes you, but know that Nulian and Gerzin did expect to lose one of this clutch."

He looked up with a grief-stricken face and tried to speak, but failed. He dropped his head and wept. Gerzin dropped his head to Alec and nudged him hard. Alec fell to the side without a fight, thinking Gerzin was angry with him.

"Thank you, my King. You did a very difficult thing and saved the lives of three of our clutch. I am in your debt, my friend," Gerzin said. He nudged Alec and scooted him along the ground until Alec relaxed and patted him.

"I am glad to have been of help, and I am very sor—" Alec said. Nulian stopped him with a harsh snort.

"No more apologies from either of you. We are so blessed to have the gift of your friendship and are tired of you expecting perfection in all you do for us. We love you and are grateful for all we share. Now, move over so I may see my new clutch properly."

She pushed Gerzin's head up, and Alec to the side, so she could nudge the eggs into a tight group with her snout. Morgan sat against her and rested with a smile on her face.

"You were very quick, my Sister. I noticed your effort to control my pain with every touch of your flesh to mine as you worked. Thank you, Morgan. You are a wonderful Caretaker and a wonderful friend." She set her head beside her and the eggs with a deep croon to both.

Morgan laid her body across Nulian's snout and peered at the gorgeous eggs as they all sang the Song of Connection together. Alec had sat beside Gerzin and was rubbing him as he stared at Morgan. She felt his gaze and met it with one of equal intensity.

"Thank you for helping me."

"Thank you for letting me."

They sat with Nulian and Gerzin for a long time before starting to yawn.

"You worked very hard for us, my Sister. Go eat, then rest. I am fine now. Thank you both for helping our new little ones into this world. I look forward to your Quickening of them soon, my Caretaker."

They all exchanged goodnights, and Morgan started climbing the stairs. Alec followed in silence until they were alone, then caught up to pull her into his arms.

"I am so sorry for my ignorant words this morning. Say you have truly forgiven me, my love. I need to know your heart is no longer aching from my thoughtlessness."

"You are fully forgiven, my love," she said as she shifted to kiss him softly. She deepened their connection and pushed them into bonding to let their link soothe them both for a few minutes before joining the others.

"WE NEED TO TELL THE CHILDREN. Let's do it in person," Morgan said.

"Fair warning," Alec said with a light chuckle. "It seems our daughter is officially a teenager with all the bells and whistles that includes. You should have seen the temper and attitude coming out of her today."

"Yes, puberty is going to be fast and furious for them both. Imagine cramming all of that weirdness and coming-of-age stress into a few weeks or months. We will be lucky if their magic does not get away with their tempers at least once." They both laughed as she sent relaxing, loving sensations to the children who awaited them in the dining room.

"Also, Qaleb is still bruised and seems to harbor pain, my dear," Alec said. "I mention it only to ask if he can block you at all with his magic."

"I am aware of his pain and will heal him soon. Surely he will be fine with holding my hand." She wore a wicked smile as she felt jealousy rise in her husband.

"He is far too young for you, my dear. He is no threat to me," Alec said. She giggled and elbowed him in the stomach.

They entered the dining room, and both of the twins moved to hug them tight. She explained the general event without any details and asked them to return to the table.

Daniel and Taru were staring at her and Alec with mingled disgust and amusement.

"What is it?" Morgan asked.

"My Caretaker, you are covered in blood," Daniel said.

They apologized and left in a flash to change clothes before returning to the dining room.

WHEN THEY RETURNED to the dining hall, most of the large family had left. The twins, Iz, Daniel, Taru, and GranMay were still chatting with each other and Qaleb. When Daniel leaned over and kissed Taru on the cheek, Qaleb watched with interest, then looked away quickly.

"You have competition," Alec said with a raised eyebrow as he glanced between Qaleb and Taru. Morgan could not help a small laugh escaping. It got the attention of many, including GranMay.

"Have you spoken to Qaleb yet?" Morgan asked GranMay.

"He is a very sad young man but has not had much to say. He watches, listens, and learns, however. What happened to him to make him so skeptical of everything around him?" Morgan explained

all she knew as GranMay watched him. *"I have heard rumors about Veridan all my life. It is said to house a bloodline of dark magic as well as one of pure magic. Did you find evidence of darkness within him?"*

"Yes, he has substantial scarring. He has been injured by it many times in his short life."

"The boy is nearing sixteen, though he looks far younger, my dear. He made his age clear to Brya earlier when she tried to speak with him. He has no respect for women, and it has ruffled Brya's feathers something awful."

Qaleb had been watching the silent exchange between the two women.

"Is the elder female your mother, Queen Morgan?"

"No, she is my dear grandmother. She served as Queen and Caretaker before my mother. Address her as Queen May," Morgan said. He bowed his head to GranMay, who nodded with a smile.

"Why do you still refer to her as Queen, if you are now the rightful Queen?" he asked in a quieter tone.

"Once a Queen of Chemerie, always a Queen of Chemerie. She will always be given the respect she has earned for her service to our brethren." He nodded but still looked confused.

"What is the tradition in your country when a King or Queen steps back to allow the younger to carry the burden of service? Do they not remain a respected part of the country's leadership?"

He looked down at his plate as anguish rose within him again. She realized too late what she had just asked.

"I am sorry. I did not mean to remind you of your loss, Qaleb. I cannot imagine your pain in losing a mother and father in the same day. While I cannot take that pain away, I can take the physical pain from you so you can rest tonight. Will you let me help you again?" He nodded so she held a hand out to him.

Qaleb glanced at Alec and did not move.

"My husband does not object to my healing anyone, young man. Now, take my hand and let me help you," Morgan said in a quiet yet stern voice. Qaleb slowly moved his hand up but still looked to Alec for a nod of permission.

"Do not give him that gesture. He will have to come to terms with our structure and respect me," Morgan said to Alec.

"Now who is making rude assumptions, my dear? I would never have done that," Alec fired back. Qaleb misunderstood when he saw that irritation cross Alec's face. He redirected his hand to lift his glass and take a drink. Morgan withdrew her hand and did not offer again for the remainder of her meal.

A few moments later, Daniel rose and came to kneel at her side, offering her his hand.

"I think I broke my finger training today. Taru asks that you check it because she found nothing. I think there is something wrong because it hurts something wicked."

She laid a hand to his and healed it in seconds.

"It was not broken, but you tore some ligaments and tendons. You really should train more responsibly," she said as she rustled his hair.

"Yes, Mother," he said as he rose and kissed her on the forehead.

Alec choked on a laugh as he was taking a drink. Morgan saw what amused him when she noticed the shocked expression on Qaleb's face. She also laughed before she explained.

"Daniel is my brother. He was joking about me being his mother because I teased him."

The young man smiled a little before looking down at his plate again.

"Qaleb has stopped eating. He pushes his food around to be polite," Alec said to her.

"You must be exhausted, Qaleb. May my son show you to your room?"

Qaleb nodded to Daniel as if she was joking about him again.

Kyan stood and moved around the table to bow to Qaleb, who rose with a smile.

"Queen Morgan, you jest with me again. You are far too young a woman to have a son this old, my Lady."

"I assure you, she is my dear mother. It will take some explaining to help you see the reality of it, however. May I suggest we hold that conversation till tomorrow?" Kyan asked in his now deepening voice. Qaleb nodded then followed him out.

"Now you owe me an apology, my dear. And I intend to make you beg for forgiveness." Alec said as he gave his wife his most devilish wink.

The wine reminded Morgan of the little boy she had left with Cara and noticed they were not at the table. She felt guilty for forgetting and rose to go check on them.

"They are not there. Cara took him to see the dragon younglings, and they are still playing in the pool room," Alec said as he took her hand. "You do not have to do everything yourself. Let Cara handle the boy. She is enjoying it immensely."

"Has his father sobered up yet?"

"He will not be clear-headed enough to talk to for a couple of days. I am not sure I want to hear anything he has to say, however. When I think of him striking a boy, it makes me want to give him the same many times over."

"I nearly did this morning. I was already angry, and I taunted him into trying to hit me. I caught myself only at the last minute before laying into him."

"He tried to strike you? He tried to strike his Queen? Why did you not banish him immediately? There is no question as to the rightfulness of it."

"Liam. The boy loves his father and has no mother. I wanted to give the man the chance to change and be a suitable father to him."

Alec kissed her cheek and smiled as he shifted back. "There is that wonderful, selfless heart of yours again. You are an amazing woman, Queen Morgan."

"I think I like you addressing me formally again. I miss the days of 'my Queen' and 'yes, my Lady'."

"Done. Formal it is from now on, my Caretaker," Alec said. She lifted his hand and kissed it as she shook her head.

"No, I think not, my love. My heart would crumble."

He tugged her hand as he stood, and she followed. Everyone rose with them and headed off to bed. When they neared the children's room, they stopped and sighed as both felt a huge amount of anger from their children.

"What are they fighting about?" Alec asked. Morgan listened in on their conversation and was a little taken off guard.

"Privacy. Sounds like Kyan suggested separate rooms, and Brya is livid. She thinks it is because of Iz that he now pushes her away," Morgan said as they quickened their pace.

As they reached the twins' bedroom door, Brya was ranting and venting her anger using anything that had annoyed her about Iz in the last few weeks.

"I think it is time they have private rooms," Alec said. *"If Kyan is asking, then he is serious about it because he knew exactly how she would react. Of course, she is exploding at everything lately."*

"I agree, but let's leave them to work it out for a bit and see if they manage on their own." He nodded and they turned to enter their bedroom.

Just as they entered, embarrassment tore through Kyan as Brya

yelled, "Are you actually hoping to kiss her soon? You think of it constantly! You do realize that you are only a child to her and know she does not think of you that way, do you not, Brother?"

Alec knocked their door open and they both jumped. He moved to stand between them while glaring at Brya.

"Our room, Now!"

Brya huffed out with another harsh glare at Kyan. Alec gripped Kyan's shoulder to stop his angry response.

"She was wrong to say those things, Son. Let yourself calm, then ask why she would when she knows it will hurt you," Alec said. Kyan used the magic to calm himself and then thought hard.

"Jealousy. She is jealous of my having Iz and her not knowing her mate yet."

"That is a big part of it for certain. There is more as well. Do you not feel it within her?"

"Yes, I feel her changing and becoming a woman. That is why I have asked for a separate room, Father. The changes are making things very difficult in many ways. Her hormone surges have begun, and I find them unsettling. And then there are her thoughts of —" Kyan stopped as Alec raised his hands to protect his ears.

"Stop, please, have mercy on your poor father. Do not tell me this about my two-year-old daughter." Kyan smiled and relaxed a bit more. "You will have private rooms. Then, you can separate when you need to. Now, I need to go see if your mother is having to hold your sister down to talk to her. Mercy, females are explosive, are they not, my boy? Just this morning your mother's pregnancy elevated hormones helped her overreact to —" Alec squinted and stopped his comment. Kyan laughed out loud as he overheard Morgan's angry response.

Alec patted his son's shoulder before heading to his annoyed wife. "Now, you have two hormonal women to contend with. Good luck, Father," Kyan called after him.

Alec entered their chambers to find Brya asleep on the loveseat of the sitting room. He moved to Morgan, kissed her cheek, then gave her a very pitiful face. She smiled and pushed him off her.

He moved to Brya and stroked her hair as he kissed her forehead.

"She was exhausted and cried herself to sleep with no help from me," Morgan said.

"Why was she so tired?"

"She has been sneaking out at night to search the city for her mate. Her temper has risen because she is getting so anxious about finding him. She was also annoyed at being ignored by Qaleb earlier. Poor Kyan caught the brunt of it when he arrived upstairs."

"Sneaking out? Why? We would let her wander the city all day if she wanted to."

"She was embarrassed to discuss her desire to find him since we still view her as a child. And, she cannot sleep from worrying about it." Alec bent over and kissed Brya again then covered her with a blanket.

"Let's not wake her. They both need some sleep and some space."

"Only a few months ago they were panicking from being separated by more than thirty feet. My head still has trouble connecting them to the babies we held on Berios," Morgan said. "Toddlers to pre-teens in under a year is just too much to process properly for any of us."

MORGAN WENT TO visit with Nulian for a while and was returning for breakfast when she felt great annoyance from Brya again. She shook her head and moved faster to try and calm her before things got out of hand. She found the young adults in the dining room. Alec had already gone to work with the Knights in training exercises.

"What has you irritated now, my dear?" she asked Brya, who was eyeing Qaleb.

"Him! He is awful, Mother!"

"How is he awful, exactly?"

"He will not speak to me and barely answers me if I speak to him. I am about to show him just how annoyed I am!"

"No. You are going to be courteous and respectful, my dear."

She sat down and ate a light breakfast as the teenagers around her spoke of the similarities and differences in their two countries. She saw Brya's point in the way Qaleb spoke to Kyan without discomfort while avoiding eye contact with Brya or Iz when they spoke.

"Explain the reason you prefer not to talk to females, Qaleb," she said. "We need to understand before we take too much offense." Qaleb reddened as he glanced at her, Brya, and Iz, before refocusing on his plate.

"I am not accustomed to being spoken to by females, my Lady. Only my mother and sister were permitted to speak to my brother and me. Any woman who spoke to a Prince was punished." He looked at Brya and bowed his head as he said, "I am truly sorry if I have offended you, Princess Brya. I do not know how to address you properly, so I was keeping my words as simple as possible. I beg your pardon."

Brya nodded, blushed, and focused on her food again.

"Well, that explains a great deal about your behavior. I would say that it was good of you to answer Brya at all. I see it as an effort to adapt to our customs and appreciate it very much. Ours is a very different way of living than you are accustomed to. I expect there to be times when a misunderstanding will result. As long as we are open and honest, we will be fine."

Qaleb glanced at Brya, and Morgan felt his desire to talk to her again. Brya, however, noticed nothing of his feelings, having raised her guard high.

"I am going for a swim. Do you want to come, Kyan, and you, Iz?" Brya asked as she moved rather quickly from her seat and toward the door.

"Sure," Kyan said after a confused pause. He had felt something from her that spurred him out of his seat.

"Qaleb, could I offer you a tour of the city? I need to drop in on some friends this morning," Morgan said.

"COULD YOU PLEASE help me understand how you could be the mother of children entering their teens? You look to be only in your twenties, my Lady. The math makes no sense to me," Qaleb asked.

"The special magic they hold, and the uniqueness of their day of conception, has resulted in their advanced growth rate. You will never believe how old they really are. Try it. Take a guess."

"They appear to be only a bit younger than me. If you say advanced, then perhaps ten," he said with a shrug. She laughed and shook her head.

"Divide by five, and you are closer."

"That beautiful young woman has only been alive for two years?"

Morgan raised an eyebrow and smiled at him without saying anything. He walked on as if he had said nothing odd. She made small talk about the city for a bit before coming back to the subject.

"Does your magic allow for magical mates to detect one another through touch, as ours does?"

"I do not know."

"If you are never allowed to speak to a female, and obviously not touch one, then how do you find your mate?"

"The line of the Lordship is set by the reigning Lord. You marry whom you are told in order to preserve the magic of the line. Or at least that is the way it was for many years. My mother and father broke that tradition. He was her second husband after Sean's father died. That is not something that is normally done. But she could not very well say no to the Crown Prince when he declared her to be his intended mate. I was the new King's first son and heir to his thrown. I now understand that Sean has resented me for taking that from him."

"Did your father accept Sean as his son?"

"To a point. He referred to us both as son, but made it clear I was the blood-heir. Neither of us liked him because his punishments were so harsh and frequent. I did my best to satisfy him, for my mother's sake. I do not believe his spirit was dark altogether, however, his prideful temper was a horrible force."

"I removed much of the scarring his punishment left behind when we bonded. While I cannot speak to his true spirit, I must tell you that the scarring was quite dark."

Qaleb looked confused as he nodded, but asked no questions.

"As for my true mate, I have no idea whether I will recognize her before or after my magic Quickens. I am in no condition to marry, however. I have no country of my own and nothing to offer a wife. If I found her now, I would deny her until I could provide for her."

"You put too much on yourself, young man. A woman is perfectly capable of providing for herself. Also, if you feel a true magical link, you will be hard-pressed to deny it. It will take your heart, and the pull will be maddening."

"I have never heard of such a thing. All couples I have ever known lived a life of indifference, merely tolerating each other, little more than that. I truly hope I can witness what you describe, my Lady."

They walked through a busy section of the city where Morgan spoke with many Chemerians as Qaleb observed in silence. As they entered a less crowded area, she touched his arm to stop him.

"I want you to know that you have a home here as long as you wish, Qaleb. I do hope your magic guides you to stay."

"How do I do that? How do I let my magic guide me?"

"Well, you start with letting yourself use it to do small things until you get a feel for its basic form. Then, when you are comfortable, you will let us Quicken your magic, and you will gain full use of it."

"What type of things shall I do with it?"

"This conversation is one example. Communicate through it often and start working on using it from greater distances. There are many possibilities. I do not know the breadth and depth of your magic, so I will have to work with you a bit. Do you want to start learning to use it now?"

"Yes. Seeing the wonderful things you do with your magic has amazed me. Before meeting you, I had only seen magic used for

control of others and for punishment."

"I suspect that both of your parents carried a type of magic, and you received your mother's. Am I right in that assumption?"

"I have no idea what type of magic I have or they had, my Lady. No one ever spoke of it. Only the King and his adult sons wielded it, and only after their Quickening on their seventeenth birthday."

Morgan stopped walking and turned to look across the city.

"I must help a friend. Can you find your way back?"

"Certainly, is there anything wrong, my Lady?"

"Not at all. It is time to share my magic with a new spirit. See you later, my friend," she said with a smile. She turned and moved swiftly through the streets toward the castle as she felt the bewilderment in Qaleb at having been called "friend."

MORGAN MET ALEC outside the home of his sister, Emma. They knocked and smiled as Emma beamed at them.

"You heard me, Cousin?"

"It concerned me, and it was emotional. Of course, I heard it. Are you ready then?"

Emma moved to the side to let them in as she called Paul. He came in and stopped in surprise to have company. He wore no shirt and Morgan saw a bad cut on his ribs covered with salve.

She moved to him without asking and pulled her hand across the wound to heal it. Paul quivered at her touch. He had never felt her strong magic directly.

"Why did you not ask me to heal this earlier?"

"I did not want to trouble you, my Queen," he said as he looked down.

"That was a lie, Paul. You thought I was mad at you and Emma for not accepting the gift I offered. I admit I was disappointed, but I understood her fear. I will also admit that I did not understand your hesitance and would like to before we continue.

Tell me the truth, please."

"*I was scared, too. I have had little contact with the magic, and its power scared me. I am sor——*"

She interrupted him with a rush of friendship and forgiveness. He smiled at the sensation, and she winked at him before turning back to Emma.

"Ready, Cousin?"

"Absolutely. What would you like me to do?"

"Just relax and lie back in Paul's lap," she said as she gestured to the couch. Alec gave her a chair so she could be beside Emma without kneeling.

"Since your child is small yet, you will not feel its reaction as it wiggles. You will feel the intense sensation of the magic passing through you. Paul, take her hands, and you will feel it a bit as well."

Emma and Paul took hands and smiled as they nodded. She pulled Emma's shirt up and laid a hand flat to her lower belly, over the child within. She placed her other hand to her Crest to focus her magic.

She had to focus hard in order to isolate the spirit of the tiny fetus. Once she found it, she was able to bond with ease. She stacked both hands over the child and sang the Song of Initiation, as she now called it. Magic flowed to the child for a few moments. Once the little one could accept no more, she let the bonding break with a strong push of confidence and healing to comfort the nervous couple.

She opened her eyes to find Emma's face covered with tears. Emma sat up and wrapped her arms around her. The intense joy and gratitude flooding through her from her cousin brought tears to her own cheeks as they held each other.

"Thank you so much, Morgan. I love you very much."

"I love you too, Emma. I look forward to seeing that precious child in your arms."

Friends and Mates

MORGAN TRANSFERRED MAGIC to three more unborn children over the next two weeks. The twins accompanied her each time. Though they were eager to use their magic and strong enough to do so, she insisted they continue to simply learn for now.

One night she sat on the window seat of her bedroom with the window open to enjoy the breeze of the late evening. She stared out the window and felt Nulian try to connect, so she dropped her guard.

"Are you alright, my Sister? I see you sitting alone, and you block sadness I still see in your eyes. What troubles you so?"

Morgan smiled at her friend as she spotted her high upon the cliffs behind the castle. She was lying alongside Gerzin with her head over his back.

"I was about to meditate and see if there is anything else I missed concerning the completion of Quickening. I will complete the twins' Quickening this week and am not at all sure what to expect. They already have incredible access to knowledge passed

via their Crests. And they already have incredible use of their magic. I wonder what this will be like for them and me.

"With Taru, we saw an increase in her ability to use the magic, but I cannot imagine the twins using it any more effectively than they have since their Quickening began. What are your thoughts?"

Nulian was quiet for a moment as she considered it.

"I expect it will increase their depth, but not their breadth of magic. Their potential is great for developing skill comparable to yours, my friend."

"I love that they could be more powerful than I am. I am just worried about not being able to do this properly because of it."

"My Sister, you will do wonderfully. You have the greatest skill in wielding your magic that I have ever seen or heard of. You do not seem to appreciate just how strong you have become. You are stronger and more efficient than any of us imagined possible. To watch your children near your level of skill is wonderful for us all. However, while we imagine that the twins will each meet your level of control in some areas, we doubt either will surpass you overall. They have only seemed extraordinary because they were born with so much available to them, and have progressed so quickly."

The love and respect from Nulian made Morgan's heart warm and her cheeks blush.

"It is your gift that makes me strong. I can never thank you enough for all you have given my family. We, and all the people who benefit from it, are in your debt forever."

"Once again, you give yourself too little credit. The gift of dragon blood would not have given any other Caretaker the skill it did you. It was your own spirit that activated the magic so profoundly."

"I did not realize that. I assumed it was the magic of your blood within me that made it possible, and I was simply learning to recognize it."

"Are you planning to complete their Quickening alone, or with the help of Queen May and Lady Taru?"

"Perhaps it is selfish, or even foolish not to include either of them. Nevertheless, my heart is set on keeping this precious experience between me and my children."

"I understand completely. That is how it should be. I was going to suggest it myself. The connection will be intense, and it should only be the three who are linked by both the Caretaker bloodline and that of my gift. Queen May will understand, however, Lady Taru may see it as a lack of trust. I would be glad to speak to her, my friend."

"I wi— actually, yes, I would appreciate that. Thank you." They each shared loving friendship with the other as they said goodnight.

MORGAN WOKE to intense jealousy from Kyan. She walked out onto her balcony and saw Iz talking with Qaleb in the garden. They were walking at least three feet apart, and Qaleb was looking at his feet as they talked.

Morgan felt Kyan on the main terrace and his emotions were getting out of hand.

"They are only talking, Son. You must trust her."

"It is not her I do not trust. Qaleb has been watching her with interest since he first saw her," Kyan said.

"He may not know of your connection to her. You should speak to him about it in a rational mann—"

"I believe Iz is about to."

She and Kyan were both hit by strong emotion from the two in the garden. Each acted to listen in on their conversation.

"I do not care if you believe me or not, Qaleb. I have told you he is my magical mate, and I will marry him as soon as it is appropriate. When I do so, it will be because it is what my heart wants, not because

I am being told to!"

"But how can it be appropriate? He must be far less mature than you if he is but two years old. He may look older, but he is just a boy," Qaleb said.

Iz spun on him and her glare backed him up a step.

"That boy is already far more man than you! He would never question a woman if she declared her connection to another. Certainly not in a feeble attempt to save face for having been turned down for a date!"

Morgan felt the pride and joy in Kyan as he ran through the castle to catch Iz on the other side, out of sight of Qaleb.

She disconnected from him and Iz as she looked to Qaleb, who pretended to not notice her gaze.

"She is right to be angry, Qaleb. You should never have questioned her word. And yes, she is the magical mate of my son."

Qaleb turned to look at her as he dealt with shock and shame.

"I am sorry. I will never speak to her again," he said as he dropped his head and started to turn away.

"I am not asking that. However, you need to be more respectful of women, or you will have a very difficult life, young man."

She managed two strides back into the bedroom before she stumbled and almost fell over. Her head spun, and she flushed as she struggled to process the enormous emotional rush she had just felt within her son.

KYAN RAN through the castle at top speed in order to reach Iz as she crossed the lawn and moved around the back of the castle. He rounded the corner of the castle and slid to a stop right into her. He stood his tallest but still looked up a bit to meet her gaze as he caught his breath.

"I have never felt so much pride in my life, Iz. Thank you for those words."

Iz was still flush and her eyes bore into his.

"I will never deny my bond to you, Kyan. I am proud of our link and do not care if you always look younger than me. I meant it when I said you were more of a man than he is. You are far more mature in both mind and heart."

Kyan lifted her hand to his lips and kissed it as he held her eyes.

"I felt your jealousy as he spoke to me," she said. "You need not feel it, because you already have my heart."

As she leaned in to kiss his cheek, he shifted and kissed her on the lips instead. With her gasp and shiver he stepped back, released her hand, and dropped his head. She took his hand back and touched his chin to make him look up at her as she smiled. He gripped her hand tight as he shared his most sincere feelings. She looked away as her breath caught and her face reddened, then gave his hand a tug as she started walking. He fell in step wearing a mischievous smile.

ALEC SAT STRAIGHT UP in bed and looked at Morgan as she righted herself from the startling rush of emotions from Kyan. They both felt queasy, and neither was brave enough to voice what they had felt for a few seconds.

"I am guessing our son just had his first kiss, my dear. I sincerely hope his Quickening will enable him to keep such emotions to himself a bit better. You did say you meant to do that soon, correct?" Alec asked as he rubbed his face.

She nodded and swallowed hard as she fought to forget her son's personal feelings.

"Oh Yes! I think their birthday tomorrow is a perfect day for it."

THEY SOON JOINED the twins and Iz in the dining room for breakfast. Morgan glanced at Iz and she blushed. Alec avoided the eyes of both Iz and Kyan, focusing on Brya as he spoke.

"How do you feel this morning, my dear?"

She looked straight at Kyan and then Iz and paused before answering. Morgan was afraid she was about to be cruel again out of jealousy.

"I am fine, Father, and you?"

"That was very kind, my dear," Morgan said to Brya.

"I love them both and am happy for them. I realize how silly it was for me to put my frustration on them. It will not happen again," Brya said with a smile to Kyan.

"I feel the sadness behind your words," Morgan said. *"I realize this is difficult in many ways. Please, remember that I am here to listen anytime you want to talk."*

"It is difficult. I know I must let go for him to be closer to Iz. It is hard knowing we may never be as close in adulthood as we—" She stopped when Kyan's head shot up to look at her with pained eyes. He laid his fork down as he pushed against the guard she had just raised.

"Then I will speak aloud, my Sister. I love you as much as ever and have no intention of letting you go on any level. I would never ask that of you, nor could I stand it. Please, do not ever think that of me again," Kyan said. Brya's eyes were welling as she nodded.

Kyan gave Iz's hand a squeeze, then both twins got up and left together in silence. Iz watched them go with a smile then started to leave as well.

"Stay and finish your breakfast, my dear. We need to talk," Morgan said.

Iz's face went white as she looked down at her plate.

"No, I am not going to discuss that, it is not a problem. However, I will be completing my children's Quickening tomorrow and expect Kyan will be quite different afterward. I have a hunch this will accelerate their maturation even further, just as the initiation of Quickening did. Also, I would like for you to stand with Alec and the rest of our closest family."

"I would love to. Thank you, my Queen," Iz said as she blushed and smiled. "Do you expect it to be as painful as the initiation was?"

"I wish I knew that answer. This is a first for all of us. We will face what comes and do our best."

"Iz, you need not worry," Alec said as he gave Morgan a proud smile. "You have seen your Queen's skill. It always seems to match the challenge when need arises."

Morgan returned the smile for a few seconds, then sobered as her thoughts went to the amount of uncertainty she had to carry into this ceremony.

KYAN AND BRYA went to the garden gazebo and bonded deeply to one another. They had been angry too much lately and had not bonded in days. They each apologized for their harsh attitudes and forgave at once. While in the bonding, they shared all the little things they had learned in the last few days, and Kyan felt something new within his sister.

"Oh, Brya, you can now bear children. Congratulations."

"It is a wicked mixture of blessing and curse. The change has greatly increased my drive to find my mate. I have been focusing hard to block the feelings, but it is exhausting."

"Then that is a task we will accomplish together. We will find your mate, my Sister."

As they broke the bonding, Brya noticed they were being watched. Kyan did also and scowled as he started to turn a glare toward Qaleb.

"No, he is only curious and means nothing by it. I feel his desire to speak with you so I will go. Remember, he does not understand our culture, and did not mean to offend you by asking Iz for a date. Do not hurt him, Brother," she said with a wink. Kyan smiled as she stood and left. He stayed where he was and watched her until she entered the gardens.

"Please join me, Qaleb. We should talk," he said as he moved

to sit on the bench which circled the inside of the gazebo.

Qaleb entered the gazebo and bowed. He then stood straight and rigid as he looked over Kyan's head and not in his eyes.

"Please relax and have a seat. I appreciate the respect, but I would prefer you be yourself."

Qaleb sat and leaned forward with his elbows on his knees as he placed his palms together in front of him. "I beg your pardon for my words to your mate, Prince Kyan. I will never speak with her again if you wish it, your Highness."

"I would never ask that of you or her. She has the right to speak to anyone she wishes, as do you. I just want to make sure you now understand the nature of my connection to my mate, as well as that to my dear Sister."

"I have made no advance toward your sister, Prince Kyan."

"No, but I felt the jealousy from you as you watched us during our bonding a few moments ago. You are attracted to her, are you not?"

Qaleb looked to his hands and nodded a bit.

"My sister seeks her true mate and is quite focused on it. She will not be open to a simple date, I am afraid," Kyan said as he stood and stepped forward to pat Qaleb's shoulder. "Just saving you some trouble, my friend."

"HELLO, QALEB," Brya said as she fell into step with him that afternoon. "Where are you headed? Can I help you find anything?"

"Your father invited me to the training grounds." "I am headed there myself."

"May I walk with you?"

"Certainly, I welcome the company," Brya said. "Have you trained in sword fighting a great deal already?"

"Yes, I am told I am quite good. I would love to spar with someone and work off some tension if it could be arranged."

"I am sure it could," she said with a wicked smirk he did not see.

When they arrived at the training grounds, Alec met them with a smile.

"Would you like to get a bit of exercise through sparring, Qaleb?"

"Very much, Sir. May I fight one of your best swordsmen, so it is a good match?"

"Certainly, Brya seems available," Alec said. Qaleb looked between them and did not move to select a sword as Brya did.

"Sir, do you mean for me to spar with a female?"

Brya walked forward, took the sword Maric offered, and threw it to Qaleb without warning. She laughed a little as he fumbled it.

"Fight or get a sharp jab in the buttocks. Your choice, boy."

She raised her sword and moved in. Qaleb parried the lunge just in time to avoid the jab she had promised and turned on her with his sword raised.

"King Alec, as her father, do you truly approve of this match and allow me to proceed?"

"Just do your best, young man. No one here will be surprised when you lose," Alec said.

That was all the motivation Qaleb needed. He threw himself into the fight full force and attacked.

They fought at a furious pace for ten minutes with neither overwhelming the other.

"Hold! Break for a drink and cool down a bit," Alec called.

The two lowered their swords, but still stared into the eyes of the other. Knights brought each a drink and they took it without breaking eye contact. When Alec and the other Knights withdrew, they both raised their swords and gave eager smiles.

"Ready...Resume," Alec said.

They launched at each other again, and the level of aggression increased. They fought all over the training grounds as they lunged, parried, twisted, and turned, each trying to out-match the other. Many of the Knights and Squires had stopped their exercises to watch and cheer the intense match.

Kyan and Iz arrived. He tensed as he watched Brya.

"Uh Oh!"

"What worries you, Son?" Alec asked without looking away from the match.

"This is not good, Father. She is quite angry and is toying with him."

"That is exactly what I expected her to do. She has put up with a number of disrespectful comments. This is a good way to humble the boy and help him respect the power of women."

Kyan and Iz both wore wicked smiles similar to Alec's as they watched the contest. Just as Alec was about to stop the fight, Brya did an acrobatic move to flip over Qaleb, striking a harsh blow to his shoulder with the flat of her blade. It did not cut him, but he fell forward from the force of it.

As he hit the ground, he immediately swept her legs and knocked her to the ground. He leapt to land on top of her, but she raised her feet and threw him to the side just in time.

She came up with her sword held high and caught him under the neck as she moved to stand. She smiled as she put slight pressure on the blade.

"Do you yield, Sir?" she asked. His eyes flared, and he lurched to the side to free himself. He circled her again with his sword held high, and his neck bleeding down his chest.

"Let me heal that before we continue," she said as she lowered her sword and held out her free hand. He grabbed her wrist, pulled her off balance, and forced his blade to her neck. "That was not very gracious, Sir Qaleb. Do you intend to win that way, you coward?"

Qaleb growled at her and shoved her back. "Fine, continue then!"

"Enough. It is a draw this time around. You can fight again another day," Alec said as he started forward.

Neither lowered their sword until he stepped in between them and opened a hand to each. They both yielded and gave him their sword, but neither dropped the hard glare.

"May I heal your neck, my friend?" Kyan asked as he stepped up to them. Qaleb nodded, and continued to hold Brya's glowing eyes as Kyan closed the wound.

"Thank you, your Highness," Qaleb said as he shifted to bow to Kyan. "That was kind and painless." He then bowed to Iz. "Good afternoon, Lady Iz." He shifted, bowed once more to Alec, then left the training grounds without another glance at Brya.

"Egocentric buffoon!" Brya said as she headed off. "I am going to swim off some annoyance. See you all later."

BRYA SPRINTED across the lawn and hit the lake fully clothed. She swam hard and then dove under to swim in the quiet of the water. She was pulling along with long smooth strokes when Zirath rose from beneath to lift her to the surface with his body.

"Quit, you big goof. I am fine!"

"I still think of your near-drowning, my friend. It was too hard on my heart," he said. Brya gave in and laid her head on his neck as he scooted along the water.

"I love you too, Zirath. Sorry I snapped at you."

He crooned as they glided across the lake to the falls. Brya rolled into the water and moved to the rocks to sit under the falls. She let the water massage her shoulders as her mother often did, and it felt wonderful.

As her body and mind calmed, she felt someone watching her. Her annoyance shot right back up when she found it was Qaleb, the evil little man himself. She refused to look at him and fought to ignore his presence altogether.

QALEB WALKED FAST through the city as he struggled to calm down. He could not get her eyes out of his head. After a few minutes, he slowed down to wander through the gorgeous garden behind the castle. As he reached the back edge of the garden, he heard a loud splash in the lake, then watched as a young dragon surfaced carrying someone on his back.

His chest tightened as he realized it was Brya, then let out a breath as she moved and repositioned herself on the dragon's back.

He could not pull his eyes away and watched as she climbed from the water to sit under the falls.

"She is amazing. A young woman so physically strong that she held her own against me fighting my hardest. And she is so confident in her skill that she challenged me to start with. And her magic, she has amazing skill much like her mother. How can one woman be all those things and be so beautiful that I struggle to take my eyes from her? The man who is her mate is a fortunate spirit indeed."

BRYA COULD NOT HELP but overhear Qaleb's thoughts about her from so near with no warning to block him. She was careful to not look at him. Instead, she turned away as if readjusting how the water stuck her back and neck.

She smiled and blushed while acting oblivious to his presence until he moved away.

When she turned back around, Zirath was watching her with a cocked head.

"What?"

"You are blushing a great deal, my Princess. Did you hear the thoughts of the young man who was watching you?" Zirath asked.

"Yes, did you?"

"No, I would have to purposefully connect through touch to hear his words. Were they good words or bad words he spoke?"

"To my utter amazement, they were good words, my friend."

She dove in and swam for the opposite shore, where she found her mother awaiting her with a small smile.

Brya walked to her and hugged her.

"I expect you heard those flattering comments, just as I did?" Morgan asked.

"Yes, and I find it hilarious," Brya said with a laugh. "He was livid when he could not beat me today. Then to secretly think me fascinating is just too much."

Morgan smiled and hugged her tight again.

"I hope you will give him a better chance to be your friend now. When you get annoyed with his manner, perhaps remember what he truly thinks of you."

"That or pummel him, whichever seems most appropriate at the moment."

Launch

KINDRED HALL was packed with Elder dragons, younglings who had never witnessed a Quickening Ceremony, and as many human Chemerians as could possibly squeeze in to fill the gaps and balconies. All were dressed in their finest attire, and excitement filled everyone.

Morgan stood in the middle of the Hall, surrounded by Elder dragons, with Alec, GranMay, Daniel, and Taru close by. Everyone in the Hall went quiet as Morgan and Nulian looked to the large balcony at the top of the main stairs.

Maric represented the Admiralty to formally announce Prince Kyan and Princess Brya. They stepped to the railing, then bowed as the room erupted in applause. Both were beaming as they moved down the stairs together. Once on the main floor, each moved to embrace Alec and GranMay, then stood tall in front of Morgan with proud, anxious smiles.

"Are you ready, my children?" "Yes, Mother," they said in unison.

Morgan reached out and placed a hand to each of their Crests, making both gasp and shiver as the markings on all three burst into a very bright glow.

"Take hold of each other's hands and bond deeply. I will join you, and the Elders will begin their Song of Transfer. This will be the most intense bonding you have ever experienced. Make no attempt to limit or control the process. Remain open to the Elders, no matter what you feel. Trust in the magic, and in our love, my dear ones. Begin."

The twins closed their eyes, focusing their minds and magic. Morgan waited as they relaxed within the deep bonding, then joined them. She let herself enjoy the precious touch of their spirits before welcoming the Elders to begin.

Nulian and the other Elders lowered their heads to place them very near the bodies of the three magical humans as all began to hum a deep resonating sound. The songs of the Perian and Alerian dragons joined into a beautiful harmony. Their songs grew more complex, and the cadence changed a few times as the levels of transfer and activation increased.

Morgan felt the magic of the dragons flowing from Nulian, through her, and into the twins. She also felt the magic within her children multiplying and changing. Both tensed their bodies, yet neither raised their guard as their pain intensified.

Their bodies were maturing at an incredible rate as the dragons reached their highest rate of sharing. A fast stream of images and sounds flashed through them as the dragons transferred vital knowledge. The twins trembled as their bodies screamed in pain, yet neither let out a cry or acted to defend themselves. Their trust in their mother and the dragons was without limit.

The final phase was a sharing of power and knowledge between Morgan and her children. Despite the normal feeling of weightlessness bonding imparted, pain rose in all three of them as the magic surged. All became hot as the dragons' song changed yet again. Their

Crests were casting brilliant light over the Hall as their body temperatures climbed rapidly.

"Be ready to support them," Morgan told Alec and Daniel as she released the bonding and connection to her children in one quick move. She staggered back against Nulian as the twins collapsed into the men's arms. Sweat poured over her shaking body as she struggled to breathe.

"What have you done, my Sister?" Nulian asked. *"Drop your guard so I can help you."*

Morgan's knees buckled, and she slid down Nulian's snout to the floor.

"Was...only...way..."

NULIAN AND THE OTHER ELDERS shifted their focus to Morgan as all began to hum their healing song together.

Alec was trying to wake the twins, having not noticed Morgan fall. She had held her guard at its highest until she passed out. He jerked with the shock of her pain as her guard dropped and bolted to her side as did Taru and GranMay.

All three recoiled from a burning sensation the instant they touched her.

"The magic within her is more intense than I have ever witnessed," GranMay said.

"What happened?" Alec asked as he looked to Nulian.

"She pulled the excess magic away from the twins to protect them from the same fate."

"We must pull the extra magic out of her before the temperature injures her brain," Taru said. She turned to Daniel to shout, "Give me something to change. Get some sand or coal!" Daniel bolted off at once.

Taru and GranMay looked to each other and nodded as they laid hands to Morgan again. Both grimaced as they tried to bond to her.

GranMay was red and shaking in seconds. Alec pulled her back as she started to fall over.

Taru achieved bonding to Morgan, which allowed some of the magic to flow to her. When she felt her own system shutting down, she broke the bonding. She opened her eyes to find she had also fallen over.

Daniel came back in and handed her three pieces of coal. Taru put one between Morgan's hands and placed her own hands to each side. She focused and hummed the song she had hummed with the children the first time she did this.

"Use it, my Queen. Reform the coal with me. Make it ordered and regular," Taru said to Morgan. She tried for over a minute, but the coal remained unchanged. She opened her eyes as they filled with tears and looked up to Alec. "I cannot reach her."

GranMay stood, walked to the twins, slapped their faces, and shook them as she shouted with her voice and her magic. They jerked awake but struggled to understand her words.

"Wake up and help your mother before we lose her! Quickly! You must help her use the magic she holds," GranMay said. Seconds later, both were darting to Morgan.

They laid hands to her and assessed the situation. Each picked up a piece of coal, stacked their hands over Morgan's Crest, and nodded to Taru to resume her efforts. They entered bonding with Taru and focused to connect with Morgan as they sang the song.

Their own Crests glowed brightly as did their hands. Their strong blood-link to Morgan had allowed them all to bond to her and use the magic she held. The coal on the palms of each twin and Taru began to shrink. The last bits soon fell away to reveal small perfect diamonds.

"That helped, but she is still far too hot," Alec said as he laid a hand to her forehead.

"Everyone move back, please," the twins said as they worked

together to lift Morgan to a standing position. They held her body between theirs and hugged each other around her.

As they bonded to each other, and then to her, they sharpened their focus on the air around them. They used the excess magical energy within Morgan to accelerate the gaseous molecules closest to their bodies. The effect was fewer molecules in the two inches around their bodies than in the air beyond that. This meant they were now the least dense thing in the area. The result was lift. They floated from the ground due to the temporary low-density cloud surrounding them.

It took an enormous amount of energy, and Morgan's temperature soon dropped to normal. The twins held their focus and let her wake in this odd situation. She blinked to make sure she was seeing what she thought, then laughed out loud as she looked to GranMay.

"Well, GranMay, it seems you were right. They did figure out how to fly without a dragon," she said. The twins let the molecules slow and diffuse their normal way, which dropped them back to the floor with a little jolt.

Alec moved in to take Morgan into a fierce embrace.

"You love to scare me to death, Woman!" he said, making everyone laugh.

"I do not actually enjoy it, but I do seem to be good at it." He squeezed extra tight before releasing her. They both looked into the faces of their children, and their breath caught.

"Mercy, your appearance aged at least another year, maybe two," Alec said. "You are now adults and responsible for your own choices and decisions."

The twins looked at each other to survey the changes and then looked back to their parents.

"We may be adults in many ways, but we are still your children and always will be. We will never stop asking your advice or trusting your judgment," they said. They hugged their parents hard as

Kindred Hall erupted in applause and many friends moved in to greet them.

KYAN TURNED TO IZ, who smiled and flew into his arms for a hug. He lifted her off her feet and she giggled at his joy in spinning her in a circle.

"Perhaps now I can be more than a cute little boy to you," he said in his much deeper voice. Iz pulled back and put a hand to his face as she took in his new features.

"You now look like the man I have seen since I first touched your hand," Iz said.

Brya watched them with a huge smile and said to them both, *"You look very much the same age now. And as Father says, you are adults and make your own decisions."*

Kyan winked at his sister, then kissed Iz on the lips, without a care in the world who watched.

Alec and Morgan laughed as they watched them. Morgan quieted as she saw Brya's smile slip a bit.

"You will find him when the time is right. Trust the magic, my Daughter," Morgan said. Brya looked at her and nodded as she smiled.

Nulian nudged Morgan and crooned. Morgan turned to lean against her snout.

"I love you, too. I am sorry to have worried you again. But you know I had to do it. You would have done the same."

"I knew you would protect them, and hoped it would not take you from us. Had I mentioned my worry, it would have neither changed your determination to complete their Quickening nor the result. I am quite thankful to still have you, my Sister," Nulian said. Morgan hugged and stroked her a moment longer before saying goodnight to all the Elder dragons as they filed out of the Hall.

A small orchestra had begun playing music, and many were

moving onto the floor to dance. Alec moved up behind Morgan and offered a hand with a bow.

"My Queen, may I have this dance?" She turned with a smile as she took his hand and moved into his arms.

"That brings back memories, very good memories," she said. Alec pulled her tight to him as he smiled. "Oh my, I certainly would not have allowed such close quarters then, my good Knight." He loosened his grip and she pulled him back to her with a devilish smile.

Kyan offered a hand to Iz and led her onto the dance floor. They moved as one, with graceful fluidity, because of the connection they shared.

"I have never felt our link like this before. Your Quickening changed it a great deal," Iz said as her cheeks flushed.

"It did, indeed, my Lady. It is a unique and wonderful sensation. I am quite encouraged to see the difference in your eyes as you look at me."

"Well, you are quite handsome, and I have not had that long to take it in just yet. Do not worry, I am sure the new of it will wear off soon." He laughed and spun her around to make her squeal.

"Would you like to take a walk in the garden, my Lady?"

"You are very transparent, my Prince. I know quite well you hope to get another kiss if you get me away from the crowd."

"That is exactly what I am hoping for, my dear."

Iz stepped back, turned, and headed for the terrace door. Kyan followed with a smile.

Morgan felt the emotion from her son and smiled as she and Alec turned to watch him follow Iz out onto the terrace.

"He is a very happy young man tonight," Alec said. "Our children are adults and are soon to have spouses of their own. I feel incredibly old just saying that."

"But you do not look a day over forty, my love," Morgan said with a laugh. He squeezed her tight as he thought many things wholly inappropriate for anyone else to hear. She blushed as they continued to dance. "Remind me to overstate your age more often. You have a fantastic reaction to it, my husband."

BRYA DANCED with Daniel before passing him to Taru. She moved to the side of the dance floor and noticed Qaleb standing alone in the corner.

She used her magic to touch his guard and caught his eye as she glanced at the dance floor.

"I have never danced, my Lady. However, if you are willing to give me a chance, I would be honored."

"If you are willing to let me lead, I will accept."

"I believe you and your mother have shown me that a woman is more than capable of leading the way, my Lady," he said as he bowed. They moved onto the dance floor and walked toward one another through the crowd.

Qaleb bowed again and offered his hand. Brya held his eyes as she took it in hers, paused a second, then looked away. She placed his other hand on her waist, then began to move with the music.

"Use your magic to anticipate my moves. It should be fun and will give you valuable practice," she said.

He focused on her and was soon able to anticipate her moves as she thought them a split second before acting on them.

"I would be happy to help you claim your magic's potential. It will be a wonderful way for us to get to know each other. I honestly think we could be strong friends," Brya said. He diverted his eyes from hers as she felt his emotions and heard his thoughts.

"I had also hoped to feel the link with you. I admit myself disappointed, Sir Qaleb." Qaleb blushed as he looked into her eyes again. She squinted and laughed.

"We will need to work on your dancing as well."

He had lost focus and was no longer following her lead but rather moving in repetitive motion as he looked at her.

"Just let the magic lead you. Let go of needing to control it. Connect to me and let it take you," Brya said.

"I do not know how to do that, my Lady. I am sorry," he said as he flushed.

"Yes, you do," Brya said as she deepened their connection. Qaleb looked into her glowing eyes as he took a deep breath and shivered with the sensation of her magic moving through him so intensely. "Do not think, just trust what you feel. Let it lead you." He nodded and started to follow her again. Very soon, there was no hesitation. They moved as one and with purpose as each focused on the other.

When Morgan and Alec approached, Qaleb released her and moved away.

"Brya has every right to dance with whomever she wishes, my friend," Alec said with a smile as he patted his shoulder. "Do not be embarrassed that you were fortunate enough to be chosen."

"But I am not her mate, King Alec. I envy the man who is, and wonder if he would feel the same as you do," Qaleb said.

"He will if he is worthy of her," Morgan said. "It seems we will have two mates to find in the years to come. You two can support each other in that effort as strong friends."

Brya and Qaleb smiled at each other then said goodnight to Morgan and Alec before heading outside.

They were walking along a garden path when Brya laughed and redirected their steps.

"I was going to ask Kyan if they wanted to do anything together, but it seems my brother is busy at the moment."

"Can you and your brother experience all the other does through your special link?"

"Yes. However, we have recently started to block the most personal from the other for privacy. I felt the essence of his feelings just now and knew to go no further. He is having a personal moment with his mate."

"*Lucky them,*" Qaleb thought.

"Agreed," Brya said.

Qaleb blushed.

21

Flawed Fathers

MORGAN SAT IN BED early in the morning hours gazing out the windows.

"What troubles you, my love?" Alec asked as he kissed her bare shoulder.

"We should go to Berios now. With the twins Quickened, and none of the babies I need to share magic with due for at least two months, it seems the right time. However, Kyan cannot take Iz as he will wish to. I was just working up the nerve to tell him."

"I will do it if you prefer," Alec said.

She kissed him then headed for the bathroom.

"Well, since you insist, you go tell him then. I will be hiding in the shower to give you plenty of time." She closed the door with a laugh just as he reached for it.

Alec headed out into the hallway and was hit by a small boy running down the hall. It was Liam and he was crying. As Alec knelt to ask what was wrong, Morgan flew out the bedroom door past them.

"Cara is in pain! It's the baby," she explained as she sprinted down the hallway.

Alec scooped up Liam and woke the twins. All followed Morgan and arrived to find her kneeling on the floor beside Cara's body. The twins moved to the other side of Cara and knelt to lay a hand to their friend.

Cara was unconscious, pale, and bleeding.

"She is in active labor, yes?" Brya asked as she looked at Morgan. "Yes. And the child is not mature enough to survive it yet," she said

as she continued to focus. As she tried to halt the premature labor, she searched for the problem that initiated it. It was a tear in the placenta. She repaired it, then focused on the contractions. Nothing she tried would stop them or ease their intensity.

"Control her pain. I will handle the delivery and the baby," she said to the twins.

She had called to GranMay earlier and quickly did so again. To help push the child through the birth canal, she added to the intensity of Cara's muscle contractions. With the twins focused on Cara, she concentrated on connection to the spirit within the tiny infant. A weak connection formed and broke over and over.

GranMay arrived and moved to help her receive the child. The instant the infant was out, Morgan went to work on the tiny figure. She tried to bond, but could not despite the skin contact.

Her focus shifted to its heart and lungs to get them started. She restarted both several times, only to have them go still again and again. GranMay put a hand to her shoulder.

"You must stop now, my dear. The child cannot be saved. You have done all that could be done," GranMay said.

"No, we must try our best. Kyan, Brya, join me. Focus on his heart and lungs."

The three tried again and again to heal the underdeveloped infant. Despite the considerable amount of magic they wielded, they could not force his body to sustain life.

"Enough! He is gone. Let him go, Morgan," GranMay said with a tone that made them all stop and look at her. She gently took the child from their hands and wrapped him delicately in a small blanket.

"All of you step out, please. I wish to be alone with Cara for a bit," GranMay said as she looked at the twins. The twins were both crying as they nodded and left the bedroom behind Morgan and Alec.

Morgan moved down the hallway a few yards, then turned to pull the twins into her arms. They had just experienced their first loss of life and were both shaking. She felt the same emotions in them that she had carried herself for far too long.

"As horrible as that was, it has allowed me to finally see a truth that I have refused to accept for years," she said. They both met her eyes as they struggled to stifle their emotions. "Do you remember me speaking of my dear friend, Balia?" With their nods, she continued, "I considered her death a failure. I thought myself too weak and inexperienced to wield the magic properly. Despite the wise words and encouragement from your father and Nulian, I have carried that guilt every day since.

"Now, I finally see that her death was not my fault, just as this was not. We did not fail that child. We must accept that our magic is not meant to prevent death any more than it is meant to create life. Despite all we wield together, it was not enough to change that child's fate. No matter how much magic we wield, we will never be able to heal a body that is unable to sustain its own life. Please try to focus your mind and heart on the gift that our magic is. You must not let the pain of loss lessen your gratitude for being able to wield it in so many wonderful ways."

The twins had relaxed and stopped crying as they listened to her heartfelt declaration.

"I understand your words, Mother, but it still hurts so much. To touch the spirit of the child, then feel it slip away was torturous. It still feels like failure to me," Brya said. She buried her face in her mother's shoulder and wept again. Kyan moved to lay his head against his father's shoulder as he fought tears.

"You are not weak to cry at the loss of life, Son. Never be ashamed that you feel such things deeply," Alec said as he wrapped his arms around the young man.

"May I come in now?" Morgan asked GranMay as she shifted Brya to Alec and Kyan.

"You alone, please," GranMay said.

She entered the room to find Cara holding her son's tiny body, taking in his form as tears slid down her face. At first, Morgan found her calm expression unsettling, worried she was in denial or shock. However, she found feelings of acceptance growing stronger, easing the pain of grief within the poor woman.

"How did you help her accept and calm so fast?" she asked GranMay.

"I was able to speak to her of this type of loss from experience. By sharing with her the journey my heart took, she was able to make that journey far faster."

Morgan stared at her Grandmother for many seconds before forming a response.

"As many times as we have bonded, I have never found that memory. Why did you keep it from me?"

"Why would I share it? It was a very long time ago, and it is painful to think of," GranMay said.

"Will you tell me about it now?"

"There is not that much to tell. I lost a child just this way in between Maric and Christina. It was a girl. The next Caretaker, or so I thought. I had spent the better part of four months preparing myself to let go of my family at her birth. When I lost her, I was overcome by grief and only came out of it with the help

of my dear friend, Zetia. The next year I became pregnant with your mother," GranMay said. Morgan knew there was much more to the story, but respected GranMay's preference to keep it to herself.

She leaned over and kissed both Cara and the sweet child.

"I am sorry for your loss, my friend," Morgan said.

"Thank you all for your help. You and the twins eased the pain in my body, and Queen May has eased my pain of heart. I can now let go," Cara said as she handed the baby to GranMay with a small smile and tear-soaked cheeks.

"Do you prefer a ceremonial burning or burial?" GranMay asked.

"I have never thought about it. I would like to use your traditional method, I think," Cara said.

"Who would you like to join you in saying goodbye?" Morgan asked.

"Only you and your family, my Queen, including my dear cousin and Daniel, of course. Liam may be disappointed, but I think it is inappropriate at his age."

Morgan nodded and squeezed her hand. GranMay moved to wrap the child further to form a small bundle while Morgan used her magic to connect to all the requested mourners and ask them to head to the burning dais in the garden.

GranMay and Morgan helped Cara dress, then led her out into the garden where the family waited. They all moved to a large pool in the center of the garden which held an ornate stone dais in the middle.

Cara stepped into the pool and took the child from GranMay, who steadied her as she swayed. GranMay stepped into the water, then kept an arm around her waist while ushering her to the dais. She then embraced Cara, kissed her forehead, and looked into her eyes with a loving smile.

"Trust that his spirit will fly forever free among those of your pure- spirited ancestors. He will be among them to greet you when your day of passing comes. This is only a farewell, my dear. Not a goodbye," GranMay said as she leaned down to kiss the small bundle. Cara was weeping but nodded and kissed the child once more before letting her take him. GranMay laid him on a pile of tightly woven hay and flowers at the center of the dais, covered him with several bouquets, then escorted Cara back to the side of the pool.

Morgan, as Queen, stepped forward to pour an oil containing a great many herbs and aromatics over the child. The oil would burn very hot and make the process far faster than without an accelerant. The aromatic ingredients were present for more obvious reasons.

As she moved back, Taru moved in with a lit torch, an honor given to her by Cara. She lit the dais, and all present began to sing the Song of Connection strong and proud. Their song continued until the flame had died very low, then all gave their condolences to Cara before departing.

KYAN FOUND IZ in the garden. She was playing with Liam to help keep his mind off the pain he witnessed in Cara. As Kyan walked up, Liam moved to stand against Iz's leg and hid behind it. Kyan knelt down and smiled at the boy.

"I am Kyan, and I will never hurt you, Liam. Please, let me be your friend," he said. He held out a hand to shake with the little boy and was relieved when Liam moved to accept his hand with a shy smile.

"You can go see Lady Cara now, but be quiet and gentle," Kyan said. Liam nodded and ran off to see the dear woman who had been caring for him.

"The Queen could not save the child?" Iz asked.

"No. Brya and I both joined her in the effort, but we could not save him. His body was not ready to sustain life. We talked through the pain of it together. It was very hard to accept," Kyan said as he looked away. Iz stepped to him and took his hands.

"Talk to me now, Kyan. Share your pain with me."

"We had to endure feeling life come and go within the baby, never being able to make it stay. But, as difficult as this was for all of us, it actually helped Mother release ill-placed guilt from a haunting loss. It is amazing how even the most tragic things can result in positive effects as well."

Iz asked what loss he spoke of and he spent a few minutes telling her of Balia.

"It was the first thing Mother had tried to do with her magic that did not work for her. It was a difficult way to experience the limits of the magic for the first time."

"I remember attending the burning that day. It was the first time your parents walked together, as mates. He rode with her through the burning, and they announced their engagement soon after that. I actually remember watching them fly as I thought how hard it must be for her to find balance between being strong and independent versus letting others support her. I hated knowing it took such a painful event to push her into embracing a love she needed and deserved."

They were both thoughtful and walked in silence for a bit before Kyan gripped her hand a bit tighter and sighed.

"We will leave for our journey to Kalias and Berios soon. We will be gone for many days, possibly for weeks."

"You do not want me to go because it is so dangerous. And, you do not want to say that to me, fearing it will hurt me."

"I would not be permitted to anyway, but you are correct in saying that I prefer for you to stay in the safety of Chemerie. I want you nowhere near Hoge or Martus, my dear," Kyan said. She nodded with no argument because she had never expected to go with him.

Kyan felt the anguish within his sister and redirected their path toward her. Brya was sitting alone in the garden crying. Kyan stopped as he felt Qaleb's approach. He waited as Qaleb joined Brya to offer a supportive one arm hug. He explained to Iz what he felt from them both.

"But, Brya said they are not mates. Should we not discourage such infatuation on his part?"

"Brya can handle herself. Besides, she needs the friendship as much as he does. Trust her to keep it in check," Kyan said.

"I will say nothing, but if she is as attracted to him as she seems to be, then keeping herself in check will be quite the challenge with her newfound maturity."

MORGAN MET with Alec and the Admiralty one last time to make sure all were in agreement with the plan for traveling through Kalias to reach Berios. Afterward, she and Alec went to bed early with intentions to leave before dawn.

As she climbed into bed, she located both of her children and was happy to find them in their rooms preparing for bed. She was not happy with Qaleb's location, however.

"Qaleb is nearing our daughter's door."

Alec was up in a flash and out the door. He waited in the shadows of the hall to see how Brya handled it. To his surprise, Qaleb knocked on Kyan's door.

"I expected you would come to me. Come in," Kyan said.

Alec moved back into his room and sat with Morgan as they eavesdropped on the boys' conversation.

"I am a good fighter, and I want to help. Please, explain to me why I cannot accompany you," Qaleb said.

"It is not up to me, Qaleb. Mother and Father set that standard, and I will not speak against them." Qaleb was pacing the room with a deep scowl.

"I would not expect you to speak against them. I simply want to understand why they do not allow me to come. Have I done something to make them think I would be a burden rather than a help?"

"Mother knows just how much danger lies in this for all of us. She would not allow me and Brya to go if she did not need our strength of magic to build the portal. She and Father are being cautious, risking as few lives as possible. I know of nothing you have done to give them cause for mistrust."

Qaleb was biting his lip, still pacing.

"Is it because of the dark magic within my family line? Does the Queen not trust me because of that?" Kyan laughed a little, and Qaleb's scowl deepened as he stopped.

"She would never judge you based on your parents. My father is the son of a very dark man, yet he carries only the purest of magic within him. Mother is well aware of the dark magic you have been tortured by and has also seen the purity of your spirit. Had she had any lack of trust in you, she would never have allowed you into the country, much less into our home."

Qaleb sat down with a sigh and hung his head.

"Yes, I know you are right, of course. I am just feeling quite useless, my friend. Compared to you, Brya, and your incredibly magical mother, I am a bit of a useless addition."

"You are not useless. You are a friend to us all, and that is quite valuable. In fact, I would ask that you be a comfort to Iz while I am away. She tries to hide it, but she is very worried." Qaleb looked surprised as he rose to leave.

"I will certainly try to be a comfort to your mate. Thank you for trusting my honor. Also, could I ask that you not tell your mother I questioned her decision? I do not want her to think I doubt her leadership, because I absolutely do not."

"You may as well tell her right now because she has heard every word we have said. You really do not appreciate her skill yet, my friend." Qaleb blanched and grimaced.

"My apologies, Queen Morgan. I did not mean to insult your leadership," Qaleb said as he glanced at the ceiling and shuffled his feet.

"I am not offended. And I commend your desire to protect your friends. However, just as you do not appreciate my skill, you do

not appreciate theirs either. They will need many things from you as their friend, but protection is the least of them. Goodnight, Qaleb."

"*Goodnight, Queen Morgan,*" Qaleb said as he left Kyan's room.

QALEB WANDERED the castle for nearly an hour before he found himself on the same corridor as Cara's room. He heard a noise and saw the little boy called Liam exit Cara's room on tiptoe.

Liam scampered down the hall as quiet as a mouse. Qaleb followed as Liam went to the main entrance to the dungeons and snuck past the guard by slipping between him and the wall.

Qaleb was too large to try that move, but he was able to distract the guard with a well-thrown stone down the hallway. He crept down the dungeon stairs and heard Liam speaking.

"Father, will you talk to me this time, please. I am sorry you are down here, but you were very bad to hurt me," Liam said. The man did not answer, so Liam crept closer to the bars of the cell. "Please, Father, speak to me. I love y—"

Qaleb jumped as a large pair of hands shot through the bars and grabbed Liam around the throat.

"I do not want to speak to you, brat! It is because of your weak little mind that I am in here at all. You will pay for this, boy!"

Qaleb shot down the remaining stairs as he pulled his knife, then stabbed the man's arm to break his tight grip on the boy's throat. As the man jerked in pain, Qaleb pulled the boy free.

The man continued to scream insults and curses as Qaleb shook Liam and waited for him to take a regular breath. Once Liam was awake and safely away from the bars, Qaleb lunged, reached through the bars, and grabbed the man's throat while pushing the sharp edge of his knife to it.

"You will not hurt that boy ever again! Not if I have say in it!"

The man struggled against him until the knife cut him a bit. Fear filled his hateful eyes as he froze. The noise of the yelling and the scuffling had attracted the guards, who were at Qaleb's side in just seconds.

"Release him, young man. He will be no more trouble to the boy," one Knight said. As one Knight pulled at his arms, the other hurried to open the cell door.

Qaleb was releasing his grip just as he saw the man's eyes roll back. He let go, and the man fell limp to the floor.

"I did nothing but graze his neck. I did not squeeze hard enough to choke him," Qaleb said as he moved back. The guards moved inside the cell to check the man.

"He is not breathing," one said.

Qaleb shifted further back as Brya leapt down the stairs, turned into the cell, and knelt to lay her hands to the man without acknowledging anyone else present. She pushed healing energy until he started to breathe again. As the man woke and started to growl, Qaleb moved to her and pulled her away. Once outside the cell, she knelt to catch Liam as he hurried to her.

She stood with the boy wrapped in her arms and turned to Qaleb. "Yes, you did do that! Your magic acted with your anger. You thought of choking the man, so that is what happened. Your lack of control over your magic is the exact reason you are not joining this Quest!" She took a few seconds to reign in her temper as she caressed Liam's back and swayed with him. "I am very proud of your protection of Liam. It is fortunate you were here when he needed your help. Come, let's get him back to Cara before she misses him."

Qaleb followed her to Cara's room and waited outside the door. When she came back out, she moved down the hall a bit then paused to look at him.

"I must get more rest, Qaleb. But I would like to understand the rage I felt in you. It was so strong that it woke me. Tell me a bit as we walk, please." Qaleb fell into step while staying a respectful three feet away.

"My rage was for the boy's mistreatment by his father. I suffered a great deal of pain at the hand of my own father, and no one ever raised a hand to stop him. I could not watch it happen to another. I was thinking the man deserved to die for hurting the boy. Especially his own son, who had just said he loved him."

Brya nodded but stayed silent until they reached her bedroom door. "You were right to be angry. However, had you taken his life out of rage it would not have been just. You will have to release this anger if you wish to properly wield your magic. You cannot let emotion control it."

Qaleb nodded and avoided her eyes as he turned to leave. "Sorry to disturb you. Goodnight, Princess Brya."

"I am neither mad nor disappointed," Brya said. He stopped and turned to look at her.

"But I am disappointed in myself, my Lady. I nearly killed a man because I cannot control my magic."

"You will control it, Qaleb. It will take time and a great deal of effort, but you will. Learn from this, but do not torture yourself over it."

"Thank you for your kindness, Princess Brya," he said with a bow. Brya smiled and turned to enter her bedroom without a word.

As Qaleb moved down the hall toward his room, Brya connected to him again.

"Goodnight, my friend, I will miss you while I am away." "I will miss you very much as well, my dear," Qaleb said.

He stopped in his tracks as he realized what he had just said.

"I care for you too, my friend."

He continued down the hall, smiling with the realization that he had his first real friend, and that friend was a girl.

22

Crossing Kalias

MORGAN, ALEC, Brya, Kyan, Daniel, and Taru all met in the dining room for an early breakfast more than an hour before dawn. Everyone was quiet, but it was not due to the hour. They were all going over the million possible problems that could arise during the Kalias leg of their adventure. GranMay joined the group a few minutes later and shook her head as she surveyed the group.

"My word! What a glum bunch you are. Is this not a quest to achieve a wonderful feat and see our dear friends again? How about some cheer for the idea of our return to Erion via a new portal which we have constructed ourselves?" Everyone started chatting as her excitement infected them all.

They soon headed out to the courtyard where the dragons and the rest of the Knights who would accompany them were waiting.

Morgan boarded Nulian alone and looked around her as their group settled. She took in the riding partners. The twins rode with

Gerzin, GranMay and Taru were with Panish, Alec was aboard Menkar, and Daniel aboard Falin. Five more dragons were carrying Maric, Burke, and three other Knights, all of whom were focused and anxious to be off.

Lirpa was not geared up and was hovering around Falin as she clawed the ground. She had agreed, after much insistence from Morgan, to stay home since she was so near her laying. At the moment, that decision was not making her happy at all.

Morgan scanned and saw the huge group of Alerian dragons was ready for departure. They had elected not to take any Perian dragons due to their sensitivity to the dark magic within Harrick and Martus.

"May the magic lead and protect us, my friends," Morgan said to all in the group as she and Nulian lifted off. Many of their brethren had gathered to see them off, and all cheered good wishes as they departed.

THE GROUP FLEW to the portal room within the great stone island. The dragons, Knights, and many craftsmen of Chemerie had worked to seal the caved-in wall and remove the water from the portal chamber. It was now dry and lit with candles. A wide tunnel now entered from high in the chamber, allowing even the largest of Elders to access the portal.

Nulian landed on the massive purple portal, and Panish landed beside her. The two great dragons just fit as they squeezed themselves and wrapped their tails around each other. Morgan nodded to Taru and GranMay and they all sang the song written on the walls of the chamber with the dragons. Soon they felt the familiar feeling of the purple liquid rising up their bodies. Then a flash of light, a quick drop, a second of weightlessness, and they were across.

The instant they arrived on Kalias, Morgan and Taru raised their guards and acted to block Hoge, Martus, and Harrick. They kept strong focus on that task as the dragons moved out of the portal chamber to make room for the next group and to put less rock between the women and the men they sought.

Morgan found the men within their castle asleep in their beds.

"This is fortunate, I am glad our planets are on similar lunar cycles," Taru said with a smile to Morgan.

Nulian and Panish moved to the crest of the mountain bearing the portal chamber to await the others. Soon the entire party was through and gathered near them.

Morgan and Nulian lifted off first and flew ahead toward the castle alone. Morgan had insisted she make sure there was no trap set before the twins came near the castle.

As she neared the castle, she felt Harrick wake but blocked him with ease. He was far more feeble after their last encounter. When she neared the dragon chambers, her heart sank. Heavy stones blocked the entrance. Hoge had discovered the portal and acted to block its use as an entrance to his city. Fortunately, he had only human labor to build the blockade.

"How long do you think it would take for you and Panish to clear the stones away enough to pass?"

Nulian swooped a bit lower to inspect the entrance. *"At least twenty minutes, perhaps more, depending on its depth."*

"It is about twice as deep as it is wide," Morgan said as she searched the cavern's structure.

"It could take as much as half an hour, my Queen," Nulian said as she turned back.

Morgan explained the dilemma to everyone as they flew.

"Taru, can you use the stars to estimate the time of night here? How long do we have before daybreak?"

"I would say we have less than an hour. Perhaps, half an hour, my Queen."

"Then we have no time to waste. Let's proceed." She and Nulian turned toward the castle with the entire party close behind.

"Hoge is now awake," she said as she increased her efforts to block him. "He seems unaware of our presence thus far."

As the group neared the castle, Nulian dropped to skim the tree-tops. They flew silently and reached the dragon chamber entrance without incident. Gerzin was flanked by two other dragons as he kept the twins high above harm's way.

Morgan, Taru, and GranMay held on tightly as Nulian and Panish started to work on the boulders at once. Morgan and Taru were so focused on blocking Hoge, Harrick, and Martus that they failed to notice the Ceruk guards approaching them from behind.

"Morgan, behind you!" Daniel yelled from aboard Falin as he swooped overhead. She silenced the attacking guards by holding their feet and jaws still.

"Many more approach!" Morgan said to everyone.

"Ahh!" Taru shrieked, grabbing her right leg, which had just been pierced by an arrow. Several more arrows failed to find purchase through the dragons' thick hides and scales.

"Kyan, Brya, use your skills to disorient the Ceruk ground troops and allow our brethren a safer battle," Morgan said. The Knights and dragons landed and formed a semi-circle around those clearing the stones away. As Alec and Daniel dismounted, Menkar and Falin roared at the attacking Ceruk troops and used their tails to send many flying far from Nulian and Panish. Maric and Burke led the other Knights in taking down any of the Ceruk guards who managed to fight through the twins' magical attack enough to pose a threat.

Morgan continued to block the three evil men within the castle until alarm bells sounded. She shivered as a fierce push of the dark magic hit her, then reinforced her guard many times over. With a hand to Nulian, she let her magic build within her, then pushed back hard against all three men.

Harrick fell at once. Taru was helping, but her focus was not sharp since she was in considerable pain. GranMay had pulled the arrow out and was healing her leg as quickly as she could.

"Hoge and Martus are on their way," Morgan said as she untied her leg bindings.

"I had hoped he would come out to play," Daniel said as he brought a Ceruk guard down with one fierce blow.

"Do not engage him, Daniel. I will handle him," Morgan said as she dismounted and moved to stand just behind the line of Knights.

"Mother, please allow us to help you," the twins said. She glanced up at her children high above, where she had asked Gerzin to stay.

"Knowing you are safe allows me to focus. Soon you will fight your own battles. I prefer that not be today."

"Careful please," Alec said as he saw her markings glowing very brightly and felt her guard raising between them. She nodded but continued to stare in the direction Hoge was approaching.

"Come, my Sister. I want you to learn from this encounter," Morgan said to Taru, who dismounted and moved to her side. Her leg was not fully healed, but she was focused and determined to fight. *"For now, connect only to me, and only enough to feel how I use the magic for both defense and offensive moves. Block them with your full guard and make no move of your own, unless I suggest it."*

Taru nodded and her eyes began to glow with the intense magic now building within her.

AS HOGE AND MARTUS stepped into sight, they each received a huge blast of intense pure magic from Morgan. Both staggered and grabbed their heads as they cursed and howled with rage.

Hoge was the first to raise his guard high enough to find his footing and move forward. He looked up and smiled as he blocked more of their efforts.

"Ah, yes, the lovely Caretaker has returned to tease me with her delicious magic," he said with an arrogant smile and wink while reinforcing his guard. His smile broadened as he started pushing a much stronger offensive against her.

She let a disgusted expression fill her face as his dark magic touched her, then shifted to a smirk as she matched and overpowered him again. He failed to take the next step he attempted and snarled as he pushed another attack. She countered him yet again, still not using even half of her capacity for attack.

Sweat soaked his body, and he began shaking as she increased her attack again and again. He closed his eyes, clenched his fist, muttered something over and over, then sent a blast of darkness that struck Morgan like a hard slap to the face.

Hoge snarled and lunged forward in attempt to grab her.

She did not flinch as she held his eyes and doubled her offensive, shredding his guard. His entire body clenched, his breath caught, and his legs buckled. He roared, grabbed his head, and dropped to his knees, gasping and shaking.

"My Queen, our way is almost clear," Nulian called aloud, as to not distract her magical battle.

"Get the twins through as soon as possible," she said as she gave Hoge a smile and returned the wink he had offered her. She started to turn, but halted as Hoge chuckled. Taru was moving toward the man with rage-filled eyes, all of her markings glowing very brightly.

"Sweet Taru," he said as his body shook from Morgan's continued assault. "So decadent you are. Breaking you will be even more satisfying. Perhaps this time you will have enough fight to save your precious dragon friends!"

Taru halted, then looked to Morgan.

"Wield it well, my Sister," Morgan said as she nodded.

Taru looked back into Hoge's eyes as she stepped a little closer.

"Your evil reign ends today!"

With the last word, Hoge lurched back and landed on his back as he grabbed at his throat and chest. Taru was holding his lungs still as she attacked his mind and magic with her own. She limped a slow circle around him as he writhed with wide panic-filled eyes. When she drew close to Morgan again, she stopped and forced a deep breath while freezing the sweat coating her body. Hoge gasped and coughed as she released his lungs, but was too weak to do anything more than glare at her as she took another step closer to look down into his eyes.

Morgan sent reassurance to Daniel as she made certain Hoge could not make a move to grab Taru. He and Alec were very close, swords at the ready, bodies primed to attack.

"The tortured child within me wants very much to watch you die. Fortunately for you, I am an apprentice to a noble Caretaker and choose to let you live. How well will you fare without your precious darkness?"

She smiled as she stepped back. Morgan moved to support her elbow and urged her toward the dragons while pushing pride and healing magic.

"Though you had more than enough reason, I am proud you chose not to take his life," Morgan said. She focused to heal Taru's leg as they walked, then cringed as she felt a flash of pure hatred and frigid dark magic.

"NO!" Daniel screamed from behind them. Morgan spun with a roar of fear-driven rage as his pain tore through her. Time seemed to stand still as she met her brother's eyes, holding them as his knees buckled, and blood poured from his mouth.

Hoge was headless, Martus had no heartbeat, and a large serrated dagger was buried deep in Daniel's chest.

BLOOD POURED from Daniel's chest and mouth as he struggled for breath. He grabbed both Morgan and Taru as they and Gran-May knelt and laid hands to him to start pushing healing. He gurgled and coughed blood over his chest as he tried to speak.

"I...love...you...aaa—"

"Fight, Daniel! Fight!" Taru screamed as he went limp and still beneath their hands. She ripped his battle gear apart and laid her hands flat to his chest to push healing. Morgan and GranMay were also pushing all they had as fast as possible. GranMay had used much of her strength healing others and was caught by Maric as she fainted. Taru pushed all she had with tears streaming down her face.

"She is too weak after fighting Hoge. Pull her back before we lose her too!" Morgan shouted. Alec and Burke did as she asked. It took both men to hold Taru as she fought and screamed.

"Children, come to me," Morgan called. Gerzin had already reached the ground, and the twins were by her side in seconds. They placed their hands over his wound as well.

Morgan looked up as she put one hand over her own Crest, and the twins copied her.

"Together, focus first on the wound to his heart," she said. They all closed their eyes and their markings set ablaze in light. She directed their magic to heal the horrible wound. His serrated heart was tedious to mend. If done poorly, it would never support him. She cursed as she felt the huge pool of hot blood reach her knees and fought to focus. Once his heart muscle was properly mended, they sealed the sack around his heart, and moved the liquid out of it. Though it was now fully healed, Daniel's heart did not start beating on its own.

She pushed harder and harder to assure no mark could be found, but still his heart did not beat. GranMay reached for her hands to stop her but she slapped her away.

"No one touch him! Get back!" she shouted as she pushed the children's hands off and their bodies away from Daniel's.

With her hands stacked over her Crest she focused on her brother's spirit and let magic build higher than she ever had before. She trapped it behind her guard as she held it at its highest and gritted her teeth as her entire body started to burn. She was shaking and sweating but let it keep building. Then, in one quick move, she pushed with all her might and slapped her palms against his chest, roaring through the painful release.

Daniel's body jerked and his back arched when the magic shocked his system. His heart leapt in his chest and started a fast uneven rhythm. While others let out breaths of relief, she placed her hands back over her Crest and let her magic build again. Her hunch was right, his heart stopped again.

She let the magic build so high she growled from the pain of it. This time she held her hands just above his chest and started to push healing. The magic focused on that task and concentrated in her hands and arms. She pushed and held them off of him as long as she could then dropped them to drive all she had through him in a fierce jolt that rocked them both.

Daniel gave another mighty jerk and took a great, raspy gasp. She rolled him as he started to choke on the blood in his airway and helped him clear his throat. He was still unconscious, but he was alive.

She kissed his forehead then moved so Taru could reach him. Alec caught her as she fell to the side, spent, and dizzy.

"That was truly amazing. Take strength from me, my dear," he said, placing her hand to his chest. The twins moved to her and sent healing energy until she was strong enough to right herself.

"We must go. Help Taru with getting Daniel aboard Panish," she said as she pushed the twins away. Alec supported her as they moved to Nulian.

"He is alive. Why do you still worry so?" Alec asked.

"He lost too much blood. It was not carrying oxygen to his brain for too long. I saved him...but at what cost?"

Everyone moved to the bottom of the intricate tunnel system to reach the portal room where Morgan insisted all go before her. An instant before passing out of Kalias, she felt Harrick's rage and sorrow as he found his grandson's lifeless body.

23

Love and Friendship

THEY ARRIVED ON BERIOS to tumultuous applause and roars. The huge chamber was filled with their party and many of

the dragons of Berios. Morgan slid to the ground and smiled as she found Daniel awake and on his feet. She was soon taken into his trembling embrace as tears of relief flowed down her cheeks.

"I almost lost you, big brother. I hope I did no damage in my method to save you."

"I am alive because you loved me enough to try something new. Even if it leaves me crippled in a hundred ways, I will still be grateful. I love you, little sister." His legs almost buckled as he held her, so she insisted Taru get him back aboard Panish.

"Please take them to the gazebo so he can rest well, my friend," she said to Panish.

She greeted many dragon friends as she moved through the crowd, but focused to pass calming energy to Hytha, who was a storm of emotions as she hurried toward them. Hytha soon moved into the chamber, nudging many aside in her haste.

"I know, my friend. Your eggs are in need of Quickening. Take us to them now," Morgan said as she continued to calm her through a gentle caress. Hytha crooned with joy as she turned and took flight. Morgan and Alec boarded Nulian, who set off at once.

"You have a job to do, my children. Follow me with Gerzin."

Hytha led them to a cave system within the same mountain that held the gazebo. Nulian dropped low to the ground and moved through the tunnels, following Hytha. She stopped just outside a cavern filled with a hot spring waterfall and pool. Morgan and Alec moved into the chamber to join Hytha. When she did not kneel to begin the Quickening, Hytha crooned and nudged her.

"What is wrong, my Queen? Is it too late?" Hytha asked.

"No, my dear, it is not too late at all," Morgan said as she moved to the eggs and knelt to place her hand near them. "They feel quite healthy. I am reserving this moment for the twins. They have Quickened themselves, and it is they who should Quicken your very special eggs." She was quiet a moment as she continued to touch the beautiful iridescent eggs. "Their magic feels wonderful, my friend. It is strong and quite unique from ours or the Perians'." Hytha was pacing around the pile of eggs while glancing toward the chamber entrance every few seconds. "You may not recognize my children, my dear. They have grown a bit since you last saw them."

"Please tell me when they arrive. I do not wish to be rude, my Queen," Hytha said.

Brya and Kyan both burst out laughing. They had been standing beside her for over a minute already. Hytha studied them, then nudged each as she crooned.

"You two look very handsome, just like your parents. While saddened to have missed your Quickening ceremony, I am most honored to have you Quicken my clutch."

"It is we who are honored, Lady Hytha. Is Tagien in agreement with our performing the Quickening?"

"He trusts the judgment of his Queen and would not object. Please proceed."

They stroked her once more, then moved to kneel in front of the eggs together. Both looked to Morgan with confident, patient eyes as they awaited her instructions.

"You are now Caretakers, just as I am. You have watched me do this many times and the knowledge is within you. Seek it, and let it lead you."

She leaned back into Alec's arms as he wrapped her tight. They watched with prideful hearts as their children lifted one egg each to hold it in their left hands, which bore the image of a hatchling dragon. They sang the first verse of the Song of Quickening, then placed the egg between their two palms. After another full verse of the song, they shifted the egg to only their right hands, which bore the image of a major dragon.

"Do you believe that the dragons within those eggs will look like the dragons on their palms?" Alec asked. She nodded with a big smile.

"That is how I knew they should be the ones to perform this Quickening. They will have a very special bond to these hatchlings, and with all the hatchlings of the original breed."

"What do you mean by original breed?"

"I have not shared that bit of information with anyone yet. I wanted to tell you first. It seems there was originally one breed from which Alerian and Perian evolved. We are not making a new breed, we are rejoining what has been separated far too long. I put it all together just recently, during my meditations since the twins' Quickening."

"I think we need to take up the habit you started with the children. You and I should share more every day so I can keep up

with you, my dear," he said as he kissed her neck. She laughed and shivered.

"I will never complain about sharing with you, my mate."

Once the twins completed the Quickening, they stood and moved to hug Hytha together.

"You have some very powerful hatchlings, my friend. We expect they will hatch a bit quicker than usual. They are growing fast, just as we did," the twins said as they caressed Hytha. She noticed their palms and nudged Brya to see one better. Brya closed her hands and hid them with a smile.

"Oh no, you will have to see them for yourself. No hints, my dear. We want you to enjoy the surprise of their beauty at their hatching," Brya said. Hytha crooned and rubbed both of them again.

"I invite you both to join me at the hatching so you may greet them with us," Hytha said. The twins beamed and shared their gratitude with each caress. "And of course, you are always welcome, my Queen, and you, my King." They thanked her as well and hugged her before leaving.

Tagien had been waiting outside in a larger cavern and crooned his thanks to all as he moved to join his mate.

MOST OF THE GROUP camped out near the lake. Alec and Daniel insisted that GranMay and Morgan use the bed at the gazebo and sent Taru and Brya along as well.

As Morgan lay in bed looking up to the stars, she felt a great wave of pride flow over her. She turned to see the teary eyes of GranMay looking at her.

"I am so glad you did not listen to me when I tried to stop your efforts to save Daniel. How did you know to do that, my dear? And what exactly did you do?"

"I did the only thing I could think of. I thought of the way doctors on Earth use electric shock to restart the pacemaker of the heart. So, I used the magic as a huge burst to jolt his system. I used it in a weaker form with Valen. To save Daniel, I had to also push it as healing, let it build very high, then release all I could in one instant." GranMay stroked her cheek sweetly as tears filled her eyes.

"I am so proud of you. Your skill with the magic is incredible and truly formidable when wielded by your strong spirit and keen mind," GranMay said. Morgan smiled and took her hand.

As they lay holding hands, Morgan flinched. GranMay sat up wearing a harsh scowl.

"What's wrong? Are you injured and hiding it again?"

Morgan moved her hand to her swollen belly and smiled as her grandmother's face brightened. They enjoyed feeling the child within her kicking for the first time. They woke Brya and Taru as well, and both climbed onto the bed to feel it.

"Shall we all bond to the little one and sing him mother's favorite lullaby through our magic?" Brya asked. They all nodded with smiles as they laid their hand flat to her belly and sought the spirit of the little child within.

Once they were all bonded, they began to sing the beautiful song together. Morgan felt all of them pushing healing energy to her as well. She smiled but did not break the song or the bonding to her growing boy.

The infant settled down as their song soothed him. She soon fell asleep within the bonding as her exhaustion took her. The rest of the women moved to cover her and tuck her in.

"I cannot imagine being as strong and confident with the magic as she is," Taru said. *"I would have lost my mate today had she not been there."*

"We will learn from her for many years and watch her grow even stronger," Brya said. *"I could only hope to wield the magic with the grace she does. She is so powerful yet so loving to all she meets. Even those who do not deserve it."*

"All true, yet she is still but a child in many ways. Remember she is only twenty-one years old tomorrow," GranMay said.

"Tomorrow is her birthday?" Brya asked. *"With all the turmoil of our Quickening and coming here, I did not realize. Oh, I feel awful!"*

"It is also her wedding anniversary," GranMay said. *"Let us celebrate it tomorrow in grand style to make up for our lack of recognition today. Speak with Kyan, tell him to consider our limited supplies and discuss possibilities with Alec. I suggest a big birthday breakfast to start the day off right."*

THE NEXT MORNING the women all rose and dressed amongst happy chatter. No one mentioned the significance of the day. They let Morgan think they had forgotten altogether. Each held her guard high to not give their surprise away. Morgan was so preoccupied with getting to work on the portal, she did not notice.

They boarded Nulian and Gerzin, then headed for the lake where the others were camped. Nulian dropped to skim the trees so Morgan would not see the large group awaiting her. When they swooped up over the final tree line, the group of men and dragons let out tremendous applause and roars.

'Happy Birthday, Caretaker Morgan' was spelled out in ice floating on the lake. Kyan's work of course.

The dragons had hunted to provide a boar, which had been cooking all night. There was a variety of fruits, vegetables, and berries as well as sweet bread cooked up by the Knights over a fire.

"Thank you, my friends. This is a wonderful surprise," she said. She laughed and blushed at the crazy level of attention.

She slid down Nulian's leg into the waiting arms of Alec who kissed her with meaning.

"Happy birthday, and happy anniversary, my bride." "Happy anniversary, my husband."

Everyone ate and enjoyed relaxed fellowship time. As Morgan finished her meal, Alec appeared at her shoulder with a small package. It was crinkled a bit after having ridden in a pocket during the trip.

She opened it to find a beautifully crafted ring, which bore a gorgeous deep blue stone surrounded by small diamonds. It was far more elaborate than anything she had made herself.

"Do you like it?"

"I love it! It is beautiful," she said as she stood to hug him tight. He slipped the ring onto her finger and kissed her again.

"Did you really not know, or are you just letting me think I surprised you?"

"No, I did not know at all. When did you do this? And how?"

"Taru and I schemed this one together. I designed it and drew it for her. She made it just before we left so there would be little chance of you finding out about it. Keeping secrets around you is quite near impossible, my dear. Only your concentration on our task kept our secret."

"You kept something from me, my husband. I must be more aware of your thoughts at all times I see," she said with a raised eyebrow before kissing him again. "Fortunately for both of us, Taru has little difficulty keeping secrets."

She reached into an inner pocket of her cloak and pulled out a package for him.

"Taru helped me with part of this, as well," she said through a laugh. They both turned to look at the blushing Taru who stood behind Daniel wearing a sneaky grin.

Alec opened the package to find a handsome amulet with the exact pattern of her Heraldic Crest. It was strung on a woven cord of dark blue to match their robes. And in the center of the entwined dragons was a blue stone much like that of her original Caretaker's amulet.

She slipped the amulet over his neck and admired the way it laid against him. She put her hand over it and it warmed with the heat that always accompanied their touch. They smiled at each other and thought, *"I love you,"* at the same time. They laughed at their tendency to do that and hugged.

Daniel interrupted with a clearing of his throat. They looked to him and found he was sweating a bit and blushing.

"Our Queen and King, we are blessed by your selfless service to our country. Your love and trust of one another is an inspiration to us all." He started to sing and everyone around them joined him. The humans with the lyrics, the dragons with the beautiful harmony.

Morgan listened as her brother sang in his beautiful tenor voice. He hated to sing in front of anyone, so this was a true gift. She realized the tune was the first she and Alec had danced to, and turned to find him bowing. She stepped forward to take his hand as soon as he stood from the bow, laughing as he lifted her to spin them into a waltz.

They were filled with love and respect from all their brethren around them. The sensation was a warm rush which moved all through her. Alec was staring into her eyes and the heat between them started to raise her temperature.

As the song ended, Brya and Kyan ran to hug them.

"Goodness, you are hot, Mother! Could you not control it?" Brya asked as she laid her hands to Morgan's flush cheeks.

"Had I wanted to, I could," Morgan said with a smile. Brya blushed a bit and diverted her eyes. Alec scooped her into his arms and shook her to make her laugh.

"We are proud of our love and the magic between us. We are not embarrassed, so you need not be either," Alec said.

"I do not mean to bring you down, but something troubles GranMay. She has barely smiled since you all arrived and holds her guard very high," Kyan said as he hugged Morgan.

"I feel her anxiety and have heard her thoughts. She is questioning your prophecy that she is to travel with you and Brya. Now

that she is on Berios, she feels the pull to stay as she planned for so long. You and Brya need to bond with her and share the power of your certainty in the task. It will ease her heart." He nodded and took Brya's hand as they headed toward GranMay.

MORGAN MINGLED with the Knights and dragons for a while to give the twins time with GranMay alone. She laughed herself to tears at the antics of Hirk and Brit trying to catch their new little brothers and sisters in a raucous game of tag. The new hatchlings were three months old now and each the size of a small bear.

One hatchling broke from the game and moved to her, where he dropped low to the ground and bowed his head.

"Caretaker Morgan, could you touch me like you do the dragons of your world?"

"Do you mean bond to create a link between our spirits, as I do all the hatchlings born from Chemerian dragons?" He nodded and shimmied closer. Morgan looked to Asira. *"Is this something you want for him, my friend?"* Asira moved forward and touched her snout to her as she crooned.

"I have taken you as my Queen because I love and respect you, my friend. I would be honored for you to become Caretaker to my younglings, my Lady," Asira said.

As Asira spoke, all of her new clutch came forward and lay down beside Morgan with eager expressions. Hirk and Brit joined them and held their heads over the top of the little ones.

"I am very happy to know you all wish to feel the bond to humans. It is by far the most wonderful part of our magic. I am honored to share that connection with you," she said as she greeted each with a gentle caress. She considered the group then sat down amongst them. "All of you come closer and put your snout against my body somewhere. Just relax and let me touch your spirit to form a strong connection."

Brya, Kyan, and GranMay moved up to stand by Alec. They watched with proud smiles as Morgan deepened her connection to each of the younglings. Everyone present felt the magic radiating from her as she started to sing the Song of Connection.

"Brya, she touches all at once. That will strengthen their bond to one another as well as creating a link to humans. She gives two gifts at once," Kyan said. Brya and Kyan watched and listened with their magic to learn as much as they could from their amazing mother.

24

Truth in Fables

MORGAN ASKED THE KNIGHTS and many dragons to begin scavenging large amount of the ore known to contain the portal metal. She then called to ask all the Elder dragons to join her and her family near the lake.

"Our task to rebuild the portal to Berios still has one major component missing. We must discover the source of the dense purple liquid. Knowledge within us explains the material required to form it is here on Berios. Do any of the Elders who have lived here know of its source?"

The Perian Elders looked to each other and not one showed signs of adding to her knowledge.

"We have no knowledge of it, my Lady. We only know of that within the portal to Kalias," Asira said.

"We start with the fact that it is a material which is present here, but not on Erion," she said. "Any ideas about that, my friends?" she said as she looked to her Chemerian brethren.

Morgan listened to the many conversations going on between the dragons without interrupting, then looked to Nulian as the group quieted.

"Elosh, the Eldest male among the Berios dragons, has a vague memory of a unique and rare mineral found within a mountain system about two hours' flight away. However, it is a brilliant blue color, my Queen," Nulian said.

"It is a place to start. Let us go find a bit to study," Morgan said as she ran to vault up to Nulian's back. She felt annoyance and frustration from both Daniel and Taru, then looked back to find him walking away from his wife, ignoring her call.

With a strong push of reassurance to Taru, Morgan slid to the ground then jogged to catch up to Daniel. He stopped but did not look at her. His face was pale, he was sweating, and he was panting from the slight exertion of a fast walk.

"I told her that she has to accept the truth. She disagreed and insisted on pushing pointless healing. I refused it, and it ticked her off!"

"I assume you refer to your being left weak from losing so much blood yesterday."

"That and my scrambled brain. I don't trust it, and I am not going to put myself in a situation where either weakness could cost anyone else. I'm tired, I'm frustrated, and I just want to be left alone. Please, just go, take her with you and let her be of use. If she brings up my condition, do not give her false hope for it changing when you have no clue if it will."

He marched away from her without ever looking at her directly. Her chest ached as she moved back to Nulian and Alec. Neither pushed her to talk as they felt her guard raise. After they were in flight, and her chest had stopped aching so much, she connected to Taru and found a storm of emotions.

"I am sorry that he has been left weak and angry, my Sister.

Please, give him time to process it."

"He has no place feeling shame for his injury, my Queen. He saved our lives and should be proud of that action!"

"I agree. What does he mean when he says his brain is scrambled?"

"He has struggled to find the right word a few times, could not call Falin's name this morning, and his memory of the entire trip through Kalias is a fractured haze. He is quiet and withdrawn. I have no idea if it is fatigue, anger, or a loss of focus on the world around him."

"Let us hope that his body, mind, and mood have all improved by the time we return. If they have not, we must give him the time he needs and not frustrate him further with coddling."

Taru nodded, but her heart was heavy as she flew further away from her troubled mate.

"DO YOU HAVE any information as to who built the portals to begin with? Either by actual memory or by fable?" Morgan asked Nulian about an hour into their flight.

"There is one silly fable concerning it, but it is nonsense."

"Well, go on then," Morgan said as she used magic to urge her to speak. Nulian sighed and grumbled many times before speaking.

"The fable speaks of an aquatic race of people. It suggests they were the ones who first created the liquid within the portal and found the skill to harness its magic to link worlds together. They shared the use of the material with the dragons in return for a protective magical barrier around their city to keep it hidden from all."

"Why does that sound so far-fetched? Had anyone asked me if dragons existed five years ago, I would have told them to seek medical care. Share the entire fable, please, as it was told."

Nulian snorted and grumbled a bit more, but began the poetic fable.

> There is a race of men who sing in sky and sea.
> > Their comfort in water has seen no bounds,
> > > nor has their skill in controlling sound.
> To the dragon they opened a universe of connection,
> > in exchange for immunity to magical detection,
> Therein they live, safe in their home,
> > having chosen solitude,
> > > lest the danger of being known.
> To call upon them is to speak to the wind,
> > for they find no other race
> > > worthy of being called friend.

"Is the mountain pass we are going to near an ocean or very large lake?"

"Yes, my Queen, it borders the ocean. Elosh says the mineral is only found in the cliffs nearest the sea," Nulian said.

Morgan was quiet for a while as she tried to decipher the poetic fable again and again.

"To sing in the sea, as in breathe under water," she proposed. "To live in a place free of magical detection could mean it has a barrier of magic that is impossible to detect. I would have made it to protect from both magic and sight, were it me. A visual camouflage that also prevents magic from penetrating it. Perhaps a glass infused with magic in a way similar to the portal liquid." Nulian did not respond beyond obvious annoyance. Morgan patted her hard and laughed. "You call it a silly fable, but I see it as the only clue I have at the moment."

They flew on for another hour before reaching the edge of the sea. Everyone fanned out and searched the cliffs for a cave entrance for another hour before finding a small opening.

Only the humans of the group would fit inside. Morgan asked Taru and GranMay to remain outside and communicate with the dragons about other possible sites to search.

Alec led the way into the cave system carrying a lit torch. They examined the walls and floor as they moved along the tunnel.

After over a mile of tunnels, Morgan and the twins felt the tickle associated with the dragons of their markings squirming about. The twins were both startled, having never felt the sensation, and inspected their Crests and hands with interest.

"Stop, and stay quiet, everyone," Morgan said. She used her magic to locate the source of the magic and found it to be moving.

"Is it a Nyek, Mother?" Morgan smiled and nodded.

"You two go ahead after it if you like. We will continue this way," Morgan said. They headed off down a different tunnel as Morgan followed Alec.

Her night vision made her view of the tunnel very different from the others'. It was not until she watched the twins disappear down the dark tunnel behind them that she realized just how much.

"Alec, wait. Douse the torch and come back to me. I think I just found the stones Elosh spoke of."

"Why am I stumbling around in the dark, my dear?" Alec grumbled as he tripped and bumped his head.

"There are bright blue crystals all along the walls. I can see them if there is no ambient light. Their glow is bright to my eye. Do you see anything at all?"

"Only blackness."

Morgan focused to increase the glow of her Crest so he could see, then used a small chisel to fill her shoulder bag with many of the crystal clusters.

"I will carry it," Alec said as he reached out in the darkness.

"I think you should worry more about walking. You are quite clumsy today." She leapt out of his reach, then laughed as she ran ahead in the darkness, hiding in the shadows.

"I feel you, my mate. Do you forget so quickly the power of our link?" Alec asked as he approached her. She pounced and pushed him against the wall.

"No, my love, I feel it every second of every day," she said as she kissed him with meaning. She gasped as he lifted her off her feet and spun around to pin her to the wall instead.

They were still discussing the intensity of their link when she felt Brya and Kyan approaching. Assuming they were in the cover of complete darkness, she did not stop the intense conversation with her husband.

"Mother!" Brya snapped as she and Kyan both halted and quickly looked away from their entangled parents.

Morgan felt embarrassment from Kyan and grimaced with the realization that her children had developed the use of their night vision.

"We will be along in a moment. Go on without us, please."

Her children were out of there in a flash, both considering methods for removing disturbing memories from their minds.

"Now we cannot even hide in the dark, my dear. We will have to behave, I suppose," she said to Alec as she started to push him away.

"Not likely," he said as he resumed their intense discussion.

MORGAN AND ALEC emerged from the cave to find the twins evading their gaze.

"You are too grown to still be surprised that your parents are passionate," she said.

They both looked up at her, then smiled as they looked away again.

"Your Crest is glowing beautifully, my Mother," Brya said as she struggled to stifle a laugh.

Alec adjusted her shirt with a smirk and a gentle touch to the scales of her Crest as he finished. She shivered and he chuckled as he pulled her closer.

Both jumped a bit as Nulian's head appeared at their side.

"Did you two find anything other than each other within that cave?" Nulian asked.

Kyan and Brya burst with laughter as did GranMay and Taru. "You are just jealous," Morgan and Alec said in unison.

Brya and Kyan were fighting to quiet their laughter but lost the battle as their parents were nudged hard with a snort and fell over. Everyone laughed hard for many minutes before a reasonable thought could be formed by any.

Taru moved to Morgan as she inspected her bulging bag.

"What did you find, my Sister?" she asked as she knelt beside her. That question brought the twins to their senses and they came to look as well. Morgan opened the bag and let the stones pour out on the ground.

"Ah, well. Those are very nice, dear," GranMay said as she looked over the dull gray rocks before them.

"In the darkness, they glow a bright blue color. I suppose their glow is too weak to be distinguished in the light," Morgan said.

"I could see nothing even in total darkness," Alec said.

"I can see the blue hue of them quite clearly," Nulian said as she moved to inspect the stones.

Morgan picked up one of the rocks and everyone gasped as it burst into a bright glow in her hand. Everyone else lifted one and found it glowed in the hand of everyone present.

"The intensity of the glow is in proportion to the magic we carry,"Morgan said. She placed her stone between her hands and focused to push magic to it. As she pushed magic the stone's glow brightened and it began to take on a slight purple hue.

"I think you found our missing ingredient. Try to accelerate its atoms. See if it will turn to liquid," Kyan said. They all tried to make the atoms within the stone move faster, and force a state change, but none were successful.

"Well, Elosh did use the word 'unique'. Quite an accurate summary," Morgan said as she rose to her feet and paced again. She carried the stone and tried a few different approaches with no success as she considered the fable again.

"The fable spoke of masters of sound. What type of sound does it refer to, Nulian?"

Nulian huffed as she raised her head and paused a few seconds before looking back down.

"It is sound that cannot be made by any other than those with the skill to wield it." Morgan raised an eyebrow. "I told you it was silly, my Queen."

"Could it be a skill we can learn? Or do you think it truly unique to their race?"

"That is how the fable was told to me, but I put no faith in it having any truth to it," Nulian said. "As I have told you multi—"

"Only they can hear it. Only they can make it. So, we must find them," Morgan said as she continued to pace.

"Who are you talking about, my dear?" Alec asked.

"No one," Nulian said with a grumble. Morgan gave her an annoyed look as she explained the fable to him and the others.

"We are seeking another race of magical beings who think they cannot be found. That sounds like a grand challenge," the twins said.

Nulian just shook her head as the group discussed the different aspects of the fable for many more minutes.

"My Queen," Asira said as she shifted closer to the group. "Now that I hear what you speak of, I believe I have a memory that is relevant. Shall I share it with you?"

"Yes, please," Morgan said as she moved to lay a hand to her cheek.

As Asira focused on the memory, images and sounds passed to Morgan. After reviewing the memory many times, Morgan thanked her with loving feelings.

"Everyone come, let me share it with you," Morgan said as she sat amongst her family and offered her hands. Soon, they each saw what she had, and most sent feelings of astonishment to the rest. The exception was Taru, who was smiling. "What connection did you just make, my Sister?"

"I did not know I had this memory. It came forward in response to the one you shared," Taru said as she held her hand back up. Morgan viewed the memory and was also smiling when they broke the bonding.

"It seems this is no fable at all," Morgan said. "The beings we seek do exist. They are much like humans, yet rather unique as well. They are here and on Kalias. It seems reasonable to suspect they are on Erion, as well. We have been unaware of them due to both their ability to block our magic and the protection the dragons provided for their homes."

She stopped to smirk at Nulian, who had dropped her head closer to listen.

"Taru was saved by one of these people as a small child. She had tried a dive from too high. She was unconscious and sinking fast when one of these people lifted her back to the surface and to the shore. Here, bond again and view the memory for yourself. Pay close attention to the actions of the man just before he leaves her." All bonded again and viewed Taru's memory.

"To be so like humans, yet view us as so dangerous that they hide themselves away. I hate to think of what happened to cause such fear."

"Interesting, but disappointing really," Alec said with a sigh. "I was hoping we would find an exotic race of mermaids." Everyone laughed as Morgan elbowed him, making him fall off the log again.

"He called me friend. That suggests they would be willing to talk to us," Taru said with a hopeful smile at Morgan.

"Mother, are we to seek the people of that race here on Berios? Or return to Kalias to seek the ones who helped Taru?" Kyan asked.

Morgan was again pacing and did not answer.

"You know my preference, my dear. I would rather we not return to Kalias until it is necessary," Alec said. She nodded and paced for another moment.

"Was that a freshwater lake?" she asked Taru.

"Yes. However, if you swim very deep the water often tastes salty, as if it were fed in some way by an ocean current. I used to swim as far down as I could and there were caves leading off the bottom. I was forbidden by Father to enter them alone, and never tried," Taru said.

"You mean your dragon father?" Brya asked. Taru nodded.

"He knew of the people and their desire to be left alone, I imagine," Kyan said. "Perhaps Elder Elosh has more information to help us now that we know what to seek." Asira gave a sad croon as did Nulian who nudged her friend's snout.

"My father is growing very old and his access to his memories is fading," Asira said. "While the information may be within him, it is likely out of his reach."

"Would he allow me to bond deeply enough to reach the memories he can no longer reach?" Morgan asked.

"You could not, my Queen," Nulian said. "Your blood is far too removed from that of the Perians. I believe Lady Taru may be able to do so, with your guidance."

"You know I am willing, my Sister. Only tell me when," Taru said. "Alright then, let's return to camp for the night. We will ask to join with Elosh in the morning," Morgan said. As they boarded the dragons, she felt longing from the twins and remembered the search for the Nyek.

She turned to find that neither the twins nor GranMay had risen from their seats. Both of her children looked to her with apologetic eyes.

"We wish to stay and seek the Nyeks during the night, Mother. Will you allow it if GranMay stays with us?"

"Are you willing to stay out here with them?" Morgan asked GranMay.

"It seems I am meant to, my dear. Just leave us the provisions we carried along. We will be fine," GranMay said with a smile. Morgan moved back and knelt to hug her tight. She pushed healing energy as she did so, of course.

"Well, my children, this will be the first time I have been away from you that you were not safe within the castle. My heart aches a bit already," she said. They both put a hand to her cheek and passed love between them.

"You made us strong, Mother," Brya said. Kyan finished, "And you know we can defend ourselves against most any threat."

"That is a comfort, but the worry of a mother remains. Just be on your guard at all times," she said. "And watch out for GranMay too," she added with a wink.

She, Alec, and Taru boarded Nulian and Panish. They asked Asira, Falin, and Menkar to stay with the others and left for the camp. Gerzin followed them after making several wide circles to check the area nearest the twins.

"This is unsettling, my dear. I hate leaving them. I know they appear as adults now, but they are still our little ones to me," Alec said. Morgan nodded as she fought tears.

"We both know that we must begin to let them live by their own decisions and their own magic. That does not seem to make it hurt any less," she said. They held each other as both ached more the farther they got from their children.

Zoli

BRYA AND KYAN stood arm in arm as they watched their parents flying away. They both felt the anxiety within their parents and now felt guilty for asking to stay. GranMay moved to embrace them both.

"It will be hard for all of us to let you two be the adults you are so soon. But your parents are strong and smart. They will be fine because they know how capable you are of taking care of yourselves," GranMay said.

"We know. It is hard for us too, GranMay. We feel the distance just as they do right now," Kyan said.

"Then turn your focus to making a suitable fire for us to keep the chill off during the night. And then I would like for you to share with me all you know of these creatures we seek."

The twins hurried to build a fire and fix pallets for sleeping later. They then sat to each side of GranMay and joined hands to hers. They passed all the information they had of the Nyek along with the basic images Morgan had shared.

"I have to say, I do not see the need for me in this, my dears. If you can now feel their presence, then why do you need me?"

"We are barely two and a half years old, GranMay," they said together with smiles.

"We need a chaperone with wisdom of life, and you are the wisest in our family," Brya said.

"Wise, do you call it? That is certainly a bit nicer than old," Gran-May said with a chuckle.

The twins helped her stand and walked to each side of her as they entered the cave. They did not take light, wanting to do nothing to spook the Nyek away from them. Once deep within the cave, they took a seat.

The twins focused to open to the tunnel system around them and searched for the faint touch of magic that the Nyek emitted. With their hands all clasped, they transferred the feeling to GranMay when they found one.

It was coming nearer to them so all stayed still and quiet. The Nyek moved to the tunnel adjacent to theirs and stopped.

"We should try to speak to it, to convince it we are friends. Shall we try together, Brother?" Brya asked. He took her hand, and they spoke together. *"We are friends and mean you no harm. We hope to help your kind grow in number on this world, and on our own world of Erion. How can we show you we are friends to the Nyek?"*

The Nyek had jumped when they started speaking, then climbed to the top of the tunnel to hide within a deep crevice in the wall. They waited for a reply but instead felt the little creature begin to move further away.

It was now blocking them even harder, making it impossible to pinpoint its position. They tried to call after it and plead for it to stay, but it moved deep into the tunnel system. When they started to go after it, GranMay stopped them.

"If you chase after it you will only scare it more. It fears either us as humans or the magic. Either way, you must allow it to come to you. Let us go eat. We will try again a bit later."

They agreed and took her arms to lead her back outside, where they sat and ate with little conversation. After they ate their sandwiches, GranMay began to cut up some fruit and berries as she sang a favorite tune.

Brya and Kyan shivered as they looked up at each other and smiled.

"Keep singing, GranMay. The Nyek seems to be attracted to either that or the fruit you hold because it is at the mouth of the cave watching us with great interest," Kyan said.

GranMay did not break her song or even hesitate in her work. She placed a few pieces on a napkin and set it just behind her without turning around.

"Is it interested in the food?" GranMay asked. She got her answer as she felt joy and excitement rise in her grandchildren. She looked to Kyan and saw he was looking at the napkin behind her with adoring eyes.

She turned her head just enough to see a gorgeous blue and grey animal. It seemed a bit larger than those in the memories she received from the children. The Nyek finished the fruit and started to back away. "Hello, friend. Would you like some more?" GranMay asked. She made no move toward the Nyek but placed a bit more on the napkin with a slow-moving hand then returned to mixing the fruit and berries together as she hummed.

"It moved further away as you brought your hand near, but did not retreat. It is now taking the fruit again. Oh, GranMay, it is gorgeous, and I can feel the strong magic within it from here," Brya said.

"Brya, we may have spooked it because we carry so much magic. It seems comfortable with GranMay, so let us not try to connect

until it grows more trusting of us," Kyan said. She agreed, and both lay down with easy movements to admire the beautiful Nyek.

GranMay continued to sing and hum her tune as she handed bowls of the mixed fruit and berries to the twins. She set a small bowl beside her to tempt the Nyek to come closer. As they all ate in silence their guest crept forward and grabbed a berry with its front paw then moved back out of the light of the fire.

The beautiful creature did this many times before it stayed by the bowl to eat. As it ate it looked around at all of them with cautious inquisitive eyes. Brya smiled but held her tongue, as did Kyan.

"We are very happy you let us see you, my friend. You are a beautiful Nyek. We have been hoping to meet one of your kind," GranMay said. The Nyek took a couple of small steps away as she started speaking but stopped to look at her with obvious curiosity. It tilted its head from side to side as she spoke as if trying to hear her better.

"May I touch your magnificent coat? It is so beautiful, I am very curious to know how it feels," GranMay asked. She held out a hand but did not actually reach for it. She was giving it the option of coming to her by choice or not.

The Nyek stepped closer to her and reached out its head to smell her hand. It then made a soft trilling noise and they all felt the message as the feeling of hunger passed over them.

"You have a big appetite for such a small creature. You may have a little more, but we must save the rest for breakfast. Here you are," GranMay said with a chuckle and a smile. She held out a biscuit to the Nyek, letting it sit on her hand without setting it on the ground.

The Nyek stared from it to her eyes and back. It then hummed a sweet crooning sound, and GranMay laughed.

"Alright, I will put it down, but I do hope you will then trust me."

They all watched as the Nyek ate the entire biscuit, thereby causing its belly to bulge a bit. As it ate, GranMay settled down on her pallet.

"I have sung to you, and I have shared my food with you. Will you repay the favor by letting me touch you now?"

The Nyek walked forward and climbed up on her stomach to sit tall and stare down into her eyes. It trilled again and they all felt a sense of gratitude from the little one. GranMay lifted her hand and held it near its head without touching.

The Nyek moved into her hand and turned to the side to let her stroke its back. It curled around her arm then settled down to lie on her chest. GranMay took in a deep breath the instant she touched the Nyek because she received a huge burst of magic.

"My hand is tingling even now and my whole body tingled when actually touching it," GranMay said to the twins.

"I am horribly jealous," Brya said as she smiled at the beautiful Nyek.

The Nyek lifted its head and looked at her.

"Did you hear my thought, little friend?" Brya asked. The Nyek answered with a bob of its head.

"You heard their plea to you earlier, yes?" GranMay asked. The Nyek turned its head back to her and bowed its head in answer. "My great-grandchildren want to talk with you, but do not want to frighten you. They are very magical for certain, but they have very kind hearts as well. They want to help your kind and would never hurt you."

The Nyek looked at Kyan and Brya and bowed its head while trilling. The twins received a peaceful feeling of welcome, which they agreed must mean they were welcome to speak to it.

"The great magic we hold was given to us so that we could achieve certain tasks. One of these is to seek out Nyeks and bring them to live in safety among our people, where they will be loved and cared for. We hope to help the Nyek become far more numerous," Brya said. Kyan continued, "You are the first we have discovered, and we have many questions. Would you help us by answering a few?"

The Nyek trilled as it laid its head down and closed its eyes. Kyan and Brya looked at each other and shrugged.

"I am not sure what I felt in that message," Brya said.

"It was like a feeling of ennui. We bored it to sleep," Kyan said. They both laughed and watched the Nyek close its eyes and go to sleep atop GranMay. GranMay continued to stroke the animal as she dozed off. The twins were jealous but did not want to risk scaring the creature away, so they lay back down to sleep themselves.

"I WILL STAY at the campsite with Daniel. You two take the gazebo and enjoy your anniversary, my friends," Taru said to Morgan and Alec. She waved as she and Falin dropped to land near the lake. Morgan and Alec sent thanks as they turned with Nulian for the gazebo and a quiet night of peace.

Nulian dropped them off and said goodnight as she headed for a high peak nearby where Gerzin awaited her.

Alec had unpacked some food for them and set a plate out for Morgan as she sat down in the chair across from him.

"This place always makes me think of our first night here together. I had never been so happy in my life as I was that night here with you," he said as he smiled at her.

"I feel the same way. Though the night we were here welcoming our children into the world was as amazing to me."

"I meant before that night. I agree that the birth of the twins and holding them with you was amazing." He ate a bit more, then asked, "How is our growing little boy today?"

"He is restless tonight. He needs a lullaby, I think. You should sing to him later."

Alec moved to kneel beside her. He kissed her belly and began to sing to his unborn son. He sang and rubbed her belly as she slid her fingers through the thick waves of his dark hair.

"You are a wonderful father, Sir Alec. I am a very lucky woman," she said as he finished his song.

He looked into her eyes and said, "Yes, you are."

She burst out laughing and pushed him back from her as she stood to get ready for bed. They both crawled into the plush bed and snuggled under the warm blankets.

"I miss them," Alec said after a few quiet minutes. "Me too."

"Have you connected to say goodnight?" "No, I thought I should leave them be."

"Neither of us will sleep if you do not check in with them, my dear," Alec said as he nuzzled her neck. She nodded and focused to connect to her children, then smiled.

"I did not speak but touched them enough to be sure they were well. They are both asleep, as is GranMay. There is an unusual amount of magic around GranMay, so I assume they found a Nyek after all."

"Thank you. Now I can sleep well." He rolled over and jostled to get comfortable. Morgan gave him a few seconds then sat up to glare at him.

"Are you really about to go to sleep without kissing me on our anniversary?" He rolled back with a devilish grin and pulled her close to him.

"No, I just love to hear you ask for a kiss, my love," he said in a deep whisper. He rolled her over to look into her eyes for a few seconds before dropping his head to let his lips brush hers.

"I love you, Morgan. I hope you have truly been happy with me as your husband because I could dream of no other woman to be my wife."

"Everything about you has been a dream to me. I have been so happy since you came into my life. I often wonder if I will wake on the window seat of my home on Earth to find this was all an elaborate dream. A perfect and beautiful dream."

The couple stayed up late discussing their three years of marriage and all the wonder they had experienced together.

THE TWINS WOKE the next morning to a soft trilling as a feeling of welcome filled them. They opened their eyes to find the Nyek sitting between their heads, looking from one to the other. They lifted onto their elbows and bowed their heads to the amazing and noble little creature.

"Good morning, little friend. May we touch your fur?" Kyan said. The Nyek trilled again and sent welcoming feelings as it lay down between them. Both twins hesitated. "Friend, you do understand we have a great deal of magic within us, and you will surely feel it when we touch you, yes?"

The Nyek trilled a short burst of impatience. Brya laughed and said, *"I think it is saying that it knows quite well, and we insult its intelligence by asking."*

"You go first, Sister. One at a time for now," Kyan said.

Brya reached out and touched the blue-gray fur with her fingertips. "Ouch!" she said as she pulled her hand back. "Mercy, that tingles so much it stings."

The Nyek looked at her and trilled, sending sympathy followed by reassurance. Brya touched it again and smiled.

"The amount of magic being transferred dropped," she said.

"That was very kind, thank you," she said as she ran her hand down its back. She shivered as she felt the magic shoot through her from her hand to the tips of her toes. Even after she lifted her hand from its fur she felt her Crest continue to tingle like mad and glow brightly in the morning sun.

"I can feel the magic you received. That is a great deal from one stroke of his fur," Kyan said. The Nyek stood and turned a scowl on him with a hiss.

"Our friend is a she, dear. You'd best apologize, at once," Gran-May said.

Kyan bowed his head to the Nyek.

"I am deeply sorry for offending you, my Lady. I have not touched you, so I had no way of knowing. Please, accept my most humble apology."

The Nyek held the stare for a few more seconds, then stepped to him with a trill, which told him he was forgiven. She dropped her head to his hand, and he caressed her fur with a great shiver.

"You are amazing, my friend. I consider this moment to be a highlight of my life, for certain," Kyan said. He looked to Brya and said, "It feels much like touching Mother when she drops her guard completely."

The Nyek trilled and sent curiosity as she tilted her head to the side a bit and looked to GranMay.

"My granddaughter, their mother, carries a great deal of magic within her as her children do. She received the gift of dragon blood, which enhances her natural power. We would love for you to accompany us to our campsite and meet her. Would you like to join us, my friend?" The Nyek looked back to the cave and trilled a long sweet trill, which sent a feeling of yearning.

"Are there others here you do not wish to leave? They are certainly welcome, as well," Brya added.

The Nyek dropped its head, moved to GranMay's side, and trilled a pitiful sound so quiet the twins barely heard her. GranMay opened her arms and caressed the Nyek as it crawled into her lap.

"Profound loneliness," GranMay said. "She has been alone here for many years, I believe. And she accepts our invitation."

"What shall we call you, my friend?" Brya asked.

The Nyek looked perplexed by the question and did not reply. GranMay pointed to each in the party in turn. "My name is May, she is Brya, and he is Kyan. What name do you use?"

The Nyek looked over to the rock face of the cliff then scampered to it. She rose on her hind legs and scratched at a spot with her front claws.

Kyan stood and moved to see what she was scratching at and saw a dark green streak through the rock. He took a hammer and chisel from his pack and moved in as the Nyek backed away.

He knocked loose a small chunk of the rock which held the green crystal. With it wrapped in his hand, he concentrated on the green material to melt the ore and let it flow into his palm. With a large amount of the green material in his palm, he laid the other hand over it and focused to move the atoms as close as possible, as he had done to make diamond before.

When he opened his hand to reveal a gorgeous green crystalline gemstone, the Nyek trilled in appreciation and nudged the stone with its nose.

"Your name is the name of this gemstone?" Kyan asked. The Nyek nodded with a slow bow.

"Now we only need to know the name of the gemstone," he said with a smirk. Asira lifted her head and moved to them to inspect the gem in Kyan's hand.

"The dragons call it Zolirine, my friend," Asira said.

Kyan looked at the Nyek, who gave a short trill and a quick nod. "Do you prefer the whole word or a shortened version, such as Zoli?" Brya said.

The Nyek made a long trill that conveyed a feeling of achievement. "It is a pleasure to meet you, Zoli," GranMay said. "Now, let us pack up and return to your parents, children. I am sure they are quite eager to have you back with them. I know your mother will enjoy meeting our new friend."

Kyan hurried to lift GranMay's bag before she did. She smiled and kissed his cheek before turning to Zoli.

"Would you like to ride with me aboard Lady Asira?"

Zoli crouched as she looked at the great dragon and trilled a low rumble which sent strong feelings of fear and distrust. GranMay moved to kneel by her and stroked her fur as she passed confidence and trust.

"Do you fear the dragon or the flight itself?" GranMay asked. Zoli looked to the sky as answer. *"I happen to be wearing a cloak my granddaughter gave me, which was made to carry dragon hatchlings. It has wonderful cloth-lined pockets which the new hatchlings love to curl up in. I think that you would feel safe wrapped tight within one. Would you like to try it and see if it suits you?"*

Zoli nodded and jumped to her knee then crawled into the pocket GranMay held open. She twisted and turned for a moment, then settled down as she trilled comfort and contentment.

GranMay boarded Asira, and the twins boarded their own mounts. The dragons were away and flying for the camp when GranMay felt Morgan touch her spirit.

"Good morning, GranMay. I am glad to feel you coming this way at last. I see you have found a new friend. Actually, I feel fear from the little one. Is it alright?"

"She is not fond of flying but has taken refuge in one of my cloaks wonderful pockets. Her name is Zoli, and she is curious to meet you, my dear. The children told her that touching her was much like touching you when your guard was down. She found that very interesting, indeed." She felt surprise from Morgan and chuckled. *"We will be with you soon, my dear."*

Elder Elosh

MORGAN AND ALEC had traveled to the campsite as soon as they woke. They were sitting with Taru and Daniel, having breakfast, when Morgan felt her children and GranMay returning. She and Alec had both relaxed in knowing the children were coming to them, but her heart was heavy as she took in the feelings within her brother. He was stoic and avoided her eyes until he rose and walked away from the group alone.

Taru laid a hand to her arm and pushed reassurance. She replied with a bit of gratitude as she fought to keep her emotions in check.

"I spoke with him last night," Taru said. *"He remains grateful to be alive. However, he is wrestling with many feelings."*

"I have been very purposeful in blocking his thoughts. I will let him share them when he is ready."

She moved to take her plate to the lake and rinsed it clean before returning it to the supply basket. She noticed Alec had left and was headed toward Daniel, who was just entering the woods.

"I prefer you not make an argument on my behalf," she said to him.

"He is my friend, and I am worried about him. I speak for myself, not for you, my love."

She smiled as she felt the sincerity and love for Daniel in his words. Her gaze fell on the great Elder Elosh, who was lying beside the lake. He was surrounded by younglings and seemed to be telling a story to them.

"Should we wait until Elder Elosh has finished visiting with the younglings to speak with him, my Sister?" Morgan asked Nulian as she moved to stand by her head.

"They will not leave him, my Queen. He will be accompanied by many younglings at all times for his final days. It is for his comfort, and it allows the younglings to respect the nobility of life and death."

"Is now a good time to join them?"

Nulian crooned a mournful sound as she looked at the aged dragon. "You should not wait, my Sister. He grows weak and will soon sleep again."

Morgan patted her and sent loving support before she and Taru headed over to visit with Elosh. As they approached, Elosh picked up his massive head and bowed to them in greeting. They all bowed to him as well to show their respect.

"You seek information, do you not, my friends? Do you wish to know more of the race who first made the purple fluid within the portal?" Elosh asked in his low, coarse voice.

"You are perceptive as usual, Elder Elosh. Do you have more to share with us?" Morgan said.

"Not at my immediate use, no. But as I have seen the strength of your heart and purity of your spirit, Queen Morgan, I will allow you to seek the information within me through bonding. I can do little else now but share my knowledge before it is lost forever." He lowered his head to lay it in front of her.

"Actually, Elder Elosh, we believe Lady Taru will be able to access more of your information as ..."

"No, only you. I feel trust for you and do not know her," Elosh said.

Morgan felt the hurt within Taru as she looked to the ground.

"Do not take it as an insult, my Sister. He does not judge you. He is comfortable with me because we have met and spoken many times over the last two years," she told Taru.

Morgan put her hand to Elosh and said only to him, *"My friend, will you look within me and seek the true nature of Taru. I completed her Quickening, and you will feel her spirit through me. I ask you, as your friend, to please consider it."* Elosh paused a few seconds before he sought bonding.

He deepened the bonding so quickly that she had to be careful to control the passing of magic between them. He sought the essence of Taru from her Quickening. He then shifted focus to Taru's history. He studied all she offered for many minutes before pulling back from the bonding.

"I will allow her to bond to me through you, my friend," Elosh said. "Come, my Sister," she said to Taru with a smile.

"I do not want to enter where I am not completely welcome, my Queen. It feels very wrong," Taru said.

"Goodness! I trust you both completely, and we need this information to build the portal home. Please, bond to one another for no reason but to feel the purity of each others' spirits so we may move forward."

Elosh picked up his head and glared at her before giving a little snort and turning his head to look out over the lake.

"It is not your place to give an order to an Elder dragon, my Queen. That was very disrespectful," Nulian said with a deep scowl. Morgan winced at the anger and disappointment from Nulian, and blushed as she realized the tone she had used.

"Forgive me, please. I meant to make a request, Elder Elosh. I did not intend for it to sound like an order. I humbly ask again now. Will you please bond to Taru enough to seek her spirit and see her purity for yourself?"

Elosh continued to look over the water as if he no longer wanted to talk to them. Morgan was just about to turn and leave when he laid his head in front of Taru. "I will allow it."

Taru stepped to him and placed both hands to his snout. She shivered at the touch, and her markings burst into light as Morgan had never seen. The dragons on her body shifted, making her shiver again. When she dropped her guard she gasped and flinched back as she looked up into Elosh's eyes.

"As I told my dear Queen, I do not want to enter where I am not completely welcome. If I am to know the touch of your spirit, I very much want it to be a choice you make without hesitation, Elder Elosh," Taru said with a smile.

"I do nothing I do not wish to. Not even for your very insistent Queen. Now, let me connect and bond so I may touch your spirit, young one."

"I am honored to do so, my Elder," Taru said as she laid her hands back to Elosh.

She allowed the connection and bonding while keeping herself calm and compliant. Emotions threatened to make her tear up the instant he found the memory of Grith, her dragon father.

Elosh spent a great deal of time touching each of her memories of her time with Grith. When he reached her last memory of Grith, she felt sorrow from him. Seconds later, his guard fell away, flooding Taru with love and acceptance.

"As a child of my dear Great-uncle Grith, you are welcome to seek whatever you wish, my Perian Sister," Elosh said. Taru smiled and leaned in to lay her head against his. She had recognized the familial link the instant she let his magic touch hers and

was thankful he welcomed their connection.

She sought his spirit and found it to be very complex. He had a sort of haze over most of his memories, which required a great deal of focus to pass through. Once beyond the foggy wall, she found many old memories of his ancestors. She focused and thought, "formation of the portal liquid," allowing her magic to guide her to the proper memories.

She soon received a fuzzy image of many thin, pale people standing in a great circle, each holding a glowing blue crystal. The group was singing a complex song where every person seemed to have a different part, which they sang over each other in perfect harmony.

The song was not what you would hear among humans. It was a sound similar to that of a wood flute and more music than song. She could not make out distinct words of any language she knew and had the feeling there were no words at all.

Taru was a little shocked as each of the people took out a small knife and pricked their finger to let a few drops of their own blood fall onto the stone in their hand. They then held the stone between their hands as the song took on an even more complex nature.

As the music continued, each person in the group took their turn to walk forward and place their stone within an ornate metal ring. Taru noticed that the glowing stones were now a deep purple color, the simple combination of the dark red blood with the bright blue of the stones.

Once all had laid their stones together, the group knelt close to the metal ring and laid their hands against it. The instant the last to kneel touched the ring, the stones' glow increased dramatically and lit the great cavern in which they worked. Taru recognized the cavern as the portal room within the rock island of Erion.

The music quieted and an Elder moved to stand within the circle formed by the stones. It was a very old man who had white eyes as if blind. He began to sing a new addition to the song. As he sang, the stones started to change from solid to liquid around his feet. Taru could not understand all he said but noticed as the liquid reached his feet, he said very clearly, "To Kalias, to home."

The Elder started to sing the exact song Taru knew to be written on the walls of that portal room. As he repeated them, the purple liquid spread to the edges of the ring, then began to climb his body. The words appeared on the walls in bright white script. With the last letter of the last word, the man's body became pure white light, which dropped into the pool, illuminating it for several seconds before fading to leave the liquid undulating slightly within the ring.

Taru was dumbstruck when all the people remaining in the room broke down into tears. One young woman leaned forward to lay her hand to the purple liquid. "Goodbye, Father. You honor us with this gift of spirit. My heart burns with pride, yet, it will never again be whole without you."

A man older than the woman helped her to her feet and held her. "It is considered the most noble of deaths among our people to give your life force to form a portal to a new world. You must be happy for Lavun, my dear. He has done an honorable thing for our people and our noble dragon friends. The dragons of Kalias can now join us here on Erion. In exchange for this portal, they have sworn to remove their memories of our cities. We will live unbothered for as long as we wish. It is a gift of protection from the dark ones on both worlds because no human could reach the depth of our city without the aid of a dragon. We may one day decide to trust humans again, but it will be our choice to make."

Taru backed away from Elosh's spirit to break the bonding but stayed connected to speak with him alone.

"How do you have this memory if the dragons' promise was kept?"

"One of my ancestors bonded to one of the spirits you saw around the circle and gained this knowledge through their special

link. The knowledge has passed through blood for many genera-tions, and the secret kept, until this moment. Use the knowledge well, my Sister."

"What are these people called?"

"Primin, my Lady. They are the oldest race of man I know of."

Taru sent admiration and loving friendship with strong force before she broke the connection and leaned away from him.

"Thank you very much, Elder Elosh. You honor me by allowing me to share your knowledge."

He crooned before closing his eyes to fall fast asleep.

TARU SHARED all she learned with those around her and was just finishing as the twins and GranMay arrived at the camp. The twins ran to hug their parents, as Daniel went to hug GranMay and offer her his arm.

They walked over to join the rest of the group, where they sat among the boulders around the lake. Taru repeated all she had learned for the three newcomers.

"Did you learn anything about the Primin who lived here on Berios?" Morgan asked.

"No, I saw and heard only mention of Kalias and Erion. I have no idea if they are here as well, my Sister," Taru said.

A sharp trill came from GranMay's pocket, making everyone who had not yet met the Nyek jump. GranMay smiled and opened her coat.

Zoli stepped out to perch on her knees. She turned to look at Morgan and bowed as she trilled to send a feeling of respect. Zoli met the eye of everyone in turn then leapt to Morgan's lap. Morgan felt a burst of magic flow through her the instant she touched her legs.

"I am Morgan. It is an honor to meet you, Zoli. Your magic has me tingling all over with just this simple contact. You must carry a great deal within you, my new friend."

Zoli nodded and moved to nudge her hand. She turned her palms up, and Zoli inspected both, as well as her Crest, with interest.

"May I touch your fur?" Morgan asked. Zoli nodded and stood as she placed her hand on the Nyek's head.

Everyone gave sounds of surprise as the Nyek changed to a bright white with a spotted pattern like a leopard as Morgan's hand moved down her back. Morgan shivered at the fast transfer of magic and looked to see how all her markings glowed brightly.

"That is a lovely coat change, but you were very attractive before, as well," Morgan said. She continued to stroke her for a bit as she thought about the possible presence of Primin inhabiting Berios.

Zoli trilled assurance and confidence and met her eyes.

"Did you just respond to my thought, little friend?" Morgan asked with a lifted eyebrow. Zoli nodded and purred. "Does that mean you know of Primin on Berios?"

Zoli nodded again.

"Can you show me where to find them? We need their help to build a portal,"

Zoli turned her head to the lake and trilled. Morgan looked at the lake she had swum in so many times.

"They have a hidden city within this very lake?" Zoli nodded and trilled reassurance.

"They have lived right around us each time we have come to Berios, and we never knew they existed," Morgan said with a glance at both Nulian and Alec. Both wore similar looks of surprise and concern. She straightened her face and looked back to Zoli. "Do you know how we could contact them?"

Zoli looked at her and tilted her head as she trilled confusion. "We need to find them and speak with them."

Zoli shook her head and resumed her purring.

"Do you mean you do not know how to contact them?"

A trill that conveyed rudeness left the Nyek as she looked at the lake and growled.

"They are rude to those who seek them?"

Zoli nodded and settled down to lie in her lap. She had just settled when she jumped to her feet and turned to study Morgan's abdomen.

Morgan smiled as the Nyek gave a soft trill and touched her nose to her belly. Her son began to wiggle around at the Nyek's touch.

"I see you felt the presence of my son, who grows quickly these days," Morgan said as she rubbed her belly. As she thought to stand, Zoli jumped up to her shoulders and laid across them. She used her long tail to hang down and loop under Morgan's arm for added balance.

Morgan stood and walked to the edge of the water. Everyone joined her and stared at the water as well.

"Taru, you can hold your breath the longest. Would you care to take a ride with one of our dragon brethren and see just how deep this lake is?"

"Absolutely," Taru said as she smiled and turned to face the group of dragons lying along the shore. "Who would care to go for a fast and deep swim with me?"

Falin was up and aloft in a second. He landed in front of her just long enough for her to jump aboard. He soared over the water, looped up, then dove straight into the middle of the lake. Zoli trilled, conveying a feeling of worry and caution.

Morgan passed the sentiment to Taru as she connected to her to track her movement and monitor her health.

"Nulian, will you be ready to dive if she stays too long, please?"

Nulian grumbled but flew to a high ridge nearby.

"She is a great deal like you in that respect," Nulian said. *"Therefore, I fully expect that she will indeed push the limits of her ability."* Morgan smiled at her friend's sarcasm while monitoring those under the water.

Daniel soon started pacing the bank.

"Use the magic and call out to them from there before you head up," Morgan said to Taru. *"Continue calling and explain our need as you rise, my Sister."*

Taru did as she asked for another two minutes before Falin urged her to return to the surface. They soon came flying up from the water, and Daniel let out a great breath as he rubbed a hand through his hair. He smiled at his wife as he shook his head.

"You worry far too much, my love," Taru said.

"I'm sure I always will, because you seem to enjoy giving me reason to do so."

Falin swam to the shore and Taru leapt to the bank where she wrapped Daniel in a huge hug. She was getting him all wet and giggled while he squirmed to get free without success. Daniel went still and his smile slipped as he noticed many watching them.

"What did you learn, Lady Taru?" Morgan asked.

"I saw nothing out of the ordinary, my Queen. We went nearly two hundred feet down, I would estimate."

"Did that depth bother you?"

"No, my Queen," she said. *"But I do not believe Falin would care to go any deeper."*

"Alright. Relax for a bit, everyone. I will seek more from the ancient knowledge within me for a while." As she walked, Zoli began to purr, which sent a warm calming wave through her.

Primin

"I HONESTLY WONDER if there is a way to get the Primin to speak with us when they have worked so hard to not be found. If they will not speak with us, then we will never fulfill this task. Berios will be lost to our family as a safe haven in times of crisis, and as a sanctuary for me when I need to be free of all the minds of Erion," Morgan said to Zoli as she wandered along the lake's edge. She glanced up at Nulian, where she lay along the high ridge. "The real loss is to our dragon Elders who come here for peace and quiet in their later years. This has been their well-deserved oasis of sorts."

Zoli trilled compassion, so she raised a hand to stroke her under her chin. She continued to walk for a while and soon found herself near the base of the falls. She sat and gazed at the lake and falls while contemplating their options.

As she sat staring at the falls with unfocused eyes, she saw movement from side-to-side. She focused her excellent vision and realized she had not imagined it. There was a figure standing behind the falling water watching her.

She opened herself to feel the being and only felt a faint presence. Not enough to represent a human the size of the figure she was looking at.

"Zoli, do the Primin have the ability to block magical detection as the Nyek do, my friend?" Zoli nodded and trilled assurance.

Morgan focused hard on the figure behind the falls.

"I know you do not wish to be disturbed, but we desperately need your help in rebuilding the portal to Erion. Please, consider helping us. I am sure you have observed us over the last few years, and know us to be kind and of pure spirit. I will not attempt to reach your city again. I ask that you come to us, and give us the opportunity to earn your trust."

She stood, bowed to the figure behind the water, and walked away. When halfway back to the others, she felt a touch of magic against her guard, which she dropped enough to receive thought only.

"Come tonight when the moons are at their highest. We will speak with you, Lady Morgan of Erion. Only with you," the voice said. She smiled as she continued a slow pace toward the camp.

"I will be here. Thank you for granting me an audience."

When she reached her family, she held her guard high and kept her face placid.

"I think we should continue to prepare what we can as we work to solve the remainder of this puzzle. I ask that the Knights go to gather the blue stones. We will need a great many of them to build such a large portal. Taru, will you go with them to help ensure they gather the right material? My hope is that Daniel will accompany you."

They both agreed and moved to organize the Knights.

"I felt you disconnect from me, my dear. I also saw you bow toward the waterfall. Did you contact the Primin?" Alec asked. She answered with a smile, a wink, and a kiss to the cheek.

LATE THAT NIGHT, Morgan kissed Alec and stood to leave. He stood to follow, and she stopped.

"They asked for me, alone. Your accompanying me may remove any chance we have at restoring the portal to Erion. I respect your desire to protect me, but ..."

"You are not invincible!" he shouted as a sudden storm of emotions roared through his entire being. He stepped closer, making her tense as his anger and disappointment seared through her. "It is time you force yourself to envision the scenario where Daniel was not at your side on Kalias! See that dagger ravaging your own body! Face the truth in that moment being your last! Your magic would not have saved you. Our children nor Queen May could have saved you. Accept that truth! Only then could you ever truly respect our desire to protect you!"

He marched out of the gazebo, then waved his arms at Gerzin and Nulian, who were lying on a nearby ridge. Morgan failed to control her temper as she leapt down the stairs and shoved him in the back. He spun on her and did not flinch as she screamed back at him.

"I have envisioned that scenario repeatedly since the second I felt his heart stop! In that moment, I welcomed death as I never have! You have never shared someone's fear in such a moment, the helplessness, the sheer terror that grips them as their body fails them completely. How can you begin to judge me when you have no idea what it is like to wield so much power, then try to accept anyone enduring such pain in your place?" He reached for her arms, but she slapped his arms away. "I have fought to convince myself that Daniel dying to save me was right on any level. It is what our country needs its Caretaker to believe, but my spirit cannot accept it! My insistence to walk into this and any other conflict alone is not an arrogant belief that I am invincible. It is a conviction to not have anyone die in an effort to save me as if my life were more valuable than theirs!"

"That is not a decision for you to make! Our conviction to die in your place is not one of devotion to you alone. It is an act of devotion to every precious member of our Chemerian family! Being the one for whom we fall is a profound and weighty duty, for certain. You are choosing to bear it as a burden, to take on the full weight of our country's future, and it is crushing your spirit. It is time you embrace it as the honor it is, respect those who proudly stand at your side, and truly recognize that our conviction to fight and die for our country is just as fierce as yours. We love your beautiful spirit and are deeply grateful to serve such a powerful Queen. Please, my Caretaker, let us love you as deeply as you love us."

She had turned away from him to gaze out over the valley as tears slid down her face. He moved to stand close behind her, making her shiver as his deep respect and love flowed over her with his last words. His arms wrapped and held her as she fought to accept the truth in his words.

"I admit feeling overwhelmed by my need to protect. I never meant to suggest that your desire to serve our country was any less valid than mine. Almost losing Daniel has left me more aware of my mortality than I have been since facing Harrick and feeling Martus's lance drive into my back. It is sobering, and I promise to be more mindful of my vulnerabilities. We must both respect the duty and convictions of the other. However, in times when our convictions conflict, you must believe that my following the magic is not being disrespectful to you."

He sighed, laid his head to hers, and spoke with conviction.

"Being led by the magic, and being led by your heart's desire to put yourself between us and all danger, are not the same. I am asking that you be honest with yourself in discerning the two."

She turned her head to rest it against his and did her best to convince herself that she could do as he asked.

"I promise to try. Surely I can trust you and Daniel to call me out if you feel I have failed to do so."

He chuckled as he shifted to kiss her cheek and urge her toward the dragons who were just landing beside them. Nulian hummed to pass deep respect as she moved to touch her snout to Alec.

"You are bold in your devotions to your mate, and to your Caretaker, my friend. I am grateful for both."

"Does that mean you have seen me as arrogant or reckless in my magic as well?" Morgan asked.

"No. It means that I have allowed love and pride to blind me to the truth in your inherent vulnerability as a human. It is also true that your human brethren can provide protections we cannot. Our might and magic are strong, but I could not have saved you from that dagger as Sir Daniel did. We will work together to find ways to use your formidable skills while keeping you out of harms' way wherever possible."

"What of this meeting with the Primin then? They asked that I come alone. Are we to ignore that request?"

"I suggest you use your skills of communication from a safe distance and assess the dangers from there. You need not put yourself near them if it seems unsafe."

"I imagine you will all be insisting I use that tactic a great deal more," Morgan said as she and Alec stepped into Nulian's offered palm.

"We will, indeed, my Queen," Gerzin said with a deep chuckle that made them all laugh as well.

MORGAN AND ALEC sat down on a boulder far from the falls as Nulian lay down in the shallow water near them. They waited for twenty minutes past the moons' cresting before Morgan started pacing.

"If they are so intimidated by our race that they will not speak with two at a time, then we have little hope of working with them, my dear," Alec said.

She turned to look at the falls as she felt the approach of uniquely different magic. Many figures appeared on each side of the falls. Their skin was pale, eyes pale hues of purple and blue, hair dark, and all had lithe frames. As they moved further from the falls, she noticed their skin had a pearlescent quality in the moonlight.

As she and Alec bowed, a male Elder stepped forward two paces and gave a curt nod. She tried to connect to the Primin's mind enough to speak but was blocked by a strong guard. Unwilling to force her way, she waited, then allowed the Elder to initiate connection.

"You alone, Lady Morgan of Erion. Trust enough to come to us, or there will be no further contact."

Morgan glanced at both Alec and Nulian as she assured only they would hear her words.

"They carry no weapons and are all Elders. I do not think they mean to attack me. I think it worth the risk to trust enough to stand a few yards from him." She held Alec's eyes, waiting for his input.

"Yards, not feet," Alec said. *"Respect that we know nothing of their physical speed and agility, so keeping that distance seems wise."* Nulian nodded in agreement, so Morgan started moving across the boulders to land on a ledge near the Primin.

"Speak your mind, Human. We will hear your words, and you will then leave us be."

"We need your help to replace the portal to Erion," Morgan said in a calm respectful tone. "It was destroyed in a quake earlier this year. That portal is a very important part of my country's culture and very precious to us. What would you have us do to prove our spirits worthy of your help?"

"No human can prove their spirit pure, as it is not possible. Your hearts are inherently bent on power and control and we desire none of it around us. The portal was not destroyed by accident. We destroyed it purposefully. We will not replace it."

"You killed a great and very dear Elder dragon in your action! I was under the impression you respected their noble race. Why would you have done such a horrible thing?"

"That was a regrettable result of a rightful act. We had no intention of harming Elder Palish. We cannot change it, however." Morgan fought to control her rage as she held the Elder's cold eyes.

"If you knew him well enough to know his name, then there is no way you did not know his spirit to be among the purest imaginable. If you forgive such a negligent act so easily, then you have no place judging humans as impure."

Frowns and whispers moved through the crowd of Primin behind the glaring Elder. All hushed as he lifted a hand.

"We have a great deal of respect for the magic of the dragon, but do not agree with their decision to align themselves with humans. It is ludicrous that such a powerful species would serve a lower species such as yours. It is not logical, as the dragon has nothing to gain in the partnership."

All of the Primin jumped as Nulian's great head came up out of the water beside Morgan. The Elder dragon had approached stealthily, with her guard high, to get very near her Queen. Nulian kept her head at the height of the Elder Primin as she studied him for many seconds.

"Elder Primin, how can you judge something of which you are ignorant? If you wish to judge our alliance with humans, then you should experience the bond between the two species before doing so."

The Elder Primin had not flinched as Nulian brought her head near him and still looked at her with a placid expression.

"We are not interested in knowing anything about your connection to humans, Elder Nulian. We simply want the humans to leave this planet and not return."

"Yours is a very selfish and elitist race, Primin. You speak of the flaws within the human race, yet ignore the obvious deficiency within your own. You speak of the human seeking power, while you wish to control all around you," Nulian said. She slowly leaned in to get very near his face. "You, Sir, are a hypocrite, and not worthy of speaking with, my Queen."

Nulian backed her head away from him and kept it between the Elder Primin and Morgan. She nudged Morgan and used the contact to reconnect, *"Get on now. Quickly, my Sister."*

"Nulian, we must convin—"

"Move, now, my Queen!"

Morgan vaulted to her back and held tight as Nulian shot through the water for the opposite shore. She felt both Gerzin and Panish drawing closer at a very fast speed.

"Nulian, did you summon them?"

"Yes. The Primin have acted against our kind, and it will not go unanswered."

Morgan tried to calm her angry sister with magic but made little progress with her own still roaring hot within her.

"They said they did not intend to harm Palish, my dear. We mu—"

Nulian stopped abruptly and swung her head around to look at her. "Harm Palish? What are you speaking of?"

Morgan tried to raise her guard, but Nulian was pushing hard against it.

"Do you wish to experience it the way they told it, or in my words?" "Your words. Hold nothing from me, my Caretaker."

"The Primin destroyed the portal on purpose to prevent me and my family from coming back here. They said they did not intend to injure Palish and consider it a regrettable result."

She had to take her hand off of Nulian as the rage within the dragon reached enormous levels in seconds. Nulian moved to the shore in a fast dash and crouched low.

"Dismount, my Queen."

"What are you going to do?"

"Get down, Morgan!"

Morgan slid down as Nulian turned her head toward where Panish approached. A great roar filled the valley as he doubled his pace toward the falls. Nulian launched into the air to sweep a circle, shot up, then dove in unison with Panish.

Gerzin circled the lake until Menkar and the rest of the Chemerian dragons landed near Morgan and Alec, then dove to follow Nulian.

Morgan knelt at the water's edge as she pushed to connect to Nulian. Her breath caught, and she clutched her chest as she felt the pain and rage within her powerful friend. She sent a quick summons to the twins and GranMay, then refocused on tracking and trying to connect to Nulian.

The enraged Elder dragons were both reliving the pain of the day they lost their brother. Panish's anger was beyond a point where reasoning with him was possible. The dragons had entered a labyrinth of water-filled tunnels making it very difficult for Morgan to stay connected.

The twins each took one of Morgan's hands the second they reached her. She used their added strength to sharpen her focus on Nulian, Panish, and Gerzin. They ascended through the tunnel system then emerged in a great cavern deep within the mountain bearing the waterfall.

All three dragons began to sing a loud and angry roaring song. Morgan felt their rage turning into song and had no idea what was happening. Many Primin entered the chamber where the dragons stood. Each fell to the ground in front of them, grasping their heads *and shaking.*

"Disconnect now, my Queen! Do not reconnect," Nulian said.

Morgan dropped the connection to Nulian, released the twins' hands, and stood to let Alec wrap her in a tight embrace as her emotions took her. As she cried, she heard Brya gasp and reached out to block her magic.

"Do not attempt to connect to Nulian, Panish, or Gerzin until they return to us," she said.

"MY QUEEN, Nulian's rage has overtaken her senses. She and Panish will kill them all if we do not stop them. Their anger feeds off that of the other," Gerzin said as he swam up through the lake to burst through the surface and land abruptly near Morgan. "She tried to reason with the Primin. Their refusal to help you, as repayment for their murder of Palish, has broken her will to hold in her rage. Please, try to reach her, my Queen."

Morgan nodded, laid her hands over her Crest, and focused her magic on connecting to her blood-giver. She flinched and leaned back against Alec as she was hit by the intense emotions ripping through her dear friend. That intense emotion crushed any guilt she felt for disobeying her Elder's order, allowing her to push harder than she ever had against Nulian's guard to assure she would hear her words.

"My Sister, you are not just in killing them now. Hear me, Nulian. It is not a just act, and you will never forgive yourself. Stop, Nulian! Stop Panish, so he does not live the rest of his life with this on his heart. Killing them will not bring Palish back to you. Please, come to me, my Sister."

Morgan was encouraged as she felt Nulian stop pursuing the Primin. She thought her plea had worked until Panish roared with pain-driven rage. Nulian responded to her brother's call in kind.

Morgan opened her eyes and laid a hand to Alec's chest as she pushed her devotion and assured he felt the urgency of the moment.

"I must go, and you cannot follow. I am sorry."

"Do not apologize for your skill. Go; bring them back to us," he said as he shifted to kiss her forehead.

He pushed her off, and she vaulted up to Gerzin. He took to the air as she slid her hands into the tight gaps between his large scales to grip their smooth edges. She dug her feet in as best she could, then lay down flat to his body as he dove for the lake. They sliced through the surface and traveled fast into the darkness of the deep lake. She had to focus to keep from panicking when the pressure and darkness of such an extreme depth hit her.

Gerzin was stroking hard to carry them as fast as possible. She tried to look forward but the speed of the water hurt her eyes too much. It took all of her new strength to hold onto the great dragon as he twisted and turned through the tunnel system.

The closer she got to Nulian, the more deeply she felt the rage within her. She tried to connect again but could not break through her guard while working so hard to keep herself stable. Gerzin started to ascend through the labyrinth just as she started aching for a breath.

As they drew closer, she was able to connect to Nulian enough to feel her rage and get a glimpse of her surroundings. She and Panish had a large group of Primin cornered and were roaring at them.

"As quick as possible, or we will be too late," she said to Gerzin. He pushed hard through the last of the tunnels and broke the water's surface in a great cavern.

Morgan leapt from his back then ran full speed as she let her link to Nulian lead her. Nulian's rage was too fierce to hear her words through magic. She had to reach her.

"No!" she screamed aloud and in thought when she felt Panish direct a strike at an attacking group of lance-wielding Primin. Her call reached him. He pulled back at the last moment, yet grazed the men with his talons enough to cause significant injury.

Morgan shot into the massive cavern where the dragons had the group cornered against the far wall. Just after she entered, a second group lunged for Nulian.

"Stop!" Morgan said as she used her magic to stop them in their tracks. She held them still as she kept running across the giant cavern floor to reach her friends.

The Elder Primin shouted an order, and a split second later a lance pierced Nulian's side. Morgan shared her pain and stumbled hard to the ground.

Nulian released a horrifying roar then lunged for the Elder who gave the order. The group pulled him to the middle and she roared mere feet from their faces.

"Him or all! Choose!"

The group of Primin did not let her have their Elder and two lifted other lances which they directed her way. Morgan was back on her feet and running hard when she saw Nulian raise her front foot to strike the group. She leapt in front of them, raised her hands, and screamed, "No, Sister!"

Nulian had already committed to the strike. She could not stop her foot, but did retract her talons just before impact. The huge foot slammed into Morgan, throwing her twenty yards across the cavern where she crashed into a stone wall.

Nulian and Panish froze, as did every Primin present, all eyes on Morgan's still form. Deep croons of remorse and worry left both dragons as they touched their snouts to their Caretaker and felt the great damage within her.

Many bones were fractured. Blood poured from a deep gash along her forehead and a gruesome open fracture to her right arm. The dragons hummed their healing song and flooded her body with magic as intensely as they could.

They felt her life slipping away as her breaths became shallow and wet. Nulian was pushing so hard she was falling weak herself and lay down as her legs buckled.

"I will die before giving up. Do not interfere, Brother," Nulian said to Panish.

"I will die with you if we cannot save her," Panish said as he continued to give all he had.

Just as the dragons were losing consciousness, they saw a Primin crawl over their snouts to reach Morgan. The Primin laid his hand over the wound on her forehead while singing a gentle, soothing tune. He then moved his hands to her mangled arm, which he manipulated as his song grew louder. After a moment, he released her well-healed arm and started touching other parts of her body to heal internal wounds as well.

Nulian was gasping for breath as she continued to push her magic to Morgan. The Primin scooted Morgan away from her, ignoring her weak growl. When he finished healing Morgan, he moved to kneel between the huge snouts of Nulian and Panish. He was not an Elder, yet spoke with authority.

"My father was wrong. He has been removed from his position as our leader. I speak for my people now, and I humbly ask you to accept strength of magic from me, dear dragons. Please let me undo the damage you have done yourselves in attempt to save your brave friend," the Primin said.

Nulian did not have the energy to reply, so she blinked once and stared back at him. He scooted forward with caution as he glanced from her to Panish, whose eyes were closed, then placed his hands to her hide. He passed energy to her until she was strong enough to raise her head and reach out to Morgan. She nudged her Queen and crooned as tears left her eyes.

"She will be fine after much rest to regain her strength," the Primin said. Nulian nodded but said nothing. The Primin healed Panish, then turned to walk away. He was stopped by the head of Panish as it swept in front of his path.

"Thank you for saving our Queen. I would never have expected such an act of kindness, but am very grateful. When she wakes, we will take her and never bother your kind again," Panish said. He then moved to lie close to Nulian and put his snout to Morgan, as did Nulian.

The Primin walked to a group of his people who all started conversing in whispers. A moment later, he walked back to where Morgan laid and knelt facing the dragons.

"Your human sister's selfless act has shown me, and those of my generation, that there is much our Elders have hidden from us. We were told the human was incapable of love and bore evil spirits. They lied to keep us away from them, and they were wrong." He laid a hand to Morgan and passed energy until she woke.

Morgan blinked as she woke and laid a hand to Nulian and Panish. Both dragons crooned as they passed their sincere love.

"I am so sorry, my Sister," Nulian said. "I am ashamed of my loss of control. Thank you for protecting me from myself."

Morgan tried to sit up, then fell back down as she squinted and gripped her head. "Goodness, my dear, I do wish you would stop spinning the cavern about like this."

Nulian chuckled, despite the guilty ache in her heart. Panish joined her as the Primin leader leaned over to touch Morgan's arm and pass more healing energy.

"Thank you, my dear. That fee—" Morgan muttered as she struggled to clear her head. Recognition of the foreign magic jolted her eyes open. She froze as she held a pair of striking amethyst-purple eyes, then forced a deep, shaky breath as she fought to raise her guard. The male Primin smiled and offered a hand. She ignored it while sliding back from him. *"I wish to leave here, my Sister."* Nulian offered her palm and hummed to share more healing magic. Morgan crawled into it, then groaned as her head throbbed and spun far more with the movement to the saddle.

Once still, Morgan met the Primin's gaze, then carefully bowed her head a bit. "Thank you for trying to heal me. I am glad to know a Primin can be kind, even to a human." She urged Nulian to leave and squinted as she leaned forward against the saddle's front bolster. *"Get me to my children, my Sister. There is something very wrong with my head,"* she said while panting through fierce waves of pain and nausea.

Nulian and Panish stood with hums of respect to the Primin, then moved at a quick pace through the tunnels to reach the cavern containing the pool of water. They wasted no time and entered the water, making a quick path back to the surface of the lake.

When Nulian slid into the bank, Morgan waited for her palm, then took her children's hands as soon as they reached her. Both pushed healing as they laid their free hands to her head. After only a few seconds, she was clear-headed and out of pain.

"YOU WERE FOLLOWED, Mother. There are many spirits rising," Kyan and Brya said as they focused on the water with scowls.

Everyone in their party turned toward the lake as a large group of Primin emerged and walked forward to stand just in front of Morgan. The male who had helped her stepped forward and bowed low with a brief pause.

"I am Primin Orin. I am now the leader of our people. It was a true honor to have witnessed such a profound act of friendship. The deep love you hold for your dragon brethren drove you to risk your own life to save them from a life of guilt and sadness. In that act, you saved the life of many of those here, and we are grateful. You have a very strong and very pure spirit, Lady Morgan of Erion. I would be honored to earn the right to call you friend."

"How do you know the purity of my spirit, Primin Orin?" Morgan asked with a scowl.

"This Primin saved your life when Panish and I could not, my Queen," Nulian said as she bowed to Orin. "He did so by his own choice and not out of fear of our wrath, as we were near death ourselves. Once you were out of danger, he then chose to save us, despite our actions."

Primin Orin returned Nulian's bow but wore an unsure expression as he studied Morgan. She stepped to him and offered a hand.

"It seems you have already earned the right to call me friend,

Primin Orin. Thank you for your great kindness."

Orin held her eyes with an intense gaze as he stepped forward to take her hand. She felt both the unique nature of his magic and his profound adoration through the touch. The effort was powerful, and she could not suppress a shiver as he pushed a strong wave of respect. Alec's angry jealousy urged her to release the Primin and step back, closer to him. He took her hand as she reached him and continued to glare at Orin. She tried to calm him while keeping her flush face as placid as possible.

"Primin Orin, will you and your people help us replace the portal to Erion?"

"We will indeed. We hope to see much of you, and that seems the best way to assure we do," Orin said.

"That is wonderful news, my new friend," she said with a smile. She relaxed as the tension around the group dropped. "I hope our peoples will learn much about each other and build strong bonds of trust between us."

Orin smiled, then shifted his gaze to study Alec. "Primin Orin, this is my mate, King Alec."

"I thank you for offering aid to my wife, Primin Orin," Alec said in his deep tone as he bowed to Orin.

"It was my honor, and pleasure, to do so," Orin said as he returned the bow.

"These are our children, Brya and Kyan, and my grandmother, Queen May," Morgan said as she gestured to each.

A murmur went through the crowd of Primin, and Orin bent down to let a smaller woman whisper in his ear. He stood straight again with a slight scowl.

"Queen Morgan, did you say they were your children? The same twins born to you here on Berios less than three years ago?"

"Yes, they are. But no, human children do not normally grow at such a rate. They were conceived on a special day given the magic they carry. The combination made them mature very rapidly."

"Yes, conceived on Berios and on the Day of Light. A very auspicious combination indeed. Of course, much of their rate of growth is a reflection of the dragon blood within them. The same is true of the child within you, my Lady."

He then bowed to the twins and kept eye contact with Brya while he stood. Kyan took her hand and his face darkened. Orin smiled and looked to GranMay.

As he stepped closer to her, his smile widened.

"I feel the wonderful purity of a Nyek around you, my Lady. May I meet the lovely creature?"

"That is up to her, Primin Orin. And she has not chosen to show herself. Perhaps another time," GranMay said. Orin bowed his head and moved back to Morgan.

"I must return to handle the mitigations with the Elders and the new leaders of our people. Shall we form the new portal this evening, my friend?"

"That sounds wonderful. We have collected ample amounts of the metal ore and have a party collecting the crystals as we speak." Orin had raised both eyebrows in surprise when she mentioned the crystals.

"You are very well-informed, Queen Morgan. I imagine you would have found a way to construct the portal yourself, had we not agreed to help you. You are a very driven and resourceful woman, indeed."

"Thank you, Primin Orin," she said as the strong admiration flowing from him made her flush again. "We all look forward to working with you this evening."

Orin smiled and stared into her eyes a few extra seconds before offering a bow to Nulian and Panish.

"On behalf of my people, I offer my sincere apologies and heartfelt condolences for the untimely death of your brother. It was a horrible result of a very ill-conceived idea by our Elder council. I am forever in your debt in hopes of one day proving our people are not all so narrow- minded." He bowed again, then turned to enter the water with his brethren.

A BREATH OF RELIEF ran through the group as the Primin dropped beneath the lake's surface. Alec wrapped Morgan from behind and kissed her neck as the rest of the group moved toward the camp.

"You made quite an impression, my bride. That man likes you very much."

She laughed and shifted away from him as she turned to give him a broad smile.

"As shamefully pleasing as it is to feel your jealousy, you know there is no need for such concern, my mate. I am, and forever will be, yours."

She laughed at his prideful smile then headed to speak to Nulian. The mournful dragon had retreated to the far end of the lake where she lay with her head and tail dipping slightly into the water. Morgan crawled over her tail, then climbed up to lay back along her snout.

"Let go of the guilt, please. I made the choice to take the hit, and I am fine." Nulian groaned at the thought of the horrible impact again.

"I nearly killed you, and could have killed your unborn child. I am quite ashamed of myself."

Morgan slapped her and pushed annoyance as she said, "Listen! I did what I did to keep you from living with guilt, and I did so by choice." She shifted to lie back down. "I love you, so I forgive you. Now, say thank you, and get over it!"

Nulian chuckled. "Thank you, Morgan. I love you."

"It is nice to hear you use my name without the serious tone it is usually given in," Morgan said with a smirk.

Nulian laughed again, and both of the exhausted friends soon fell fast asleep.

Vengeance

MORGAN HAD FALLEN deeply asleep lying on Nulian's snout. She woke to Alec's gentle touch to her Crest.

"Time to wake, my love. You need to eat. Then we will go to the gazebo for some proper sleep."

She sat up slowly with a grumble.

"I was very comfortable, my dear. But now that I am awake, I am very hungry."

"I have a meal waiting for you," Alec said with a laugh. She slid down from Nulian's snout into his arms and kissed him lightly. She ate three platefuls of food before stopping herself. She was still a little hungry but put her plate away and moved to perch on Menkar's leg. He crooned as she leaned against his chest with a yawn.

"I feel your fatigue, my Queen. Would you like to return to the gazebo?" Menkar asked.

"In a bit, but you know Nulian will wish to carry me, my friend."

He grumbled and said, "She is selfish with you, my Queen. I

respect the bond you share with her, but I miss your touch."

Morgan smiled then climbed up to sit on his back. "Well, are we going for a flight or not, my friend?"

Menkar crooned and let out a pleased little roar as he took off with unusual grace, knowing she was riding without restraint. They soared high and far for a while as she relaxed against him, enjoying a deep connection.

"It is wonderful to fly with you, my friend. I am touched that you wanted me to. I will admit I thought you content with the men of my family as your riders."

"I love the King, Prince, and Admiral dearly, but I also love my Caretaker and Queen. It is an honor to carry you, and I love the feel of your magic moving through me." He flew lazily for a bit longer, then made a rather sharp turn back toward the camp.

"Did you just get reprimanded for taking me up without a saddle?" "Yes, but it was my father, not Nulian. He has been quite tense of late. I believe it is associated with my young sister, Hytha, and her first clutch. I dare not push him, my Queen."

Morgan thought about Drieden and his worry, then connected to him gently.

"Elder Drieden, what troubles you about Hytha's clutch?"

"Nothing, my Queen."

"I do not appreciate that, my Elder. If you do not wish to discuss your feelings with me, that is fine. Please, do not lie to me."

"Did Father refuse to talk to you, my Queen?"

"Not exactly. He made it clear that he does not wish to share with me."

The two friends flew in wide circles around the lake.

"I want to take a swim before returning to the gazebo. Shall we?" Morgan said.

Menkar dropped quickly and glided in low to skim the surface and make a sliding entrance across the water. Morgan took a deep breath just as he tucked his head under, and they submerged together.

He stroked at a medium pace so she could keep her eyes open. As she looked down into the deep darkness below, she found a pair of eyes looking back at her.

"We are being watched by the Elder who was just ousted from his position as leader of the Primin. I would not be surprised if he meant me harm."

"Do you wish to surface, my Queen?" Menkar asked as he made a turn upward.

Morgan did not respond because she could hear nothing beyond the high-pitched constant note in her head. She rubbed her ears and fought to connect to Menkar without success. As the sound intensified to a painful level, she became very sleepy.

Though she fought to raise her guard, she could do nothing to block the shockwave of sound that hit her next. Dazed, confused, and struggling to tell up from down, she focused on Alec. Everything went suddenly silent, her body went limp, and the force of the rushing water pulled her free of Menkar.

She watched him turn back to reach for her, then clench as a violent shockwave of sound hit him. He writhed in pain, roared reflexively, then fought for many seconds more before going silent and still. She could do nothing for him, or for herself, as darkness closed in.

ALEC WAS TALKING to Daniel and Taru when he felt the jolt of fear and heard Morgan's panicked call. He turned and ran full speed for the water as he yelled, "Nulian, Morgan is in trouble!"

He hit the water and swam hard until Nulian swept him into her front foot and dove. She swam hard and growled deep in her chest as she saw the motionless body of Menkar slowly rising to the surface. She then put on a burst of speed as she saw Morgan sinking fast below them.

Her body buckled as the horrible sound waves the Elder Primin produced hit her and amplified all through her as blinding pain. She released Alec to keep from crushing him and swam hard for Morgan.

Alec's ears hurt far more from the depth at which he was now swimming than from the sound waves. He finally reached Morgan and was encouraged to find her heart still beating. With an arm wrapped around her middle, he started to swim for the surface as hard as he could kick. He climbed about twenty yards before being slammed into by the Elder Primin, whose eyes shone with rage.

The Primin was very nimble in the water. He moved too fast for Alec to see him coming as he flashed by them over and over. With each pass, the Primin's dagger cut deep gashes across Alec's arms and back.

Alec kept one arm wrapped tightly around Morgan's waist, pulled his own dagger, and continued to kick as he looked for his attacker. A flash from his right made him strike just in time to wound the Primin as he flew by.

The Primin let out a high-pitched shriek and darted into the darkness again. Alec watched but kept kicking. He was getting very dizzy, having run out of air long ago.

The Primin emerged from the darkness with his knife bared to impale Morgan. Alec shifted her body behind his just as the Primin reached them. As the Primin slammed into him, Alec wrapped him with arms and legs, ignoring the dagger now buried deep in his abdomen.

He twisted the thrashing man around, hooked an arm tightly around his neck and locked his legs around his torso. With his grip tight, he arched his back and twisted to snap the Primin's neck. After kicking the Primin's lifeless body away, he pulled the dagger from his gut and started fighting to reach Morgan again.

He kissed her lips, used the last of his physical strength to push her toward the surface, and watched her rise as he focused his mind on his children.

THE TWINS had been struggling against the restraint of Panish and Drieden, who held them back by Nulian's order. When they heard their father in their head, their magic acted with their fear. Both Elder dragons roared in pain and swung their heads. The twins slipped free in their distraction and sprinted for the water. Nulian woke with the jolt of their fear and shifted to block them.

"Father calls! Save Mother, GranNulian," the twins screamed in unison.

Nulian shot into the water with a stern order for them to not follow. Menkar dove just behind her. Seconds later, Nulian burst from the water with Morgan in her grasp.

GranMay and the twins all laid hands to Morgan as soon as Nulian laid her down.

"She has a heartbeat, her lungs are clear, and she just took a breath on her own," Brya said. Everyone stared at Morgan and watched as her chest rose and fell at a normal pace.

"Yet, she is not waking. Something is still very wrong," GranMay said.

"I cannot connect to her. What is going on?" Kyan shouted as he pushed harder. Everyone tried with all they carried to reach her mind, yet none could connect.

"That Elder Primin has placed a magical barrier around her consciousness," Nulian growled. "She is trapped within it, and we are held outside of it."

"Where is Father?" Kyan asked as he and Brya stood and stared at the lake. "Menkar is still searching."

Drieden took flight, then dove. He forced Menkar to rise, then dove to search for Alec. Menkar surfaced just long enough to take in a deep breath and dove again.

"They cannot find him," Brya said as she gripped Kyan's hand.

Both placed their other hand to their Crests to let their magic build and allow them to reach as far into the deep water as possible.

They searched for a long moment before both fell to their knees. They had reached the bottom of the lake and found nothing.

They tried to search within the tunnels to the Primin city, but could reach only a few hundred feet into them. Still, they found nothing of their father's spirit.

"GranNulian, Drieden, and Menkar have pushed too far and are near death themselves. We cannot feel Father anywhere in the open water. He is within the cave system somewhere, or he is dead," Kyan and Brya said.

Nulian, Panish, Asira, and Gerzin all dove at once. The minor dragons made a large circle around their human brethren and stood at high alert as they scanned the area around them.

"Both of you come help Zoli. She grows weak, yet your mother is still not coherent. Do nothing but give her your magical strength until you are too tired and weak to continue. Do not push too far," GranMay said. They knelt as each placed a hand to their own Crest and stacked the other atop Morgan's. They pushed all they had to the point of complete exhaustion and passed out.

"At least this way their anguish is lessened for a bit," GranMay said as she pulled them back from Morgan and knelt at her head again. "Carry on, Zoli."

"Queen May, did you do that on purpose to make them sleep?" Falin asked.

"Yes," she said as she placed her hands to Morgan's cheeks. "They would have stopped me from doing this. I love this woman more than my own life. I am giving it to her by choice. Do not interfere!"

Zoli let out a high-pitched trill and pounced to nip at GranMay's hand. She growled and moved to snug herself up to Morgan's throat and chest. Her eyes never left GranMay's as she trilled and purred even louder. Morgan started to mumble and toss her head.

GranMay had pulled her hand away and now glared at the Nyek. Zoli held her gaze as she shifted to trill directly into Morgan's right ear. She shifted and trilled in the other ear for a moment, then back. GranMay jerked as Morgan's screams through magic blasted in her head.

"I am here, Morgan! Can you understand me?" GranMay said. She heard only incoherent screaming, but she heard something. Tears streamed down her face as she looked at Zoli. "It is working. Please, keep going."

The Nyek nodded as she continued her efforts. GranMay placed her hands back to Morgan's temples, and Zoli growled.

"I am only going to try to speak to her, I promise," GranMay said.

Zoli stopped growling and trilled a bit to send trust to GranMay.

That sentiment tore at GranMay's heart since she had just lied to her little friend. She had every intention of giving all she had in an effort to save Morgan.

She tried to connect but could not penetrate the barrier around Morgan's mind. After many fruitless attempts, she removed her hands and looked at Zoli with tears streaming down her cheeks.

"I can do nothing to help her. Let us hope the magic you offer will help her fight her way out of this."

ALEC WOKE to intense tingling in his abdomen and a gentle touch to his cheek. His eyes were too heavy to open. He realized the magic touching him was not Morgan's and jerked upright as the memory of his last conscious moment came back to him.

His abrupt move nearly knocked over the small Primin woman helping him, but he caught her just before she fell backward.

"How did I get here? Where is Morgan?"

"I felt your magic as I was traveling near the outer rim of the city, and found you near death within the east tunnel," the nervous Primin said. "I brought you here to heal your wound, clear the water from your lungs, and encourage your heart to beat again. There was no female near you, and I felt no other magic nearby."

Alec dropped his head to his chest at the mental image of Morgan drifting motionless in the black depths of the lake. Then he thought of his dragon brethren and knew they would never have left her there. He moved to get up but pitched to the side instead.

"Careful! The magic used against you may have damaged your ears such that balance will take a while to return. You are fortunate that you do not carry more magic, or the wicked method used against you would have left you deaf or worse."

Alec's head snapped up to look at her. "Explain that again, please." The Primin saw the fear in his eyes and suddenly shared it.

"Was the woman with you the very magical woman I saw here last night?"

"Yes! What did you mean?"

"I would rather a Primin much older than I explain it to you," she said as she shook her head and started to stand.

Alec took her arms gently.

"Just tell me what you know, please."

"If she had a great deal of magic, then the weapon used against her had that much more devastating an effect. It uses the magic within. She will likely be deaf if she ..."

"If she lives at all," Alec finished. The girl nodded.

"Her only chance is to get our healers to her quickly. Wait here, I will return."

The girl dashed away before Alec could get to his feet. He tried to stand again, but the floor began to tilt as his head spun, making him topple and land hard on his knee.

He sat back down for a moment before he was startled to his feet again. He was stumbling forward as soon as he heard the roaring of dragons within the tunnels around him.

He yelled to them again and again until he heard Nulian in his head.

"My King, are you well? Are they holding you by force?"

"No. A young female Primin saved my life. Tell me of Morgan."

"She was alive when I left her side, my King. But she does not wake."

"Oh, thank the magic," he said as he rubbed his face. *"The Primin said she may be deaf and may still die if one of their healers does not reach her soon. The girl ran to get someone. Call to them, Nulian."*

Nulian used her magic to assure the Primin they would not hurt them, that they were only seeking their King. She pled for their help and asked them to please come quickly.

The young girl came running around a tunnel bend and had two older men on her heels. One was Primin Orin. The two men carried Alec forward to the cavern where the dragons waited. Nulian was crooning and nudging Alec immediately. He rubbed her as he looked to the Orin.

"Your father has injured my wife greatly. Will you help her, Primin Orin?"

"I will try. We must go quickly," Primin Orin said. "Wait here. One of my brothers will arrive shortly and protect your ears as he escorts you to the surface."

The three Primin dove into the water and were out of sight a second later.

"Go, my friends," Alec said as he backed away from Nulian. "Help them if you can. I will be along soon."

Nulian dove, but Gerzin laid his snout to Alec's side and hummed a deep tone that sent devotion and love. Alec leaned into him as his heart ached.

KYAN AND BRYA SHOT TO THEIR FEET as they felt the Primins' approach. Their rage flared, and each let their magic build as they waited, then released it as the first Primin reached the surface.

The young female grabbed her head and dove back under the

water with a shriek. The twins stayed focused, unfazed by her pain.

"Stop! Leave them be so they can help your mother. Your father is alive due to their kindness," Nulian said.

The twins halted their attack and ran into the water toward the Primin. They apologized as they helped the men who carried the girl.

"Please let us remove the pain we caused her," Brya said.

The two male Primin released their friend to let the twins carry her and hurried toward Morgan. Orin knelt beside Morgan and bowed to the Nyek upon her.

"May we offer our magic, my friend? We know the injury and may be able to reverse some part of it," Orin said.

The Nyek moved down Morgan's chest to sit over her belly without interrupting the steady stream of magic she provided.

Orin looked up to Alec as he arrived. "I must lay my hands to her chest and head. Will you permit it?"

Alec knelt and pulled Morgan's cloak and shirt out of the way. "Do what you need to. Just help her."

Orin nodded, then looked down at Morgan's chest and went still. He looked at his partner, and both frowned.

"What is it? What stops you?" Alec asked.

"Neither of us has ever encountered a mark of the dragon. We do not know how our treatment will affect her. I am not certain we should do this," Orin said as he gazed at Morgan.

"None of the most magical among us can reach her through the barrier your father put in place," Kyan said. "Please, if you can reach her, and tell her how to break free of it, then do try, Sir."

Orin nodded to Kyan and Alec in turn before he and his partner placed their hands over Morgan's Crest. Both flinched at the contact and quickly closed their eyes.

"Everyone, move back and cover your ears, please," Orin said without opening his eyes. They all did as he asked.

The Primin started to sing a song of very complex harmony,

which rose in volume quickly. They seemed to be putting very little effort into the extremely loud music they produced.

Once the song reached a nearly painful level for those around them, they each placed their free hand to Morgan's head. The song dropped in volume but doubled in complexity.

After only a moment, the second Primin took his hand away and stood.

"I can offer no more. Orin will offer all he can alone now," the man said as he moved to stand behind Alec.

Orin lay down beside Morgan and scooted close to sing directly to her ear without removing his hand from her Crest. Alec was so worried about losing her he did not react to the very personal contact.

29

Silence and Sacrifice

MORGAN WOKE IN A SMALL DARK BOX. As her hands slid over the frigid surface of her prison, she reached out with all of her senses. The silence she found was utterly complete, and wholly terrifying. Vague memories of swimming with Menkar quickly dissolved into the nothingness consuming her.

Her magic could not penetrate the walls of the box that held her. She screamed again and again, pleading for someone to free her. No one answered, no one was there to help.

The only sounds were her frantic breaths and pounding heartbeat. There was nothing beyond her own self, no sight, no sound, no magic, no warmth except the tears streaming down her face.

She called out to her children and to Alec. Pleas went out to every member of her family and each of her dragon brethren. And still … there was only cold, empty, nothingness. Her body and mind were exhausted. The silence was heavy, the loneliness an icy presence pulling heat and hope from her body. She should sleep … just sleep …

Music, beautiful soft music washed over her like a warm breeze. A lovely voice added words to the music, sending another wave of warmth that pushed back the icy cold. She strained to listen and pushed against the walls around her, but the words remained just out of focus.

She reached out with her magic, focusing on the music, and felt the box weaken at last. Hope grew inside her chest like a small fire finding fuel in her bones. She let her magic build until she could stand no more, then released it as one great force while kicking hard against one wall.

Light flickered around her like cracks through ice. The music grew louder, and the fire inside of her burned hotter with every loud beat of her heart. Over and over, she let her magic build to that painful level, then unleashed it against the walls of her prison. She fought with her magic and her might, punching and kicking, as the music grew louder, and her body grew stronger.

ORIN HAD BEEN SINGING and passing his magic to Morgan for over five minutes. He began to tremble as he weakened.

Alec moved to stop him, but hesitated when he saw Morgan's eyes flickering and heard her start to mumble. He knelt at her side and tried to connect to her.

"Fight it, Morgan! Fight against it with all you are!"

Zoli moved to lie against Orin, purring loudly to share her magic with him. As he was strengthened, Morgan began to open her eyes slowly. She held her eyes open, but they were unfocused, staring blankly into the sky.

Alec called to her in thought continually because he knew she may not be able to hear with her ears. He took her hand, and his whole body clenched from the intensity of the storm of magic within her.

"Fight, Morgan! Come back to me," he screamed in thought as

he squeezed her hand.

She blinked a few times as she began to murmur in harmony with Orin's song. Orin reached over and turned her head to face him, then laid his hand to her cheek as he stared into her eyes.

The volume of his song increased again, and it changed cadence completely. Kyan felt the young female Primin shift beside him and glanced at her to see a look of surprise.

"What is he doing that makes you uncomfortable, my Lady? Do not lie to me," Kyan asked as he forced a deeper connection to assure she had no option of doing so.

"He is using a very personal method to reach her. It is normally reserved for mates only. I am sure he has tried everything else and is simply trying all he can to save your mother."

Kyan's face darkened as he relayed the information to Alec. Alec's entire body primed as he glared at Orin, but he did not stop the interaction.

Orin continued to sing to Morgan for a few more minutes, then stopped abruptly and lifted his hands as they burned against her skin. He continued his intense stare as she focused her eyes on him.

"You saved me, and I thank you, Orin. But if you ever attempt that again, I will hurt you very badly." As she sat up, he softened his expression to a smile.

"I am glad to see you are back to yourself, Lady Morgan. You are as bold and strong as ever. I hoped a threat to your relationship with your mate would make you fight the hardest. It was my last option, and thankfully, it worked."

She turned away and rubbed her face as he spoke, then looked to Alec as he touched her shoulder.

"How do you feel, my love?" he asked as he pulled her into his arms and kissed her head.

She scowled, then her breath caught as she shifted to look up at him. Tears filled her eyes as she reached up to touch his lips.

"I can hear nothing of your words, or anything else. I… I am deaf."

Alec tucked her head to his chest and held her tight as the reality of that truth gripped her. He looked at Orin sternly over her head as his anger grew.

"She can hear nothing! She did not hear your explanation!" Alec said.

"I am so sorry … I could not repair all that had been done. It is possible that she will hear again one day. Our Elders have known it to happen before. Reversal of the effect takes great magic, time, and a great deal of willpower."

"Those things she has in abundance," Kyan said as he and Brya moved to hug her with tears of relief. Both smiled and caressed her face as she shifted to look at them.

"Your loss will not hurt you. We are blessed by our magic to share all we think and feel, Mother. We are just so thankful to have you alive and with us."

Morgan failed to return their smiles and pressed her face into Alec's chest as she gasped and broke into hard sobs. Nulian crooned sadly, as she felt Morgan's pain and heard her thoughts. Alec swallowed hard, then lifted Morgan's chin to make her look him in the eye.

"I know that depth of sorrow must be associated with our unborn son. Have we lost him?"

"He is alive… but he will be deaf as well. I am so sorry."

She pushed her face into his chest again as tears came hard and fast. Kyan and Brya looked to Alec as he explained. Both wrapped Morgan and held her shaking body. Orin heard Alec's words to the twins and staggered a bit as he stood.

"I did not realize the damage had reached the child. I am very sorry for the horrible damage my father has caused your family, King Alec. I will see to it he is kept far away from you from this day forward."

"You will not have to. He is dead at my hand. He tried to take my wife's life, so I took his. I will not apologize for the act, nor do I regret it," Alec said as he glared at Orin.

Orin bowed slightly then turned to walk away with his kin. They reached the water before he stopped and turned back around to look at Alec as he connected only to him.

"Sir Alec, I must fight you to the death. It is our custom to avenge the murder of a blood Elder in battle. Tomorrow at noon, right here."

Alec nodded then glared at the water where Orin dove and disappeared.

"What did he say to make you so angry? Did he explain what he tried to do?" Morgan said as she looked up.

"What do you mean? What did he try to do?"

Morgan diverted her eyes and said, *"We can discuss it later, my dear."*

Alec lifted her to her feet, and she was hugged by all those present. Zoli moved to her shoulders as she hugged GranMay and settled down. GranMay explained how the Nyek had sustained her for so long in hopes she would break through on her own. Morgan nuzzled Zoli as she sent feelings of profound gratitude and friendship.

DURING THEIR FLIGHT TO THE GAZEBO, Morgan placed her hand to Alec's stomach where the wound had been from the Primin Elder's knife.

"You were healed by another. I can feel their magical traces. Tell me all that happened, please."

He told her all he knew, stopping before explaining Orin's challenge. She felt the attempt at deception and squeezed his hand.

"Orin has challenged me to a fight to the death tomorrow because I took the life of his father. I do not believe he truly blames me. But it is their custom, and as their leader, he cannot go against it."

Morgan tightened her grip on him.

"I will not let him hurt you. I cannot."

"I can wield a sword quite well, my Caretaker," he said as he kissed her head.

"What of his magic?"

Alec did not answer for a moment.

"You should consider that it was my lack of magic that saved you today, my dear. All those with any greater magic than I were overwhelmed by the Elder's attack."

Morgan was silent as she pulled his arms tight around her and dozed during the flight to the gazebo.

They settled into bed after Nulian left them. Alec turned to her and kissed her as he pulled her tight against him. Through their connection, she heard all of his thoughts and spoken words with ease.

"I almost lost you again, and believed myself lost as well. My heart is ragged from all it has endured this day." He felt fear and profound loss within her and his heart ached as well. "The children are right, my love. You are blessed by the magic and will be able to communicate at nearly the same level without the audible interaction. You have become accustomed to holding your guard high enough to block all unsolicited conversation from your mind. Perhaps now you will allow more of that in to assure you hear all you need to."

"I agree. It is not my loss that hurts so much. It is knowing our son will never hear at all. He will never know your lovely voice or those of his brother and sister." She stopped as she felt him react to her spoken words. "I sound odd when I speak, don't I?"

"You pronounce your words fine, my dear. You were just whispering and I could barely hear you."

"I will not use my voice very much until I can speak without brining attention to my injury."

"I think that would be a great loss to all who love the beautiful sound of your voice. I will not push you to speak, but ask that you please consider that viewpoint, my dear."

They lay quietly in each other's arms for many minutes before Alec rolled to look into her eyes.

"What did he try to do?"

"Please, don't worry about it, I stopped him before he was able to accompli—" She stopped as strong annoyance and insult moved between them.

"Accomplish what, exactly? Tell me the truth, please." He felt the worry in her as she moved his hand to her Crest and looked into his eyes.

"This," she said as she illustrated the intended level of bonding the Primin had been trying to achieve with her. When fury filled his eyes, she lifted to kiss him deeply and used their powerful link to slowly calm his jealous rage.

MORGAN WOKE TO find Alec moving silently through an exercise routine to loosen his muscles in preparation for the duel with Orin.

"Do you expect me to simply watch you fight in this barbaric ritual?"

"Yes."

He had not paused and continued his exercises without another word. She watched him for a few minutes while monitoring his emotions.

"Did you let his attempt to bond intimately to me fuel your desire to fight him?"

"Yes."

"I will agree that he deserves a swift kick in the buttocks, but I do not think it warrants killing him."

Alec stopped and turned to her with a stern expression.

"Morgan, I did not lay down this challenge, but I will not cower away from it. Nor will I accept you fighting it for me. Do not ask that of me, my dear."

Morgan washed up and dressed before speaking to him again.

"This has all taken a very ugly turn. We need the Primin's help to rebuild the portal, yet, just when we have their friendship, the table turns. Now we face a fight to the death between the male heads of both parties. It is ridiculous, and I hope to talk some sense into him before this match begins. If it is to happen, I hope you will not ask me to watch you die. That is a promise I will not keep, my mate."

"Are you so sure he will defeat me?"

"I am deaf because their magic is powerful and quite different from my own. I am not sure how powerful, and neither are you. Of course, I am worried."

"If he chooses to fight me as a man, and not use his power, I will defeat him easily. If he uses his magic, it will be a very different fight. Either way, I will not refuse this challenge."

"I would never call you a coward. Well, except that one time I was trying to make you mad. You know I do not see you that way. Your bravery saved me the first time we met and many times since then. It is Orin I do not trust to give you a fair fight."

He turned around slowly as she stepped up behind him, smiled broadly, and leaned in close to kiss her nose.

"My Queen, are you not the woman who can block most any-one's magic if she wishes to? You can help me today by taking his magic out of the equation."

She matched his smile and said, *"Now that is a plan I can support, my King."*

NULIAN LANDED in the field near the lake only briefly before launching again.

"What is wrong, my Sister?" Morgan asked as she pushed calming to ease the Elder's anxiety.

"I cannot allow this ridiculous battle. Gerzin spent the entire night trying to convince me that I had no say, but I disagree. I love

my King and have devoted myself to protecting my brethren. I am not going to let him walk into a slaughter," Nulian said as she soared away from the lake.

"I cannot hear your conversation, but I am bright enough to deduce the subject," Alec said through his link to Morgan. *"Nulian, as your King, and as your friend, I am asking you to take me to the lake, now. I am no coward and will not be seen as one by my brethren. Would you yourself walk away from a challenge such as this, my friend? Answer in your heart, honestly."*

Nulian thought of it, then grumbled as she turned back for the lake.

"You can help me and the twins assure this is a fair fight by blocking Orin's magic, my dear," Morgan said to her alone.

"If his father's attack yesterday is any evidence, we may fail in that endeavor, my Sister," Nulian said. Morgan's anxiety level climbed fast as she considered that possibility. When Nulian landed near the lake, she waited for them to dismount, then nudged them against her side.

"My friends, my heart is still not over nearly losing you both yesterday. You are very precious to us, and we cannot watch either of you die and not act. You cannot expect that of us."

"I do not wish to fight him, Nulian," Alec said. *"There is no good way for such a battle to end. Either I die, or I kill the man who saved my wife's life. However, if he forces the matter, I will fight. And yes, I do expect you to respect me enough to follow my wishes, my dear."*

Nulian did not move her snout when he pushed against her.

"You force me to go against your wishes, my King. It hurts me to anger you, but it would hurt far worse to watch you die."

Alec's face grew red and he said, *"King or not, if you are truly my friend you will respect my choice and let me pass, Nulian."*

Nulian moved her snout and released him. He moved away from her a few feet before noticing Morgan had not joined him. He turned to see her leaning against Nulian and not looking at him.

"Do you intend to ignore my wishes as well?" he asked as he walked back to her. She did not answer and did not make eye contact. *"Clearly, you think that if you do not promise me now, then you are not breaking a promise when you interfere. It does not work that way, and you know it. Either you respect me, or you do not. You know me well enough to understand why I must do this. I am trusting you to let me fight my own battle, my mate,"* he said as he slid a hand over her neck to lift her head and look into her eyes. *"Love me enough to let me be the man you know me to be."* He kissed her deeply, then headed for the camp without looking back.

He was only halfway to the camp when she fell into step and took his hand. She looked forward and said nothing, but he smiled and gripped her hand as her devotion moved through him.

They ate a light breakfast with the children and GranMay with little conversation. The twins and GranMay were eyeing them curiously, having noticed their tense silence. Morgan looked skyward to the east and smiled.

"Our friends return from gathering stones. They will be here in an hour," Morgan said to everyone around the lake. She looked to Alec as she blocked all others, *"They will be here before the confrontation, at least."*

"Their presence will not change anything, my dear."

"If the Primin refuses a fair fight, without magic, I will consider it an act of war against us! Do not question that for an instant," Morgan said as she gave him a hard glare. She looked back to the ground at her feet as she rubbed her palms to relieve their tingling, which was intensifying with her rising anxiety level. *"Tell them."*

Alec told their children and GranMay of the challenge. All three started arguing instantly. GranMay was the first to read the look on Alec's face and quieted the twins.

"I intend to accept the fight if he will not withdraw the challenge.

To refuse it is a cowardly act I cannot accept. I would hope you know me well enough to know that," he said. He glanced at Morgan and continued, "Your mother has decided that she will demand that Orin agree to fight without his magic. If he refuses to fight me under those conditions, she is determined to declare it an act of war against us and will send our men and dragons against them all." He stood and walked toward the clear part of the field as he added, "Children, fetch your swords and come help me warm up a bit."

The twins were dumbstruck and did not move. They looked to Morgan, but she shook her head.

"*Do as he asked,*" she said as she gave them a stern glance. They moved without argument. She continued to stare at the ground and rub her hands together. GranMay moved to sit beside her and put her arm around her. They connected and blocked all others.

"*Part of what fuels Alec's desire to fight Orin is the Primin's attempt to bond far too deeply to me yesterday. Orin claims it to be the way he forced me to fight hard enough to break free of the magical barrier, and that is what I told Alec. But he and I know that the man had other intentions. The truth is, I will enjoy watching Alec thrash Orin for his disrespectful action. That said, I do not wish to see either killed.*"

"*Alec is brave and noble. Those virtues are much of the reason you fell in love with him so quickly. You must respect his wishes, my dear. If he is to die, then let him die a noble death and not that of a coward. It is his choice whether he takes Orin's life. The challenge was made of him, not you.*"

Morgan hated to hear so much truth in her words. She sighed, kissed her wise grandmother's cheek, then moved to sit on Nulian's front leg.

"*Would you walk away from a challenge such as this, my dear? If Gerzin interfered, would you not be furious and hurt that he did not respect your wishes?*"

"I know you are trying to convince yourself as much as me, my Queen. Yet, neither of us is any closer to letting Alec die than we were the second we heard of the challenge."

They both watched Alec and the twins stretch for many minutes and then begin sparring rather aggressively. Morgan loved watching him fight with his sword. He was highly skilled and she loved the way he moved as if the sword were part of his body.

"If Orin agrees to fight without the magic, Alec will be left with the choice of whether to take or spare his life," Morgan said.

"Not an easy choice, unless Orin forces his hand."

"I think it to never be an easy choice, even when given no other. However, I am done sparing lives when it puts others at risk as a result. Alec is not wrong when he says I would have died had Daniel not taken that dagger for me. I think I will find ending a dark one far easier with that truth so painfully clear. Orin is not dark, yet he threatens the one I hold most dear. I can and will end him if he strikes with that level of malice."

"A wise and honorable decision, my Caretaker."

DANIEL WAS LIVID when he learned of all they had missed the day before and of the challenge laid before Alec. He asked to fight in Alec's stead and was promptly refused by a nearly insulted Alec. He then took Morgan's hand and pulled her away from the group to look her hard in the eyes as he tapped his temple, requesting a private connection.

"Why did you not tell me of this before now?"

"I chose not to worry you unnecessarily. Now was soon enough to start worrying when we cannot change his mind." She turned back to watch Alec sparring with a worried face. Daniel took her shoulders and turned her to face him again gently.

"I was referring to your injury, not the challenge. Did it harm your child?" Her face answered the question, so he hugged her tight.

"He lives, but he will also be deaf."

"I am so sorry. Now I understand Alec's fury and desire to fight this Primin."

"Do you think he blames Orin for his father's actions?" Morgan said as she pushed back to scowl at him.

"Maybe not, but think about it. His wife is deaf, and his son will be as well. Blame is not the issue. The sheer rage festering inside him is the issue. Orin offers the opportunity to release that anger."

"Oh my gosh, Daniel. I think that is exactly what Orin has done. He was devastated when he heard of our child being deaf. He apologized on behalf of his father with calm words, but I felt the anguish within him. He lied. I'll bet you there is no custom requiring him to fight. It is his own guilt driving this challenge. He is giving his life as repayment for his father's damage to me and our son."

She turned toward Nulian.

"Where are you going?" Daniel asked.

"To talk to Orin."

"No, you're not!" Daniel shouted aloud as he leapt to grab her arm and spin her around to face him. His yell got the attention of the Knights around them, but he did not let her go or soften his scowl. *"You are not going back down there."*

"Do you honestly think you are going to stop me, Brother? I am not that little girl crying in her window seat anymore. I make my own decisions," Morgan said as she jerked her arm away and shoved him back many feet.

Daniel ignored the anger and insult she pushed on him as he moved to put himself between her and Nulian.

"I'm not about to just let you go when you nearly died at their hand yesterday. I love you a bit more than that, little sister. You'll have to hurt me to get away from me!" Morgan's rage woke Nulian, who moved her head to just above Daniel's.

"What has you two so red in the face, my Caretaker?"

"He refuses to move so you can take me down to speak with Orin."

Nulian laid her head back down and snorted.

"Well, tell him he may as well move because I will do no such thing."

"You know how important this is to me. Do you seriously respect me so little that you would refuse?" she shouted out loud and in magic.

"As I told you long ago, I would rather you hate me than lose you, my Queen." Morgan growled at them both and shed her cloak as she walked resolutely into the water. Just before diving in, she felt the Primins' approach and gave both her brother and mentor an annoyed glare while connecting to Alec.

"The Primin are almost here," she said as she redirected her steps to meet him at the bank while forcing herself to calm down. She stood beside Alec and offered Orin a stern glare when he exited the water. His expression was somber, his clothing more substantial, and he now wore a long, thin sword.

She walked three paces forward and stopped as she raised her hand, palm forward. Orin smiled as he stepped closer to lay his hand to hers, then slowly laced their fingers as he shifted closer still. She felt anger rise in her husband but ignored him as she connected to Orin and blocked all others.

"There is no such custom that would require this challenge. I know what you are doing and cannot let this proceed. You are not to blame for your father's actions, Orin. You saved my life, and I am very thankful. Now, let me save your life by walking away from this conflict." She passed feelings of forgiveness and friendship as strongly as she could and felt him shiver as it moved through him. He responded with a great deal of sorrow for her and her child.

"I must do this, my friend. Your mate has the right to punish my people for the damage done to you and his unborn child."

"He will not fight you once I tell him your reasoning," she said with a smirk.

"Then do not tell him, my friend," Orin said with a sad smile. Her smirk slipped and she gripped his hand a bit tighter as her temper flared.

"I cannot let you do this. You must know my heart cannot do that!"

"I admire you a great deal and am quite jealous of your mate, Queen Morgan. The magic around your spirit is the strongest I have ever felt, and it has touched me most profoundly. Nevertheless, I will not let you stop this. My people will subdue you and your children if necessary. Please, do not make me give that order. Allow me to fight him honestly. Give him his rightful revenge and allow me to die in honor for my people."

Morgan felt his desire to do this mixed with great sorrow for his father. She also felt a hint of something else and smiled.

"How can you be so sure your brethren can successfully subdue me, Orin?"

"I know the magic you hold and I know ours can match it, my Lady. Again, I beg you, do not make me give that order."

"You are the strongest of the Primin and you cannot fight me if you are fighting my husband. Who do you suggest will do this magical management while you are occupied?" Morgan asked as she eyed the Primin behind him.

"Look over my left shoulder, my friend. You will see two women and two men older and more powerful than I. You do not feel their magic because they block you, even now."

Morgan smiled and shook her head as she felt the obvious deception within his words. She held the smile until he sighed. He held her eyes as he pushed determination through their touch.

"The choice is yours. Allow me to fight him or all of our people will end up in battle. I have laid the challenge and will not be so

cowardly as to walk away now."

"Why can you not simply let go of this ill-placed guilt? You did nothing, Orin. You are not responsible for your father's evil actions!"

"Because I released him from his guard. I trusted him to obey our wishes to leave you be. It is my fault that he was able to reach you at all! The guilt I carry is very well-placed, I assure you!"

They were both flush, and their hands tightly gripped as Alec stepped to Morgan's side with a glare at Orin. Morgan took a quick breath as her mate's hand laid lightly to her back. Orin lifted an eyebrow as he felt and saw her reaction to Alec's light touch.

"I will tell him all you have said, and he will choose. That is the only fair thing to do," she said as she released Orin's hand. He nodded as she dropped the connection.

She turned to lay one of Alec's hands over her Crest to form a deep private connection.

"You need to know all I just learned before you do this."

She let him experience it all as she had. When she finished, he nodded and turned to pace in silence as he considered the situation.

"Let me speak to him through you, please," Alec said. She connected to both of them with a slight glance at Orin. Alec gave no indication that he was communicating with Orin as he continued to pace.

"Do you really wish to die for your father's cruelty in this way? Or, do you want to lead your people to a new future with the people of Chemerie as your allies?"

"It is not a matter of want. It is a question of honor and a debt unpaid," Orin said.

"I think it very much a matter of want. You want to act as martyr, which requires I take your life. However, knowing your reasoning, I am no longer willing to do so. I want your life to be offered not to my blade but as the required spirit offering to form the portal to Erion. I would think that to be a much more honorable way to die, Primin Orin."

Orin looked to the ground as he considered Alec's proposal, and Morgan felt his remorse.

"I would indeed think that a more noble way to repay this debt. Unfortunately, I cannot be the portal spirit as I am not an Elder. The magic of the Primin changes with age and I do not yet have the skills necessary to do so."

"If we duel, and I choose to spare your life, what then?"

"In the very unlikely event that you found me under the point of your sword, chose to spare my life, and consider the debt paid, then I would have no choice but to accept that defeat. It is a very dishonorable way to settle the matter, and I will fight with all my might to not have that happen. I would rather die," Orin said as scowled and tensed.

Alec stopped and looked him straight in the eye.

"Are you really certain of that?"

Orin glanced away for a second, and Alec moved to stand in front of him. He spoke loudly so all could hear.

"I killed your father because he intended to kill my wife and unborn son. I believe my actions were justified. I would expect any intelligent man to see that, Primin Orin. Are you so narrow-minded that you do not see the justice in my actions?"

Orin was silent for many seconds as his neck flushed.

"I do see the honor in protecting your wife, King Alec. Nevertheless, the matter is ..."

"Do you condone your father's actions?"

"No! He was wrong to attack your Queen. We all agree on that."

"Then why would you feel it necessary to pay for his evil with your own life when I have not asked for it, Sir?"

Orin was now very red in the face.

"I offer myself as martyr to allow you the revenge you deserve for the harm done to your family by my people."

Alec stepped back and surveyed the crowd of Primin.

"He says I was wronged by his people. Who among you wronged me?" None of them answered, but many shifted uncomfortably under his gaze before he looked back to Orin. "Did you yourself wrong me? Or can you point to any one of your brethren as having personally wronged me?"

"No, King Alec. Only my father wronged you. He is now dead, so you have only me to place your blame upon."

"I think it is my choice who I wish to blame, Primin Orin. I am a man who only blames the one who gave the order or wielded the weapon for the injury received. Did you do either in this instance? If you did, then I will gladly take your life. If you did not, I have no quarrel with you."

"No, I did not order the attack, nor did I wield the magic which did the injury, King Alec."

"Then I hold no grudge against you, Primin Orin. You have said you see the honor in my actions to protect my wife. Do you hold any grudge against me for the death of your father?"

"No, I do not hold a grudge for you in that matter."

"Then I suggest that we consider the matter settled and move on. I have not forgotten that you saved the life of my mate, and would be honored to call you friend, Primin Orin," Alec said as he held out a hand.

Orin stared into his eyes hard as he considered this resolution of the matter. He turned his head to look at the Primin Elders beside him, and all four nodded with small smiles. Orin took a deep breath of relief and grasped Alec's hand. The crowd of Primin, human, and dragon erupted in applause and light roars.

Alec still held Orin's hand as everyone's attention moved away from them. He pulled the Primin sharply to his chest and squeezed his hand as he held his eyes with a vicious glare.

"If you ever make a move of familiarity against my mate again, I will end you!"

30

Friendship Forged

"YOU MAY BOTH SPEAK NATURALLY as long as you do not block me. I will connect to you and hear everything," Morgan said to Alec and Orin as they gathered amongst the visiting crowd of their peoples. They both nodded. *"Does your offer to rebuild the portal still stand, Orin?"*

"Absolutely, my Lady. However, my people will need time to discuss the details," he said with a smile.

Morgan saw him glance at the group of Elders.

"I do not want one of your people to give their life before their natural time to die, my friend."

"That is very kind of you to say. But you must understand that we consider the offering of one's spirit to form a portal the most desirable, noblest way to die. We believe the spirit of the giver is immortalized in the portal and lives free on both of the worlds the portal connects."

"If your people believe the portal liquid to house the spirit of one of your people, how could your Elders have purposefully destroyed one?"

Alec asked. Orin did not answer, but his forehead wrinkled at the question. "My apologies, it is not my place to question your Elders."

"I appreciate your point of view, yet I also understand theirs. Driven by fear alone, most were convinced humans would be the death of our people. When you and your family started coming here, it caused a great deal of discontent within the Elder council. Some wanted to approach you and judge you for themselves, while others wanted to stop your return.

"Unfortunately, my father was of the latter opinion and moved to strike without the approval of the entire council. The Elders you see with me today had refused to interact with him in any way since he acted so maliciously. They now support me as leader of our governing Council, comprising all adult generations, and are as interested in forging a meaningful relationship with your people as I am."

"What can we do to help you?" Morgan said. *"We can form the metal enclosure ourselves if you wish. Also, if you have not already chosen a suitable mate, we can assist in the search."*

Orin broke into a small laugh as he looked at her fondly.

"You are very driven, my Lady. Do you ever allow yourself the pleasure of relaxation?"

"Yes, but now is not the time. We brought all of our magical family here to give us the best opportunity to build the portal. Our country is guarded by many Knights and dragon brethren, but there is no Caretaker present at the moment. We have been away far too long for me to relax, my friend."

"I will hold a council meeting today to hear pleas from all who wish to offer their spirit for the portal. Once the privileged one is chosen, we will be ready to proceed. It is fortunate you have brought so many magical ones with you because we will need your assistance. Many of our Elders have grown quite weak. Though they have the knowledge of how to form the portal, they themselves can no longer properly wield the magic within them.

"As for the location, it needs to be a nearly flat region large enough for the portal to accommodate your Elder dragon brethren. I will leave you to choose it and to form the circlet. We will go now, and begin the selection process," Orin said. He bowed low and stepped to his Elder brethren, who also bowed before entering the water with Orin.

ONCE THE PRIMIN WERE AWAY, Morgan asked for a forum with all of her brethren in the party. Everyone gathered to listen as she explained the process to be undertaken and the requirements for the location. She asked Daniel to organize the transport of the ore and stones to the portal site once it was chosen. Once they were away, she and Alec moved to Nulian and Asira, where they lay on the bank of the lake.

"Well, do either of you have a good spot in mind for the portal, my friends?" she asked.

Both had a few possibilities in mind and offered to take her and Alec to view them. They flew over many miles of rough countryside before they agreed on a perfect spot.

It was a small meadow on the crest of a ridgeline nestled between two larger mountain ranges. The larger peaks to the sides offered protection from the harsh winds of winter on Berios, and the height of the peak made flooding a remote possibility during the wet season.

While the portals on other worlds were often hidden, there was no need to hide this one as the planet did not hold any dark spirits who would misuse it. Morgan and Nulian passed the coordinates to all the other dragons, and Daniel's teams started to transport the raw materials to the location.

MORGAN AND ALEC sat atop a ridge overlooking the portal location. They were taking a few moments of quiet before beginning the great effort to build the portal that afternoon.

"What did you say to Orin just before letting go of him today?"

"I made sure he understood my opinion of his attempt to bond intimately to you. I believe I made my point clear."

She shifted in his arms to give him a wicked smile. *"He actually admitted being quite jealous of you."*

"As he should be, my beautiful bride," he said as he kissed her softly before pulling her back into a tight snuggle. He soon felt anguish filling her and leaned down to kiss her cheek.

"I cannot imagine never hearing your voice again, never hearing you say 'I love you' in that deep rich tone that makes me shiver. To think of never hearing my children call me…"

Alec wrapped her tight then placed his hand over her Crest to assure she felt every ounce of love he held. She took in a deep breath as it moved over her and calmed.

"We communicate quite well in silence, my mate. I do not have to hear your voice to feel your love inside of me. I know it will be hard, but try to remember our fortune in having such a deep connection with each other and with our children."

"Wise as usual, my dear Elder mate," she said with a smirk. He bit at her neck, making her laugh and wriggle madly as he held her tight. He harassed her until she relaxed and was again free of sorrowful thoughts.

MORGAN, BRYA, KYAN, AND TARU worked for many minutes to extract the pure metal from the natural ore. Morgan had asked that the Knights lay it out in nearly the same circular path it would take when formed to lessen the work later. Once they had plenty of the metal extracted, they all gathered around GranMay where she now knelt by the circle of metal.

As they all laid a hand to GranMay and entered bonding, Zoli moved from her pocket to lie across GranMay's shoulders. The Nyek trilled and they all felt the large amount of magic she offered.

"This should go very quickly, indeed. Let us begin, my dears," GranMay said with a soft chuckle. She placed her hands to the metal in front of her and closed her eyes. The rest began to focus on the proper shape and appearance of the circlet and pushed their magic to GranMay. With the added magic of Zoli, the task took half the time it had in their practices on Erion.

As GranMay completed the task, they all let the bonding drop gently and helped her to her feet. Morgan felt amazement from the Primin just as she saw her family shift to look behind her. She turned to find all of the Primin applauding with looks of amazed glee on their faces.

"Why the level of surprise, Orin? How is our method different from yours?"

"Our people would have worked for hours to form a circlet of that size. We are truly amazed at the speed and efficiency of your performance," he said with a bow. Morgan relayed the conversation to her family, and all bowed with grace.

"How are we to help you with the rest, my friend?" Morgan asked. She had connected to all involved in the build so they could communicate naturally, and she would still hear their thoughts.

Orin moved forward and picked up one of the small stones then smiled as it glowed brightly in his hand. He handed it to her and smiled as it glowed very brightly in hers as well.

"Your magic does the task for you. You need only sing the song with us, and offer the stone in turn as we reach that part of the song," Orin said. Morgan stared at the stone a few seconds, then handed it to GranMay and shifted her gaze between those of her family.

"I cannot trust my voice and will not risk interfering in this process. Trust their guidance and enjoy learning all you can from this experience," she said as she turned to move toward Alec. Orin watched her go until she reached Alec, who gave him a nod as he took Morgan's hand.

Brya and Kyan moved dutifully to the edge of the circlet and took a stone in their hands to await further instructions. Taru and Gran-May joined them with smiles and nods as they pushed encouragement to the anxious twins.

Alec gripped Morgan's hand as he was hit by the intense anguish within her. He did not acknowledge it, knowing she was struggling to keep her composure. He passed supportive strength the best he could and she squeezed his hand hard.

Orin and the other Primin placed themselves around the rest of the circlet and each lifted a stone. Orin smiled at the humans within the group and bowed.

"We will use our magic to activate the stones. For the stone to be fully activated, the holder must provide a bit of their magic through blood. I am told it will work for humans as well as it does for our people. When we reach that segment of the ritual song, simply prick your finger and allow a single drop to touch the stone. This will complete the activation and the stone will be ready to be transformed into the portal window.

"When it is your turn, place your stone to touch the one laid previously. When all the stones have been laid, the chosen one will offer their spirit to connect this portal to that on Erion."

All within the circle nodded their understanding. Orin began the song and the Primin joined him.

"*You will hear only one of the strands being sung. Sing it once you get the tune. Continue to sing it until the chosen one is gone,*" he said to the humans. They nodded and each listened to the tune they heard. As they learned the tune, they began to sing along and their voices mingled with those of the Primin.

Morgan smiled as each of her family members connected to her so she could hear their individual songs in her mind. She soon started to hum along with the core melody all of their versions shared. Through Alec, she heard all he did. While glad to hear what they shared, she knew she would never be able to participate unless she regained her hearing.

She and Alec watched as the group each pricked their fingers and allowed their blood to fall onto the stone they held. Morgan felt the dramatic increase in the magic flowing within the circle of singers as the stones in their hands turned a deep purple color.

As the last of the group walked forward to lay their stones against the rest spiraling out from the center of the circlet, an Elderly woman walked forward to stand at the center. She made eye contact with each of those in the circle around her, humans included.

Her song shifted to add a lovely new layer to the chorus, and all within the singing circle changed the cadence in response. The stones glowed brighter and brighter, then started to liquefy around the woman's feet. She had a look of joyful pride on her face, and Morgan felt her excitement as the liquid climbed her body. Within the woman's song were the very clear words, "To Erion, to Chemerie."

The woman's body burst into intense white light then dropped into the pool. The liquid glowed brightly and doubled in volume to completely fill the circlet then lay slightly undulating within it. Morgan felt intense heartache within Orin and found his face to be wet with tears as he dropped his chin to his chest.

"She was his mother. He has lost both parents to our desire for this portal," Morgan told Alec.

"You must not think that way. His mother made a choice she was clearly happy with," he said.

Morgan sent friendship and condolences to Orin. He raised his head at her magical touch and smiled.

"Thank you, Lady Morgan, for your concern. I am happy for her, but I will miss her greatly," Orin said as he rose and walked to her and Alec.

"Your path home is forged once again. Safe journey and farewell, my friends," Orin said. He bowed to them both and moved to stand with his brethren beside the portal.

"We should make sure it works somehow before just sending everyone through," Morgan said.

"The only way is to request a volunteer to go through and return to confirm it is safe," Alec said.

She gave him an annoyed glance and stepped forward. He slid an arm around her waist to hold her back as he called out to the group.

"I ask one of my brethren to volunteer to test this new portal before our Queen does so herself."

Falin hurried and landed on the pool. He turned his head to Nulian who started singing the tune to teach it to him. He joined on the third repetition and sang it fluidly. As he continued, the purple liquid slowly crept up his body.

Morgan pulled away from Alec as light burst from the pool, to start pacing the second Falin fell through it. Her heart was racing and she shot Alec many harsh glares. He was unfazed by her annoyance but also grew anxious after two minutes.

"How long should this take normally?" Morgan asked Nulian after three minutes.

"Less than a minute, my Sister," Nulian said as she shifted and clawed the ground. Morgan stopped and stared at the purple pool as her chest ached. She knelt beside the circlet and fought tears as another minute passed.

A great breath of relief left everyone as the pool glowed brightly and Falin stood in front of them once again. Morgan leapt forward to wrap her arms around his snout and hug him tight.

"What kept you? You scared me to death!"

"It is Lirpa, my Queen. The eggs come with difficulty, and she is enduring horrible pain," Falin said. Morgan explained to Alec as she laid a hand to Falin and told him to sing. She tried to sing along but kept contact in case it did not work.

NULIAN ARRIVED just after Morgan and Falin, then quickly caught up. All landed outside the dragon chambers and hurried to Lirpa, who lay writhing in pain in the middle of the large laying room.

Morgan's assistant, Willow, was there, looking exhausted and worried to death. Morgan laid her hand to Lirpa to control her pain and help her calm.

"It has been nearly a full day, my Queen. Still, they do not come. I was near taking them myself. Please, my Queen, take them out," Lirpa said.

"Let me see what is wrong first, my dear," Morgan said. She moved along her side, then placed her hands to either side of the eggs bulging low in her abdomen to study their position in the birth canal.

As she worked, Willow hovered just behind her and talked frantically. Nulian nudged her with a quiet croon and shook her head. Willow scowled a bit but respected the Elder dragon by going quiet and stepping back.

"Two eggs have moved into the birth canal side-by-side, which makes it impossible for any to move through. I am going to try to move them around to free their path. Relax your muscles, my friend. Let me have control for a bit."

Nulian placed her snout to Lirpa and hummed her healing song strong and steady. Lirpa crooned and nuzzled her.

Falin shifted tighter against his mate and added his healing song as he caressed her neck with his snout. Lirpa laid her head to his as they watched Morgan work. Morgan started to push on Lirpa's belly to get the eggs to roll over one another.

"Willow, come, push as I direct you, please," she said as she glanced at her friend. They worked together to first move the eggs by pushing down on the two blocking the canal. They both strained as they forced the eggs to move within Lirpa.

Finally, the lowest eggs slipped past one another, and the rest fell in line behind them.

"This should go quickly now, my dear. I will control your pain so it will be as pleasant as possible." Lirpa sat up a bit to watch her first eggs emerging while she and Falin both crooned loudly together. Once all seven eggs were delivered, both parents moved to nuzzle them.

Morgan moved back from them and put an arm around Willow.

"Thank you for comforting her, my dear," Morgan said.

"I have only been here since dawn, my Queen. Iz and Qaleb sat with her all night. I insisted they sleep for a bit, and Sir Burke helped force them away for a while. Oh my! They will be so upset that they missed the laying after all." Morgan located them in guest rooms of the castle and woke both.

"Wake up, my friends. There are a couple of very happy parents down here that you need to come visit." She laughed as she felt both of them startle then bolt down the hallway.

"My dear, may Alec and the twins join us as well?" she asked Lirpa.

"Of course, my Queen. They are our family as well," Lirpa said. The twins moved to Lirpa first to hug and caress her as they congratulated her and Falin. Brya jokingly scolded her for not waiting for them to return, and all were laughing.

The twins' laughter halted as they looked up to watch Qaleb and Iz enter the chamber at a run while holding hands. Morgan saw the anger in her son's eyes as the emotion filled him.

"Do not jump to conclusions. They have had time to get to know one another well, now. Do you actually feel that kind of emotion between them?"

He concentrated and soon smiled as he and Brya moved to greet them. Morgan turned and walked away a bit as she took a few calming breaths to release the anxiety that had built within her over the last few minutes. Her back was to the rest of the group and her guard at its normal high level.

"Welcome home, my Queen," Qaleb said as he moved up behind her. He waited for her response a few seconds then started to turn away.

Brya had turned at his words and beamed as she stepped closer to him.

"Qaleb, she did not hear your words," she said. "She was injured and is now deaf. Please, tell her again. Use your magic, my friend." Kyan and Iz had also looked to him with prideful faces and nodded their encouragement.

Morgan turned as Qaleb attempted to connect, then smiled as she allowed it. He dropped to one knee and bowed his head to her.

"Welcome home, my Queen. I proudly offer my spirit to your service," he said. Morgan stepped forward and touched his shoulder to ask him to rise.

"I am honored, and very proud, Qaleb. Thank you for the commitment to our country, and to our family," she said with a huge smile. She opened her arms to offer a hug and he froze as his eyes widened. She stepped forward and took him into her embrace. As her magic filled him, he relaxed against her.

"I have never been held or felt love like this from any but my own mother. Thank you for your acceptance, despite my family's history, my Queen. I will not disappoint you."

"I know." She released him after a long moment and held his shoulders to look into his eyes. *"If the time comes for you to free the Veridan people from the oppression of the dark magic, your Chemerian brethren will be with you."*

"Thank you, my Queen."

A HUGE FEAST AND CELEBRATION was held that evening to welcome the Caretaker family back home, and to celebrate the new portal connection to Berios. Morgan was standing alone at the edge of the festival area, looking out over the crowd. She watched those dancing and singing to the music the musicians made. She saw laughing faces and friendly conversations. For her, it was like a silent movie as she held her guard high to force herself to experience the truth of her deafness. Her magic was a wonderful gift and she was grateful to have the skills it offered, but losing natural sound was still a painful loss.

As she wandered the back section of the garden, she came to terms with the things that would and would not change for her. The one thing that continued to make her heart ache was knowing that her child would never know sound at all.

As she continued meandering along, she felt her son kicking as his magic washed over her. She smiled as she rubbed her belly and sat down to bond deeply to him. He was quickly approaching his time for birth, and she estimated it to happen within the month.

She pondered their connection and decided to try something. She focused on her son's spirit and sang to him in thought. Her heart nearly burst as she felt the child begin to move in rhythm to the music. Tears slid down her face as she continued to sing to him, then even faster as she realized the significance of the song. It was the song she heard when her own mother's voice first entered her head through the Book of the Caretaker.

A few minutes later, she felt Brya and Kyan coming to her.

"I am fine, my loves. You should enjoy the party." They continued toward her and sat to either side with loving smiles as they laid hands to her belly. She put her arms around them and pulled them close as they bonded to her and their little brother. When she began to sing, the twins looked up at her with huge smiles and joined her through their wonderful magical link.

31

Prejudice and Malice

MORGAN FELT a great deal of anxiety from Drieden as he flew over the castle heading for the Elders' Chambers.

"Drieden, I am here if I can help you in any way, my friend," she said. He turned and landed beside where she lay on the lawn.

"I apologize for being so disrespectful when you tried to soothe me on Berios, my Queen," he said. She rubbed his snout and sent forgiveness, but did not push him to talk. "I am worried for Hytha's clutch, my Caretaker. They grow very quickly and will hatch very soon. I want them to grow up here in Chemerie, but I do not believe Tagien or his parents want that.

"It is a great worry to me, as I want them to have the magical bond with my human brethren that their mother has. I do not know how to address the topic with Tagien's family without seeming disrespectful. It is a very delicate matter, and I am not delicate."

Morgan never stopped stroking him as he shared his worry with her. "Is it the link to the Caretaker you worry about, or do you think as much about the camaraderie with the Chemerian people?"

"Both, my Queen. Our lives here are rich and wonderfully full of friendship and love. I simply want that for all my family."

"The hatchlings already have a strong link to the twins, my friend. My children bear their likeness on their hands, and it was they who performed their Quickening. As for their link to Chemerie, I think you need to ask Hytha her thoughts. I believe she will put your heart at ease."

He looked at her with a slight lift of one brow ridge, and she gave him a big smile. He nudged her with a deep croon then backed away to take off with a strong leap.

She smiled, then lay back on the soft grass to resume her very serious task of taking an afternoon nap.

KYAN PAUSED AT THE DOOR of his parent's chambers and asked permission before entering. He moved to the terrace where Morgan and Alec each sat reading and relaxing in the afternoon breeze.

He wore an anxious smile as he sat at the foot of a lounge, facing them.

"This looks serious. Any guesses, my dear?" Alec asked as he put his book down and shifted to face his son.

"One, but he will not like my answer," Morgan said as she did the same.

"Then we agree on that answer, my wife."

"May I participate in your conversation for a bit?" Kyan said with a smirk. Everyone laughed lightly as Morgan lowered her guard.

"I believe you know what I am about to ask, so shall we skip the formality and have your answer?"

"Alright, you will not marry until Iz is eighteen, and only with the permission of her father," Morgan said. Both Kyan and Alec looked at her with lifted eyebrows. She laughed. "It appears that was not the question you were thinking of."

"No, but it is nice to know where you stand, Mother," Kyan said as he laughed. He then grew serious again, and his parents quieted as well. "I would like your permission to ask Iz to join me on our quest for the Nyeks of Erion."

Morgan and Alec looked to each other as she blocked Kyan from their words. After a short discussion between them, she included Kyan again.

"I want you to consider something before we answer," Morgan said. "Ask yourself what Iz's personal goals were before learning she was your mate. You know that Iz has been studying for years to complete her training and go through trials to become a Knight of the Guard. Would she regret giving that up? Should you ask her to?"

"She does not see it that way, Mother. She wants to be with me as much as I want her to."

Morgan paused a moment for him to notice his tone. He softened his eyes and passed his apology through his magic.

"She may not realize it now, but what of a few years from now? And what of the magic you gave her? I realize you could teach her many things yourself, but is her mate the most logical choice to train with?" She walked to him and put a hand on his shoulder. "You are a grown man, so we will not make this decision for you. I simply think you should consider those questions, for her sake, before you ask her."

Kyan had his head bowed a bit and was looking at the ground in front of him. She felt the anguish growing in him and knew he was realizing her point was valid. A moment later, he rose and left the terrace.

She covered her face with her hands and moaned.

"I hate to make him hurt so," she said. "But I do think it the right and responsible thing for him to do for his mate. Do you think my point a valid one, my dear?"

Alec walked to her and kissed her cheek.

"You are a wise one, my young wife. You thought of their happiness in the future and not only in the short term. I think he and Iz will both see the wisdom in your words eventually."

"Yes, but until then, they will follow my wishes with a bit of resentment." Alec wrapped her in his arms as he turned her to look out over the gardens, then hummed as he kissed her neck.

"I am quite glad that you have chosen to no longer deny us your beautiful voice. I have missed it very much," he said in a tone so deep that she felt the vibrations through her back. "Forgive me if that seems selfish."

She smiled and turned to caress his face, tracing his lips.

"It isn't selfish. It was missing your voice that helped me see how foolish I was being. I see no reason to allow that man's evil action to limit my connection to my family any more than my gifts can prevent."

He dropped to hold his lips very close to hers and said, "I love you," in his deepest tone. She smiled as she felt the vibrations and heat of his breath while hearing his words through their connection.

Their kiss was interrupted seconds later as Drieden's voice boomed in her head. She jumped, froze as she listened, then bolted into their bedroom.

"Drieden says there is something wrong with Hytha and the clutch. Grab a coat and let's go," she said as she put on riding clothes and her cloak. Alec said nothing but followed her request.

Both ran out onto the terrace as Nulian landed. As they flew hard toward the Berios portal, Morgan told her family of the news and promised to keep them informed when possible.

"We will join you in an hour if we hear nothing before then, Mother," Kyan said. She knew just where he got that headstrong attitude and did not bother arguing.

THE INSTANT THEY ARRIVED on Berios Morgan felt great fear within Hytha. Nulian flew at a fast pace to reach the mountain housing Hytha's clutch then moved through the tunnel toward her brooding chamber.

Hytha moved to Morgan as she entered the chamber and crooned as she laid her head to her body. Morgan stroked her to comfort her, as did Alec.

"One of my eggs is missing, my Queen. Someone may have taken one of my hatchlings." Morgan turned to the eggs and counted. One was indeed missing.

"We have looked everywhere we can reach. Will you look within the tighter areas of the cave to be sure it did not somehow roll off of the pile as we slept? I would be embarrassed if that is the reason for its absence. That is why I asked you to come. I know my Queen and King would never make me feel foolish."

Morgan and Alec searched in every small crevice or tunnel anywhere near the cavern the eggs were in.

"I am sorry, my dear, but we do not see it with our eyes, nor do I feel its magic within the cave system." Hytha gave an angry growl as she curled around her clutch and breathed hard.

"Tagien has gone to search for it. But how is he to find a single egg with no clear direction to search? I need you to help locate it, my Caretaker. Please, use your magic and cunning to find my hatchling."

Morgan stroked her neck to share calming, supportive feelings in an effort to ease her fear and anger.

"We will find your egg. Stay with your clutch and leave it for no reason. Drieden will be with you. I will keep you up to date as we search, my dear."

She and Alec ran to mount Nulian, who moved back to the mouth of the tunnel where Drieden waited.

"Drieden, one of the eggs is missing. We will start the search. I ask you to stay here and let no one in except Tagien or us." Drieden nodded, then moved to block the tunnel entrance with his great body as he growled and scanned the area around them.

Nulian took to the air and made circles around the cave, widening their search with each turn. Morgan focused on the feeling of the magic within the eggs and used it as her guide. Feeling no hint of the egg, she reached out to Tagien who was a few miles away.

"Tagien, King Alec and I want to help locate the missing egg. I must ask you, who has had the strongest objection to the joining of the breeds?" She felt his heartache as he hesitated a few seconds.

"The most opposed have been the two Eldest females of the Perian dragons of Berios. One is my great-grandmother. She feels I have tainted our family bloodline. She has refused to speak to me since learning I am mated to Hytha."

"Will you tell me where she is, so I may speak with her, please?" *"She would not hurt my eggs, my Queen. She may be opposed, but she would never actually hurt any dragon."*

"Then my speaking with her, and asking her advice, should do no harm, my friend." Tagien knew her real reason and grumbled such that she heard it through the connection.

"She is within the ancient lair near the portal to Kalias. Her name is Ildora. She is the Eldest female upon Berios. Do be careful with your words, my Queen."

"I will be as diplomatic as possible, my friend," she said before blocking him from the rest of her conversation. *"Nulian, did you know of this rift within his family?"*

"I know Ildora, and do not care for her in the least. She is prej- udiced against most any but her own bloodline and far too old to be reasoned with. I have not seen her out of the ancient lair in many years. She is quite old, my Queen, and is most certainly near her day of passing."

Morgan passed annoyance as she waited for an answer to her actual question.

"Yes. I did know," Nulian said. *"I did not mention it because I knew you could not change the mind of such an unyielding old dragon. I am sorry if you see it as a deception. I simply did not see it making a difference."*

"It may have made a grave difference. Please, take me to see her now."

"Ildora will not speak to you. She speaks to none but her family line."

"She may not speak, but she will hear me. If I can penetrate your guard when you are angry at me, then I can likely force her to at least hear my words."

"If you offend her, there could be a great deal of negative repercussions, my Caretaker. Please heed Tagien's advice and be careful of your words."

As they flew, Alec massaged Morgan's shoulders and passed calming feelings.

"Perhaps a mediator would help sway the Elder to speak with you," he said.

Morgan nodded as she thought about the ill-tempered Elder dragon, then sought the spirit of Asira.

"Are you a blood-relative of Ildora, my friend?"

"Distant, but yes. I am, my Queen."

"Will you act as a spokesperson for me so she will hear my words?"

"I would do so gladly, but she will not listen to me. She and I had a disagreement over Hytha and Tagien's mating and have not spoken since."

"I need your private and honest opinion, my friend. Do you think Ildora would go so far as to harm the younglings to stop this mixing of her bloodline?"

Asira raised her guard very high, so only Morgan could hear her answer.

"I do think her capable of such, my friend. She has become obsessed with the purity of her bloodline the closer she gets to her time of passing. I believe her to no longer be in her proper mind, my Queen."

Morgan rubbed her face as she took that in and realized just how horribly this could go. She knew who she needed to consult about mediating for her, but hated to do it. With encouragement from Alec, she connected to Tagien's mother.

"Elder Tevish, I must ask if you believe it possible Ildora could act against Tagien and Hytha's clutch?"

"Of what do you speak? Has harm come to them?" Tevish said.

"Yes. As of this morning, one of the eggs is missing. I am considering the possibility that someone who was opposed to the mating of the two breeds may be acting against the eggs. Do you think Ildora capable of it?"

"I will have an answer for you very soon," Tevish said as she redirected her flight toward the ancient lair.

"She is closer than we are," Nulian said as she put on a burst of speed.

Morgan called to Tevish, but the Elder was in a rage and would not answer. Nulian dropped to the lake just long enough for Alec to leap into Gerzin's palm. The males followed but did not enter the Elder Female's private chambers.

WHEN NULIAN AND MORGAN reached the Elder Female's chambers, Tevish was yelling and snarling in a full rage. Ildora was lying on the ground staring at her with disdain.

"Lady Tevish, please try to calm, and allow me to have a word with Elder Ildora," Morgan said as she slid down Nulian's foreleg to shift closer to her chest.

"This is not your concern, Lady Morgan. This is a family matter," Tevish said.

"I consider all dragons to be my family. I love Hytha and Tagien very much. I am going to find the egg, and will not accept being told to stay out of it!"

She focused on Ildora and attempted to strengthen her connection to her. Ildora turned her head slowly and dropped it to look into her face as she snorted.

"You will not enter my mind, Human!"

Morgan continued to increase the pressure she applied to the Elder's guard in small increments. She made progress with each move then gave one strong push to pass her guard enough to sense her emotions and hear her thoughts.

"Are you in any way responsible for the missing egg?"

As the answer hit her, she dropped the connection and staggered back against Nulian. She fought nausea while staring at the ancient dragon who chuckled deep in her throat.

"She…she took the egg while they slept, and has left it to hatch and die alone. She would have taken all had Hytha not been wrapped around the pile so well. Nulian, I have never felt hate like this within a dragon. There is no evil dark magic to blame. It is her own heart which wants to bring this agony to them," Morgan said. She felt the same shock within Nulian as she was nudged toward her palm.

"Come, my Queen. I will tell Tevish and let her deal with her grandmother herself. We must leave at once," Nulian said. Morgan dodged her palm.

"No, I must find out where she has left the egg. I must touch her to … to force my way into her mind while she is alive. Tell Tevish. Then do what you must to subdue her. We must have the truth. I must do this to have any chance of saving the hatchling."

"Move into the next hallway and wait for my call, my Sister. Please, stay clear no matter what you hear or feel within us," Nulian said. Morgan moved away but paused at the archway.

"Tell me you agree that we are just in this, Nulian. She has acted with great malice against the most innocent of all." Nulian looked at her and pushed a fierce wave of confidence as she nodded then moved closer to Tevish.

Morgan moved around the corner into the next tunnel and many yards from the opening. She focused on her connection to Nulian and listened as she shared the truth with Tevish.

The roar Tevish released shook Morgan to the bone and made her breath catch in her throat. She wrapped her arms around her torso and held herself tight as Tevish's rage tore through her.

The two younger females moved toward Ildora and demanded she tell them the location of the egg. Ildora moved with surprising speed and agility as she stood and moved toward the chamber exit.

Tevish grabbed Ildora's tail with her teeth and bit hard as she pulled. Ildora roared and turned on her with bared teeth and hateful eyes.

"I will not allow my bloodline to be tainted by the survival of those half-breeds! I will kill them all before they mate. Had you listened to your Elder when the matter came before me, this would not be necessary. You forced my hand, Tevish. Unlike you, I have the courage to protect the purity of my family line!"

"Where is it?" Tevish roared as she side-stepped to counter the far larger Elder's movement.

"Do you dare attack your clan's Eldest female? Do you truly wish that shame on your children?" Ildora said in a loud and booming voice.

Nulian saw the pain in Tevish as she thought of attacking her own grandmother, then moved forward with a deep snarling growl that got Ildora's attention.

"You are not my Eldest female, nor do I fear you, Ildora. I will not hesitate to strike if you do not tell me the location of the egg at once." Ildora and Nulian circled one another and growled with bared teeth.

Morgan was pacing the corridor just outside Ildora's chambers while monitoring all three dragons. She flinched as Ildora used her tail to slash Tevish across the neck and face.

As Tevish slammed into the wall, Nulian glanced her way, and Ildora struck. Morgan felt the burst of triumphant rage within Ildora and sprinted toward the chamber. She tripped and fell hard to the floor as Ildora sank her teeth into Nulian's neck.

Nulian let out a great howling roar as the powerful jaws threatened to crush her spine. Ildora suddenly jerked, released the bite, and roared as her front legs buckled.

Nulian shifted to see Tevish's teeth buried in her grandmother's neck, just behind her head. She quickly turned and lunged to tackle and pin Ildora. Tevish released the bite and worked with Nulian, shifting their weight until Ildora's attempts to thrash were futile.

"My Queen, co—" Nulian called.

"Right here," Morgan said as she climbed up to reach her neck. She was being showered with Nulian's blood as she struggled to reach her largest wounds.

"Please, focus on Ildora," Nulian said as she and Tevish strained to keep the far-larger Ildora pinned.

Morgan ignored her and pushed healing to close the deep gouges along her throat. Only when they were completely healed, did she turn her focus to Ildora.

Before she touched the enraged Elder dragon, she took a few deep breaths and placed her hands over her Crest to calm and focus her magic. She looked into the eyes of both Nulian and Tevish as she steeled her spirit for what she was about to do.

"You are fully just in this, Queen Morgan," Tevish said as she strained against the snarling Ildora. Morgan nodded, then slid off of Nulian to land against Ildora. The second she laid her hands against the dragon's hide, she attacked her guard. Ildora bucked and roared in pain as she fought the intrusion. Morgan clung to her scales to not lose contact as she countered each magical attempt to block her. When she passed Ildora's guard to reach deep into her mind, the great Elder let out an agonized mewing roar and started trembling beneath them.

"Please, Ildora. I can and will take the information I need to save that little one! How much that costs you is your choice. Where is the egg?"

Ildora did not respond beyond sinister snarls and continued attempts to block her.

Morgan cursed, forced a deep breath, then released a powerful blast of magic to forcibly bond to the most powerful dragon she had ever touched. Every cell of her body burned with fiery pain, nausea gripped her insides, and her body poured sweat as Ildora roared and writhed.

As Morgan drove them into a deep bonding, her body shuddered and her Crest burned white-hot on her chest. There was no blissful weightlessness this time; it was a constant barrage of piercing pain. This was not the beautiful bonding of willing spirits. This was domination. This was what evil spirits coveted. Tears flooded her face as her Crest seared through her chest, but she did not let up on her attack.

As she sought the ancient dragon's memories, she found a dense fog obscuring every thought within the Elder's mind. Everything was a jumbled, confused mess of rambling thoughts and fractured emotions. It took her a long moment of sifting through the storm of information before finally reaching the pertinent memory.

She watched Ildora enter Hytha's brooding chamber and lift the top egg off the pile in her teeth. Rather than crush the egg in her powerful jaws, she left the cave and flew far to the East, where she dropped it from a mile above the surface. Morgan's body clenched as she watched the egg's fall, then relaxed as it splashed into a large lake.

Guilt and shame rose within Ildora as she viewed the memory

while having Morgan's emotions flooding through her. Morgan released the bonding and connection, then hurried toward the cave opening at a run. Nulian and Tevish released Ildora and moved back with caution. The Elder female offered no fight, then curled up into a tight ball without a sound.

AS MORGAN VAULTED UP to Nulian's back, she felt Brya and Kyan arrive along with Daniel and Taru. They were carried by Menkar, Sirzi, Lirpa, and Falin.

She brought everyone up to speed as Nulian flew hard to the East with Gerzin and Alec. The twins and Taru were closer to the region where the egg was dropped.

Just moments into the flight, Kyan and Brya felt their Crests tingle like mad. They saw their markings begin to glow brightly and both shivered as a strong wave of magic moved through them.

"The special hatchlings are coming, Mother. They call to us," the twins said.

"Go to them. Try to help Hytha relax and enjoy the birth of her children."

Lirpa and Taru found the lake that matched the description Morgan had given.

"The egg landed nearly dead center of the lake, so start there. I will be there shortly to help you," Morgan explained.

Lirpa and Taru sliced through the surface of the cold mountain lake.

Lirpa swam hard and was soon at her limit of depth. Taru swam down a bit further and found the rough and jagged rock floor of the lake around her. Lirpa soon grabbed the arguing Taru by the coat and started pulling her upward.

Taru slipped free of her coat and swam back toward the bottom. She stopped and held still to let her magic open to the area around her, but felt nothing. Unable to locate the magic within the egg and growing dizzy as she ran short of oxygen, she was thankful when Lirpa grabbed her around the torso and took off for the surface.

Lirpa was growing too disoriented to focus when she was grabbed around the wing joints and pulled upward. It was her dear Falin, who had grown impatient when she did not surface.

When they reached the surface, the other dragons moved to carry both the exhausted ones to the shore. Morgan and Alec had just arrived. She laid a hand to each of her friends to give them strength.

"We found the bottom and searched, but did not see it. I tried to use my magic and felt nothing. I am sorry, my Sister," Taru said.

"Do not apologize. You risked your life for the hatchling and that is more than we could ask," Morgan said. She stood and moved toward the lake as she touched Alec's guard to summon him. When he arrived, she took his hand and gripped it hard.

"If I enter the lake and go to that depth, it is possible it could affect our child. But if I do not go, the hatchling will most certainly die."

"Be careful, my Caretaker, and kiss me before you go." She smiled and kissed him with meaning as she pushed pride and gratitude. He released her and stepped back with a confident nod.

She moved toward the water but stopped as Nulian cut off her path. "You risk too much in this. I cannot let you do it."

"Who am I, Nulian?"

Nulian looked at her with startled anguish.

"You are my Queen, whom I love and swore to protect," Nulian said. With Morgan's continued stare, she added, "And, you are my Caretaker." "I am also the Caretaker of the dragon within that egg. Now, let me do what you know I must. I could not live with myself if I left it to die. It is not a matter of choice at all. It is who I am." She patted her friend then held her stare as she took off her heavy cloak and boots.

Nulian felt the intense emotion she had pushed with her words and bowed her head as she offered her palm.

"It is my honor to carry you, my Caretaker."

"I love you too, my Sister. Let us enter at speed, so we have ample breath to find the egg."

Morgan looked into Alec's eyes. Each shared their love and devotion through their link before she and Nulian lifted off.

Nulian flew high and shot down very quickly for the lake. Morgan looped her hands in the wrist loops and ducked behind the front bolster to protect her bulging belly from the impact of the water. Nulian arched her neck to lessen the impact on her as well.

Once through the surface, Nulian stroked her wings hard and drove them down as both opened and tried to detect the magic of the hatchling. When Nulian reached the bottom Morgan swam free of her and searched for the magic of the egg.

"My dear, you must move away for me to detect the subtle magic of the egg," Morgan said. Nulian hated her words but knew their truth, so she moved up a hundred yards.

Morgan felt the unique magic of the hatchling and moved toward it. She found a sheer rock wall and moved up as she followed the egg's magic. The magic of the egg pulled at her, and she soon found herself at the mouth of a tight tunnel, into which a fast current flowed.

She gripped the rough stone to fight the current and looked up to hold Nulian's eyes.

"I must try. You know I must."

Just as Nulian shot toward her, she let go and allowed the current to pull her into the dark tunnel.

32

Bound by Birth

NULIAN WATCHED as Morgan released her grip on the wall and slipped into the dark tunnel a second before she reached it. She clawed at the mouth of the cave in a desperate rage, tearing stone away only to reveal more of the small tunnel. At first, she could track Morgan's movements, but now she could barely feel her Caretaker's magic. She called and called, but got no reply. Her heart was breaking more with each second, any concern for her own survival forgotten.

Her weak, uncoordinated efforts were interrupted when Gerzin and Menkar grabbed hold to pull her up as fast as possible. She roared angrily in reflex, her lungs filled with water, and she was unconscious in seconds. The males broke the surface with a huge splash and dragged her to the bank where Taru waited.

Taru laid her hands to Nulian and pushed her magic strong and steady. Nulian's heart was still beating, but she had to cough hard to clear her lungs. She gasped and coughed many times before she could explain what happened to Alec.

"Falin, please return to Erion, speak with Queen May, and bring back a large amount of strong rope. Taru, go with Menkar and seek the aid of the Primin. Make it clear to Orin that it is Morgan who needs him. Hurry, please. If she is still alive within the tunnels, we must reach her."

"I can reach her, my King. I will go quickly," Taru said.

"Hold!" Alec barked. "That is a mere hope, not a certainty. I am certain that you are the only one who can reach and speak with the Primin. Please, go."

Taru moved to Menkar, and they were off. Daniel stood beside Nulian and stared at the water.

Alec moved away to pace alone. He had often felt helpless when it came to helping Morgan, but this moment was the most profound thus far. He had felt the pain within her just as Nulian had. Neither had told the others, so their worry would not triple as his had.

MORGAN MOVED into the tunnel system and let the magic of the egg guide her. As she approached the egg, she was hit with an incredible blast of pain in her abdomen.

"Oh no, not now. You must wait, my boy."

All of the muscles around her child were tight. She was going into labor.

She struggled to reach the egg as her pain increased. As the tunnels shifted, the current helped her move along a sidewall toward the egg. Finally, she found it and gripped the wall to hold still long enough to scoop it up and push it under her shirt to rest above her swollen belly. Relief washed over her as she found it undamaged, the hatchling's spirit still strong and stable.

Fighting the current to move back toward the lake was difficult. She made good progress until she was hit by a tremendous round of contractions. Her grip slipped, and she was pushed back many feet before grabbing hold again to dangle in the current. Her head started to spin as she accepted she could not fight it current any longer.

"Ok, my boy, we need air. Help me focus. Find us an air pocket, a spot of lower density."

She opened to feel the layout of the tunnels she was now in and found a small air-filled cavern further into the rocky labyrinth. Just before she let go to move with the current, the egg started to tremble and jerk as the hatchling began to fight to free itself of the shell.

"Good gracious, you too? This is not the time to be impatient, little ones."

She moved as fast as possible, letting the current carry her forward toward the small cavern. She took two wrong turns and had many bruises and cuts by the time she broke the surface in the cavern. Two deep gasping breaths and she gagged on the disgusting smell of the air.

There was barely enough oxygen in the air to sustain her, but she had no choice. She moved to a small ledge, climbed up, then rested against the wall as she used her magic to warm herself and dry her clothing a bit.

The next round of contractions was fierce, and her lurch almost made her drop the egg. She clutched it to her chest as she panted, then gritted her teeth to keep herself quiet as she saw the egg's shell crack and a small piece lift free.

The pain of the contraction lessened a bit as she gazed in mesmerized wonder at the gorgeous female hatchling now staring back at her.

"Welcome, little one… I… am Caretaker… Morgan… and I… " she tried to say. She was getting dizzy and very tired. The hatchling moved from its shell to nuzzle her neck, then pushed its shell off of her chest. It clawed at her shirt and looked at her as it chirped.

She opened her shirt to bare her Crest, and the hatchling lay down with a sweet croon. She took in a gasp as the magic of the minute-old dragon rushed through her and took the sharpest of the pains away.

"Thank you, my new friend. Shall we bond for a bit?"

The hatchling crooned and passed loving support. It laid flat against her and began to hum the dragon healing song as it sought to form a bond to her.

She was amazed to see how capable the dragon was so soon out of the shell. Her pain was climbing again, so she let the hatchling connect and bond. Once the bonding was established, she was able to relax far more. She stayed within the bonding until she felt the hatchling growing weak, then broke it herself.

She groaned as pain rose again and was not surprised to find her son was ready to join the hatchling.

"I will need to sit up, my dear. Hold on tight. I need to help my boy out so he can meet you," she said as she wrestled with her damp pants.

The next contraction filled her with fear. The hatchling crooned, and she felt its offense at her thought of being alone. She smiled and kissed it on the snout.

"I am very happy you are here to share this with me. I cannot think of a more wonderful greeting for my son."

She closed her eyes to focus on the spirit of her son. Once within that bonding, she was able to calm herself and enjoy the moment with him. She felt the hatchling push against her guard and included her in the bonding as well.

The combination of their spirits was intoxicating and cut her pain by half. With the next sharp rise of pain, she opened her eyes, leaned forward to push with all her might, and reached down to catch her son.

Tears streamed down her face as she felt his joy the instant her hands touched him. She gathered him up to lay him on her chest without breaking the bonding. The hatchling wrapped itself over her son, and she wrapped her arms around both. Her magic responded to the need, and her skin warmed to soothe the babies lying against her. A few seconds later, the hatchling nudged her to make her open her eyes. She had almost fallen asleep.

The little one crooned and rubbed her snout across her son's back. A faint glow filled the chamber and a lovely rush of magic made the boy wriggle and coo.

Morgan sat up a bit and studied her son's body. She traced her finger over the many small scale regions which traveled down the center of his back. When she rolled him over, tears flooded her face again as she found more lines along his clavicle that joined and dropped to the larger patch of his Crest.

"Hayden," the hatchling said. Morgan gave her a curious look. *"Sister Balia said to name him Hayden."*

Morgan stared at the gorgeous dragon for many seconds before she could say anything intelligent.

"Please explain more, my friend."

"Sister Balia spoke to me and encouraged me to be patient. She said you were coming for me, and I must wait to feel your touch before breaking my shell. Just as you lifted my shell, she said, 'Name, my Sister's second son Hayden and tell her I love her'."

"Hayden," Morgan said as she broke into a hard cry. She kissed her son and the hatchling then hugged them both tight against her.

"Will you share her touch to your spirit with me, please?"

The hatchling lay flat again and pushed to bond. She deepened the bonding and soon felt the familiar strong love of her friend fill her.

She smiled in spite of the ache of longing within her. Tears slid down her cheeks as she realized that Balia had never really left her. She was always with her.

"Thank you very much, my friend," she said as she caressed the hatchling.

"What shall be my name, my Caretaker?"

"I think we should let your parents name you, my dear." The hatchling nodded then crooned to Hayden and nuzzled him.

Morgan felt hunger within Hayden and shifted him over to feed him. The gorgeous little boy looked into her eyes as he ate, and she sang to him through their magic. She heard him begin to hum along through the magic and smiled at his ability to use his magic so soon just as the twins had.

"He sings to you, my Caretaker," the hatchling said. Morgan was so groggy she did not register what the hatchling had said for many seconds.

"He is making audible sounds to the tune I sing to him?"

"Yes, and he is quite in tune," the hatchling said.

She smiled and continued her song as tears continued to flow. Once Hayden was full and drifting off to sleep, she wrapped him with her top shirt. After fighting her damp clothes back into position, she laid down to cuddle the little ones, and exhaustion took her.

TARU AND MENKAR returned with Orin near the same time Falin returned with the bundle of rope. Orin jumped nimbly to the ground and moved to Alec.

"Thank you for coming, Primin Orin. I am grateful for your help. Has Taru told you what we know?"

"Yes, and I know the tunnel system well. I will find her easily. It is not wise to bring her out against the current. There are other routes which are longer, yet safer," Orin said as he started to turn away. Alec touched his arm to stop him.

"You need to understand a bit more of the situation. Morgan may have gone into labor. She may still be in labor or have given birth to our son. The possible scenarios you will meet when you get to her are many and complicated. I have asked for the rope to allow the strength of the dragons to assist in pulling Morgan free. It is the safe removal of my son that I do not know how to accomplish."

"I will reach her and do my best to help her and your son," Orin said. He turned and hit the water at a full run then dove.

33

Hythiens Among Us

ORIN SWAM HARD and shot into the tunnel system as he focused on the magic he knew to be Morgan. He moved to the cavern where she slept and to her side. His breath caught in his throat at the sight of blood pooled around her legs, but his heart lifted when he saw the child breathing easily against her chest.

He knelt beside her and took in her features before laying his hand to her cheek to wake her. As he felt the profound fatigue within her, he started to pass healing energy. She woke disoriented and reached up to take his hand as she mumbled.

He grasped her hand and continued to pass healing energy as he gazed at her. The lovely dragon markings on her chest were visible only above the child and hatchling dragon wrapped over him. He reached out to touch her Crest but drew his hand back as the hatchling hissed.

Morgan opened her eyes and blinked as she became aware of both her surroundings and her company. She pulled her hand away from his as she muttered, "Thank you."

"Congratulations, my Lady. You have had a very difficult day, yet have managed to birth both a human son and a dragon," he said with a smile. She smiled as she caressed both little ones. "Please let me give you more strength. You will need a great deal to get free of this tunnel system."

She tried to sit up and grimaced at the aches and pains shooting through her. He moved to support her back and help her scoot enough to lean on the wall. With her permission, he leaned in to get a closer look at Hayden.

"How lovely. He has a great many dragon scales, as does your friend, Taru. He is very handsome." He then studied the dragon hatchling. When she shifted to tuck her head a bit, he backed away. "This dragon is absolutely beautiful. I have never seen such features or coloration. Who are its parents?"

"This lovely young Lady is of the original breed of dragon to inhabit this galaxy. She is a beautiful result of recombining the Alerian and Perian breeds. Her parents are Hytha of Chemerie and Tagien of Berios," Morgan said as the hatchling pushed her head into her hand. She felt an odd wave of relief from Orin and looked up to find him wearing a proud smile.

"You have a beautiful voice, my Lady. I am so very glad to know you did not allow my father's cruel actions to take your words any longer."

She nodded and started to move the little ones. When she grimaced again, Orin held up a hand with a pleading look. She sighed and took his hand. He pushed his magic as he gazed into her eyes. She dropped her eyes to her little ones and focused to allow the transfer of healing energy while blocking any attempt for more. He did not try. He only gave her energy at a steady pace for many minutes until she was feeling strong enough to build her own magic further.

She carefully shifted Hayden and the hatchling off of her Crest and swaddled them inside her top shirt on the floor. As they settled, she stacked her hands over her Crest to allow her magic to build within her. When she felt strong again, she opened her eyes to find Orin studying her with an adoring expression.

"I am very thankful that you have come to help us, Orin. However, I need to make something very clear," she said. "I feel the emotion you hold for me, and do not share it. I am faithful to my mate and seek the link-of-spirit to no other. You hope that I will reach for you, but ... "

Orin moved very close and slid his hands lightly over her bare arms as he dropped his guard.

"Feel it, Morgan. Feel the powerful combination of our magic," he said as he moved a hand toward her Crest. She grabbed his wrist to stop him, then took a quick deep breath as he pushed a nearly overwhelming flood of fierce emotion over her. "Look me in the eye and tell me that this does not make your heart lift and your magic soar. Tell me that it is not enjoyable to you, and I will never bring my feelings to you again."

Morgan had to focus hard to keep her face placid and hide how jolted she was by the joining of their magic. He took her silence as consent and leaned in to kiss her.

"There is no comparison," she said just before his lips touched hers. He paused, misunderstanding her meaning, and tried to kiss her again. He managed only a slight brush of her lips before she laid a hand to his chest to shock him with a jolt of anger. "As intense as this may seem to you, it pales in comparison to the profound sensations I experience when touched by my rightful mate."

Orin held her eyes as he laid his hand over the one she had pressed to his chest. When he spoke again, his tone was passionate with a hint of pleading.

"I can feel your emotions, just as you can feel mine. Despite your efforts to hide them, I feel both the physical and emotional reactions you are having as we touch. Please, stop fighting it, Morgan. Open yourself and enjoy it with me."

He slid a hand up to the back of her neck and pulled as he tried to lean in again. Her anger spiked and her magic acted. He gasped and flinched back from her touch just as the hatchling leapt to her shoulder to hiss with bared teeth mere inches from his face.

"Back away before one of us injures you badly." As he slid many feet away, she fought to calm herself. She urged the hatchling to return to Hayden as he started to cry. Once he settled again, she looked to Orin with a stern glare.

"It is clear to me that you have never touched your rightful mate. The power of your magic would undoubtedly make your link with her incredible, as mine is to Alec. I felt your sincere belief that we are linked, but you are wrong. I am not your mate, and never will be. If you choose to touch me inappropriately again, I will hurt you and never speak to you again."

Orin dropped his head and forced a slow deep breath before meeting her eyes again.

"You do not understand my state. Thoughts of you and your powerful spirit consume me. I long for you as I have no other. A woman believed to be my mate pursues me intently, yet I have refused to touch her. If she touches me, she will feel my love for you, and it will hurt her badly. Despite many hours meditating and exhausting myself, I cannot quiet the thoughts or quench the desire. You remain ever-present in my mind." He stood and turned away to stare at the water. "I will accept your decision and will never bring this to you again."

She caressed the hatchling and Hayden while giving him a minute to calm.

"Will you remain my friend or will you accept all or nothing from me, Orin?"

"I will always be available to help you and your people in any way I can. However, I cannot imagine anything more for now, my Lady."

"How do we get home?" she asked as she scooped up Hayden. Orin moved to her and looked at the hatchling, who was perched on her shoulder again.

"You will not have the protection of your shell, and the water pressure is very high. It will likely cause you great pain if you do not allow me to shield you with application of my magic."

"What application do you speak of?" Morgan asked as she felt unease from the hatchling.

"It is the use of pressure created by sound waves behind the eardrum to counteract the pressure exerted by the water. I can bond to them and protect them while I carry them out." Morgan nodded as she gazed at Hayden sleeping in her arms. "You will be able to carry yourself most of the way. Your mate has provided a rope held by the dragons to assist in freeing you of the current." He held out his hands to her and gestured to Hayden. "Please, trust me, Morgan. I will protect them."

Morgan kissed Hayden and handed him to Orin with a heavy heart.

The hatchling did not move. "Please, go with Orin, little one."

"The Primin's attention should be focused on only one. He can return for me, or I will ride with you. I will not take attention from Hayden, my Caretaker," the bold little hatchling said.

"I will take your son to his father, assist the dragons to extend the rope to you, then take the hatchling up as you leave. I will be back shortly, my Lady," Orin said as he stepped closer to the water.

"Be safe, my friend," Morgan said. His face fell as he started to turn away. "Yes, I do consider you my friend, Orin. I hope you find your mate soon so we may all be strong friends."

He smiled as he began to sing with Hayden against his chest. He held a hand over his head to hold him tight against him as he bonded to him. His song increased in volume and complexity before he jumped in and disappeared.

MORGAN DROPPED to her hands and knees as fear gripped her. She focused to follow their progress but soon could not locate them through all the dense rock. She waited with the hatchling for many minutes before Orin shot from the water with a smile and cheerful tone.

"There are many very excited people adoring your son, my Lady. They request your presence. Shall we go?" he said as he opened his arms to the hatchling. Morgan smiled and nodded to the hatchling, who nuzzled her cheek before moving to Orin.

Morgan almost kept up with Orin until he put on a great burst of speed once she reached the rope. She pulled herself along a few feet, then grabbed hold as the rope started to move forward, propelling her along much faster.

She shot from the mouth of the tunnel and was grabbed by a joyful Nulian who passed enormous waves of love and relief as she stroked upward. They broke the surface to roars from all the dragons and cheers from her family.

Nulian set Morgan down on the bank in front of Alec, where she was taken into a strong embrace. He held her without a word or a move for many long seconds then kissed her lips, cheeks, and forehead.

"You are an incredibly devoted Caretaker, and I am very proud of you," he said. Morgan could think of no better thing he could have said and pulled him close to kiss him again.

"So what do you think of your second son?"

"He is alive. That is all I learned thus far. I was a bit preoccupied and let the twins take him," Alec said as he stroked her face and held her tight.

A wave of jealousy hit her and she knew it to be Orin. She did not turn or acknowledge it in any way.

Kyan and Brya moved to them with huge smiles. She kissed and hugged them both, as they flooded her with healing magic.

"Your little brother has a surprise," she said as she took Hayden from Brya to uncover him.

Everyone reached out to trace his dragon scale lines with their fingers. Hayden giggled and grabbed at their hands. They all laughed with him as they felt his joy.

A new wave of jealousy hit her. It was from the hatchling who was on Taru's shoulder staring at her. She handed Hayden to Alec, then opened her arms to the hatchling, who soared to her and laid against her chest. The hatchling crooned as she kissed and caressed her.

Alec had been so focused on Morgan, he had not taken in the hatchling's appearance. As he shifted closer to Morgan, Hayden's scale areas glowed brighter. When the hatchling leaned closer, Hayden reached out to touch her. He cooed and gurgled as the hatchling crooned in return. Alec almost cried as he caressed both.

"Just when I thought our family could not get any more wonderful, you bring these two beautiful children into our life. You are an amazing woman, my mate."

"Does our brother have a name yet, Mother?" Brya asked.

"Yes, his name is Hayden." She turned her head to look at Nulian as she continued, "The pure and wonderful spirit of Balia touched the hatchling within the shell. She saved her life and named our son." Nulian moved closer to touch her with intense croons. Hayden giggled as her deep tones tickled him.

"Welcome, Hayden," everyone said.

"We should go and get this precious young Lady to her parents and siblings," Morgan said as she stroked the hatchling. The little dragon pressed itself against her chest and tucked its head in her shirt.

"I wish to stay with you, my Caretaker."

"Let us go to your parents, and we shall discuss it. You may feel differently once you are surrounded by their love and the love of your siblings."

The little one tucked her head deeper and said nothing more.

AS EVERYONE MOVED to mount their dragon brethren, Morgan looked to see Orin smiling at her with a heavy heart. He bowed to her and boarded Menkar with Daniel.

"Goodbye, Orin, and thank you."

"Be well, Queen Morgan of Chemerie." He bowed his head to Alec as Menkar launched. Morgan watched him fly off as she contemplated their conversation.

Alec moved to her and urged her along to board Nulian. Once they were settled and flying high above the others, he connected to her and lifted her chin to look into her eyes.

"That man had you alone for many minutes. Do I now have reason to beat the life out of him or to shake his hand?"

"A bit of both. I was very clear on my devotions and do not think he will question our link again. However, we will not see much of him until he feels the link to his rightful mate."

Alec did not question her, but she felt the uncertainty he was attempting to hide as he shifted his gaze to Hayden.

"Do you doubt my words in some way?" she said as she shifted to kiss his cheek and nudge him until he looked into her eyes again.

"I am not blind, my bride. I do not need your magic to know his feelings for you surpass simple fascination. I do not doubt your love for me or the validity of our link. It is knowing how wonderful your touch feels to me, how it is likely enhanced by his magic, and how …"

She slid a hand into his hair and pulled to take his kiss as she dropped her guard completely. He held her tightly and matched her intensity as their link burned through them.

"Nothing of that man's touch or magic could ever pull me away from you, my mate."

MORGAN AND HER FAMILY flew with their dragon brethren toward the mountain bearing both Hytha's lair and the gazebos. As they neared the mountain, all the adult dragons started to hum together. Their hearts were joyful as they welcomed the new dragon clutch. The twins landed with Sirzi and moved into the tunnel to reach their special new friends.

Nulian landed gently and offered her palm to ease her riders to the ground. Alec held Hayden while Morgan held the anxious hatchling as they moved into the cave.

As they neared the brooding chamber where her family was gathered, the hatchling began to hum and relax. The instant they were within sight of the chamber she took flight, soared into the brooding lair, and landed among her siblings who played between the great bodies of her parents.

"Welcome, our Daughter," Hytha and Tagien said.

Morgan and Alec stayed back and watched with elated hearts as the family all crooned and nuzzled one another. Brya and Kyan sat among the hatchlings who crawled all over them with croons and chirps.

Hayden started to cry, so Alec handed him to Morgan. He did not settle with her touch, but she was smiling as she moved to hand him to Brya. "Someone is jealous." Brya laid him in her lap, and the hatchlings all gathered around.

Hayden's Crest and other scale areas were glowing intensely, as were the Crests of Morgan, Brya, and Kyan. He cooed as he touched the hatchlings. All were gently touching their snouts to him and sharing magic.

Kyan and Brya began to sing the Song of Connection as they touched Hayden's Crest and each others'. The hatchlings moved to touch them and joined their song. Soon all bonded to one another, and the glow of the children's markings lit the room.

Morgan and Alec moved to congratulate Hytha and Tagien. They all watched with pride at the amazing magical sharing occurring between their children.

"The Hythien breed is among us once again. And the Caretaker line is ready to serve it. I am blessed to witness this day," Nulian said as she moved to lay with her head just in the chamber.

Hytha and Tagien looked at each other with surprise and pride. The obvious combination of their names to form the name of the original breed suggested their destinies had been set long before they were ever born. Morgan and Alec settled down, and she snuggled into his arms as they watched their children continue to bond with the new clutch of beautiful hatchlings.

As the song ended, the female hatchling who had been saved by Morgan moved to her parents. She crooned as they dropped their snouts to her and nuzzled both.

"What shall my name be?"

"Your name is Mythan," Hytha said.

Tagien repeated her name with a deep rich humming croon as he pushed pride and devotion over his daughter. "A fitting combination of both your mother's name and that of your Caretaker, my Daughter. We would not have you were our Queen not so brave and devoted to us all," Tagien said. He and Hytha looked over at the sleeping Morgan nestled in Alec's arms with love and pride in their eyes.

Mythan crooned and rubbed her parents again before moving to Morgan. She chirped to Alec, who smiled as he moved his arm. She nuzzled his cheek then settled herself against Morgan's Crest where she fell fast asleep.

Quest

MOST OF CHEMERIE met their Caretaker family on the castle lawn. GranMay had organized a celebration dinner and festival in honor of Hayden's birth and the birth of the first Hythien dragons in hundreds of years.

Morgan sat in the gazebo with Alec, Hayden, and Mythan as their brethren moved by in procession to see the new son and the new breed of dragon. Everyone was amazed at Hayden's markings and enamored with the beauty of Mythan.

Both of the young ones grew tired and cranky, so the twins took them to rest. Morgan and Alec visited with their friends and family for a while before she stopped and gazed out over the large group of dragons filling the lawn and lake area. She was near tears as she watched Panish playing with a group of younglings and laughing.

"He is nearly himself again. Qin's love has allowed his heart to mend," GranMay said as she moved to stand beside her.

"I cannot hear him, but I feel the happiness within him. I also feel the reason for his high spirits today. Qin is holding their first clutch," Morgan said. As she gazed over her beloved dragon brethren she spotted another wonderful surprise. "Oh, look, GranMay. Valen has just found her magical mate at last."

Valen was staring intently at a large Alerian male who had been among those of Kalias. He bowed low to her then approached. Valen held her head high and proud as the male circled her then dropped her snout to nip at him when he attempted to touch her neck. They continued the playful nipping and pushing for a bit, then took to the air to fly together.

"We may soon have many Hythien younglings among us," Alec said as he watched their courting. Morgan had not responded because she was watching another interaction with great interest.

Daniel had just lifted Taru into his arms and was spinning her around as they laughed. Morgan was hit with tremendous happiness and pride from both of them as she connected.

"Am I right in thinking that amount of joy is associated with your discovering Taru carries a child?" she asked Daniel as she and the others moved to them. Daniel and Taru nodded and were attacked with hugs from the gathered family.

"How long have you known, my Sister?" Taru asked. Morgan just smiled and hugged them both.

THE MOOD ON THE LAWN was one of joyous celebration, yet Morgan struggled to hold a smile as she glanced at Alec and started toward the castle. After congratulating Daniel and Taru once more, he made their excuses and caught up to her. Once they found themselves alone in their chambers, he took her into his arms and held her tight as they both allowed tears to fall.

"I have no idea how I was supposed to prepare myself for this day," Morgan said. "I am not at all ready to let them go. I am not sure my heart can take it."

"I doubt there is preparation enough, but we know they must go."

The twins soon entered their room without knocking and joined their embrace. They had felt their pain and knew its source to be the same as their own. The four held one another and cried for a few moments before anyone spoke.

"We feel the pull and know we must go. Our hearts are so torn. We do not want to leave you and Hayden. But it is the magic which pulls us, and we know it is the one thing we must trust in before all else," Brya said. Morgan had stopped her crying altogether and now looked at the twins with pride in her eyes.

"Your tasks will take you on a great adventure, and I want you to enjoy every minute of it. Remember, the magic has blessed us; we will be able to keep up with each other any time we wish with our skills. We may not be able to see or touch, but we can hear and feel. That will make this far less painful for all of us."

"We will miss so much of Hayden's growth. He will not know us by the time we return," Kyan said.

"Do you really believe that? I am certain the magic you share will make your bond to him clear no matter how long you are apart," Alec said. Kyan nodded and smiled. "Besides, I imagine you will be singing lullabies to him and speaking with him via your magic. He will know your spirit well before you return."

GranMay entered and moved to the hugging group. She nudged her way in as she said, "I am a jealous old woman and demand to be hugged this instant." Everyone laughed and moved to encircle her as they squeezed her tight.

"All right now, let us discuss the details of this grand adventure, so I will have a clue what to pack."

GranMay moved to the love seat of the sitting area as everyone followed her and took a seat as well.

"Who will be included in our traveling group, my dear?" she asked Morgan. "I have some ideas, of course, but I thought I would be respectful and ask you first."

Everyone laughed and shook their heads.

"Please, GranMay, do tell us your ideas," Morgan said.

"First of all, I do not think Lady Iz nor Sir Qaleb should accompany us, and I assume you are of the same opinion given teenage tendencies and the amount of free time we will have."

"That was a disrespectful assumption, GranMay," Brya said. "Kyan has chosen not to ask Iz to join us for responsible reasons. And as for Qaleb, I would not allow any inappropriate interactions with him. He is my friend, and he would not make such an advance."

"My dear, I have heard the thoughts of that boy as he looks at you and have no doubt he would indeed make such an advance if he thought you accepting of it," GranMay said.

"I realize he has feelings for me and, truthfully, I have feelings for him as well. But we are not magical mates and will not cross that line. The problem is that you see us as children incapable of controlling our emotions!"

Alec rubbed a hand over his face as his tension grew. Morgan took his hand and gave a little smile.

"Both of you take a moment, please," Morgan said. She pushed calming to her husband as she gave the rest a minute. "I fully expect you to have conflicts like this throughout your trip. GranMay will have to see you as adults, and you will have to act as such. The matter of Qaleb joining you is not one to argue over. I would not have allowed him to join the quest because he has much to learn and needs to be here studying with me."

Brya nodded and leaned over to take GranMay's hand as she said, "I am sorry for my tone. I love and respect you, GranMay."

"I am only looking out for you, my love," GranMay said with a smile as she squeezed her hand.

"What others shall we ask to join you then? I think a couple of Knights would be appropriate to help with the physical labor and for physical protection as well," Alec said. The twins glanced at Morgan and all three smirked. "I will continue to provide additional protection despite your abilities. I do not mean it as an insult but an act of caring."

"We know, Father. We appreciate the care you show for us all," Kyan said.

"Which Knights do you suggest, my dear," Morgan said.

"I would think Maric and Burke would be ..." Alec started to say. He stopped as Morgan shook her head.

"While I doubt Maric would hesitate to accept, you have forgotten Burke and his wife are expecting another child within the next four months," Morgan said. Alec nodded and considered the other choices.

"You should know Daniel has asked to accompany us. He feels it a fitting responsibility since his role as your protector has become ambiguous," GranMay said. "Of course, he asked before finding out Taru was pregnant and may feel differently now."

"I know he still wishes to go, but I think he should stay here since we do not know the rate at which Taru's pregnancy will progress," Morgan said. She looked to Alec to ask, "I would think any of the Knights who wish to go on such a long adventure would be appropriate. How many do you think would be interested?"

"Quite a few, my dear. The duty of protecting the Prince and Princess is an honorable one and one they would be proud to accept. I suggest discussing it with Maric, and letting him choose a partner he could work well with for a long period of time."

"Good idea. Being on that long of an adventure with someone annoying would be quite the trial."

"Tell me about it, look what ..." Kyan started to say. He was stopped by a hard push into the floor by Brya. Everyone laughed at them and relaxed a bit more.

"Have you asked Zoli if she wishes to accompany you or stay

here?" Morgan asked GranMay.

"I have not asked because I imagined she would want to be with Hayden as she is now. The children tell me the Nyeks often spent great amounts of time with the infants of the Caretaker line in the past. I want her to do whatever feels the most natural to her and not feel pressured to join us."

"She has become quite attached to you. I imagine she will want to accompany you," Morgan said. GranMay smiled but said nothing. "As for packing, I would suggest carrying as little as possible with the expectation of picking up food in the villages and towns along your path." Everyone nodded, and she leaned forward with a deep breath as she looked at the twins. "GranMay and the dragons are well aware that there are many peoples of this world who fear the dragon and have no trust for magic. You will have to keep your Crests and hands hidden as you meet new people.

"The dragons will do their best to avoid the townships but will not be able to avoid being seen altogether. Use your skills to be aware of all around you at all times. Your magic will make this a far safer trip, but only if you are vigilant in its use."

"We will be careful and responsible for all our sakes. We have already discussed many ways to be as efficient as possible with our skills and link," Kyan said.

"And we will consult with you anytime we are unsure of how to act. Between the wisdom of GranMay, and the magical link to you, we are sure to be fine, Mother," Brya said.

Morgan, Alec, and GranMay laughed out loud.

"It was very respectful of you to say that, but we know you two can take care of yourselves without our help. We just hope you will seek our advice some of the time," Morgan said. "I will speak with Nulian about which of your dragon brethren will accompany you. You should get to bed and get a good night's rest in those comfy beds." She stood to hug them goodnight, but Brya hesitated.

"When you speak with GranNulian, you should consider that Zirath will most assuredly come with us, even if you asked him not to. We would prefer he accompany us as well," Brya said.

"I would never ask him to stay if his heart tells him he should be with you. He is your brother, and I fully expect he will demand to accompany you. Even if it means ramming his head into Menkar's chest again," Morgan said. They all laughed as GranMay and the twins headed off to bed.

Morgan and Alec checked in on Hayden and found him snuggled between Zoli and Mythan. His markings glowed brightly as strong magic flowed between the three of them.

When they returned to their room, she called to Nulian but found she was not on Erion.

"Sirzi, do you know if something has happened to call Nulian to Berios, my friend?"

"I have heard nothing, nor have I felt anything worrisome from her, my Queen. I am sure she will return shortly. Shall I go and bring her to you, or is there something I can help you with while she is away?"

"No, there is nothing pressing just now. I was only concerned when I could not feel her. Goodnight, my dear."

MORGAN TOSSED AND TURNED for nearly two hours waiting to feel Nulian pass back over to Erion but still could not detect her dear friend.

She searched and found Drieden, many of the Elder council, Menkar, Lirpa, and Falin were also off-world. She was a little annoyed that Nulian had not explained her departure and was now more worried knowing so many were gone at the same time.

She rose and was dressing when she felt Nulian return at last. She connected to her and felt great anguish from her friend.

"What has happened, my dear?"

"Elder Elosh has passed, my Sister. I was asked to participate in his ritual burning. I am sorry if you missed me, but I did not want to disturb your happy time celebrating your son."

"I am sorry to hear of his passing, but I am glad you were there to support Asira and her family. I did miss you, but I understand. I expect you are quite exhausted after ..." She smiled as Nulian immediately took flight to come to her.

"I am never too tired for your touch, my Caretaker. I need its comfort just now. There was a second reason for my hasty departure. The Elder Council of Berios summoned me to speak to them about the actions of Ildora. She was to be banished until I said I thought it a harsh action, given her condition of mind. My heart questions that decision greatly."

"I agree with you. They should remove her from a position of power and keep an eye on her, for everyone's sake. However, she deserves to be given love and respect for the life of service she has given to her brethren. It is not her fault she has grown ill of mind," Morgan said as Nulian soared into a smooth landing beside her terrace.

"That is very much what I just said to them, my Sister. We think much alike these days," Nulian said as she dropped her head over the railing.

Morgan leaned into her and rubbed her neck. Nulian hummed as their magic soothed her.

"You should see my boy's crib. He is snuggled between Zoli and Mythan. The magic they share is very strong," Morgan said as she caressed her friend.

"There is sure to be a powerful bond between Hayden and Mythan, given their births were so near and their bonding so soon. It will be a wonderful thing to witness."

"The twins and GranMay will leave me tomorrow. My heart is tearing at the thought, my dear. I need to ask you who of our dragon brethren will accompany them. Maric and one more Knight will join their party." Nulian was quiet for a long time as she considered the question.

"Given the importance of the party members to our country, I feel I should go as Eldest Female," Nulian said. Morgan had expected that answer but had hoped it would not come. "However, I will stay with you, my Queen. I will ask the other Elders who would wish to accompany them, rather than deciding for myself. I suspect Panish will insist on accompanying Queen May as he loves her most dearly, and I believe Menkar will ask to go. Falin and Lirpa will wish to go. However, I worry for Falin's stamina as yet. He has a far bigger heart than wingspan, and a delicate ego as well."

"I expect we would be challenged to stop Zirath from accompanying them, my dear." Nulian grumbled. "You must not make him stay to protect him. He loves them and has been raised as their sibling. Balia would be proud of his bond to them and would want him to go."

"I will miss all their spirits around me, my Caretaker."

"We will both ache the entire time they are gone."

NEARLY ALL OF THE INHABITANTS of Chemerie were crammed into the garden lawn and lake area to say farewell to the questing party.

Morgan and Alec watched with heavy hearts as Kyan and Brya bonded once more with Hayden.

Iz stood with quiet composure behind Kyan, while Qaleb stood just behind Alec. GranMay was hugging Kisik farewell, when Zoli rubbed against her leg, purring and trilling. GranMay knelt and lifted the Nyek to her shoulder with a smile as she moved to Morgan.

GranMay placed her hand to Morgan's Crest and moved into bonding. They passed profound love and devotion through their shared magic for a long moment alone before GranMay reached out to take Alec's hand and include him. She smiled as tears filled her eyes.

"I could not be leaving my beloved country in the care of any more devoted than you two. Take care of yourselves as well as you do your brethren, my dears. You have many challenges of many forms ahead, and I look forward to watching you handle them with grace and pure spirit. I love you both very much." She released the bonding then kissed them before turning to Daniel, who waited to walk with her to Panish.

Morgan had felt her grandmother's anguish at leaving be replaced by acceptance that left her calm. She was quite jealous that she could not find that acceptance. Her heart felt as if it would rip any moment.

The twins handed Hayden to Emma and moved into their parents' arms. The four bonded deeply together for many minutes without trying to express their feelings in words. They let their magic convey all they felt, and it was profound for all. The twins let the bonding drop then gave quick kisses before turning for their mounts. Kyan moved to hug Iz once more and kissed her lovingly before running to vault up to Menkar's saddle.

Daniel and GranMay were just releasing a deep connection that left his cheeks wet. He hugged her tight for a long time, then helped her into Panish's palm with a loving kiss on the cheek. He returned to stand with Taru, Morgan, and Alec with his head down, then turned with a light smile as he waved to the twins again.

Brya was aboard Sirzi, GranMay aboard Panish, Maric aboard Qin, and senior Knight Sir Hollace was aboard Kerek, a major dragon who had come from Kalias. Lirpa, Falin, and Zirath were accompanying them as well. Lirpa and Falin each wore harnesses so they could switch out with the larger dragons to carry riders or supplies.

The moment for departure was upon them, and everyone grew quiet as they looked to Morgan. She smiled as she shifted her gaze between each member of the questing party, sending love and pride over them all. As she and Alec bowed formally, she reached out to connect to all of her Chemerian family.

"Be well and let the magic guide you, my brethren. Leave us confident in our love for each of you. We are deeply proud of your devotion to this noble quest, but will miss you every moment you are away. May the magic keep you until our spirits touch again."

The crowd repeated her last words then broke into excited cheers and applause as all of the questing party bowed as one.

Morgan felt her knees go weak as the questing group launched. She disconnected from all but Alec and kept her guard high so the twins would not feel her pain, knowing that they did the same for her.

She had to actively block the anguish from all of her family to keep from bursting into tears. Alec wrapped her tight as they continued to watch the group fly away.

"I cannot imagine letting you go at the same time," she said. *"I am so thankful I never had to do that, my love."*

Emma brought Hayden to her as he began to wail. She held him to her and gave what comfort she could, but he continued to cry until he fell asleep. Willow moved forward as Mythan became agitated. The hatchling covered Hayden with her wing and snuggled up to him. Alec leaned down to kiss both little ones, then kissed Morgan gently before offering a confident smile.

"All of the children being born with your gift of magic, a clutch of the original breed, two teenage pupils, and this beautiful boy will keep you busy, my dear. The magic has provided ample distraction to keep you from worrying so much about the twins' travels," he said as he kissed her forehead. She sighed and shook her head while blocking all from their words.

"Worry will be a constant, given what awaits them, my dear," she said as she focused on the sky where the dragons carrying her children were almost out of sight. *"The magic pulls them to go, and me to stay. Yet it makes me keenly aware of the challenges they face in this quest."*

"What has the magic shown you?"

"While they will enjoy many moments of joyous triumph, they will endure equal portions of impossible choices, painful truths, death, and darkness. Both their skills of magic and their strength of spirit will be tested many times over before we hold them again."

"You have taught them to trust in the magic they hold, and to wield it well, my love," Alec said as he gazed at his new son asleep in his mother's arms. "I am confident they will do both and return from this grand adventure even stronger than they leave us."

Kisik chuckled and clapped Alec on the shoulder.

"And a grand adventure it promises to be. We should all worry more for Maric as he navigates the three strong wills of his Caretakers. That boy does well facing a hoard of Marock, but melts like butter under his mother's tenacity. Just imagine him attempting to mediate a feud between her and the equally fierce will of Princess Brya."

Everyone laughed and relaxed as his hearty chuckle infected them all.

Morgan looked to Iz and Qaleb with a confident smile. Both relaxed as her magic moved over them and stepped closer to gaze at Hayden and Mythan.

"Do you believe this handsome young man will grow as fast as his siblings did, my Queen?" Iz said as she gazed at Hayden, who was waking.

"I certainly hope not," Morgan said as she shifted to kiss her son's head. "Between his extra markings and his unique link to the original breed hatchlings, I am certain we are in for an equally unique adventure raising this little man."

They all laughed as Hayden wriggled and cooed as if in complete agreement with his mother. ⬡

Continue the adventures of the Caretaker in
THE BOOK OF THE CARETAKER
BOOK 3

Queen's Aegis

The Evil Twin

THE QUESTING GROUP reached the shoreline of the northern continent just before dusk. The dragons were fast asleep after hunting to fill their bellies. The humans prepared their dinner and began an archery challenge to pass the time. This had become a common activity among them.

Sir Hollace was by far the best shot. He had been making his own bows for years and practiced often. He gave Brya and Kyan some pointers, and both were far more accurate as a result.

The group ate and discussed the plans for rescuing the Nyeks being held captive in cages. Brya grew more irritated the longer they talked. Her insides ached as she considered the distance that would lay between her and Kyan.

"Brya, you know this is the only logical approach. I do not like the distance either, but you going to that castle is too dangerous."

"Understanding the logic does nothing to remove the foreboding making me ache. It is a feeling of lingering loss which worsens the closer we get to this wretched castle."

"I will admit I have felt something since this afternoon as well. But we cannot leave those Nyeks enslaved, and I will never agree with you going there. If you make a mistake, as you did in looking at King Sean of Veridan, these people will beat you right then and there."

"Not likely," Brya said as she scowled. *"I would not let that happen easily."*

"We would both fight them. But consider the odds. There are twelve huge men for every woman. You would have many attackers in seconds. That is not a scenario I wish to risk, Sister. Please do not push this."

Brya nodded as she conceded, but the haunting feelings only worsened in doing so.

THE NEXT MORNING the group flew two hours inland and landed in a meadow four miles west of the castle holding the Nyeks.

Kyan and Maric readied their packs and hugged Brya and Gran-May farewell. Brya had trouble letting Kyan go as her heart raced.

"Keep safe please, I love you," she said as her eyes welled.

"I love you too. Take care of yourself and GranMay. See you soon."

He hugged GranMay tight once more and flooded her with confidence and love.

"I love you, my dear boy. Be safe and return to us unharmed before all else," GranMay said. She held him a few extra seconds before giving him a little shove to get him started.

Maric kissed and hugged his mother once more, then moved off to catch up to Kyan.

Brya paced and chewed her nails for the next half-hour as she watched them from the tree line. As they dropped over a ridge, she used her magic to follow them. She sat beside GranMay for a bit but was soon pacing again.

"Dear girl, do find something to keep you occupied," GranMay grumbled. Perhaps exercise of some kind, or go exploring nearby. You are making me quite anxious with the pacing."

Lirpa moved to Brya and nudged her gently as she crooned. Brya stroked her and felt her concern.

"How about a flight, my Princess? We can check out the landscape and perhaps find a good spot to take a swim." Brya kissed GranMay then vaulted up to Lirpa's saddle.

Falin and Zirath joined them to fly just above Lirpa. They flew for a few minutes making wide circles around the camp before choosing a good location to take a dip. It was a small river about a mile to the northwest of the camp.

Brya dismounted, then went still as she felt the familiar tickle of her dragon markings shifting. The cause was faint magic coming from the woods near the large pool. She removed her top clothes and entered the water as she spotted the little head of a Nyek watching her from atop a large pile of boulders. It was slender as if starved, and she wondered if it had escaped the castle. Though it was quite curious of her, each sound the dragons made caused it to slide back a bit.

"My friends, do you mind taking flight for a bit. There is a Nyek watching me, and I would like to try and befriend it. You are a wee bit intimidating," Brya said. None of them took flight. Instead, they moved far away from the pool to crouch near the opposite tree line.

As she swam in the cool water, she eased her way closer to the end of the pool where the Nyek was hiding. She stopped and looked at the little creature with a small smile.

"I am a friend of the Nyek, and will not hurt you. I am not like those within the castle to the east. The strong magic within me may make you unsure, but please give me a chance to show you my honest desire to help you." She only spoke aloud, knowing it was unwise to try and use her magic to connect.

After a few minutes more, she spotted the skinny Nyek as it leapt to a boulder closer to her. It was blocking her from feeling anything more than a trace of its magic, yet it watched her intently.

"May I approach you?" The Nyek moved back a bit and crouched low to the ground. "Alright, I will not. I will let you come to me when you are ready." It watched her every move as she swam to the bank and laid atop a large flat boulder.

She closed her eyes and tried to relax in the warm sun while checking Kyan's progress. Seconds later, she was startled as the Nyek landed on the boulder just behind her head.

"Well, hello th—" she started to say as she tilted her head back to look up at the little creature. Something about its eyes made her go silent. Before she could act in any other way, the Nyek leapt to her chest and dug its claws into her body, with one paw digging into the scales of her Crest.

Her body bucked, and a shriek left her as her Crest and skin seared everywhere the creature touched her. Fiery pain shot through her like lightning, shocking her, taking her breath, and blurring her thoughts. Terror filled her as she realized the pain was not a magical assault. It was her own magic being stripped away by force. The creature glaring at her with its claws sunk deep into her body was stealing her magic at a rate far faster than she could ever replace it.

The dragons had shot forward with roars, then halted as the creature slid up her chest to sink its long sharp teeth into her neck with a sinister growl. Lirpa made the slightest move toward them, then froze as the creature drove its teeth deeper, making Brya jerk and cry out. Its message was clear—come any closer, and she dies. Zirath took to the air and headed for the major dragons at his fastest pace as he continued his frantic call to them and Kyan.

Brya's writhing weakened to shaking, and her screams became raspy, gasping cries. She could no longer move and knew death was imminent if she did not stop the drain of her magic very soon. With her eyes closed, she shut out everything to focus on the pure spirits of Kyan and GranMay. She called out to them but had no idea if they could hear her past the creature's wicked attack. It was all she could do, she had no more to give, she was utterly spent, and her body was shutting down.

"Why?" she muttered to the creature taking her life.

Pure evil poured over her like frigid water running through her veins as the creature growled again. This was no Nyek. It was an evil spirit who was taking her pure magic and turning it to wicked darkness. A last attempt to raise her guard brought another sinister growl from the creature as it ripped at her skin with its claws and jerked its head to tear at her neck. She flinched only a little, and her cry was barely audible as her body went cold and heavy. Blood now poured from her neck and the many rips on her body.

Lirpa and Falin were calling to their Chemerian brethren in thought as they clawed the ground and growled agonizing sounds. Both were shaking, and tears slid down their faces as they watched their Caretaker's life fade. They both fought to connect to her, to offer what comfort they could. Their attempts were useless, growing more and more futile as the creature grew stronger by the second.

Brya was cold, limp, and knew she had but seconds. She stopped trying to fight and focused her final thoughts on her love for her family and dear friends. Her fear faded away as she thought, "This is not goodbye, only farewell. Our spirits will touch again." ⬢